THE YALE EDITION OF THE

WORKS OF SAMUEL JOHNSON

VOLUME XVI

Rasselas and Other Tales

SAMUEL JOHNSON

Rasselas and Other Tales

EDITED BY GWIN J. KOLB

NEW HAVEN AND LONDON : YALE UNIVERSITY PRESS

1990

The preparation of this volume was made possible (in part) by a grant from the Program for Editions, and publication assistance was provided by the Division of Research Programs, of the National Endowment for the Humanities, an independent federal agency.

Set in the Baskerville types by Keystone Typesetting, Inc., Orwigsburg, Pennsylvania. Printed in the United States of America by Murray Printing Company, Westford, Massachusetts.

Library of Congress catalog card number: 57–11918
International standard book number: 0–300–04451–8

The paper in this book meets the guidelines for permanence and durability of the Committee on Production Guidelines for Book Longevity of the Council on Library Resources.

IN
GRATEFUL AND AFFECTIONATE MEMORY OF
Bertrand Harris Bronson
(1902–1986)

PREFACE

The combination of works making up this volume is almost unique. Only once before (Philadelphia: Hagan and Thompson, 1850) have *Rasselas*, "The Vision of Theodore," and "The Fountains" formed a discrete collection of Johnson's writings. Yet, as the Editorial Committee of the Yale Johnson recognized from the outset, the conjunction of the three narratives is preeminently fitting, probably inevitable: the three constitute Johnson's longest fictional pieces and, although they embody different literary genres, some of their main themes and emphases exhibit unusual similarities. *Rasselas* (1759), perhaps the most widely read of all of Johnson's compositions, occupies first place in the volume; "The Vision of Theodore" (1748) and "The Fountains" (1766) follow in chronological order.

The texts provided below have not entailed complex editorial labors and decisions. After examining the relevant evidence, I concluded, like several of my predecessors, that Johnson lightly revised the second—and only the second—edition of *Rasselas*. I have therefore inserted these revisions into the text of the first edition, which served as the basic copy-text. Collation of the editions published during Johnson's lifetime revealed no authorial changes in the text of "The Vision of Theodore," which is consequently that of the first edition. Collation of the manuscript draft of "The Fountains" and the first—and only—edition published during Johnson's lifetime revealed that the printed version, replete with authorial changes, should obviously be the copy-text.

The introductions to the three works are intended to make clear the known or probable circumstances which, according to modern scholarship, principally attended the creation and early existence of the works. Some topics—composition, publication,

generic classification, and reception, for example—are addressed
in all the introductions; others—notably the Abyssinian and
Egyptian background of *Rasselas*—have resulted from a felt need
to explicate selected aspects of individual works. Apart from the
sections on genres, I have not attempted critical analyses or interpretations of the texts; I hope, however, that the materials in the
introductions and in the annotation on the texts will aid the
production of fresh evaluations and interpretations. The annotation concentrates on clarifying the meaning of numerous words,
relating specific notions to Johnson's expressions of the same or
similar opinions elsewhere, and indicating antecedents—even,
occasionally, likely sources—of various parts of the texts. The
notes on *Rasselas* are admittedly full; the importance of the work
both in the Johnsonian canon and also in English literature justifies, I believe, that fullness.

During the lengthy preparation of this edition, I have received
valuable assistance and encouragement from many individuals
and institutions. One group of benefactors is unfortunately beyond the reach of my expression of thanks: Arthur Friedman
(who long ago pointed out to me the desirability of a fresh edition
of *Rasselas*); R. S. Crane (who gave me his annotated copy of
Rasselas); Robert Metzdorf (whose joint participation in this edition was cut short by death); Allen Hazen (who invited me to
prepare this volume for the Yale Johnson); James Clifford (whose
conversation and letters produced significant information for the
enterprise); Napier Wilt (who as Dean of the Humanities Division
at the University of Chicago provided me with indispensable
financial support); and George Sherburn, Donald Bond, Louis
Landa, and L. F. Powell (who enthusiastically urged the completion of the project). Happily, a larger company of friends can still
be saluted for their diverse but essential contributions to the
undertaking: Walter Blair, Donald Greene, James Miller, Edward
Rosenheim, Robert Rosenthal, Joshua Scodel, Robert Streeter,
Stuart Tave, John Wallace, and Karl Weintraub—all of the University of Chicago; Paul Alkon, of the University of Southern
California; Donald Eddy, of Cornell University; David Fleeman,
of Pembroke College, Oxford; Patricia Hernlund, of Wayne State
University; Robert Mayo, of Northwestern University; Graham

Nicholls, of the Johnson Birthplace Museum; Howard Weinbrot, of the University of Wisconsin at Madison; and Richard Wendorf, of the Houghton Library, Harvard.

To this number should be added the members of the Editorial Committee of the Yale Johnson, whose comments and suggestions have much improved the editorial features of this volume. I must pay special tribute to Mary Hyde Eccles, who continues her extraordinary kindnesses to me and my research; Herman W. Liebert, who has been unfailingly helpful in a variety of ways; Walter Jackson Bate, cherished supporter and fount of knowledge; O M Brack, Jr.; Bertram H. Davis; James Engell; James Gray; Jean H. Hagstrum; Benjamin B. Hoover; William R. Keast; and Bruce Redford. I am also warmly appreciative of the constant care, generosity, and patience with which John H. Middendorf, the General Editor of the series, discharges his responsibilities.

I shall never forget munificent grants from the Guggenheim Foundation and the American Council of Learned Societies. The efficiency and courtesy of the respective staffs have enabled me to work profitably and agreeably in the University of Chicago Libraries, the John Crerar Library, the Newberry Library, Northwestern University Library, British Library, Bodleian Library, Yale University Libraries, and the Rylands Library of Manchester University.

Many previous editors have contributed to my commentary on *Rasselas;* three—G. B. Hill, O. F. Emerson, and John Hardy—merit more recognition than is afforded by the list of Short Titles below. My research assistant, David Cahill, has substantially increased the accuracy of my references.

It is a great pleasure to record the following permissions: by the University of Chicago Press for reprinting parts of my essay on "The 'Paradise' in Abyssinia and the 'Happy Valley' in *Rasselas*," which appeared in *Modern Philology* (LVI [1958], 10–16); by the editors of *Novel* for reprinting parts of my essay on "Mrs. (Thrale) Piozzi and Dr. Johnson's 'The Fountains: A Fairy Tale,'" which appeared in *Novel* (XIII [1979], 68–81); by the University Press of Virginia for reprinting a revised version of my essay on "The Reception of *Rasselas*, 1759–1800," which appeared in *Greene*

Centennial Studies: Essays Presented to Donald Greene in the Centennial Year of the University of Southern California, edited by Paul J. Korshin and Robert R. Allen (1984); by the English Department of Harvard University for reprinting a revised version of my essay on *"The Vision of Theodore:* Genre, Context, Early Reception," which appeared in *Johnson and His Age,* edited by James Engell (1984); and by the Rylands Library of Manchester University for printing portions of MS. English 654 (Mrs. Piozzi's transcription of Johnson's "The Fountains: A Fairy Tale").

Finally, my largest measure of gratitude I owe to my wife Ruth, who has sustained and shared my labors for over forty years, and to our children, Jack and Alma Dean, who have sympathetically watched my "wrestling with *Rasselas"* for much of the same period.

G.J.K.

The Editorial Committee wishes to express its sincere gratitude to all those individuals, institutions, and organizations whose generous contributions to the Friends of the Edition have helped to make possible the publication of this volume: Malcolm J. Abzug, Lionel Basney, Robin Bromley, Morris R. Brownell, Emily C. Bucher, Donald E. Burgess, Sara B. Burroughs, Colin Campbell, W. Bliss Carnochan, Arthur H. Cash, Chester Chapin, Philip B. Daghlian, Bertram H. Davis, Harry C. DeMuth, Mary Hyde Eccles, James Elliott, Frank Ellis, Richard Enemark and Nancy Lawton, Jennifer B. Fleischner, Paul Fussell, Jr., Henry C. Gibson, Jr., Homer Goldberg, Richard Goodyear, Edward Graham, Isobel Grundy, Mary N. Gunther, Jean H. Hagstrum, Elizabeth A. Hedrick, Anne Himmelfarb, Benjamin M. Hines, Ari Hoogenboom, Herman V. Ivey, Thomas Jemielity (in memory of his mother), The Johnson Society of Lichfield, Mark C. Jones, Eugene Katz, Judith Keig, William Kinsley, Gwin J. Kolb, Lanshaw & Co., John M. Lindsey, Gregory Lowchy, Clark Luikart, Sandra E. Lundy, Maureen MacGrogan, Helen Louise McGuffie, Ann P. Messenger, W. H. Miller, Barbara Millman, Herbert C. Morton, Daisuke Nagashima, Yoshiyuki Nakano, James F. Nash, William D. Nesbit, Catherine N. Parke, R. G. Peterson, Charles E. Pierce,

Jr., The Lynn R. and Karl E. Prickett Fund, Richard A. Rabicoff, James E. Radford, Allen Walker Read, Allen and Susan Reddick, Arthur G. Rippey, Deborah Rogers, Robert W. Rogers, Loren R. Rothschild, Michael A. Scully, Stuart Sherman, Neille Shoemaker, Mary Margaret Stewart, Joseph E. Stockwell, Jr., Erica Strasser, Paul E. Strauss, Hitoshi Suwabe, Janice Thaddeus, Lars Troide, John A. Vance, John M. Walker, Jr., Ian Watt, Howard D. Weinbrot, Josephine C. Wiseman, Qian-Zhi Wu, Guozhang Xu.

The preparation of this volume was made possible in part by a grant from the Program for Editions of the National Endowment for the Humanities. For this support the Editorial Committee is sincerely grateful. The General Editor wishes also to thank Mary Alice Galligan, of the Yale University Press, for seeing this volume through to completion with experienced attention, good sense, and quiet, cheerful authority; and John P. Zomchick, of the University of Tennessee, and Jennifer Thorn, of Columbia University, for their valuable assistance in a variety of editorial tasks.

Changes have occurred in the Editorial Committee since the publication of the previous volume. We are pleased to announce the appointment to the committee of James Engell, J. D. Fleeman, Bruce Redford, and Howard D. Weinbrot. But it is with deep sorrow that we report the loss by death of Bertrand B. Bronson, a member of the committee since its inception, a scholar whose profound learning and constant helpfulness will be greatly missed. As a sign of our admiration and affection, this volume is dedicated to him.

CONTENTS

ILLUSTRATIONS

Letter from Samuel Johnson to William Strahan, 20 January 1759

INTRODUCTION

The primary document containing information about the composition of *Rasselas* is the following letter—still extant—which Johnson wrote to his friend and frequent printer, William Strahan:

Sir
  When I was with you last night I told you of a thing which I was preparing for the press. The title will be

The choice of Life
or
The History of ——— Prince of Abissinia

  It will make about two volumes like little Pompadour that is about one middling volume. The bargain which I made with Mr Johnston was seventy five pounds (or guineas) a volume, and twenty five pounds for the second Edition. I will sell this either at that price or for sixty the first edition of which he shall himself fix the number, and the property then to revert to me, or for forty pounds, and share the profit that is retain half the copy. I shall have occasion for thirty pounds on Monday night when I shall deliver the book which I must entreat you upon such delivery to procure me. I would have it offered to Mr Johnston, but have no doubt of selling it, on some of the terms mentioned.
  I will not print my name, but expect it to be known.
                                 I am Dear Sir Your most humble Servant
                                                      Sam: Johnson
Jan. 20. 1759
Get me the money if you can.[1]

---

1. *Letters* 124, the text of which differs slightly from that of the manuscript.

From this letter we learn that by Saturday, 20 January 1759, Johnson had initiated a discussion concerning the sale of the book, given it a title (without, however, naming the hero), determined its approximate length (which he compared to the size of the lately published *History of the Marchioness de Pompadour*), apparently written a large number of its pages, vowed to deliver it (presumably to Strahan) two days later, and decided not to include his name on its title page while expecting his authorship "to be known." From the letter we also deduce a direct causal relationship between the composition of the work and Johnson's obviously pressing need for money.

Other letters of the same period contain clues to the reason for Johnson's financial plight—namely, the last illness and death of his ninety-year-old mother, who lived in Lichfield with Johnson's stepdaughter, Lucy Porter, and who was buried there on 23 January 1759. On 13 January, after hearing of her worsening condition from Lucy Porter, he wrote to his mother:

> whatever you would have done, and what debts you would have paid first, or anything else that you would direct, let Miss put it down; I shall endeavour to obey you.
>
> I have got twelve guineas to send you, but unhappily am at a loss how to send it to-night. If I cannot send it to-night, it will come by the next post.

On 16 January he told his stepdaughter: "I hope you received twelve guineas on Monday. . . . I will send you more in a few days." On 23 January—three days after his letter to Strahan—he wrote: "I shall send a bill of twenty pounds in a few days, which I thought to have brought to my mother; but God suffered it not." Two days later, stating his inability to "get a bill . . . to night" for the twenty pounds, he promised to send the money "on Saturday" (27 January); and on Saturday he informed Miss Porter: "I have sent you a note of twenty pounds with which I [would] have done what you suppose my dear Mother would have directed. I repose wholly on your prudence and can send ten pounds more when you please." In each of his next three letters, he mentioned the payment of his mother's debts. On 6 February he observed that "My Mother's debts, dear Mother! I suppose I may pay with little difficulty"; on 15 February he directed that "Kitty [Chambers, the maid-servant] shall be paid first, and I will send her down money to pay the London debts afterwards"; and on 1 March he repeated his direction, saying that the maid-servant should "be paid first, as my dear dear Mother ordered," and requesting his stepdaughter to "let me know at once the sum necessary to discharge her other debts, and I will send it you very soon." Finally, in letters dated 23 March and 10 May, Johnson referred to one (if not the chief) putative source of the amounts of money he had been sending, or promising to send, to Lucy Porter during the preceding months. "I am going to publish a little story book," he told her in the first, "which I will send you when it is out." And in the second—written, of course, after the publication of *Rasselas*— he asked Miss Porter to "tell me how you like my little book."[2]

Statements in early biographies of Johnson and elsewhere reinforce and extend (not always accurately) the evidence afforded by his letters regarding the composition of *Rasselas*. In the *Gentleman's Magazine* for December 1784 (LVI, 908), Thomas Tyers observes that "it is reported, [Johnson] wrote [*Rasselas*] to raise a purse of pecuniary assistance to his aged mother at Lichfield." In his *Life* (1785), William Cooke, after suggesting that Johnson's translation of Lobo's *Voyage to Abyssinia* was the seed of the "novel," remarks that the immediate cause of the work "was the want of *twenty pounds*, to enable him to go down to Lichfield to pay the last duties to his mother who was dying." In his *Memoirs of the Life and Writings of . . . Johnson* (1785), William Shaw provides a somewhat different relation: "It is known," he says, "to many of the Doctor's friends, that his *Rasselas or Prince of Abyssinia*, was an early conception, on which his ideas were matured long before the completion of the work. He shewed the first lines of it to a bookseller, who gave him no encouragement to proceed. . . . The outlines of this immortal work could not procure the author credit for twenty guineas. His mother was dying of a good old age. He wished to raise this sum that he might be able to see her on her death-bed. He sat down to finish his plan, and notwithstanding his expeditious composition, she died before he could

2. *Letters* 118, 119, 125, 126, 126.1, 127, 128, 129, 130, 131.

INTRODUCTION

make it convenient to visit her. . . . the *Prince of Abyssinia* was sold
to another bookseller, and had a very considerable sale."[3] In his
Life (1787), Sir John Hawkins also refers to the "report" which
"says, but rather vaguely, that, to supply [his mother's] necessities
in her last illness, [Johnson] wrote and made money of his *Rasselas*"; then Hawkins continues: "The fact, respecting the writing
and publishing the story of Rasselas is, that finding the Eastern
Tales written by himself in the *Rambler,* and by Hawkesworth in
the *Adventurer,* had been well received, he had been for some time
meditating a fictitious history, of a greater extent than any that
had appeared in either of those papers, . . . and having digested
his thoughts on the subject, he obeyed the spur of that necessity
which now pressed him, and sat down to compose the tale . . . ,
laying the scene of it in a country that he had before occasion to
contemplate, in his translation of Padre Lobo's voyage."[4] Boswell
is the most detailed and precise. Dismissing Hawkins's "reveries"
about the work, he declares: "I have to mention, that the late Mr.
Strahan the printer told me, that Johnson wrote it, that with the
profits he might defray the expence of his mother's funeral, and
pay some little debts which she had left. He told Sir Joshua
Reynolds [and others] that he composed it in the evenings of one
week, sent it to the press in portions as it was written, and had
never since read it over."[5] Last, Edmond Malone reported the
following account from Giuseppe Baretti:

> When Johnson had finished his *Rasselas,* Baretti happened
> to call on him. He said he had just finished a romance—that
> he had no money, and pressingly required some to take to his
> mother who was ill at Lichfield. He therefore requested Ba-
> retti to go to Dodsley the bookseller, and say he wished to see
> him. When he came, Johnson asked what he would give for
> his romance. The only question was what number of sheets it
> would make. On examining it, he said he would give him

100*l.* Johnson was perfectly contented, but insisted on part of the money being paid immediately, and accordingly received 70*l.* Any other person with the degree of reputation he then possessed would have got 400*l.* for that work, but he never understood the art of making the most of his productions.[6]

All these pieces of primary and secondary evidence thus place the actual birth of *Rasselas* in the early part of 1759—probably in the latter half of January. There seems to be no reason for doubting that Johnson, famous for his speed of composition, could have produced the book "in the evenings of a single week" or that he "sent it to the press in portions as it was written" (even though Robert Dodsley, according to Baretti, may have examined much of the manuscript on one occasion). The identification of the exact period of composition will probably never be made. But the gestation of the work may well have extended over a number of years. Boswell and Cooke discern the possible inception or "remote occasion" of the tale in Johnson's translation of Lobo's *Voyage to Abyssinia* (1735); Shaw observes that *Rasselas* "was an early conception, on which [Johnson's] ideas were matured long before the completion of the work"; and Hawkins states that Johnson, encouraged by the reception of the "Eastern Tales" in the *Rambler* and *Adventurer,* "had been for some time meditating" a substantial "fictitious history" prior to his mother's final illness.

Much more recently, Donald M. Lockhart and Arthur J. Weitzman have suggested independently, at the end of revealing essays on the Abyssinian and Egyptian background of the book, that Johnson's preparation for writing *Rasselas* occupied a much larger interval than a single week.[7] Lockhart goes so far as to conclude that "both the substance and the Ethiopian background of *Rasselas,* the latter probably in the form of notes, were already developed at least seven years before that week in January 1759,

6. James Prior, *Life of Edmond Malone* (1860), pp. 160–61. Prior says (p. 159) that Malone received this account from Baretti himself on 5 April 1789.

7. Donald M. Lockhart, "'The Fourth Son of the Mighty Emperor': The Ethiopian Background of Johnson's *Rasselas,*" *PMLA,* LXXVIII (1963), 537; Arthur J. Weitzman, "More Light on *Rasselas:* The Background of the Egyptian Episodes," *Philological Quarterly,* XLVIII (1969), 57–58.

when Johnson wrote *Rasselas* for publication." The principal basis of this conclusion is the remarkable conformity between the certain or likely sources Johnson utilized in his depiction of the Abyssinian background of *Rambler*s 204, 205 and those he subsequently employed for similar purposes in *Rasselas*. Lockhart's assertion may fail to recognize adequately the celerity of Johnson's imagination and the extraordinary power of his memory, which was capable of suddenly putting to use, for a given purpose, an abundance of minute materials collected at random earlier, with no specific end in view. Nevertheless, Lockhart's hypothesis, Weitzman's findings, and the comments of Shaw and Hawkins support the conjecture that Johnson had planned a story possessing some of the features of *Rasselas* long before he actually wrote the tale. The nature and extent of these features are discussed in the following section of this introduction.

Having possibly "meditated" the creation of a "fictitious history" for a substantial period and, impelled by the exigency of his mother's illness, having finally produced most of the text, Johnson, as his letter of 20 January 1759 to Strahan shows, turned his attention to the sale of his "little book." The letter records the three alternative prices which he offered—via Strahan—to William Johnston, a leading London bookseller and publisher, with whom he had perhaps made an earlier "bargain" regarding the translation ("little Pompadour") of a French work entitled, in English, *The History of the Marchioness de Pompadour* (1758).[8] Soon after writing the letter, however, Johnson, instead of negotiating solely with Johnston or with Robert Dodsley (cf. Baretti's account, obviously incorrect in this respect, quoted above), sold the publishing rights to a partnership consisting of Johnston, Dodsley, and Strahan. Boswell's report of the transaction ("Mr. Strahan, Mr. Johnston, and Mr. Dodsley purchased [*Rasselas*] for a hundred pounds, but afterwards paid him twenty-five pounds more, when it came to a second edition") is confirmed by entries in Strahan's ledgers and another document.[9]

8. For a detailed discussion of this possibility, see Gwin J. Kolb, "Johnson's 'Little Pompadour': A Textual Crux and a Hypothesis," *Restoration and Eighteenth-Century Literature*, ed. Carroll Camden (1963), pp. 125–42.

9. *Life*, 1.341. For relevant entries in the ledgers, see Gwin J. Kolb, "*Rasselas*: Purchase Price, Proprietors, and Printings," *Studies in Bibliography*, xv (1962),

Received May 21. 1759. of Mr Strahan
Ten pounds on acct. for the second Edition
of Rasselas Prince of Abissinia

£10 : 0 : 0   Sam: Johnson

Received June 22. 1759. of Mr Strahan Six
Guineas more on the same account
                               Sam: Johnson

£6 : 6 : 0

Received   of Mr Strahan
Eight pounds fourteen Shillings in full
of twenty five pounds due to me from
the Second Edition of Rasselas, and is
in full for the said Copy

£8 : 14 : 0

Receipts for payments to Johnson for the second edition of *Rasselas*

The ledgers also reveal that Strahan's firm printed the first edition of the tale, as well as at least the next eight "authorized" editions. On 19 April 1759 the work was entered in the Stationers' Register, and, according to most newspaper advertisements, the next day—20 April—saw its initial appearance in two small octavo volumes costing five shillings.[1] A second, lightly revised edition came out some two months later, on 26 June.[2] The proximity of the first and second editions may explain why Johnson, perhaps considering the writing and the revising a continuous operation,[3] told Sir Joshua Reynolds and others, at unspecified times, that he "had never . . . read [the book] over" since composing it. In 1781—while on a carriage trip—he "seized . . . with avidity" a copy which Boswell "happened to take . . . out of [his] pocket" and perused it eagerly.[4] And as late as 19 April 1784— only eight months before he died—his continuing parental interest in the *History* was manifested by his presenting a copy of the sixth edition (1783) to his young friend Ellis Cornelia Knight, who subsequently wrote *Dinarbas* (1790), a sequel to *Rasselas*.[5]

THE ABYSSINIAN AND EGYPTIAN BACKGROUND

For understandable reasons, investigations into the Abyssinian background of *Rasselas* have regularly begun with an examina-

---

256–59. The other document—SJ's acknowledgment of payments by Strahan for the second edition—is reproduced in the illustration facing this page. Part of still another Strahan manuscript (in the American Philosophical Society Library) contains, as Patricia Hernlund has kindly informed me, the following entry under the general heading "The Particulars of the Estate of Wm. Strahan as it stood on the first of January 1759": "⅓ Rasselas, Pr. of Abyssinia 33:6.8." A discrepancy obviously exists between the apparent date of this entry, which seemingly proves that Strahan owned a one-third share of *Rasselas* on 1 Jan 1759, and the date of SJ's letter of 20 Jan to Strahan, which certainly proves that the tale had not been sold by 20 Jan. The discrepancy vanishes, however, if one assumes that Strahan, in reckoning the value of his estate, made the entry regarding *Rasselas*—the very last of a list of twenty-eight titles—after 20 Jan rather than at the beginning of the month.

    1. See Donald D. Eddy, "The Publication Date of the First Edition of *Rasselas*," *Notes and Queries*, CCVII (Jan 1962), 21–22.

    2. *Life*, 1.340, n. 3; 341, n. 2.

    3. O. F. Emerson first made this suggestion; see *Life*, 1.341, n. 2.

    4. *Life*, IV.119.

    5. See p. xii, n. 7, below.

tion of Johnson's first book, *A Voyage to Abyssinia* (1735), his (partial) translation, from French to English, of Joachim Le Grand's *Relation historique d'Abissinie du R. P. Jerome Lobo* (1728).[6] Like several other early accounts of Abyssinia, the translation (or "epitome") contains references to the policy, "establish'd about 1260" but "abolish'd for two ages," of confining, in order to maintain political stability, "the sons and brothers of the Emperor . . . till their accession to the throne." It also includes allusions to the "barren summit of Ambaguexa," a "famous rock" located in the kingdom of Amhara, on which "the princes of the blood-royal pass'd their melancholly life, being guarded by officers who treated them often with great rigour and severity." Furthermore, among the historical personages appearing in the work is "Rassela Christos lieutenant general to Sultan Segued," who figures, too, in other early books about Ethiopia. In addition, as is demonstrated by notes below to specific portions of the tale, particular passages in the *Voyage* parallel more or less closely various parts of *Rasselas,* among them, for example, the designation of the Nile River as the "Father of Waters" and the spelling of the name (Goiama) of the Abyssinian kingdom where the Nile originates and the poet Imlac was born (*Voyage to Abyssinia,* pp. 163, 167, 85, 81, 171).

However, even if it provided Johnson with miscellaneous data for his story, the *Voyage's* description (the "barren summit" of a rock) of the royal prison is strikingly different from the "Happy Valley" in *Rasselas,* its mention of the unpleasant life led by the princes has nothing in common with the luxurious existence of the royal inmates (princes *and* princesses) of the valley, and the name attributed to "Sultan" Segued's "lieutenant general" is not exactly the same as the name of Johnson's hero. Consequently, we must look beyond the *Voyage* for possible sources of, and ana-

---

6. Although usually identified as Lobo's *Voyage to Abyssinia,* SJ's volume is a rendering of Le Grand's work, which includes, among other materials, Le Grand's French version of Lobo's Portuguese manuscript, Le Grand's sequel to Lobo's narrative, and sixteen "dissertations"—also by Le Grand—concerning Abyssinia. For additional information about the relationship between Le Grand's work and SJ's translation, see *Voyage to Abyssinia,* p. xxiii. The most thorough examination of the Abyssinian background of *Rasselas* is the essay by Donald M. Lockhart cited on p. xxiii above, to which the present discussion is substantially indebted. Footnote 2 of Lockhart's article lists a selection of previous studies of the subject.

logues to, the principal Abyssinian features of *Rasselas*. The Preface to the *Voyage* supplies useful directions for our search. This "Portuguese traveller," Johnson observes, "contrary to the general vein of his countrymen, has amused his reader with no romantick absurdities or incredible fictions. . . . He appears . . . to have copied nature from the life, and to have consulted his senses not his imagination; he meets with no basilisks that destroy with their eyes . . . , and his cataracts fall from the rock without deafening the neighbouring inhabitants" (p. 3). Later Johnson refers approvingly to "Dr. Geddes's" history of the church of Abyssinia and to the work of the "great Ludolfus" (pp. 4, 5).

Insofar as *Rasselas* is concerned, Michael Geddes's church history (1696) contains nothing that is not also found in the *Voyage*. But Hiob Ludolf's large *Historia Aethiopica* (Frankfurt, 1681)—Johnson owned[7] a copy of the English translation (*A New History of Ethiopia* [1682])—yields, on examination, more profitable results. In the translation (Table between pp. 192 and 193, p. 171) appear the characters "Rasselach" (whose possibly sibilant ending makes it the closest known approximation of the name of Johnson's prince[8]), the same historical individual as the *Voyage*'s "Rassela Christos," and "Icon-Imlac," a fourteenth-century "Prince of the Salomonean Race," who almost certainly provided the name of the poet in Johnson's tale. Furthermore, the "Genealogic Table" in Ludolf's history records the escape from "Amhara" of the fourth child (like Prince Rasselas) of an Abyssinian monarch. Finally, certain other comments by Ludolf may be the sources of incidental passages in *Rasselas*.[9]

Yet on the kind of place assigned to the emperor's sons as their prison-home, Ludolf, despite his glowing description of the tops of Ethiopian mountains (pp. 28–29), is as realistic and unromantic as Johnson's *Voyage*. "The reports," he declares scornfully, "concerning the pleasantness of those rocks [of Amhara], and the splendid attendance upon those royal exiles, are all ridiculous falsities" (p. 197). Thus, with respect to the incarceration of Abys-

---

7. Item 587 of *The Sale Catalogue of Samuel Johnson's Library: A Facsimile Edition* (introd. J. D. Fleeman [1975]) reads: "Ludolph's history of Ethiopia, and 17 more" (p. 26).

8. I have borrowed this remark from Lockhart, p. 518.

9. See p. 7, n. 5, and p. 8, n. 9, below.

sinian royalty, Ludolf, Geddes, and a number of other early writers (several of whom Ludolf cites)[1] may be said, in Johnson's
phrase, "to have copied nature from the life"; their accounts are
sober, more or less accurate, and wholly different from Johnson's
portrayal of the Eden-like delights of the Happy Valley. One of
these sober accounts, it should be pointed out—*The Voyage of Sir
Francis Alvarez . . . made unto the Court of Prete Ianni, the Great
Christian Emperour of Ethiopia* (English translation, 1625)—anticipates Johnson's location of the royal prison in a valley. According
to Alvarez, "There is . . . a valley betweene two mountaines,
which is very strong, so that by no meanes a man can goe out of
the same, because the passage is closed up with exceeding strong
gates, and in this valley which is very great, and hath many townes
and dwellings in it, they keepe those which are of the bloud-
royall."[2] Although his knowledge of the book is not certain, Johnson may have borrowed this setting from Alvarez's *Voyage,* seemingly the only pre-1759 work to specify a valley as the site of the
prison. Similarly, he may have drawn on another realistic narrative, Charles Jacques Poncet's *Voyage to Aethiopia* (first English
translation, 1709), for several details, including the size, complex
structure, and location of the palace in the Happy Valley.[3]

Numerous additional features of the paradisial prison clearly
derive, however, not from historical descriptions of Abyssinia, but
from a "romantic" kind of work, glanced at by both Johnson and
Ludolf in the passages quoted above. The most famous member
of this class of "incredible fictions" and "ridiculous falsities" is
Father Luis de Urreta's ecclesiastical and political history of Ethiopia, written in Spanish, published at Valencia in 1610, and mentioned (pp. 273–74, 281) in Johnson's *Voyage.* A total of five
chapters in Urreta's volume "would perswade us," as a later author put it, "there had been another Terrestrial Paradise con-

---

1. See Lockhart, p. 519.
2. Samuel Purchas, *Hakluytus Posthumus or Purchas His Pilgrimages,* VII (1905),
p. 80. This edition of Alvarez's *Voyage,* which begins in Vol. VI (pp. 517–43), is part
of a twenty-volume reprint of the 1625 edition of Purchas.
3. Poncet's *Voyage* forms part of the collection entitled *The Red Sea and Adjacent
Countries at the Close of the Seventeenth Century,* ed. Sir William Foster (Ser. II, Vol. C,
of the Hakluyt Society Publications, 1949). See p. 10, n. 5, below. Poncet appears
in SJ's *Voyage to Abyssinia,* pp. 134 ff.

cealed in [Amhara]."[4] The chapters depict the assorted splendors, both natural and man-made, of the elevated retreat and the life led therein by the royal captives. The prison is situated in the middle of Ethiopia under the equinoctial line and atop a mountain with an "umbrella-like"[5] upper edge. Its wonderful adornments exhibit remarkable resemblances to the embellishments of Johnson's Happy Valley, including "the spring-fed rivulets . . . , the lake, the fish of every species, the ever-bearing fruit trees, the wild and tame herbivorous animals . . . , the absence of ferocious animals, the birds singing in the trees, the extensive area enclosed by the mountains,"[6] the palace (thirty-four in Urreta, one in *Rasselas*), the treasure and jewels (Urreta devotes two chapters to a treatment of the "grandissimo tesoro," the jewels, and the other precious objects kept on Amhara), and the wise teachers who instruct the princes. Indeed, so pronounced are the likenesses between the comparable parts of the *Historia* and *Rasselas* that Johnson's indebtedness to Urreta seems highly probable even if not absolutely certain.[7]

Of the various fictions about Abyssinia in English, *The Late Travels of S. Giacomo Baratti* (1670), a spurious travel book almost surely based in part on Urreta's history, depicts (pp. 33–36, 117–20) the royal prison in terms corresponding most closely to Johnson's description in the initial chapters of *Rasselas*. Both works represent the residence ("a very delicious place in the middle of a large mountain," Baratti asserts [p. 33]) as a veritable paradise full of natural and artificial delights. Both say that all the king's children, not merely his sons, live on Amhara, share a single building, and receive instruction during their captivity. And both refer to the treasure kept in the stronghold and to the emperor's annual visit there ("The emperour visits this place once a year with his wives," Baratti informs us [p. 36]). This last comment, along with Baratti's designation of both sexes as the royal inhabitants of the retreat, suggests that the *Travels* may have provided one or more items of Johnson's conception of the paradisial prison.

4. Balthazar Telles, *The Travels of the Jesuits in Ethiopia* (1710), p. 49.
5. I have borrowed this term from Lockhart, p. 520.
6. Lockhart, p. 522.
7. See Lockhart, pp. 520–23, for a detailed discussion of the subject.

The second extended pre-1759 description in English of the delights and "rarities" of the "hill Amara" occurs in the collection of *Purchas His Pilgrimage* (1613). Admittedly an abstract of material in Urreta's *Historia,* the account contains (pp. 565–68) fewer similarities to Johnson's creation than do Urreta and Baratti. But the collection assembled by Purchas was well known and moderately accessible—later editions appeared in 1614, 1617, and 1625—and it is possible that before composing *Rasselas* Johnson examined the section on the Abyssinian royal prison, which, following Urreta, closely resembles the Happy Valley.

Whatever the precise sources of the Happy Valley (and, despite Lockhart's careful investigation, uncertainties about some of them still obviously persist), its general background is clear. Johnson, who surely knew the harsh truth about the imprisonment of the Abyssinian princes, was thoroughly acquainted with the fanciful "paradise" tradition,[8] and he deliberately chose to employ it in the opening chapters of *Rasselas.* Behind him, besides his *Voyage to Abyssinia,* were *Rambler* 204 and 205, which record the unsuccessful attempt of Seged, "lord of Ethiopia," to be completely happy for eight days.[9] In his selection of the "romantic" tradition, Johnson was at once continuing the practice of the past and anticipating the usage of the future, and thus helping to make literary history. Milton in *Paradise Lost* and Thomson in *The Seasons* had utilized the same tradition earlier; and Coleridge, at the end of his private road to Xanadu, was to do so later in *Kubla Khan.*[1] But the Happy Valley remains the most celebrated incarnation.

---

8. Pre-1759 prose manifestations of this tradition are not restricted to the works by Urreta, Baratti, and Purchas. For brief "romantic" descriptions of the royal prison, see, for example, Peter Heylin's *Cosmographie* (5th ed., 1677), Book IV.53; Giovanni Paolo Marana's *Turkish Spy* (6th ed., 1707), IV.144–45; and Alexander Hamilton's *New Account of the East Indies* (1727), ed. Sir William Foster (1930), I.26.

9. For an examination of these papers as a generic prefiguration of *Rasselas,* see pp. xxxv–xxxvii below.

1. For full discussions of the use by Milton, Thomson, and Coleridge of the Abyssinian "paradise" tradition, see the following: Evert M. Clark, "Milton's Abyssinian Paradise," *Texas Studies in English,* XXIX (1950), 129–50; Alan D. McKillop, *The Background of Thomson's "Seasons"* (1942), pp. 151 ff.; John Livingston Lowes, *The Road to Xanadu* (rev. ed., 1930), pp. 375–76, 590–91.

Aside from Abyssinia, the main geographical locale of *Rasselas* is Egypt, notably the city of Cairo, the "great pyramid," the Arab chief's "castle" (and seraglio), "the monastery of St. Anthony," and the "catacombs." None of these places elicit elaborate treatment—the setting is general throughout practically all of the tale—but most of them closely conform in their lineaments to the largely accurate remarks on the subject by early authors. Before writing *Rasselas,* Johnson, it seems clear, "must have read widely in European travel and geography books dealing with Egypt and the Near East, besides what he may have read of ancient Egypt by Greek and Roman historians."[2]

The allusions to Cairo, for example, though they may also reflect Johnson's opinion of London, wholly accord with observations in such travel books as Aaron Hill's *A Full and Just Account of the Present State of the Ottoman Empire* (1709) and Richard Pococke's *A Description of the East* (2 vols., 1743–45), which stress the size, diverse population, and commercial strength of the Egyptian metropolis.[3] Moreover, Hill's and Pococke's works, like (say) John Greaves's *Pyramidographia* (1646), contain information about the Great Pyramid of Cheops which is also provided by the narrator of *Rasselas* when he says in chapter XXXII that the prince and his party "passed through the galleries, surveyed the vaults of marble, and examined the chest in which the body of the founder is supposed to have been reposited."[4] Further, both Hill and Greaves (along with Mr. Spectator, of course) anticipate the action of the prince's party in measuring the Great Pyramid,[5] and both voice opinions (Greaves borrows his from Pliny's *Natural History*) which resemble Imlac's comment in chapter XXXII on the

---

2. I have quoted this passage from the article (p. 43) by Arthur J. Weitzman cited on p. xxiii above. The following discussion is substantially indebted to Weitzman's essay, the fullest examination yet published of the Egyptian background of *Rasselas.*

3. See Weitzman, pp. 54–55; p. 63, n. 1, below.

4. See Weitzman, pp. 46–48; p. 117, n. 1, below. According to Boswell (*Life,* II.346), SJ was acquainted with Pococke's *Description of the East,* and he apparently owned a copy of Greaves's *Pyramidographia* (item 38 in *The Sale Catalogue of Samuel Johnson's Library,* introd. by J. D. Fleeman [1975], reads [p. 4] in part: "Greave's tracts. 2 v.").

5. See Weitzman, p. 48; *Spectator* 1.

pyramids as symbols of human vanity.[6] Finally, although Johnson's indebtedness cannot be definitely proved, an episode in
Hill's *Account* exhibits marked similarities to the abduction, outside the pyramid, of Pekuah and her maids by the troop of
Arabs.[7]

The depiction of the Arab chief, his dwelling ("a strong and
spacious house built with stone in an island of the Nile"), and
harem is quite different from the accounts of desert Arabs and
marauding sheiks given by most seventeenth- and eighteenth-
century writers. For his treatment, more akin to things Turkish
than Bedouin, Johnson may have drawn on such works as Richard Knolles's *Generall Historie of the Turks* (1630), the principal
source of Johnson's only play, *Irene* (1749); John Greaves's *Description of the Grand Seignor's Seraglio* (1650), which was in Johnson's library; Alexander Russell's *Natural History of Aleppo* (1756),
which Johnson reviewed in the *Literary Magazine* (1756); and
Aaron Hill's *Full Account*. The last volume may have also provided
material for the passage on the catacombs at the end of chapter
XLVII of *Rasselas*, and Pococke's *Description of the East* perhaps
supplied facts for the references to the monastery of St. Anthony
in chapter XXXVII.[8]

Since its initial publication, commentators have employed a number of different terms to indicate the generic classification of *Rasselas*. Early reviewers called the work a "moral tale," a "novel" (but
not conforming to the ordinary pattern), a "romance" (whose
contents belie the connotations of its title), a "satire," and an
"eastern story" (or "fable" or "tale"). Later writers added such
phrases as "philosophical discourse," "philosophical romance,"
"classical romance," "oriental apologue," and "philosophic tale"
to the list. In the twentieth century, critics have relied on earlier

6. See Weitzman, p. 48; p. 118, n. 6, below.
7. See Weitzman, pp. 44–45; p. 120, n. 1, below.
8. For a longer discussion of the works mentioned in this paragraph, see
Weitzman, pp. 50–54. Also see p. 168, n. 3, and p. 130, n. 3, below.

descriptions and have also invoked the categories of "comedy" and "satire manqué."[9]

The use of these assorted concepts undoubtedly reveals essential aspects of the classifiers' assumptions and procedures: we usually find what we are looking for during the scrutiny of a literary text. But the application of so many differentiae suggests, too, that Johnson's book is a complex mixture of elements,[1] the most important of which merit recognition before an attempt is made to classify the whole amalgam.

To begin with, the designation of the *History* as a kind of novel or tale or romance rests on several manifest facts. *Rasselas* recounts the actions and thoughts of a group of individuated fictional characters who move, within a specific geographical milieu, through a temporal sequence constituting a beginning, a middle, and a conclusion (in which, admittedly, "nothing is concluded"). Moreover, like the "comedy of romance" Johnson distinguishes in *Rambler* 4, the account of the Prince of Abyssinia "bring[s] about natural events by easy means, and . . . keep[s] up curiosity without the help of wonder." Second, the nationalities of the characters, the entire setting, and some of the incidents all relate the narrative to the tradition, especially strong in the eighteenth century, of the "oriental" or "eastern tale," although at a far remove from the adventure-filled type represented by the *Arabian Nights*. Again, the decided accommodation of the plot and characters to instructive ends, the many dialogic conversations, the pervasive expression of ideas, and the steady stream of aphorisms about human life largely account for the description of the tale as "moral" or "philosophic" or as an "apologue." Likewise, the light, humorous, often ironical and mocking treatments accorded a sizable group of incidents and characters (including, occasionally, the main figures) provide a measure of support for the

---

9. See Alvin Whitley, "The Comedy of *Rasselas*," *ELH*, XXIII (1956), 48–70; and W. Jackson Bate, "Johnson and Satire Manqué," *Eighteenth-Century Studies in Honor of Donald F. Hyde,* ed. W. H. Bond (1970), pp. 145–60.

1. In addition to those cited above, numerous studies have sought to clarify the precise character and form of *Rasselas;* see James L. Clifford and Donald J. Greene, *Samuel Johnson: A Survey and Bibliography of Critical Studies* (1970), pp. 227–34; Donald Greene and John A. Vance, *A Bibliography of Johnsonian Studies, 1970–1985* (1987), pp. 71–77.

classification of the work as a brand of comedy or a variety of satire.

Faced with the task of labelling generically the entire entity named *Rasselas,* an editor, intent on aiding, not misleading, the reader of his introduction, must make a selection which subsumes the principal discrete elements of the book. The categories of comedy and satire appear unduly restrictive because they rule out the existence of many serious, nonsatiric components in the work. On the other hand, the appellations of "novel," "oriental tale," "classical romance," and the like are so inclusive that they miss the distinctive qualities of Johnson's composition. Consequently, we are left with the phrases "moral tale," "philosophic tale," and "apologue." All three convey a sense of a fundamental relationship between the narrative of *Rasselas* and the didactic or intellectual content of the text. Although not connoting the presence of other generic strains, all three also easily assimilate episodic comedy and satire within their conceptual boundaries. Admittedly, the three do not completely reveal the attributes of the subject but they are reliable as far as they go. And the addition of "eastern" or "oriental" to each, while producing cumbersome results, further sharpens the traits of the story.

Suggesting, then, that "oriental moral tale" or "oriental philosophic tale" or "oriental apologue" (choosing one of these very similar terms seems needless hairsplitting) accurately if not precisely characterizes the genre to which *Rasselas* belongs, we may briefly survey the nearest members of the work's literary family. Among Johnson's own creations, the history of Seged, "lord of Ethiopia" (*Ramblers* 204, 205), exhibits the most remarkable resemblances to the history of Rasselas, prince of Abyssinia. "In the twenty-seventh year of his reign," Seged, his kingdom peaceful and prosperous, resolves to retire for ten days from the cares of his high office and to "fill the whole capacity of my soul with enjoyment." Afterwards, he tells himself, he will be content "to then fall back to the common state of man, and suffer his life to be diversified, as before, with joy and sorrow."

The emperor's palaces include a luxurious "house of pleasure" located on an island, itself "cultivated only for pleasure," in Lake Dambea. To this delicious region, Seged summons "all the persons of his court, who seemed eminently qualified to receive, or communicate pleasure." The period to be spent in continual happiness begins. The first day passes before the monarch can decide which of the possible delights to savor first. On the second morning, he forbids anyone to appear in his presence "with dejected countenance, or utter any expression of discontent or sorrow"; by evening he is forced "to confess to himself the impotence of command, and resign another day to grief and disappointment." After a night filled with bad dreams, he spends much of the third day lamenting that "a dream could disturb him." The next day the king is happy (for three hours) until an accident mars his enjoyment. Hoping to secure "uncommon entertainment," he offers, on the fifth day, rich prizes for those persons who "distinguish themselves by any festive performances"; but anxiety, not contentment, is the result of the competition. On the sixth day, his peace of mind is broken by overhearing the censorious remarks of a courtier. On the seventh, he is saddened by memories of a defeat in battle and the jealousies of his companions. His daughter—the princess Balkis—becomes ill on the eighth day and dies on the tenth. Thus ends Seged's attempt to be completely happy for a restricted period—an attempt whose record "he has bequeathed to future generations, that no man hereafter may presume to say, 'This day shall be a day of happiness.'"

The history of Seged obviously anticipates *Rasselas* in several important respects. The most pronounced of these, of course, is the conception of the piece as an unsuccessful quest for lasting happiness. Seged limits his wishes to ten days of unalloyed joy; Rasselas seeks a choice of life which will ensure his happiness indefinitely. Second, the emperor's change of place in his search for felicity corresponds to Rasselas's departure from the Happy Valley and his entrance into the ordinary world. Seged's specific transfer, to be sure, is quite different from the prince's; for he tries to find enjoyment by moving from his usual location to a "happy" island. Nevertheless, the same two kinds of place provide settings for the actions of the royal searchers, although Seged restricts his efforts to attain continual joy to a paradisial island, and Rasselas, dissatisfied in a paradisial valley, examines the possibilities for durable happiness in the outside world. Third, the monarch's

collection on the island of "all the persons . . . eminently qualified
to receive or communicate pleasure" resembles the annual assembly in the Happy Valley of "all the artificers of pleasure" (p. 10
below). Fourth, Seged's successive efforts to induce delight parallel the prince's explorations of various modes of life which supposedly produce contentment. Finally, the narrative of Seged
uses Abyssinian material in much the same way as does *Rasselas*.
Specifically, both the monarch and the prince owe their names
(and sex) to actual members of Ethiopian royalty.[2] Likewise, the
islands in Lake Dambea and the particular one containing a royal
palace (to which Seged retreats) are mentioned, like the royal
prison of Amhara, in factual accounts of Abyssinia.[3] And Johnson's description of the "happy" island is comparable to his more
extended description of the Happy Valley.[4]

If the "history of Seged" may be considered *Rasselas*'s closest
older relation in the genealogy of Johnson's writings, the story of
Omar (*Idler* 101) is its nearest kin among members of the younger
generation. Unlike the two *Rambler* papers, however, this oriental
apologue resembles only a narrow part of the full-length tale.
Omar, after a distinguished career as a high government official
in "Bagdat," retires from his post and resolves to gain his remaining pleasure by conversing with "the wise" and receiving "the
gratitude of the good." Among the visitors who come to see and
admire him is Caled, the son of the viceroy of Egypt. One day the
youth asks Omar to tell him "the secret of your conduct, and
teach me the plan upon which your wisdom has built your fortune." " 'Young man,' said Omar, 'it is of little use to form plans of
life.' " Then he proves his conclusion by showing the vast gulf
between what he had intended to do during his active years and
what he had actually done. At the end of his recital, he summa-

2. As noted on p. xxvii above, "Rassela Christos" was "lieutenant general to
Sultan Segued" (*Voyage to Abyssinia*, p. 85).

3. See *Voyage to Abyssinia*, pp. 97, 163, 93 (where "Ganete Ilhos, a palace newly
built, and made agreeable by beautiful gardens" [located "on the north shore of
Lake Tana in Ethiopia"] is mentioned). In his *Voyage to Aethiopia* (cited on p. xxxvii
above), Charles Jacques Poncet remarks: "Towards the middle of [Lake Dambea]
there is an island, where the Emperour has a palace, which for the beauty and
magnificence of its buildings yields not to that of Gondar, altho' it is not so big."

4. See p. 9, n. 9, below for a passage paralleling a sentence in *Rasselas*.

rizes his life: "'With an insatiable thirst for knowledge I trifled away the years of improvement; with a restless desire of seeing different countries, I have always resided in the same city; with the highest expectation of connubial felicity, I have lived unmarried; and with unalterable resolutions of contemplative retirement, I am going to dye within the walls of Bagdat.'"

The figures of Caled and Omar in this essay patently bear marked affinities to Rasselas and the poet Imlac. For example, a teacher (male, much older)-pupil (male, younger) relationship is common to both pairs of characters. "Omar admired [Caled's] wit, and loved his docility"; Imlac "pitied [Rasselas's] ignorance, and loved his curiosity." Omar relates the story of his life to Caled just as Imlac tells his history to Rasselas. Omar's opinion—based on experience—regarding the futility of forming plans of life recalls Imlac's emphasis on the difficulty of making choices of life that can actually be realized. Clearly, *Idler* 101—and, earlier, *Rambler*s 204, 205—embody the same genre and contain some of the same notions and devices as does *Rasselas*.

Six of Johnson's other periodical papers (*Rambler* 38, 65, 120, 190; *Idler* 75, 99) also belong to the category of oriental apologue. The characters and settings of these pieces are all Asiatic. The actions and dialogues serve mainly to inculcate moral lessons, usually explicit, occasionally implied. The instruction propounds such themes as the vanity of inordinate wishes and of seeking happiness through wealth, the likenesses between human life and a day's journey, and the results of a person's failure to seize an opportunity when it is offered. To an observer of Johnson's entire canon, the conclusion is inescapable: the Great Moralist's work during his most fecund decade displays a repeated manipulation of the literary type which reached its amplest, most complicated flowering in the history of the prince of Abyssinia.

But the generic antecedents of the history are not confined to the writings of its author. The broad class of moral or philosophic stories of one sort or another has formed, of course, a significant part of fiction from ancient to modern times. During the eighteenth century, a good many of these stories, sometimes utilizing a mode of address and figurative language associated with an eastern or sublime style, represented a wide range of oriental characters—Indian, Egyptian, Syrian, etc.—acting and speaking in their native lands. Of such English works, selected *Spectator* essays, mostly Addison's compositions, rank among the earliest specimens. The most famous member of the group, No. 159, "The Vision of Mirzah," formally a literary "vision" as its title tells us, contains the first-person account of Mirzah, who, atop a mountain of "Bagdat," meets a supernatural "Genius" and, under his guidance, observes and comprehends an allegorical depiction of human life, death, and immortality.[5] Other papers in the *Spectator, Guardian,* and *Freeholder* relate "Turkish," "Arabian," and "Persian" tales for the edification of their readers.[6] And similar narratives, including numerous *Adventurer* essays by John Hawkesworth,[7] appeared intermittently between (say) 1714 and 1759. Sir John Hawkins stated, as already recorded (p. xxii above), that Johnson, "finding the Eastern Tales written by himself in the *Rambler,* and by Hawkesworth in the *Adventurer,* had been well received, . . . had been for some time [before the composition of *Rasselas*] meditating a fictitious history, of a greater extent than any that had appeared in either of those papers."

Compared to the history's marked affiliations with the oriental apologues in previous periodical essays, both Johnsonian and non-Johnsonian, the connection between *Rasselas* and *The Arabian Nights* brand of eastern tale seems decidedly remote (although parts of the former—notably the chapters describing Pekuah's kidnapping and imprisonment by the Arab chieftain—present an ironic contrast to the latter's amazing adventures, wonders, and romances). Nevertheless, Geoffrey Tillotson has argued that *Rasselas* is indebted for its "subject and outline" to the middle section of the collection entitled *Persian Tales,*[8] a near generic relative of *The Arabian Nights,* which, early in the eigh-

---

5. For another reference to "The Vision of Mirzah," see pp. 185–86 below.

6. See, specifically, *Spectator* 195, 512, 535, 631; *Guardian* 61, 99, 162; *Freeholder* 17.

7. Hawkesworth's essays include *Adventurer* 20–22, 32, 72–73, 76, 91, 103–04, 114. *Almoran and Hamet* (1761), quite different from *Rasselas* in plot, characters, and tone, is Hawkesworth's most ambitious, best known oriental apologue; see p. vii below.

8. In his essay entitled "'Rasselas' and the 'Persian Tales'" (p. 114), Tillotson writes: "There can be little doubt of Johnson's debt to the 'Persian Tales' for the

teenth century, was englished from the French of François Petis
de la Croix by Ambrose Philips and also by Dr. William King and
"several other hands."9 Philips's preface to the first volume of his
translation, which reached a sixth edition in 1750, makes clear the
overall design of the "feigned histories" constituting the bulk of
the *Persian Tales.* Recounted by a nurse, the tales are intended "to
reduce a young princess to reason, who had conceived an unac-
countable aversion to men, and would not be persuaded to marry.
In order to [do] this, each story furnishes a shining instance of
some faithful lover, or affectionate husband: and though every
tale pursues the same drift, yet they are all diversified with so
much art, and interwoven with so great a variety of events, that
the very last appears as new as the first."1 As the nurse finishes
one tale (sometimes containing subordinate tales), the princess
finds fault with the behavior of the lover depicted in it, and this
leads the nurse to begin another story or sequence of stories. At
the end of the collection, the princess, influenced by the counsel
of a supposed dervish rather than the stories of her nurse, alters
her hostile view of men and marries a charming prince.

Among the yarns the nurse spins is the group which, according
to Tillotson, probably provided the "subject and outline" of *Rasselas.* Bedreddin, King of Damascus, while admitting that he himself is not fully content—the main cause of his discontent, we
learn later, arises from a tragic love affair—asserts, in opposition
to his "sorrowful vizier's" opinion, that somewhere in the world
are persons whose joy is unmixed with "disquiet" (p. 131). Whereupon the vizier tells the exciting story of his life; his sorrow is
produced by the mysterious disappearance of his beloved princess. The king turns next to his favorite. His history, filled with
exciting incidents, reveals that he, too, has been unlucky in love;
he is attached to the picture of "a lady who is not in being"
(p. 163). Bedreddin inquires further in the city and his court.

subject and outline of 'Rasselas' " (*Essays in Criticism and Research* [1942; rptd with
new preface, 1967], pp. 111–16).

  9. For additional details about the translations, see Tillotson, p. 112.

  1. This passage is drawn from the edition of Philips's translation which appears,
along with *Betsy Thoughtless*, in Vol. XIII (1784) of the *Novelist's Magazine.* Subsequent passages in the *Persian Tales* are drawn from the same edition, cited by page
numbers in the text.

Everywhere the result is the same: the "happy weaver," for instance, who tells his tale to the king, is miserable because of love; the courtiers and officers of his household, none of whom tells stories, are also dissatisfied for various reasons—envy, ambition, domestic troubles, etc. Disregarding the vizier's maxim to "judge of every body by yourself" (p. 175), the king decides to travel until he finds a happy person. In disguise and accompanied by his adviser and favorite, he begins an unsuccessful journey. He meets assorted persons who are seemingly contented and hears several marvelous tales, but all the principal narrators confess an unhappiness springing from disappointment of one sort or another in their love affairs. Concluding that everybody "has something or other to trouble him," Bedreddin returns with his comrades to Damascus; "if we three are not entirely contented," says the ruler, "let us consider that there are others more unhappy" (p. 257).

The chief similarities between Bedreddin's history and *Rasselas* can be itemized quickly. Two discontented members of eastern royalty undertake extended searches for a happy person and then, unable to find one, return (Rasselas decides—without acting—to return to Abyssinia) to the places from which they set out. Both travel incognito and are accompanied by wiser men who foresee the failure of their quests, and both hear stories during their searches. In addition, a few similar remarks about happiness appear in the two texts. On the other hand, the two display fundamental differences which are readily apparent to the most casual reader. In the *Persian Tales,* as intimated above, the story, a succession of thrilling episodes, is the most important element. Bedreddin's inquiries afford a convenient entry into the realm of the adventure tale—crowded with handsome princes, lovely ladies (and some not so lovely), amorous relationships, arrant villains, hairbreadth escapes, enchanted castles, magic chests, powerful genii, and so on. Only after a tale is finished is the narrator's unhappiness really voiced. This slight emphasis arises, not from a desire to point a moral or treat a philosophical issue, but from the nurse's pretext of telling in this series experiences of unhappy lovers in order to persuade the princess that certain men, deprived of their beloveds, are forever faithful and miserable. Unlike Rasselas, Bedreddin is not intent on making a wise choice of life, and little is said about his personal dissatisfaction (notwithstanding his recital of his own unfortunate love affair); he simply believes that some persons are completely happy and tries to find at least one. Obviously, he cannot discover such a person unless the nurse's stories are to cease being what they manifestly are— adventure tales of men who say they are unhappy lovers. Therefore, although the possibility of *Rasselas*'s minor indebtedness to the *Persian Tales* cannot be wholly discounted,[2] it is certain that the genres exemplified by the two books are completely distinct.

Apart from titling his composition a history (defined as "Narration; relation" in his *Dictionary*), Johnson, who took care to classify his two additional pieces of extended fiction, "The Vision of Theodore" and "The Fountains: A Fairy Tale," never specified the literary category to which *Rasselas* should be assigned. In 1778, however, he remarked to Boswell that if his creation and Voltaire's *Candide* "had not been published so closely one after the other that there was not time for imitation, it would have been in vain to deny that the scheme of that which came latest [*Rasselas* in April 1759] was taken from the other [*Candide* in January 1759]."[3] Numerous commentators, early and recent, have also discerned notable resemblances between the two works.[4]

Unlike *Rasselas*, *Candide*, of course, cannot be labelled an oriental tale, for none of its main characters is oriental, only the concluding part of the action occurs in an eastern country (Turkey), and its style can scarcely be called elevated or sublime. But, as Johnson points out, its overall scheme readily calls to mind that of

2. The degree of SJ's acquaintance with the *Tales* remains quite unclear. Tillotson acknowledges that "he does not seem to have mentioned the 'Persian Tales' in writing or conversation, except in the 'Life of Philips' [1781], when he wrote bibliographically of the book in a way suggesting that he had handled it" (p. 114). The passage (*Lives*, III.313–14, par. 4) Tillotson refers to reads: "[Philips] was reduced to translate the *Persian Tales* for Tonson, for which he was afterwards reproached, with this addition of contempt, that he worked for half-a-crown. The book is divided into many sections, for each of which if he received half-a-crown his reward, as writers then were paid, was very liberal; but half-a-crown had a mean sound." Obviously this comment contains little information about the date or the nature of Johnson's knowledge of the *Tales*.

3. *Life*, 1.342; III.356. For the date of *Candide*'s publication, see the edition by René Pomeau (*The Complete Works of Voltaire*, Vol. XLVIII [1980]), pp. 53ff.

4. See, for example, pp. lii, lix, 254–55 below; James L. Clifford, *Dictionary Johnson: Samuel Johnson's Middle Years* (1979), pp. 217–20.

his own "little book." In each of the stories, the plot consists of a single line of incidents (interspersed with subordinate autobiographical accounts) followed by a conclusion which details the situation of a limited group of characters, including the protagonist. In both stories, the protagonists—each a naive, idealistic young man holding optimistic beliefs about human existence and happiness—leave fine dwellings (Candide is actually ejected), travel abroad, undergo various experiences involving diverse, often unfortunate individuals, and finally, far from home, arrive at changed notions regarding the prevailing state of the world and the amount of personal happiness securable in it. The protagonists, too, number among their companions shrewd counsellors (excluding Pangloss) who are partly responsible for the protagonists' movement from ignorance to knowledge of the harsh realities of life. Further, both stories utilize (in different measures, to be sure) satire, irony, and humor during their (often) omniscient narrators' relation of the happenings. Last— and most important—in both *Candide* (entitled, significantly, *ou l'optimisme*) and *Rasselas* the blend of actions, characters, ideas, satire, irony, and point of view regularly functions to present to the reader comparable—but far from identical—assessments of the human predicament. Perhaps foremost among the estimates advanced by *Candide* is the judgment that the world (excluding El Dorado), far from being the best possible, abounds with evils of all sorts and that human happiness is thus very limited and unpredictable. Among the primary lessons to be drawn from *Rasselas* is the conclusion that the human species, despite its persistent craving—and searching—for lasting contentment, is fated to enjoy only ephemeral happiness on earth and must consequently look to eternity and divine goodness for permanent felicity.

Altogether, then, their many likenesses—their glaring dissimilarities notwithstanding—seem to justify the placement of *Candide* and *Rasselas* in the same broad literary compartment. The generic term commonly applied to *Candide* is *conte philosophique*. As indicated above, "oriental philosophic tale" is one of the three designations, "oriental apologue" and "oriental moral tale" being the others, which accurately characterize *Rasselas*.

Neither of Johnson's other substantial pieces of fiction, "The Vision of Theodore" (1748) and "The Fountains: A Fairy Tale" (1766), can be labelled an oriental apologue. The first, as its title indicates, falls in the category of visionary literature and records the experience of an old hermit named Theodore (nationality unspecified) during his climb up the peak of Teneriffe. The second, also classified in its title, recounts the fulfilment—and retraction (with one exception)—of a succession of wishes made, over a long period of time, by a woman named Floretta (presumably Welsh) who, living near Mount Plinlimmon, owes her supernatural power to a grateful fairy. But common themes and motifs link *Rasselas* to "The Vision" and "The Fountains" and help to identify the trio as the creations of the same mind. In all three works, for example, happiness is emphatically the conscious goal of human life. In all three, characters are preoccupied with choices of existence which will presumably produce happiness.[5] In all three, lasting earthly felicity appears exceedingly difficult, indeed impossible, to achieve; most human wishes, as Johnson's poem on the subject (generically, an "imitation" of Juvenal's tenth satire) also stresses, are notable for their vanity. In "The Vision" and *Rasselas,* as in *The Vanity of Human Wishes* (1749), permanent happiness occurs, one infers, only after death and a moral life— and through the will of God; in "The Fountains," the possible bliss of eternity goes unmentioned, although the transience of earthly contentment is abundantly evident. Moreover, all three compositions feature central figures—Theodore, Rasselas, Floretta—whose personalities and actions form essential means of conveying the predominant themes of the texts. The earliest and the last of the three constitute minor, if memorable, treatments of the ceaseless human quest for happiness; *Rasselas,* on the other hand, has attained worldwide recognition for its unforgettable representation of the same theme.

RECEPTION, 1759–1800

By January of 1760, *Rasselas*—published, it will be recalled, probably on 20 April 1759—had been reviewed in at least fourteen

5. See the studies by Edwin Christian Heinle, Earl R. Wasserman, and Carey McIntosh cited on p. 182, n. 7, below.

different serials. The notices, invariably accompanied by longer extracts from the tale, fall into two groups: (1) six sets of original comments and (2) eight reproductions of observations appearing elsewhere, specifically seven from the Gentleman's Magazine, the eighth from the Monthly Review.[6] The second group, mentioned again later (Appendix, p. 251 below), is cited here only as a quantitative indicator of the attention accorded the work—attention which, with respect to "the miscellanies," exceeded that given "any previous work of prose fiction, French or English, for at least twenty years" and which makes Rasselas "a pivotal novel in the history of magazine fiction."[7] Of the first group, one brief notice—in Benjamin Martin's Miscellaneous Correspondence—confines its presumably positive reaction to a single not very revealing sentence: "Amidst the variety of sentiments exhibited in these volumes," says the writer, "we shall give our readers a specimen of the language and genius of the author, from Vol. 2d, Chap. 29. the Debate on Marriage continued" (III [1759], 115). The five other reviews plainly state both their authors' opinions of Rasselas and, in varying detail, the reasons for their estimates. Three are mostly laudatory; one expresses a mixture of praise and censure; and one, the longest by far, is largely negative. The purpose, matter and plan, style, and author of the tale make up the chief referents of the reviewers.

The highly favorable notices appear in the Gentleman's Magazine, the London Magazine, and the Annual Register. When assessing the opinions expressed in these three periodicals, we should

---

6. The seven serials which reprinted the evaluation in the Gentleman's Magazine are: Scots Magazine, Edinburgh Magazine, Lloyd's Evening Post, London Chronicle (3–5 May 1759, p. 423), Owen's Weekly Chronicle, Caledonian Mercury (Edinburgh), and Universal Magazine of Knowledge and Pleasure (XXIV [May 1759], 238). The Grand Magazine reprinted part of the assessment in the Monthly Review. For more details about all of these reprintings except those in the London Chronicle and the Universal Magazine, see Helen Louise McGuffie, Samuel Johnson in the British Press, 1749–1784: A Chronological Checklist (1976), pp. 20–21. Pertinent information about various reprintings also appears in Robert D. Mayo, The English Novel in the Magazines, 1740–1815 (1962), pp. 240–41, 446, 523–24, 619–20.

7. Mayo, pp. 408–09. Mayo also notes (pp. 619–20) that "a disguised redaction of . . . Rasselas" was published in the "Weekly Amusement, II (Feb 2–Mar 16, 1765)." And he has kindly informed me that other extracts were printed, still later, in the Gentleman and Lady's Weekly Magazine (Edinburgh), III (4 Feb 1774), 41–42; and the Bristol and Bath Magazine, I (1782), 243–47.

remember that at least two of them—the first and the third—
were surely disposed to esteem Johnson's compositions. The
writer of the *Gentleman's* estimate was probably Johnson's friend
John Hawkesworth,[8] who makes his short remarks at the end of a
summary (relying heavily on extracts) of the tale; weighing the
work's contents, he notes the abundance of "the most elegant and
striking pictures of life and nature, the most acute disquisitions,
and the happiest illustrations of the most important truths" (xxix
[1759], 186). Referring to Johnson himself and his characteristic
mode of discourse as well as to the substance of *Rasselas*, the
unidentified reviewer for the *London Magazine* informs his audience that "the excellent author of the *Rambler*, has lately obliged
the world with a moral tale . . . which contain[s] the most important truths and instructions, told in an agreeable and enchanting
manner, and in his usual nervous and sententious stile." "Our
readers," the reviewer adds, "will, no doubt, expect some account
of a performance which is so much admired, and we shall endeavour to gratify their expectations" (xxviii [1759], 258); five pages
(258–62) of extracts (linked by an occasional summarizing statement) follow in the May issue, and another eight (324–31) are
included in the June number.

The *Annual Register* critic, almost certainly Edmund Burke
(who first met Johnson in 1758), prefaces and concludes his
descriptive account—consisting mainly of quotations—with a total of three paragraphs devoted to the intention, narrative, style,
and author of *Rasselas*.[9] "In this novel," he asserts, "the moral is
the principal object, and the story is a mere vehicle to convey the
instruction." He continues:

> Accordingly the tale is not near so full of incidents, not so
> diverting in itself, as the ingenious author, if he had not had
> higher views, might easily have made it; neither is the distinc-
> tion of characters sufficiently attended to: but with these de-
> fects, perhaps no book ever inculcated a purer and sounder
> morality; no book ever made a more just estimate of human

8. See Clifford, p. 213. Clifford also describes (pp. 213–16) the reviews in the
London Magazine, Annual Register, Critical Review, and *Monthly Review.*
9. See Clifford, p. 216.

life, its pursuits, and its enjoyments. The descriptions are
rich and luxuriant, and shew a poetic imagination not inferior to our best writers in verse. The style, which is peculiar,
and characteristical of the author, is lively, correct, and harmonious. It has, however, in a few places, an air too exact and
studied.

Later, ending his notice, Burke says, "There is no doubt that [the
author] is the same who has before done so much for the improvement of our taste and our morals, and employed a great
part of his life in an astonishing work [i.e., the *Dictionary*] for the
fixing the language of this nation; whilst this nation, which ad-
mires his works, and profits by them, has done nothing for the
author" (II [1759], 477, 479).

Like his fellows in the *London Magazine* and the *Annual Register,*
the writer for the *Critical Review,* whose identity remains unknown, makes clear his awareness of Johnson's connection with
Rasselas: "This little tale," we are told, is "in every respect worthy
of the learned and sensible author of the *Rambler.*" To "philosophers," the critic declares, the work, which "couche[s] in the
method of dialogue the most important truths and profound
speculations," may be recommended "as a beautiful epitome of
practical ethics, filled with the most judicious observations upon
life" and "the nicest distinctions upon conduct." However, "readers of novels" are likely to find the tale "unintelligible," for, exalt-
ing "reflections" and "dissertations" at the expense of "narrative"
(which "might have been comprised in ten lines"), it contains "no
plot, incident, character, or contrivance . . . to beguile the imagination." After quoting a chapter to illustrate Johnson's "manner,"
the reviewer again expresses reservations: "Upon the whole, we
imagine the talents of the author would appear to more advantage, had he treated his different subjects in the method of essays,
or form of dialogue. At present, the title page will, by many
readers, be looked upon as a decoy, to deceive them into a kind of
knowledge they had no inclination to be acquainted with" (VII
[1759], 372–73, 375).

These relatively mild strictures are far exceeded by those of the
Monthly Review critic, Owen Ruffhead, who, although ostensibly
ignorant of the fact, doubtless knew that Johnson had written

Rasselas and whose negative evaluation probably reflects this knowledge.[1] Ruffhead begins his extended notice (containing numerous extracts) with a tribute to "fiction or romance . . . as the most effectual way of rendering the grave dictates of morality agreeable to mankind in general." "But," he hastily points out,

> to succeed in the romantic way of writing, requires a sprightliness of imagination, with a natural ease and variety of expression, which, perhaps, oftener falls to the lot of middling writers, than to those of more exalted genius: and therefore, we observe, with less regret, of the learned writer of these volumes, that *tale-telling* evidently is not his talent. He wants that graceful ease, which is the ornament of romance; and he stalk[s] in the solemn buskin, when he ought to tread in the light sock. His stile is so tumid and pompous, that he sometimes deals in sesquipedalia, such as *excogitation, exaggeratory,* &c. with other hard compounds, which it is difficult to pronounce with composed features—as *multifarious, transcendental, indiscerpible, &c.*

Had the writer, Ruffhead continues, put "this swelling language" "into the mouth of a pedant only, nothing could be more apt: but unhappily he has so little conception of the propriety of character, that he makes the princess speak in the same lofty strain with the philosopher; and the waiting woman harangue with as much sublimity as her royal mistress."

Turning to the "matter of these little volumes," Ruffhead "cannot discover much invention in the plan, or utility in the design. The topics . . . are grown threadbare: . . . [the] sentiments are most of them to be found in the Persian and Turkish tales, and other books of the like sort; wherein they are delivered to better purpose, and cloathed in a more agreeable garb. Neither has the end of this work any great tendency to the good of society": we may learn "that discontent prevails among men of all ranks and conditions," Ruffhead asserts, without making a trip to Ethiopia. Moreover, he maintains for the length of three paragraphs, "the inferences" drawn by Johnson "from this general discontent, are by no means just." Human happiness is more frequent than the

1. See Clifford, p. 215.

theme of *Rasselas* indicates. Then, through a combination of summaries, quotations, and short critical remarks (mostly negative), Ruffhead outlines the sequence of events in the tale, pausing occasionally to make clear the intellectual context of specific passages. At the end, commenting on the last chapter, he says that, "as nothing is concluded, it would have been prudent in the author to have said nothing. Whoever he is, he is a man of genius and great abilities; but he has evidently misapplied his talents." Ruffhead adds that the title page of the work "will impose upon many" readers, "who, while they expect to frolic along the flowery paths of romance, will find themselves hoisted on metaphysical stilts, and born aloft into the regions of syllogistical subtlety, and philosophical refinement" (xx [1759], 428–29, 437).

II

By June 1759—two months after the appearance of *Rasselas*— the 1,500 copies of the first edition had been disposed of, and a second edition (of 1,000 copies) had been issued. The following April saw the publication of the third edition, consisting of another 1,000 copies. Thus, by the end of its first year of publication, the tale reached, from the proprietors' editions alone, the substantial figure of 3,500. During the remainder of the century that number grew steadily with the appearance of the fourth edition (1,000 copies) in 1766, the fifth (1,000) in 1775, the sixth (1,000) in 1783, the seventh (1,000) in 1786, the eighth (1,500) in 1790, the ninth (1,500) in 1793, and the tenth (number apparently unknown) in 1798.[2]

Besides the proprietors' editions, approximately forty other editions (excluding those in the collections of Johnson's works) and translations strongly attest to the increasing scope of *Rasselas*'s popularity, which helped to account for its designation as a "classic tale" early in the nineteenth century. Following the common Irish practice of reproducing English books shortly after

2. For more information about the first ten editions, see Kolb, "*Rasselas:* Purchase Price," pp. 257–59; William P. Courtney and David Nichol Smith, *A Bibliography of Samuel Johnson* (1925), pp. 87–88. For the number of copies of the ninth edition, I am indebted to David Fleeman.

their first publication (usually in London), the Dublin booksellers G. and A. Ewing and H. Bradley brought out in 1759 what appears to be the earliest nonproprietary edition of the novel. At least four more Dublin editions were published before 1800—in 1777, 1787, 1795, and 1798. Barely honoring the protective period of twenty-eight years afforded the author by the Copyright Act of 1709, alert London booksellers began issuing editions (two) in 1787. Before the end of the century, their total ventures came to at least twelve editions (including the *Novelist's Magazine* version), a number which, when added to the ten authorized, or proprietors', editions, five Dublin editions, and a single Edinburgh edition (1789), produce a sum of twenty-eight editions printed in the United Kingdom and Ireland between 1759 and 1800.[3]

III

After the cluster of public responses that greeted its initial publication, the next large body of critical comments on *Rasselas* appeared in the early biographical accounts of the author. The five longest accounts are Mrs. Piozzi's *Anecdotes of Samuel Johnson* (1786), Sir John Hawkins's *Life* (1787), Boswell's *Life* (1791), Arthur Murphy's *Essay on the Life and Genius of Samuel Johnson* (1792), and Robert Anderson's *Life* (1795). Of this group of works, Mrs. Piozzi's alone does not undertake a critique of "that surprising little volume," as she calls the tale. Two of her three brief allusions locate the origin of specific parts in Johnson's experiences and beliefs. "Many of the severe reflections on domestic life," she reports, "took their source from its author's keen recollections of the time passed in his early years"; and the chapter on poetry is "really written from the fulness of his heart" ("very fully was he persuaded of [poetry's] superiority over every other talent") and

---

3. The information in this paragraph about the nonproprietary editions is drawn from an unpublished checklist of editions of *Rasselas* made available to me by the generosity of David Fleeman; a part of the Samuel Johnson entry in the *NCBEL* (II. col. 1130); Courtney and Smith, pp. 87–88; and my personal collection of editions of *Rasselas*. For the translations and editions of the tale published in Europe and America, see the Appendix below, pp. 253–58.

"quite in his best manner I think." The third mention likens Johnson's conversation to that of the sage in Chapter xvIII. Scattered references elsewhere reinforce one's impression that Mrs. Piozzi knew the story well and esteemed it highly.[4]

Sir John Hawkins devotes over six pages of his *Life* to a discussion of *Rasselas*, "numbered," he states, "among the best of [Johnson's] writings." The treatment, which may be indebted to the hand of Hawkins's daughter Laetitia-Matilda,[5] contains a mixture of praise, causal explanations, summary, quotation (of the passage on pilgrimages in Chapter xI), generic classification, and pointed reservations. "Considered as a specimen of our language," Hawkins begins, "[the tale] is scarcely to be paralleled." But though in form "a general satire, representing mankind as eagerly pursuing what experience should have taught them they can never obtain," and exposing "the weaknesses even of their laudable affections and propensities," the work conveys an excessively bleak appraisal of life, which derived both from the author's habitual pessimism and specifically from his sad condition at the time of creating *Rasselas.* Hawkins also ascribes to Johnson's personal opinions and psyche several discrete sections of the tale, notably "many conversations on topics . . . known to have been subjects of his meditation," the "dissertation on poetry" (compare Mrs. Piozzi's similar observation), the "chapter" on "insanity" and the imagination, and "superstitious ideas of the state of departed souls, and belief in supernatural agency." Summing up, the biographer declares "that this elegant work is rendered, by its most obvious moral, of little benefit to the reader." For, he explains, (1) "we would not . . . wish to see the rising generation so unprofitably employed as the prince of Abyssinia"; (2) "it is equally impolitic to repress all hope"; and (3) granted "there is no such thing as

---

4. *Anecdotes*, 1.151, 284–85, 347. For additional references to the tale, see, for example, Mrs. Piozzi's *Letters to and from the Late Samuel Johnson, LL.D.* (1788), 11.129–30, 266, 358, 360. In a note written on the last page of a copy of *Rasselas* (Sharpe's ed. [1818]), Mrs. Piozzi called the book "unrivalled in excellency of intention, in elegance of diction: in minute knowledge of human life—and sublime expression of Oriental imagery" (Hilaire Belloc, "Mrs. Piozzi's *Rasselas*," *Saturday Review of Literature*, 11 [15 Aug 1925], 38).

5. In her *Memoirs* (2 vols., 1824), Miss Hawkins says that she "furnished . . . the reviews" (1.160) of SJ's works contained in her father's *Life of Johnson*.

worldly felicity . . . it has never been proved, that, therefore we are miserable." In conclusion, Hawkins remarks that "Johnson had meditated a second part, in which he meant to marry his hero, and place him in a state of permanent felicity"; unfortunately, however, the continuation was not written because Johnson discovered that all earthly "enjoyments are fugacious, and permanent felicity unattainable" (pp. 366, 367, 369–72).

Except for a small qualification, Boswell's well-known assessment, unlike Hawkins's much cooler "examen," expresses uniformly fervent praise for diverse aspects of *Rasselas*, which, he grandly avows, "though [Johnson] had written nothing else, would have rendered his name immortal in the world of literature." Possessing "all the charms of oriental imagery, and all the force and beauty of which the English language is capable," he elaborates, the book "leads us through the most important scenes of human life, and shews us that this stage of our being is full of 'vanity and vexation of spirit.'" Boswell proceeds to compare the tale and *Candide*, concluding that, whereas Voltaire "meant only by wanton profaneness to obtain a sportive victory over religion . . . Johnson meant, by shewing the unsatisfactory nature of things temporal, to direct the hopes of man to things eternal." After transcribing a short passage (on "apparitions") from Chapter xxxi, he admits a possible connection—presented as a certainty by Hawkins—between Johnson's "melancholy . . . constitution" and the dark view of life depicted in *Rasselas*, adding, however, that "there is too much of reality in the gloomy picture." Boswell makes other brief remarks on human life and happiness and then ends his criticism with six lines from John Courtenay's *Poetical Review of the Literary and Moral Character of the Late Samuel Johnson* (1786) which "beautifully illustrated" the "effect of *Rasselas*, and of Johnson's other moral tales." The first four of these lines run:

> Impressive truth, in splendid fiction drest,
> Checks the vain wish, and calms the troubled breast;
> O'er the dark mind a light celestial throws,
> And soothes the angry passions to repose.[6]

6. *Life*, I. 341–44.

Arthur Murphy begins his one-paragraph, mostly laudatory evaluation of *Rasselas* with an amused "smile" at the phrases "immaculate purity" and "turgid eloquence" used by Hawkins to describe the style of the tale. "Both elegant and sublime," the story, Murphy continues, displays a gloomy picture of human life attributable to "the author's natural melancholy," which his mother's "approaching dissolution" enhanced. The reader's attention is held by "pictures of life," "profound moral reflection," and "a discussion of interesting questions." The parts singled out for mention are "Reflections on Human Life; the History of Imlac, the Man of Learning; A Dissertation upon Poetry; the Character of a wise and happy Man. . . . The History of the Mad Astronomer" (which mirrors Johnson's own "apprehensions" about insanity); and "the discourse on the nature of the soul" (which "gives us all that philosophy knows, not without a tincture of superstition"). "It is remarkable," Murphy finally notes, "that the vanity of human pursuits" attracted the pens of both Johnson and Voltaire about the same time; *Candide* "is the work of a lively imagination, and *Rasselas*, with all its splendor of eloquence, exhibits [he repeats] a gloomy picture."[7]

The last of the longer early accounts of Johnson, Robert Anderson's *Life*, relies heavily on its predecessors (eminently, Hawkins, Boswell, and Murphy) for its rather detailed examination of *Rasselas*. The tissue of borrowings is so widespread, in fact, that one may momentarily wonder what Anderson himself really thought of the tale. Nevertheless, his solid admiration seems indisputable, although tempered by criticism of certain features of the narrative and qualifications (echoing those voiced by Hawkins) regarding the book's moral instruction. Examining Johnson's character as a novelist, Anderson states flatly, "There is no doubt that great beauties . . . exist" in *Rasselas*. The work "astonishes with the sublimity of its sentiments, and . . . the fertility of its illustrations, and delights with the abundance and propriety of its imagery." On the other hand, "the *History* . . . is not without its faults. It is barren of interesting incidents, and destitute of

7. The passages from Murphy's *Essay* are drawn from *Johnsonian Miscellanies*, ed. G. B. Hill (2 vols., 1897), I.471–72.

originality or distinction of characters." Moreover, the universally "dark catalogue of calamities" embodied in the tale does not depict the human situation either accurately or circumspectly. "The moral" Johnson seeks "to inculcate, that there is no such thing as happiness, is ungrateful to the human heart, and inconsistent with the gratification of our most laudable affections and propensities." The "benevolence" of the author's "intentions is indubitable; but in the gloom which his melancholy imagination raised around him, he saw darkly." Therefore, Anderson warns the prospective reader, "to peruse this moral tale with advantage, . . . inexperienced youth" must "guard against the discouraging experience of *Rasselas,* and . . . keep steadily in view the design of the venerable moralist . . . to elevate our contemplations above this sublunary scene, and to fix our affections on a higher state of existence."[8]

Besides evoking responses in the lengthier works on Johnson's life and writings until 1800 (four of whose authors, Mrs. Piozzi, Hawkins, Boswell, and Murphy, were Johnson's close friends), *Rasselas* figures at least briefly in each of the fourteen, often derivative and repetitious accounts that have been collected and edited by O M Brack, Jr., and Robert E. Kelley under the title *The Early Biographies of Samuel Johnson.* Three accounts restrict their notices to the tale's composition or publication. Three others contain short, highly favorable but wholly borrowed critical remarks. The remaining eight present more or less original assessments which range from a single phrase ("immortal work") to a sizable paragraph. The first (1762) of these, by William Rider, describes *Rasselas* as "a novel in the oriental way, a species of writing . . . in which Mr. Johnson [who manifests "through his allegorical and oriental compositions" a striking "turn to the sublime"] is allowed to surpass all English authors." The second sketch (1764), by David Erskine Baker, which provided, directly or indirectly, the criticism found in the three accounts mentioned above, makes a still more sweeping comparison. Johnson, Baker declares, "in his Eastern stories in the *Rambler* . . . has . . . greatly excelled any of the Oriental writers in the fertility of his inven-

8. *The Life of Samuel Johnson, LL.D.,* 3d ed. (1815), pp. 491, 533, 535, 536–38.

tion, the conduct of his plots, and the justice and strength of his sentiments. His capital work of that kind . . . is a novel, entitled *Rasselas* . . . , in which, as he does at present, so he probably ever will, stand without an equal."[9]

This veritable paean gave way in 1782 to a less exalted encomium when another biographer, possibly William Cooke, placed *Rasselas* among Johnson's "lighter" writings and said merely that the "little work abound[s] with such elegance of sentiment, and moral instructions, as would be in itself sufficient to support the character of novel writing in this country." A little later (1784) two lives—one anonymous in the *Universal Magazine,* the other by Thomas Tyers in the *Gentleman's Magazine*—respectively dubbed the tale an "admirable" and an "excellent" romance. The anonymous author praises the book for affording a reader "the knowledge how to be happy in what he is" but "suspect[s] that Dr. Johnson does not wholly disbelieve the exploded doctrine of the reality of apparitions." Tyers reports Edward Young's comment "that *Rasselas* was a lamp of wisdom" and notes Johnson's "uncommon capacity for remark" and "best use of the descriptions of travellers." The next year William Cooke's biography, after sounding the usual round of applause for the "beautiful little novel['s]" "moral sentiments," "design," and "imitation of the Oriental writers," judged the conversation on marriage to be the finest discussion of the topic Cooke had ever read, "and as such must afford no inconsiderable instruction to all married people." Finally, Joseph Towers, whose *Essay on the Life . . . of . . . Johnson* (1786) followed closely behind Cooke's *Life,* also paid tribute to

---

9. *The Early Biographies of Samuel Johnson* (1974). The first group of three works mentioned includes: Isaac Reed and/or George Steevens, "An Account of the Writings of Dr. Samuel Johnson, Including Some Incidents of His Life" (p. 53); "The Life of Samuel Johnson, LL.D." (p. 236); and James Harrison (?), "The Life of Dr. Samuel Johnson" (p. 279). The second group of three works mentioned includes: James Tytler (?), "An Account of the Life, and Writings of Dr. Samuel Johnson" (p. 11); Isaac Reed (?), "An Impartial Account of the Life, Character, Genius, and Writings, of Dr. Samuel Johnson" (p. 14); and David Erskine Baker (with additions by Isaac Reed), "Samuel Johnson" (p. 21). The phrase "immortal work" occurs in William Shaw's *Memoirs of the Life and Writings of the Late Dr. Samuel Johnson* (p. 170). The quotation from Rider's "Mr. Johnson" appears on p. 2; that from Baker's "Mr. Samuel Johnson, M.A." appears on p. 6.

the disquisition concerning marriage and, further, to the character of Imlac and of the Arabian chief who captured the maid of honor Pekuah. But Towers found "the representations . . . of human life" gloomier "than are warranted by truth or reason," stated that the princess Nekayah "is made too profound a philosopher" on some occasions, and imputed the chapters on madness and the imagination to Johnson's fear of insanity and "morbid melancholy."[1]

Turning from these largely positive evaluations in early biographies, we should note some of the varied responses to *Rasselas* that additional persons, famous and obscure, both friends and strangers to Johnson, expressed during the period from 1759 to about 1800. The materials offered here are obviously incomplete and can be supplemented by other students of eighteenth-century letters. Negative opinions will be surveyed first, then mixed and favorable reactions.

In her letter of 28 April 1759 to Elizabeth Carter, Hester Mulso (afterwards Mrs. Chapone) directed severe strictures against the work and its author: "Tell me," she asks her correspondent, "whether you do not think [Johnson] ought to be ashamed of publishing such an ill-contrived, unfinished, unnatural, and uninstructive tale?" She admits that "there is a great deal of good sense, and many fine observations in it." "But," she inquires, "how are these fine sentences brought in? How do they suit the mouths of the speakers? And what moral is to be drawn from the fiction upon the whole?" For Miss Mulso, "the only maxim one can deduce from the story is, that human life is a scene of unmixt wretchedness, and that all states and conditions of it are equally miserable: a maxim which," she asserts, anticipating later criticism, "if adopted, would extinguish hope, . . . make prudence ridiculous, and, in short, dispose men to lie down in sloth and despondency." She goes on to criticize the characterization and the ending of the book. Her next letter (dated 15 July 1759), however, contains more temperate opinions. She admits the "justice" of Miss Carter's remarks (in a missing letter) about Johnson and his tale, confesses she "was very angry with him for the

1. *Early Biographies*, pp. 25, 39, 80, 109, 198.

conclusion," and "hope[s]" that in the continuation she hears he "proposes," "he will give us antidotes for all the poisonous" inferences deducible from the present story. She adds, "Though I am scandalized and grieved at the frightful picture he has drawn of family life, I cannot but admire his truly philosophical manner of placing the advantages and disadvantages of each situation before us."[2]

The poet William Shenstone's first and second impressions of *Rasselas* were more different from each other than were Miss Mulso's. Writing to Richard Graves, author of the *Spiritual Quixote,* on 26 October 1759, Shenstone commented, "*Rasselas* has a few refined sentiments thinly scattered, but is upon the whole below Mr. J[ohnson]." By 5 July 1761, however, he had apparently decided, in a letter to Thomas Percy, that "*Rasselas* deserves applause, on account of ye many refined sentiments [Johnson] has expressed with all possible elegance & perspicuity." Shenstone's later estimate was a response to Percy's comparison of *Rasselas* and John Hawkesworth's recently published Oriental tale *Almoran and Hamet,* "intended," Percy says, "as a rival to *Rasselas,*" which Percy rated inferior in interest (by virtue of *Almoran and Hamet*'s "very pleasing love-story") but superior in "style" and plausibility to Hawkesworth's book.[3]

If Shenstone's real opinion of *Rasselas,* at best hardly enthusiastic, remains ambiguous, no such uncertainty marks the attitude of the Scotsman Archibald Campbell, who in his *Lexiphanes* (1767) roundly assailed Johnson and his works for assorted flaws, especially the frequent use of hard words. Terms from *Rasselas* are cited as examples of its creator's liking for polysyllables, and we are told that whereas "one should naturally expect wit and humour in periodical essays, novels, and romances," the *Rambler*s and *Rasselas* contain "nothing but what [Johnson] calleth, 'stern philosophy, dolourous declamation, and dictatorial instruction.' "[4]

---

2. *The Posthumous Works of Mrs. Chapone,* 2 vols., 2d ed. (1808), I.108–11.

3. *The Letters of William Shenstone,* ed. Marjorie Williams (1939), pp. 528, 583; *The Correspondence of Thomas Percy and William Shenstone,* ed. Cleanth Brooks, Vol. VII of *The Percy Letters,* ed. Cleanth Brooks and A. F. Falconer (1977), pp. 101–02.

4. 2d ed. (1767), pp. 24, 30, 32, 55.

Two later critics discerned in the apologue a combination of beauties and faults, the latter being rather more pronounced than the former. William Hayley, whose *Two Dialogues* (1787) includes a *Comparative View of the Lives, Characters, and Writings, of Philip, the Late Earl of Chesterfield, and Dr. Samuel Johnson*, presents his evaluation through exchanges between two speakers, an archdeacon (and admirer of Johnson) and a colonel (and admirer of Chesterfield). For the archdeacon, *Rasselas*, the "marvellous effort of a great and tender mind," would have been acclaimed "a noble poem" by the French had it been the production of a Frenchman. "And surely," the cleric maintains, "distinguished as it is by liveliness of description, by dignity of sentiment, by elevation and purity of language, we ought to esteem it as the work of a poetical imagination." The colonel, on the other hand, declares that "with a total inability to catch or support the proper tone of any assumed character [Johnson] appears to me, among writers, very like what a deformed giant would be in a company of players. . . . An effect of this defective kind (to use the quibble of Polonius) strikes me perpetually in *Rasselas*. I hardly ever hear a sentence uttered by the Princess, or the Lady Pekuah, but I see the enormous Johnson in petticoats." Moreover, though "there may be minds to whom the pompous and dark fictions of your moralist are both salutary and pleasant," "to me," the colonel says, "they are neither; for, instead of quickening my virtues, they only communicate their own gloominess to my spirits" (pp. 48, 107–09).

Like Hayley, William Mudford, who published his *Critical Enquiry into the Writings of Dr. Samuel Johnson* shortly after 1800, also found much to commend but even more to blame in *Rasselas*. "It is entitled to every praise," he asserts with scant originality, "which can be bestowed on language, on sentiment, and on argument; it is the production of a mind abundant in allusion, and capable of sublimity. It . . . is uniformly grand even to a fault; for hence arises a want of discrimination" evident in the unvarying "exalted style" and the energetic reasoning of its characters. Mudford then proceeds to censure the tale's "subject" or theme, lack of emotional force, false portrait of the world and human nature, and harmful effects on many of its readers ("it is calculated to vitiate the principles of the ignorant, and the young; and as these may be said to compose by far the greater part of society, it is hence calculated to do much injury which can never be re-paired").[5]

The penultimate group of miscellaneous responses to *Rasselas* being surveyed is unified by a fairly consistent note of approval. The first remark comes from outside traditional literary circles. In a letter dated 18 May 1759 to Andrew Mitchell, British ambassador to Berlin, one Robert Symmer informs his correspondent that he has sent him "the *Prince of Abissinia*, a pretty little novel, which happens to be somewhat of a counterpart to Voltaire's *Candide*"—Symmer's comparison of the English and French works is the earliest yet recorded—"and may afford you . . . a few hours amusement in the camp."[6]

Although his immense respect for Johnson is widely known, Sir Joshua Reynolds's opinion of *Rasselas* has elicited small attention since F. W. Hilles made it accessible in 1936. Without bothering to date his comment, which, Hilles infers, indicates that he "contemplated writing a critique on Johnson's literary ability," Sir Joshua observed:

> If . . . we could suppose novels writ by an angel or some superior being whose comprehensive faculties could develope and lay open the inmost recesses of the human mind, give the result of their experience compressed together in characters and exhibit this in the garb of play or amusement only by being conveyd in some story mixed with interesting events which totally occupy and fix the attention and such events as might have happend to every reader, supposing his rank whether from being too high or too lower [sic] had not exempted him from such accidents, or ever being in such situations, such a novel would give in a few hours the experience of ages, such a novel is Rasilas what is here done whatever part of life it develops the result the moral is undoubted truth.[7]

5. 2d ed. (1803), pp. 82–85, 103–05.

6. For this comment, see Robert Halsband, "'Rasselas': An Early Allusion," *Notes & Queries*, ccvii (Dec 1962), 459.

7. Frederick W. Hilles, *The Literary Career of Sir Joshua Reynolds* (1936), pp. 151–52.

Reynolds's criteria for judging the "novel"—the "faculties" of the author, "the undoubted truth" of the tale, and its presumed effect on a reader—are neither original nor especially striking. Nevertheless, his comment forms one of the handsomest compliments *Rasselas* has ever received.

Last, among Johnson's other contemporaries, James Beattie and Richard Cumberland (both of whom, of course, were acquainted with him) recorded their favorable opinions of *Rasselas* publicly. In his dissertation "On Fable and Romance," Beattie, while calling Addison's "Vision of Mirzah" (*Spectator* 159) the finest eastern fable he had ever seen, labels "*Rasselas*, by Johnson, and *Almoran and Hamet*, by Hawkesworth," as "celebrated performances in this way." "The former," he adds, is "admirable in description, and in that exquisite strain of sublime morality by which the writings of this great and good man are so eminently distinguished."[8] For Cumberland, similarly, discussing Johnson's character and compositions in his *Memoirs*, *Rasselas* contains "much to admire, and enough to make us wish for more. It is the work of an illuminated mind, and offers many wise and deep reflections, cloathed in beautiful and harmonious diction." Cumberland concedes that "we are not indeed familiar with such personages as Johnson has imagined for the characters of his fable," but, he goes on, "if we are not exceedingly interested in their story, we are infinitely gratified with their conversation and remarks."[9]

The diversity of the reactions to *Rasselas* may be suggested, finally, by a trio of poems which the book evoked. One, entitled "On Reading *Rasselas*, an Eastern Tale" and obviously, as James L. Clifford has said, the effusion of an "avid" admirer of Johnson, appeared in *Lloyd's Evening Post* (2–4 May 1759, p. 428) soon after *Rasselas* was published. The following lines, chosen from a total of twenty-six, display the adulatory tone and critical emphases of the anonymous author:

> So pure his diction, and his thoughts so bright,
> His language shines an insula of light;
> A tide of vivid lustre pours along,

---

8. James Beattie, *Dissertations Moral and Critical,* 2 vols. (Dublin, 1783), II.241.
9. *Memoirs of Richard Cumberland,* 2 vols. (1807), I.363.

That ev'n his prose is melody and song;
What depth of sentiment, what height of thought,
With what sublime, exalted morals fraught![1]

Another set of (twelve, four-line) stanzas appeared first, apparently, in the *Royal Female Magazine* for May 1760 (i, 230–32) and
was subsequently reprinted several times elsewhere.[2] Entitled
"Liberty, *an Elegy*," the poem, ostensibly a lament by "Myra," an
"inhabitant" of the Happy Valley in *Rasselas*, dilates on the theme
that "the most exquisite pleasures of sense cannot make amends
for the want of liberty." An introductory letter signed "Harriet
Airy" (the pseudonym of the real author, Mary Whateley)[3] attributes the inspiration for the verses to the opening chapters of
Rasselas, described as an "elegant, eastern tale."

Yet a third poem derived from the same source takes up five
pages (97–101) of the *Miscellanies in Prose and Verse* (1766)
officially assigned to Johnson's blind friend, Anna Williams.
Headed "Rasselas to Imlac" and ostensibly written by "Stella"
(who may be Miss Williams herself), the group of quatrains,
reminiscent of Mary Whateley's piece, expresses the prince's dissatisfaction with the sensuous pleasures of the Happy Valley and
his longing to escape, with Imlac's aid, into the world outside the
prison. The final stanza reads:

Methinks already poiz'd, I skim the skies,
Groves, grots, and lawns, your pleasures I resign;
New social scenes now meet my ravish'd eyes,
The wide, the busy world, my friend, is mine.

[p. 101]

IV

Shortly after the publication of *Rasselas*, a rumor circulated, as
Hester Mulso pointed out,[4] that Johnson intended to write a
continuation. Much later a similar report, which stated that the

1. I have taken these lines from Clifford, pp. 213–14.
2. The verses also appeared, for example, in the *London Chronicle* for 26–29 Dec
1761, p. 628, and in the *Royal Magazine* for Jan 1762, pp. 9–10.
3. For this identification, see Courtney and Smith, p. 86.
4. See p. lvii above.

process of composition was actually under way, reached the London newspapers, where it was alternately asserted and denied.[5] Still later the rumor attained a kind of official authority when Hawkins, as noted above,[6] recorded it in his *Life of Johnson*. The only other evidence of Johnson's presumed intention is the tale itself, whose conclusion, "in which nothing is concluded," may seem to suggest a sequel. That such a sequel was written and enjoyed considerable popularity again attests to the attraction of the original book for readers of the last decade of the eighteenth century.

The author of the sequel, Ellis Cornelia Knight, who as a young girl was, together with her mother (Lady Knight, widow of Admiral Sir Joseph Knight), a member of Johnson's circle,[7] entitled her work *Dinarbas; A Tale: Being a Continuation of Rasselas, Prince of Abissinia*, which was brought out anonymously, inscribed "To the Queen," and published in the middle of May 1790.[8] In her short introduction, Miss Knight quickly outlines the "general plan" of Johnson's "inimitable" story, naming as she does so the principal characters—Rasselas, Imlac, Nekayah, Pekuah, and the Astronomer—who reappear in the sequel; admits that Hawkins's report regarding Johnson's presumed intention "suggested" the continuation to her; disavows any "attempt to imitate the energetic stile, strong imagery, and profound knowledge of the author of *Rasselas*"; and expresses her hope that, since Johnson himself did not delineate "the fairer prospect" "attendant on humanity," "the narrative of *Dinarbas*" will afford "consolation . . . to the wretched traveller, terrified and disheartened at the rugged paths of life."[9]

It is not necessary for our purposes to describe the particular

5. See McGuffie, pp. 255, 269, 275, 277, 278, 282, 298, 302.

6. See p. lii above.

7. See Barbara Luttrell, *The Prim Romantic: A Biography of Ellis Cornelia Knight, 1758–1837* (1965), pp. 25–28. The Rothschild Library includes a copy of the sixth edition (1783) of *Rasselas* which Johnson inscribed "To Miss Cornelia Knight from the Authour. Apr. 19. 1784" (*The Rothschild Library: A Catalogue of the Collection of Eighteenth-Century Printed Books and Manuscripts Formed by Lord Rothschild* [1954], I.315).

8. An announcement of its publication appeared in the 13–15 May 1790 issue of the *London Chronicle*.

9. *Dinarbas* (1790), pp. [iii], v–viii.

turns of the complicated plot of *Dinarbas*.[1] Picking up the story where *Rasselas* leaves off, Miss Knight introduces Johnson's characters to her own creations, notably the brave young Dinarbas, his sister Zilia, and their father Amalphis; subjects Rasselas and Dinarbas to a succession of (mostly martial) adventures; places the prince on the throne of Abyssinia and marries him to Zilia and Dinarbas to princess Nekayah; and finally makes Rasselas abolish the royal prison which Johnson had ironically called the Happy Valley. During the course of the tale, she also accords the "young men of spirit and gaiety" and the "shepherds" a far more affirmative treatment (pp. 49–54, 55–60) than Johnson had given them (*Rasselas*, chaps. XVII, XIX). In addition, at the end of her work, she causes Rasselas to offer the following assessment of human existence, which contrasts sharply with Johnson's gloomier depiction:

> Let us return thanks to Heaven [says the new monarch] for having inspired us with that active desire of knowledge, and contempt of indolence, that have blessed us with instruction, with friendship, and with love! It is true that we have been singularly favoured by Providence; and few can expect, like us, to have their fondest wishes crowned with success; but even when our prospects were far different, our search after happiness had taught us resignation: let us therefore warn others against viewing the world as a scene of inevitable misery. Much is to be suffered in our journey through life; but conscious virtue, active fortitude, the balm of sympathy, and submission to the Divine Will, can support us through the painful trial. With them every station is the best; without them prosperity is a feverish dream, and pleasure a poisoned cup.

To be sure, he admits:

> Youth will vanish, health will decay, beauty fade, and strength

---

1. For modern discussions of the work, see C. J. Rawson, "The Continuation of *Rasselas*," *Bicentenary Essays on "Rasselas*," collected by Magdi Wahba, supplement to *Cairo Studies in English* (1959), pp. 85–95; Luttrell, pp. 84–86; Robert W. Uphaus, "Cornelia Knight's *Dinarbas*: A Sequel to *Rasselas*," *Philological Quarterly*, LXV (1986), 433–45.

sink into imbecility; but if we have enjoyed their advantages, let us not say there is no good, because the good in this world is not permanent: none but the guilty are excluded from at least temporary happiness; and if he whose imagination is lively, and whose heart glows with sensibility, is more subject than others to poignant grief and maddening disappoint- ment, surely he will confess that he has moments of ecstasy and consolatory reflection that repay him for all his suffer- ings. [pp. 334–36]

The reviewer of *Dinarbas* for the *European Magazine* (XVIII [July 1790], 39–40) applauded the sequel's "delineation" of "the fairer prospects of humanity" as an "antidote" to the "poison," "ren- der[ing] the mind dissatisfied with the ends of its existence," which *Rasselas,* "perhaps" the gloomiest of Johnson's works, con- tains; simultaneously, however, the writer readily admits that the continuation "does not possess the energetic style, strong imag- ery, and profound knowledge" of the original. A second critic, in the *Analytical Review* (VII [June 1790], 189), begins by saying that "Dr. Johnson's *Rasselas* . . . is so well known, that any comments on it might appear to be almost impertinent; but it is necessary to inform the public, why the author of *Dinarbas* attempted . . . to give a happier termination to the story." After quoting part of Miss Knight's introduction and acknowledging the good sense and considerable merit possessed by the sequel, the reviewer asserts:

> If Rasselas was to have been made happy, . . . it must have been done by Dr. Johnson himself. The style without the vapid tone of tautology . . . made us recollect the *Rambler;* but if this work had not been a professed conclusion of one of that writer's productions, we should simply have remarked that, without the stiff gait of affectation, the writer had let us see that Johnson had been his model.

Last, a third notice, prefacing extracts from *Dinarbas* printed in the *Universal Magazine* (LXXXVII [July 1790], 21), implies a similar reservation by stating that the tale "certainly cannot appear with any powerful prepossessions in its favour, when considered as the supplement to a work of Dr. Johnson's."

Notwithstanding the qualified character of these and probably other reviews, *Dinarbas,* profiting, one assumes, from its explicit connection to *Rasselas,* fared moderately well at the hands of the reading public. Translated into French and Italian a year after publication, it reached four English editions (1790, 1792, 1793, 1800) by 1800 and apparently at least six more by 1820.[2] Furthermore, usually bound with *Rasselas,* as mentioned below (p. 258), it attained its first American edition (at Philadelphia) in 1792 and its second (at Greenfield, Mass. and New York) in 1795.[3] Altogether, then, during its initial decade, the sequel appeared in at least eight different printings.

V

In conclusion, we may venture brief summarizing remarks about the early fortunes of the *Prince of Abyssinia.* These comments focus on two matters, the relative popularity of *Rasselas* and the nature of the critical responses it evoked.

Comparisons, often based on inaccurate and incommensurate data, are not always either valid or illuminating. Nevertheless, it may be instructive to place the fifty editions of *Rasselas* (including translations, it should be remembered, but excluding its appearance in collections of Johnson's works) alongside those of several other tales during, roughly, the same period of time, that is, from the middle to the end of the eighteenth century. For obvious reasons, one immediately thinks of the early editions of *Candide.*[4] Regrettably, a single reasonably comprehensive bibliography of Voltaire's writings has yet to be accomplished; but limited, fragmentary sources of information permit the crude guess, possibly quite wide of the mark, that between 1759 and 1800 the total number of editions of *Candide* (including translations and its appearance in larger collections of Voltaire's works) *may* have run to between eighty and ninety.[5] Turning to selected English fiction

2. Luttrell, p. 87; my personal copies of the first four editions; *CBEL,* II.549.

3. Charles Evans's *American Bibliography* (rpt.; New York, 1941), VIII.165; X.111.

4. See pp. xlii–xliii above; Pomeau's edition of *Candide* is cited on p. xlii, n. 3, above.

5. I hazard this tentative figure after consulting the following works: André Morize's edition of *Candide* (Paris, 1957), which lists (pp. lxvi–lxxiv) forty-three

and examining pertinent lists in the *NCBEL,* one discovers the following figures, which seem to be more or less comparable to that for *Rasselas:* twenty-eight for Smollett's *Peregrine Pickle* (1751), twenty for Richardson's *Sir Charles Grandison* (1754), six for Hawkesworth's *Almoran and Hamet* (1761), seventy-one for Goldsmith's *Vicar of Wakefield* (1766), and seventy for Sterne's *Sentimental Journey* (1768).[6] These numbers, together with my guess regarding the eighteenth-century editions of *Candide,* lead to the scarcely startling inference that *Rasselas,* although not at the top of the best-selling fiction of its time (that honor goes to such works as *Candide, The Vicar of Wakefield,* and *A Sentimental Journey*), belongs securely in the class of books maintaining a large, persistent reading public and hence by 1800, if not previously, would have been deemed eminently worthy of the attention of Johnson the critic, who, at the beginning of his *Preface to Shakespeare,* remarked that Shakespeare "has long outlived his century, the term commonly fixed as the test of literary merit."

During its first forty years of life, of course, the task of determining the tale's beauties and faults rested on narrower critical shoulders than those of the author. But with no important exceptions, these lesser evaluators appear to adhere to a concept of literature which Johnson himself espoused, however much he might have objected to the way specific persons applied that concept to the appraisal of his own writings. As a group, the early critics emphasize the mimetic, the overtly didactic, and the pleasurable functions of verbal art while acknowledging the presence of "expressive" or autobiographical elements in that art. The aspects of a fictional text they discerned and discussed—truthful-

---

"impressions successives que j'ai vues et collationnées"; Theodore Besterman, *Some Eighteenth-Century Voltaire Editions Unknown to Bengesco,* 4th ed. (*Studies on Voltaire and the Eighteenth Century* [cited hereafter as *SVEC*], cxi [1973], 131–52); *idem,* "Some Eighteenth-Century Voltaire Editions Unknown to Bengesco" (supplement to the 4th ed.), *SVEC,* cxliii (1975), 105–12; Mary-Margaret Harrison Barr, *Voltaire in America, 1744–1800* (1941), pp. 12–13; and the "provisional bibliographies" of editions and translations of Voltaire in these languages: Dutch and Flemish, English, Italian, Portuguese, Scandinavian and Finnish, and Spanish (*SVEC,* cxvi [1973], 19–64; viii [1959], 9–121; xviii [1961], 263–310; lxxvi [1970], 15–35; xlvii [1966], 53–92; clxi [1976], 43–136).

    6. *NCBEL,* ii. cols. 963, 918, 836, 1197–98, 951.

ness of representation, moral purpose, generic form, plot, characterization, sentiments, style, the presence of the sublime, the
effect on the reader, for example—were commonplaces of the
century.

Judged and examined according to these widely accepted principles and distinctions, *Rasselas* prospered steadily, on the whole,
even in the company of its brilliant pendant, *Candide*. To be sure,
a succession of commentators pointed to what they deemed serious defects in the book: an inaccurate, excessively dark depiction of human existence (partly attributable to Johnson's melancholy temperament); a dismal moral productive of ill effects on
the tale's audience (especially young, impressionable readers); a
meager, unexciting plot and flat; undifferentiated characters;
and a stiff style laden with hard words. A still larger number of
critics, however, either praised all features of the work they mentioned or else suggested that its weaknesses were subordinate to
what they saw as its primary strengths—the efficacy and variety of
pure moral instruction; the remarkably truthful, elegant pictures
of life; the wealth of profoundly wise reflections and disquisitions
on human affairs; the masterly embodiment of the Eastern tale;
an eloquent, harmonious style rising, in unison with other elements, to sublimity.

Thus by the beginning of the nineteenth century, it seems safe
to conclude, when we consider both its public appeal and critical
reception, that Johnson's "little book," possibly written during
"the evenings of one week" of 1759,[7] had reached a shining place
in the firmament of English literature.[8]

THE TEXT

Establishing the text of *Rasselas* for the present edition has proved
to be a relatively simple process. No manuscript of the work is
extant. During Johnson's lifetime, six editions were published by

7. *Life*, 1.341.
8. For additional information about the reception of *Rasselas* between 1759 and
1800, see the Appendix, pp. 251–58 below, which treats (1) "Robert Dodsley's
Lawsuit against the *Grand Magazine of Magazines*" and (2) "The Reception in
Europe and America."

the original proprietors and their successors.[9] The firm of one of the "partners," William Strahan, printed all six editions.[1] The recto of one leaf (A2) of Volume II of the first edition exists in two states: the earlier reads "CONTENTS. / VOL. II."; the later, changed (it can be inferred) to parallel the corresponding phrase in Volume I, reads "CONTENTS / OF THE / SECOND VOL-UME." A collation of five copies[2] of the first edition discloses no signs of "stop press" revisions.

Set from the first edition (later state of Volume II, A2r), the second edition, published on 26 June 1759,[3] contains a considerable number of fresh readings which O. F. Emerson and subsequently R. W. Chapman attributed to the author.[4] An independent examination has led me to the same conclusion, despite Johnson's remarks, also noted by Emerson and Chapman, that might suggest no authorial revisions.[5] Three reasons underlie my conclusion: (1) the changes are such that only an author would be likely to make; (2) the changes are consonant with Johnson's revisions in other writings; and (3) the advertisement for the second edition describes it as "corrected."[6] A collation of three copies[7] of the second edition reveals no evidence of different states in the type setting.

The third edition (1760) was set from the second, and the fourth (1766) reverted to the second. Thereafter the sequence

9. Since SJ would surely have confined his textual changes to the authorized editions, I have restricted my collations to these six editions and the text in Hawkins's edition (1787) of SJ's *Works*. The latter contains no evidence of authorial revisions. For information about other editions of *Rasselas* published during SJ's lifetime, see pp. xlix–l above.

1. For details about the "partners" and the printing of these editions, see pp. xxiv, xxvi above.

2. The location of these copies is: British Library, University of Chicago Library, Harvard University Library (Hyde Rooms), University of Illinois Library, Gwin J. Kolb.

3. *Daily Advertiser*, 26 June 1759.

4. O. F. Emerson, "The Text of Johnson's *Rasselas*," *Anglia*, XXII (Dec 1899), 499–509; R. W. Chapman (ed.), *Rasselas* (1927), pp. xviii–xx. Fleeman has noted that "a good deal of the type-setting of the first edn. is retained in" the second, "which is perhaps most accurately to be described as a 'corrected re-impression.'"

5. See p. xxvi above.

6. *Daily Advertiser*, 26 June 1759.

7. The location of these copies is: British Library, Harvard University Library (Hyde Rooms), Gwin J. Kolb.

THE

PRINCE

OF

ABISSINIA.

A

TALE.

IN TWO VOLUMES.

VOL. I.

LONDON:
Printed for R. and J. DODSLEY, in Pall-Mall;
and W. JOHNSTON, in Ludgate-Street.
M DCC LIX.

Title page of Volume I of the first edition of *Rasselas*
(earlier state of Volume II, A2r)

was chronological, with the fifth (1775) being set from the fourth and the sixth (1783) from the fifth. A collation of three copies each[8] of editions three through six discloses no signs either of authorial revisions or of different states in the settings forming the individual editions.

The basic text presented here is that of the first edition (University of Chicago Library copy, earlier state of Volume II, A2r). It has been altered by the insertion of the later wording of Volume II, A2r; the substantive variants, corrected spellings, and regularized punctuation in the second edition which, it seems valid to infer, were made or approved by Johnson; and the accurate numbering of Chapters XXIX–XLIX. All of these changes are denoted in the textual notes. Other slight modifications have also been made in the accidentals. Specifically, the bodies of the initial words of Chapters I and XXVI in the chapter headings of the Table of Contents, as well as the bodies of the first words of chapters, are lowercased; and the use of quotation marks conforms to modern conventions. The name of the Happy Valley is variously printed in the copy-text in lowercase roman or italic type; it is here printed in roman with initial capitals. Italics and capitals in works quoted in the introductions, annotation, and appendix follow the style of the Yale Johnson edition.

The Yale University Library possesses a copy of the first edition of *Rasselas*—formerly in the Jerome Kern Collection and described in the sale catalogue of that collection—which Johnson apparently presented to the novelist Samuel Richardson, who seemingly wrote on the pastedown of Volume I "From the Author." Below the notation is the signature (also on the pastedown of Volume II) of "Anne Richardson," Richardson's daughter. The text of the copy contains eight small changes in what C. B. Tinker believed to be Johnson's hand.[9] It appears likely, however, that the revisions (assigned here to the textual notes) were made by Richardson rather than Johnson.

8. The location of these copies is: British Library, Harvard University Library (Hyde Rooms), Gwin J. Kolb.

9. *The Library of Jerome Kern* (1929), 1.236. The description in the catalogue mistakenly lists only "seven corrections" ("indubitably in Johnson's handwriting") and goes on to express indebtedness "to Professor Chauncey Brewster Tinker for revealing the interest and importance of these volumes." Part I of Kern's collection was sold on 7–10 Jan 1929, Part II on 21–24 Jan.

SHORT TITLES AND
ABBREVIATIONS

Anecdotes—H. L. Piozzi's *Anecdotes of the Late Samuel Johnson*, 1786, in *Johnsonian Miscellanies*, ed. G. B. Hill, 2 vols., 1897. Vol. I, pp. 144–351.

Dictionary—Johnson's *Dictionary of the English Language*, 4th ed., 2 vols., 1773.

Emerson—O. F. Emerson, ed., *History of Rasselas, Prince of Abyssinia*, 1895.

Geography—Emanuel Bowen, *A Complete System of Geography*, 2 vols., 1747.

Hardy—J. P. Hardy, ed., *The History of Rasselas, Prince of Abyssinia*, 1968.

Hill—G. B. Hill, ed., *History of Rasselas, Prince of Abyssinia*, 1887.

Letters—*The Letters of Samuel Johnson*, ed. R. W. Chapman, 3 vols., 1952; referred to by number of letter.

Life—Boswell's *Life of Johnson*, ed. G. B. Hill, revised and enlarged by L. F. Powell, 6 vols., 1934–50; Vols. V–VI (2d ed.), 1964.

Lives—*Lives of the English Poets*, ed. G. B. Hill, 3 vols., 1905.

Voyage to Abyssinia—The Yale Edition of the Works of Samuel Johnson, Vol. XV: *A Voyage to Abyssinia*, ed. Joel J. Gold, 1985.

Sigla used in the TEXTUAL NOTES

59a—1759 (1st ed.)
59b—1759 (2d ed.)
60—1760 (3d ed.)
87—1787 (Hawkins's ed. of Johnson's *Works*)
RWC—R. W. Chapman
YC—Kern-Yale copy

THE HISTORY OF RASSELAS,

PRINCE OF ABYSSINIA

THE HISTORY OF RASSELAS, PRINCE OF ABYSSINIA

CONTENTS OF THE FIRST VOLUME.

---

1. At this point, the contents page of the copy-text contains the reference "page 1." The page numbers given here refer to the Yale edition.

CONTENTS OF THE SECOND VOLUME.[a]

a. CONTENTS . . . VOLUME. *59a, later state of A2r*] CONTENTS . . . VOL. II. *59a, earlier state of A2r*   b. xxix *60*] xxviii *59a, 59b. The misnumbering of the chapters by one continues throughout the remainder of 59a and 59b.*   c. languishes . . . of *59b*] continues to lament *59a*   d. remembered . . . sorrow *59b*] remembered by the princess *59a*

e. opinion . . . justified *59b*] astronomer justifies his account of himself *59a*

THE HISTORY OF RASSELAS,
PRINCE OF ABISSINIA.

Chap. I.

Description of a palace in a valley.[1]

Ye who listen with credulity to the whispers of fancy, and
pursue with eagerness the phantoms of hope; who expect
that age will perform the promises of youth, and that the
deficiencies of the present day will be supplied by the morrow; attend to the history of Rasselas prince of Abissinia.[2]

Rasselas was the fourth son[3] of the mighty emperour,[4] in
whose dominions the Father of waters begins his course;[5]
whose bounty pours[a] down the streams of plenty, and scat-
ters over half the world the harvests of Egypt.[6]

According to the custom which has descended from age

---

a. pours *59b*] powers *59a* powers *is also changed to* pours *in the YC.*

---

1. For a discussion of the background
and sources of the Happy Valley, see
Introduction, pp. xxvi–xxxi above.

2. In Hiob Ludolf's *Historia Aethiopica* (1681), a copy of the English translation (1682) which SJ owned, "Rasselach" is identified as a son of the wife
of an Emperor Basilides (Genealogical
Table between pp. 192 and 193); *Voyage to Abyssinia* (1735) refers to the
same person as "Rassela Christos lieutenant general to Sultan Segued" (p.
85). The translation of Ludolf may be
the source of the name of SJ's prince;
see Introduction, p. xxviii above.

3. Ludolf notes (Genealogical Table)
that the fourth son of an Abyssinian
emperor escaped from the royal prison
of Amhara.

4. According to *Voyage to Abyssinia,*

"the kings of Abyssinia having formerly had several princes tributary to
them, still retain the title of Emperor"
(p. 211).

5. In *Voyage to Abyssinia,* frequent references to the Nile include the statement that the river, "which the natives
call *Abavi,* that is, the Father of Waters,
rises first in . . . the kingdom of Goiama, . . . one of the most fruitful and
agreeable of all the Abyssinian dominions" (p. 81); the specific source of the
river, we are told, is located "in the eastern part of this kingdom on the declivity of a mountain." Cf. Ludolf, pp.
34–43.

6. Many early works note the indebtedness of Egypt's "envyed fertility" "to
the annual inundations" of the Nile
(*Voyage to Abyssinia,* p. 85).

to age among the monarchs of the torrid zone, Rasselas[b] was confined in a private palace, with the other sons and daughters of Abissinian royalty, till the order of succession should call him to the throne.[7]

The place, which the wisdom or policy of antiquity had destined for the residence of the Abissinian princes, was a spacious valley[8] in the kingdom of Amhara,[9] surrounded on every side by mountains, of which the summits overhang the middle part.[1] The only passage, by which it could be entered, was a cavern that passed under a rock, of which it has long been disputed whether it was the work of nature or of human industry. The outlet of the cavern was concealed by a thick wood, and the mouth which opened into the valley was closed with gates of iron, forged by the artificers of ancient days, so massy that no man could, without the help of engines, open or shut them.

From the mountains on every side, rivulets descended that filled all the valley with verdure and fertility, and formed a lake in the middle inhabited by fish of every species, and frequented by every fowl whom nature has taught to dip the wing in water. This lake discharged its superfluities by a stream which entered a dark cleft of the mountain on the northern side, and fell with dreadful noise from precipice to precipice till it was heard no more.

The sides of the mountains were covered with trees, the banks of the brooks were diversified with flowers; every

b. Rasselas 59*b*] he 59*a*

---

7. For a discussion of the confinement of Abyssinian princes and princesses, see Introduction, p. xxx above. Among early works, the spurious *Late Travels of S. Giacomo Baratti* (1670) is perhaps unique in saying that all the emperor's children, not merely his sons, are confined in the royal prison.

8. *The Voyage of Sir Francis Alvarez . . . made unto the Court of Prete Ianni, the Great Christian Emperour of Ethiopia* (English translation, 1625) is apparently the only pre-1759 work which designates a valley as the site of the royal

prison; see Introduction, p. xxix above.

9. In specifying Amhara as the site of the royal prison, SJ agrees with almost all writers on the subject; see *Voyage to Abyssinia*, pp. 163, 167; Ludolf, p. 29; Introduction, pp. xxvii–xxx above.

1. For a discussion (and graphic representation) of these strangely shaped mountains, see Donald M. Lockhart, "'The Fourth Son of the Mighty Emperor': The Ethiopian Background of Johnson's *Rasselas*," *PMLA*, LXXVIII (1963), 520–21.

blast[2] shook spices from the rocks, and every month dropped fruits upon the ground.[3] All animals that bite the grass, or brouse the shrub, whether wild or tame, wandered in this extensive circuit,[4] secured from beasts of prey by the mountains which confined them. On one part were flocks and herds feeding in the pastures, on another all the beasts of chase frisking in the lawns;[5] the spritely kid was bounding on the rocks, the subtle monkey[6] frolicking in the trees, and the solemn elephant[7] reposing in the shade.[8] All the diversities of the world were brought together, the blessings of nature were collected, and its evils extracted and excluded.[9]

The valley, wide and fruitful, supplied its inhabitants with the necessaries of life, and all delights and superfluities were added at the annual visit[1] which the emperour paid his children, when the iron gate was opened to the sound of musick; and during eight days every one that resided in the

---

2. *Blast:* "A gust or puff of wind" (sense 1 in *Dictionary*).

3. In one part of Abyssinia, according to *Voyage to Abyssinia*, "the ground is always producing, and the fruits ripen throughout the year" (p. 90).

4. Abyssinia, *Voyage to Abyssinia* remarks, contains animals in as "great numbers" and "of as many different species, as in any country in the world" (p. 45).

5. *Lawn:* "An open space between woods" (*Dictionary*).

6. According to *Voyage to Abyssinia*, "the monkies" of Abyssinia are "creatures so cunning, that they would not stir if a man came unarmed, but would run immediately when they saw a gun" (pp. 38–39). In SJ's *Dictionary, subtle* is defined as "Sly; artful; cunning."

7. In Abyssinia, *Voyage to Abyssinia* remarks, are "so great numbers of elephants . . . that in one evening we met three hundred of them in three troops" (pp. 45–46).

8. See Introduction, p. xxx above, for a summary listing of the many resem-

blances between SJ's paradisial Happy Valley and the "romantic" description of the royal prison contained in Luis de Urreta's *Historia Ecclesiastica, Politica, Natural y Moral de los Grandes y Remotos Reynos de la Etiopia* (Valencia, 1610), which may have been a source for SJ's depiction.

9. Cf. this sentence from the account, in *Rambler* 204 (par. 4), of King Seged's search for happiness: "All that could solace the sense, or flatter the fancy, all that industry could extort from nature, or wealth furnish to art, all that conquest could seize, or beneficence attract, was collected together, and every perception of delight was excited and gratified." For a discussion of the similarities between *Rasselas* and *Rambler*s 204, 205, see Introduction, pp. xxxv–xxxvii above.

1. Among early works, only Baratti's *Late Travels* states that "the emperour visits" the royal prison "once a year with his wives" (p. 26); see Introduction, pp. xxx above.

valley was required to propose whatever might contribute to make seclusion[2] pleasant, to fill up the vacancies of attention, and lessen the tediousness of time. Every desire was immediately granted. All the artificers of pleasure were called to gladden the festivity;[3] the musicians exerted the power of harmony, and the dancers shewed their activity before the princes, in hope that they should pass their lives in this blissful[c] captivity, to which these[d] only were admitted whose performance was thought able to add novelty to luxury. Such was the appearance of security and delight which this retirement afforded, that they to whom it was new always desired that it might be perpetual; and as those, on whom the iron gate had once closed, were never suffered to return, the effect of longer experience could not be known. Thus every year produced new schemes of delight, and new competitors for imprisonment.

The palace stood on an eminence raised about thirty paces[4] above the surface of the lake. It was divided into many squares or courts,[5] built with greater or less magnificence according to the rank of those for whom they were designed. The roofs were turned into arches of massy stone joined by[e] a cement that grew harder by time, and the building stood from century to century, deriding the solstitial rains and equinoctial hurricanes, without need of reparation.

This house, which was so large as to be fully known to none but some ancient officers who successively inherited

c. blissful *59b*] blisful *59a* blisful *is also changed to* blissful *in the YC.*   d. "these *should perhaps be* those; *the words are hardly distinguishable in Johnson's hand."* (RWC) these *is changed to* those *in the YC. 87 reads* those.   e. by *59b*] with *59a*

---

2. *To seclude* but not *seclusion* is listed in SJ's *Dictionary*.

3. Cf. King Seged's action in *Rambler* 204 (par. 5): "Into this delicious region Seged summoned all the persons of his court, who seemed eminently qualified to receive or communicate pleasure."

4. *Pace:* "A measure of five feet"

(sense 5 in *Dictionary*).

5. SJ's description of this palace resembles remarks about an Abyssinian palace (at Gondar) contained in Charles Jacques Poncet's *Voyage to Aethiopia* (pp. 116, 120; cited in the Introduction, p. xxix above).

the secrets of the place, was built as if suspicion herself had dictated the plan. To every room there was an open and secret passage, every square had a communication with the rest, either from the upper stories by private galleries, or by subterranean passages from the lower apartments. Many of the columns had unsuspected cavities, in which a long race of monarchs had[f] reposited their treasures.[6] They then closed up the opening with marble, which was never to be removed but in the utmost exigencies of the kingdom; and recorded their accumulations in a book which was itself concealed in a tower not entered but by the emperour, attended by the prince who stood next in succession.

Chap. II.

The discontent of Rasselas in the Happy Valley.

Here the sons and daughters of Abissinia lived only to know the soft vicissitudes[1] of pleasure and repose, attended by all that were skilful to delight, and gratified with whatever the senses can enjoy. They wandered in gardens of fragrance, and slept in the fortresses of security. Every art was practised to make them pleased with their own condition. The sages who instructed them,[2] told them of nothing but the miseries of publick life, and described all beyond the mountains as regions of calamity, where discord was always raging, and where man preyed upon man.

To heighten their opinion of their own felicity, they were daily entertained with songs, the subject of which was the

f. a . . . had 59*b*] successive monarchs 59*a*

---

6. Urreta's *Historia* describes at length (pp. 112–18) the rich treasure which a succession of Abyssinian rulers had deposited in the royal prison of Amhara. Purchas's translation follows Urreta; Baratti simply mentions the "precious things belonging to the Emperour" which are kept in the prison (pp. 33–34).

1. *Vicissitude:* "Regular change; return of the same things in the same succession" (sense 1 in *Dictionary*).

2. Urreta (Chap. xii), Purchas (p. 568), and Baratti (p. 119) all refer to the teachers who instruct the royal prisoners.

Happy Valley. Their appetites were excited by frequent enumerations of different enjoyments, and revelry and merriment was the business of every hour from the dawn of morning to the close of even.

These methods were generally successful; few of the princes had ever wished to enlarge their bounds, but passed their lives in full conviction that they had all within their reach that art or nature could bestow, and pitied those whom fate had excluded from this seat of tranquility, as the sport of chance, and the slaves of misery.

Thus they rose in the morning, and lay down at night, pleased with each other and with themselves, all but Rasselas, who, in the twenty-sixth year of his age, began to withdraw himself from their pastimes and assemblies, and to delight in solitary walks and silent meditation. He often sat before tables covered with luxury,[3] and forgot to taste the dainties that were placed before him: he rose abruptly in the midst of the song, and hastily retired beyond the sound of musick. His attendants observed the change and endeavoured to renew his love of pleasure: he neglected their officiousness,[a4] repulsed their invitations, and spent day after day on the banks of rivulets sheltered with trees, where he sometimes listened to the birds in[b] the branches, sometimes observed the fish playing in the stream, and anon[5] cast his eyes upon the pastures and mountains filled with animals, of which some were biting the herbage, and some sleeping among the bushes.

This singularity of his humour[6] made him much observed. One of the sages, in whose conversation he had formerly delighted, followed him secretly, in hope of discovering the cause of his disquiet. Rasselas, who knew not

---

a. officiousness 59b] endeavours 59a   b. in 59a, 59b] in is changed to on in the YC.

---

3. *Luxury:* "Delicious fare" (sense 4 in *Dictionary*).

4. *Officiousness:* "Forwardness of civility, or respect, or endeavour. Commonly in an ill sense" (sense 1 in *Dic-*

tionary).

5. *Anon:* "Sometimes; now and then; at other times" (sense 2 in *Dictionary*).

6. *Humour:* "Present disposition" (sense 4 in *Dictionary*).

that any one was near him, having for some time fixed his eyes upon the goats that were brousing among the rocks, began to compare their condition with his own.

"What," said he, "makes the difference between man and all the rest of the animal creation? Every beast that strays beside me has the same corporal necessities with myself; he is hungry and crops the grass, he is thirsty and drinks the^c stream, his thirst and hunger are appeased, he is satisfied and sleeps; he rises again and is hungry, he is again fed and is at rest. I am hungry and thirsty like him, but when thirst and hunger cease I am not at rest; I am, like him, pained with want, but am not, like him, satisfied with fulness. The intermediate hours are tedious and gloomy; I long again to be hungry that I may again quicken my attention.[7] The birds peck the berries or the corn, and fly away to the groves where they sit in seeming happiness on the branches, and waste their lives in tuning one unvaried series of sounds. I likewise can call the lutanist and the singer, but the sounds that pleased me yesterday weary me to day, and will grow yet more wearisome to morrow.[8] I can discover within me no power of perception which is not glutted with its proper pleasure, yet I do not feel myself delighted. Man has surely some latent sense for which this place affords no gratification, or he has some desires distinct from sense which must be satisfied before he can be happy."[9]

c. drinks the *59a, 59b*] at *is inserted between* drinks *and* the *in the YC.*

---

7. Rasselas's plight resembles that of the retired business man in *Adventurer* 102 (par. 11) who protracts "breakfast as long as I can, because when it is ended I have no call for my attention, till I can with some degree of decency grow impatient for my dinner"; and who eats not "because I am hungry, but because I am idle; but alas! the time quickly comes when I can eat no longer."

8. Neither *today* nor *tomorrow* appears in *Dictionary.* Under sense 25 of *to,* SJ comments, "Before *day, to* notes the present day; before *morrow,* the day next coming."

9. With Rasselas's recital of the differences between man and other animals, cf. SJ's remarks in *Rambler* 41 (par. 2): "I cannot but consider this necessity of searching on every side for matter on which the attention may be employed, as a strong proof of the superior and celestial nature of the soul of man. We have no reason to believe that other creatures have higher faculties, or more extensive capacities, than the preservation of themselves, or their

After this he lifted up his head, and seeing the moon rising, walked towards the palace. As he passed through the fields, and saw the animals around him, "Ye," said he, "are happy, and need not envy me that walk thus among you, burthened with myself; nor do I, ye gentle beings, envy your felicity; for it is not the felicity of man.[1] I have many distresses from which ye are free; I fear pain when I do not feel it; I sometimes shrink at evils recollected, and sometimes start at evils anticipated: surely the equity of providence has ballanced peculiar sufferings with peculiar enjoyments."[2]

With observations like these the prince amused himself as he returned, uttering them with a plaintive voice, yet with a look that discovered[3] him to feel some complacence in his own perspicacity, and to receive some solace of the miseries of life, from consciousness of the delicacy with which he felt, and the eloquence with which he bewailed them.[4] He mingled cheerfully in the diversions of the evening, and all rejoiced to find that his heart was lightened.

Chap. III.

The wants of him that wants nothing.

On the next day his old instructor, imagining that he had now made himself acquainted with his disease of mind, was

---

species, requires; they seem always to be fully employed, or to be completely at ease without employment, to feel few intellectual miseries or pleasures."

1. Replying to an encomium on the joys of "savage life," SJ declared: "Do not allow yourself, Sir, to be imposed upon by such gross absurdity. It is sad stuff; it is brutish. If a bull could speak, he might as well exclaim,—Here I am with this cow and this grass; what being can enjoy greater felicity?" (*Life*, II.228).

2. Both with Rasselas's observations and his conclusion, cf. *Adventurer* 120 (par. 13), which reads in part: "It is

scarcely to be imagined, that Infinite Benevolence would create a being capable of enjoying so much more than is here to be enjoyed, and qualified by nature to prolong pain by remembrance and anticipate it by terror, if he was not designed for something nobler and better than a state, in which many of his faculties can serve only for his torment."

3. *To discover*: "To shew; to disclose; to bring to light" (sense 1 in *Dictionary*).

4. For SJ, to talk about one's troubles is to reveal a degree of pleasure in them. See *Life*, IV.31; III.421.

in hope of curing it by counsel, and officiously sought an opportunity of conference, which the prince, having long considered him as one whose intellects[1] were exhausted, was not very willing to afford: "Why," said he, "does this man thus intrude upon me; shall I be never suffered to forget those lectures which pleased only while they were new, and to become new again must be forgotten?" He then walked into the wood, and composed[2] himself to his usual meditations; when, before his thoughts had taken any settled form, he perceived his persuer at his side, and was at first prompted by his impatience to go hastily away; but, being unwilling to offend a man whom he had once reverenced and still loved, he invited him to sit down with him on the bank.

The old man, thus encouraged, began to lament the change which had been lately observed in the prince, and to enquire why he so often retired from the pleasures of the palace, to loneliness and silence. "I fly from pleasure," said the prince, "because pleasure has ceased to please; I am lonely because I am miserable, and am unwilling to cloud with my presence the happiness of others." "You, Sir," said the sage, "are the first who has complained of misery in the Happy Valley. I hope to convince you that your complaints have no real cause. You are here in full possession of all that the emperour of Abissinia can bestow; here is neither labour to be endured nor danger to be dreaded, yet here is all that labour or danger can procure or purchase.[a] Look round and tell me which of your wants is without supply: if you want nothing, how are you unhappy?"

"That I want nothing," said the prince, "or that I know not what I want, is the cause of my complaint; if I had any

---

a. procure or purchase 59b] procure 59a

---

1. Though SJ uses the word rather often—e.g., *Rambler* 164 (par. 9), 167 (par. 3); *Adventurer* 99 (par. 15), 128 (par. 7), 137 (par. 20); *Idler* 48 (par. 9), 78 (par. 3); *Life*, IV.181—*intellects* (meaning "intellectual powers, mental faculties, 'wits'" [*OED*]) is not listed in his *Dictionary*.

2. *To compose:* "To adjust the mind to any business, by freeing it from disturbance" (sense 7 in *Dictionary*).

known want, I should have a certain wish; that wish would
excite endeavour, and I should not then repine to see the
sun move so slowly towards the western mountain, or lament when the day breaks and sleep will no longer hide me
from myself. When I see the kids and the lambs chasing one
another, I fancy that I should be happy if I had something
to persue. But, possessing all that I can want, I find one day
and one hour exactly like another, except that the latter is
still more tedious than the former.[3] Let your experience
inform me how the day may now seem as short as in my
childhood, while nature was yet fresh, and every moment
shewed me what I never had observed before.[4] I have
already enjoyed too much; give me something to desire."

The old man was surprised at this new species of affliction, and knew not what to reply, yet was unwilling to be
silent. "Sir," said he, "if you had seen the miseries of the
world, you would know how to value your present state."
"Now," said the prince, "you have given me something to
desire; I shall long to see the miseries of the world, since the
sight of them is necessary to happiness."[5]

Chap. IV.

The prince continues to grieve and muse.

At this time the sound of musick proclaimed the hour of

---

3. The appearance of "the latter" and
"the former" contradicts Boswell's assertion that SJ "never used the
phrases . . . , having observed, that
they often occasioned obscurity" (*Life*,
IV.190).

4. Cf. *Idler* 44 (par. 3): "We are naturally delighted with novelty, and there
is a time when all that we see is new.
When we first enter into the world,
whithersoever we turn our eyes, they
meet knowledge with pleasure at her
side; every diversity of nature pours
ideas in upon the soul; neither search
nor labour are necessary; we have
nothing more to do than to open our
eyes, and curiosity is gratified"; *Ram-*

bler 151 (par. 9); *Letters* 429, 656.1.

5. With the prince's conclusion, cf.
SJ's observation in *Rambler* 150 (par.
11): "As no man can enjoy happiness
without thinking that he enjoys it, the
experience of calamity is necessary to a
just sense of better fortune; for the
good of our present state is merely
comparative, and the evil which every
man feels will be sufficient to disturb
and harass him if he does not know
how much he escapes"; *Adventurer* 111
(par. 3): Seneca "might have said, with
rigorous propriety, that no man is
happy, but as he is compared with the
miserable."

repast,[1] and the conversation was concluded. The old man went away sufficiently discontented to find that his reasonings had produced the only conclusion which they were intended to prevent. But in the decline of life shame and grief are of short duration; whether it be that we bear easily what we have born long, or that, finding ourselves in age less regarded, we less regard others; or, that we look with slight regard upon afflictions, to which we know that the hand of death is about to put an end.

The prince, whose views were extended to a wider space, could not speedily quiet his emotions. He had been before terrified at the length of life which nature promised him, because he considered that in a long time much must be endured; he now rejoiced in his youth, because in many years much might be done.

This first beam of hope, that had been ever darted into his mind, rekindled youth in his cheeks, and doubled the lustre of his eyes.[2] He was fired with the desire of doing something, though he knew not yet with distinctness, either end or means.

He was now no longer gloomy and unsocial; but, considering himself as master of a secret stock of happiness, which he could enjoy only by concealing it, he affected to be busy in all schemes of diversion, and endeavoured to make others pleased with the state of which he himself was weary. But pleasures never can be so multiplied or continued, as not to leave much of life unemployed; there were many hours, both of the night and day, which he could spend without suspicion in solitary thought. The load of life was much lightened: he went eagerly into the assemblies, because he supposed the frequency of his presence necessary to the success of his purposes; he retired gladly to privacy, because he had now a subject of thought.

His chief amusement was to picture to himself that world

---

1. Baratti's *Late Travels* (see p. xxx above) includes a reference to the music played when the Abyssinian "Emperour" "dines or sups" (p. 58).

2. Cf. SJ's remarks on hope in *Rambler* 67 (par. 1): "[N]o temper," he asserts, is "so generally indulged as hope," which "begins with the first power of comparing our actual with our possible state, and attends us through every stage and period. . . . Hope is necessary in every condition."

which he had never seen; to place himself in various conditions; to be entangled in imaginary difficulties, and to be engaged in wild[3] adventures: but his benevolence always terminated his projects in the relief of distress, the detection of fraud, the defeat of oppression, and the diffusion of happiness.[4]

Thus passed twenty months of the life of Rasselas. He busied himself so intensely in visionary bustle, that he forgot his real solitude; and, amidst hourly preparations for the various incidents of human affairs, neglected to consider by what means he should mingle with mankind.

One day, as he was sitting on a bank, he feigned to himself an orphan virgin robbed of her little portion[5] by a treacherous lover, and crying after him for restitution and redress. So strongly was the image impressed upon his mind, that he started up in the maid's defence, and run[6] forward to seize the plunderer with all the eagerness of real persuit. Fear naturally quickens the flight of guilt. Rasselas could not catch the fugitive with his utmost efforts; but, resolving to weary, by perseverance, him whom he could not surpass in speed, he pressed on till the foot of the mountain stopped his course.

Here he recollected himself, and smiled at his own useless impetuosity. Then raising his eyes to the mountain, "This," said he, "is the fatal[7] obstacle that hinders at once the enjoyment of pleasure, and the exercise of virtue. How long is it that my hopes and wishes have flown beyond this boundary of my life, which yet I never have attempted to surmount!"

---

3. *Wild:* "Meerly imaginary" (sense 11 in *Dictionary*).

4. "To a benevolent disposition," SJ declares in *Adventurer* 34 (par. 1), "every state of life will afford some opportunities of contributing to the welfare of mankind."

5. *Portion:* "Part of an inheritance given to a child; a fortune" (sense 3 in *Dictionary*).

6. In his "Grammar" (but not in the *Dictionary* proper, where only *ran* appears), SJ identifies *run* as "the preterite imperfect and participle passive" of the verb *run*. He also identifies *ran* as the "preterite" form but adds that it and others—like *began, sang,* etc.—in the same class are mostly "obsolete." Cf. the use of *run* on p. 23 below.

7. *Fatal:* "Appointed by destiny" (sense 3 in *Dictionary*).

Struck with this reflection, he sat down to muse, and remembered, that since he first resolved to escape from his confinement, the sun had passed twice over him in his annual course. He now felt a degree of regret with which he had never been before acquainted. He considered how much might have been done in the time which had passed, and left nothing real behind it.[8] He compared twenty months with the life of man. "In life," said he, "is not to be counted the ignorance of infancy,[9] or imbecility[1] of age. We are long before we are able to think, and we soon cease from the power of acting. The true period of human existence may be reasonably estimated as forty years, of which I have mused away the four and twentieth part. What I have lost was certain, for I have certainly possessed it; but of twenty months to come who can assure me?"

The consciousness of his own folly pierced him deeply, and he was long before he could be reconciled to himself. "The rest of my time," said he, "has been lost by the crime or folly of my ancestors, and the absurd institutions of my country; I remember it with disgust,[2] yet[a] without remorse: but the months that have passed since new light darted into my soul, since I formed a scheme of reasonable felicity, have been squandered by my own fault. I have lost that which can never be restored: I have seen the sun rise and set for twenty months, an idle gazer on the light of heaven: In this time the birds have left the nest of their mother, and committed themselves to the woods and to the skies: the kid has forsaken the teat, and learned by degrees to climb the rocks

a. yet 59b] but 59a

---

8. In his diaries, prayers, and elsewhere, SJ often reproached himself, of course, for his supposed laziness and procrastination. See, for example, *Diaries, Prayers, and Annals*, ed. E. L. McAdam, Jr., with Donald and Mary Hyde (Vol. I, Yale Edition of the Works of Samuel Johnson, 1958), pp. 81, 159; *Letters*, III.343–44 (s.v. "Character: [1]

Self-examination"); *Life*, I.398; V.231.

9. Infancy, says SJ in his *Dictionary*, is "Usually extended by naturalists to seven years."

1. *Imbecility:* "Weakness; feebleness of mind or body" (*Dictionary*).

2. *Disgust:* "Ill-humour; malevolence; offence conceived" (sense 2 in *Dictionary*).

in quest of independant sustenance. I only have made no advances, but am still helpless and ignorant. The moon, by more than twenty changes, admonished me of the flux of life; the stream that rolled before my feet upbraided my inactivity. I sat feasting on intellectual luxury,[3] regardless alike of the examples of the earth, and the instructions of the planets. Twenty months are past, who shall restore them!"

These sorrowful meditations fastened upon his mind; he past four months in resolving to lose no more time in idle resolves,[4] and was awakened to more vigorous exertion by hearing a maid, who had broken a porcelain cup, remark, that what cannot be repaired is not to be regretted.

This was obvious; and Rasselas reproached himself that he had not discovered it, having not known, or not considered, how many useful hints are obtained by chance, and how often the mind, hurried by her own ardour to distant views, neglects the truths that lie open before her.[5] He, for a few hours, regretted his regret, and from that time bent his whole mind upon the means of escaping from the valley of happiness.

Chap. V.

The prince meditates his escape.

He now found that it would be very difficult to effect that which it was very easy to suppose effected. When he looked

---

3. Cf. p. 12, n. 3, above.

4. The prince's extended "resolving" exemplifies SJ's comment in *Idler* 27 (par. 7): "I believe most men may review all the lives that have passed within their observation, without . . . being able to tell a single instance of a course of practice suddenly changed in consequence of a change of opinion, or an establishment of determination." Cf. also his later reflection in *Diaries, Prayers, and Annals*, p. 133: "Every man naturally persuades himself that he can keep his resolutions, nor is he convinced of his imbecillity but by length of time, and frequency of experiment."

5. Cf. *Idler* 91 (par. 1): "It is common to overlook what is near by keeping the eye fixed upon something remote. In the same manner present opportunities are neglected, and attainable good is slighted, by minds busied in extensive ranges and intent upon future advantages."

round about him, he saw himself confined by the bars of nature which had never yet been broken, and by the gate, through which none that once had passed it were ever able to return.[1] He was now impatient as an eagle in a grate.[2] He passed week after week in clambering the mountains, to see if there was any aperture which the bushes might conceal, but found all the summits inaccessible by their prominence.[3] The iron gate he despaired to open; for it was not only secured with all the power of art, but was always watched by successive sentinels, and was by its position exposed to the perpetual observation of all the inhabitants.

He then examined the cavern through which the waters of the lake were discharged; and, looking down at a time when the sun shone strongly upon its mouth, he discovered it to be full of broken rocks, which, though they permitted the stream to flow through many narrow passages, would stop any body of solid bulk. He returned discouraged and dejected; but, having now known the blessing of hope,[4] resolved never to despair.

In these fruitless searches he spent ten months. The time, however, passed cheerfully away: in the morning he rose with new hope, in the evening applauded his own diligence, and in the night slept sound after his fatigue.[5] He met a thousand amusements which beguiled his labour, and diversified his thoughts. He discerned the various instincts of animals, and properties of plants, and found the place replete with wonders, of which he purposed to solace

---

1. That is, none who had once entered the Valley through the gate were able to return to the outside world.

2. *Grate:* "A partition made with bars placed near to one another, or crossing each other: such as are in cloysters or prisons" (sense 1 in *Dictionary*). The *OED* defines an obsolete sense as "a barred place of confinement for animals, also, a prison or cage for human beings."

3. *Prominence:* "Protuberance; extant

part"; *protuberance:* "Something swelling above the rest; prominence; tumour" (*Dictionary*). Cf. the description of the "summits" on p. 8 above.

4. See p. 17, n. 2, above. Also cf. *Idler* 58 (par. 7).

5. Cf. SJ's remarks on the "pleasure of projecting" in *Rambler* 207 (par. 2). In *Rambler* 150 (par. 11), he says that "the highest pleasure which nature has indulged to sensitive perception, is that of rest after fatigue."

himself with the contemplation, if he should never be able to accomplish his flight; rejoicing that his endeavours, though yet unsuccessful, had supplied him with a source of inexhaustible enquiry.[6]

But his original curiosity was not yet abated; he resolved to obtain some knowledge of the ways of men. His wish still continued, but his hope grew less. He ceased to survey any longer the walls of his prison, and spared to search by new toils for interstices which he knew could not be found, yet determined to keep his design always in view, and lay hold on any expedient that time should offer.

Chap. VI.

A dissertation on the art of flying.[1]

Among the artists that had been allured into the Happy Valley, to labour for the accommodation[2] and pleasure of its

---

6. In *Rambler* 5 (par. 15), SJ expresses the same opinion about the benefits of observing natural objects.

1. Composing this chapter at the end of the 1750s, SJ had available the ancient tradition, as old as Icarus, of the ambitious aeronaut; the prescient observations of men like Roger Bacon and Leonardo da Vinci; the repeated experiments of aerial pioneers; and the deployment, during the same decade, of flying and fliers in (say) Robert Paltock's *Life and Adventures of Peter Wilkins* (1750) and Richard Owen Cambridge's *The Scribleriad* (1751). Moreover, as Louis A. Landa has pointed out, the "Dissertation" exhibits an amalgam of attitudes, both positive and negative, toward flying reflective of opinions expressed by earlier and contemporary scientists and ethical writers, the latter intent on delineating man's proper end and sphere of action ("Johnson's Feathered Man: 'A Dissertation on the Art of Flying' Considered," *Eighteenth-Century Studies in*

Honor of Donald F. Hyde, ed. W. H. Bond [1970], pp. 161–78). For much of the material in the chapter, however, SJ almost certainly drew on *Mathematical Magick: or the Wonders that may be Perform'd by Mechanical Geometry* (1648), by Bishop John Wilkins, distinguished Fellow of the Royal Society and perhaps the foremost aerial enthusiast of his age. The evidence for the indebtedness is presented in Gwin J. Kolb, "Johnson's Dissertation on Flying," *New Light on Dr. Johnson: Essays on the Occasion of his 250th Birthday*, ed. Frederick W. Hilles (1959), pp. 91–106. Discrete notes below detail the chief resemblances between passages in *Mathematical Magick* and SJ's "Dissertation."

2. In *Rambler* 145 (par. 1), SJ bestows high praise on such an "artist": "The meanest artizan or manufacturer contributes more to the accommodation of life, than the profound scholar and argumentative theorist."

inhabitants, was a man eminent for his knowledge of the mechanick powers, who had contrived many engines both of use and recreation.[3] By a wheel, which the stream turned, he forced the water into a tower, whence it was distributed to all the apartments of the palace.[4] He erected a pavillion in the garden, around which he kept the air always cool by artificial showers. One of the groves, appropriated to the ladies, was ventilated by fans,[5] to which the rivulet that run[6] through it gave a constant motion; and instruments of soft musick were placed at proper distances, of which some played by the impulse of the wind, and some by the power of the stream.[7]

This artist was sometimes visited by Rasselas, who was pleased with every kind of knowledge, imagining that the time would come when all his acquisitions should be of use to him in the open world. He came one day to amuse himself in his usual manner, and found the master busy in building a sailing chariot:[8] he saw that the design was prac-

---

3. The first sentence of Book II (entitled "Daedalus") of Wilkins's *Mathematical Magick* reads as follows: "Amongst the variety of artificiall motions, those are of most use and pleasure, in which, by the application of some continued strength, there is bestowed a regular and lasting motion" (p. 145).

4. In his discussion of the possible uses of water-mills, the first kind of "self-movers" described in "Daedalus," Wilkins remarks: "Herein doth the skill of an artificer chiefly consist, in the application of these common motions unto various and beneficiall ends; making them serviceable not only for the grinding of corn, but for . . . the elevating of water or the like" (p. 147).

5. After his treatment of water-mills, Wilkins details the varied uses of "mils that are driven by wind"; "there being scarce any labour, to the performance of which, an ingenious artificer cannot apply them" (pp. 147–48).

6. See p. 18, n. 6, above.

7. Among the "motions by wind or air" which, Wilkins says, "may prove of excellent curiosity, and singular use" is "that musicall instrument invented by Cornelius Dreble, which being set in the sun-shine, would of it self render a soft and pleasant harmony, but being removed into the shade, would presently become silent" (pp. 148–49). Two pages later he mentions as one of the purposes for which a pair of "sails" (placed in the chimney and moved by the pressure of ascending air) might be serviceable the possibility that they be used "for the chiming of bels or other musicall devices" (p. 151).

8. Chapter II of the second book ("Daedalus") of Wilkins's *Mathematical Magick* is devoted to a discussion "Of a sailing chariot, that may without horses be driven on the land by the wind, as ships are on the sea" (p. 154).

ticable upon a level surface,[9] and with expressions of great
esteem solicited its completion. The workman was pleased
to find himself so much regarded by the prince, and resolved to gain yet higher honours. "Sir," said he, "you have
seen but a small part of what the mechanick sciences can
perform. I have been long of opinion, that, instead of the
tardy conveyance of ships and chariots, man might use the
swifter migration of wings; that the fields of air are open to
knowledge, and that only ignorance and idleness need
crawl upon the ground."

This hint rekindled the prince's desire of passing the
mountains; having[a] seen what the mechanist[1] had already
performed, he was willing to fancy that he could do more;
yet resolved to enquire further before he suffered hope to
afflict him by disappointment. "I am afraid," said he to the
artist, "that your imagination prevails over your skill, and
that you now tell me rather what you wish than what you
know. Every animal has his element assigned him; the birds
have the air, and man and beasts the earth."[2] "So," replied
the mechanist, "fishes have the water, in which yet beasts
can swim by nature, and men by art. He that can swim
needs not despair to fly: to swim is to fly in a grosser fluid,

a. having 59b] and having 59a

---

9. The "chief doubt" as to the prac-
ticability of a sailing chariot, according
to Wilkins, is "whether in such a contrivance every little ruggednesse or un-
evennes of the ground, will not cause
such a jolting of the chariot as to hinder
the motion of its sails" (p. 161).

1. *Mechanist* does not appear in SJ's
Dictionary. *Mechanician* is defined as "A
man professing or studying the construction of machines."

2. Cf. Wilkins's paraphrase of the
same objection to schemes for flying:
"Eusebius [*Contra Hierocl.* confut.l.x.]
speaking with what necessity every
thing is confined by the laws of nature,
and the decrees of providence, so that
nothing can goe out of that way, unto

which naturally it is designed . . . infers, that therefore none will venture
upon any such vain attempt, as passing
in the air . . . ; whereupon he advises
that . . . since we are naturally destitute
of wings, not to imitate the flight of
birds" (pp. 197–98). Implied, of
course, in the first chapter of Genesis,
the concept of the proper distribution
of living creatures among earth, water,
and air had become a commonplace
long before the eighteenth century,
when such a writer as William Derham
could exclaim in his *Physico-Theology:*
"Who, but the infinite wise Lord of the
world, could allot every creature its
most suitable place to live in" (7th ed.,
1726, p. 258).

and to fly is to swim[3] in a subtler.[4] We are only to proportion our power of resistance to the different density of the matter through which we are to pass. You will be necessarily upborn by the air, if you can renew any impulse upon it, faster than the air can recede from the pressure."

"But the exercise of swimming,"[b] said the prince, "is very laborious; the strongest limbs are soon wearied; I am afraid the act of flying will be yet more violent, and wings will be of no great use, unless we can fly further than we can swim."[5]

"The labour of rising from the ground," said the artist, "will be great, as we see it in the heavier domestick fowls;[6] but, as we mount higher, the earth's attraction, and the body's gravity, will be gradually diminished, till we shall arrive at a region where the man will float in the air without any tendency to fall: no care will then be necessary, but to move forwards, which the gentlest impulse will effect.[7] You,

b. swimming *59b*] swiming *59a*

---

3. In Chapter VIII of "Daedalus," Wilkins, after analogizing the flight of a kite ("how he will swim up and down in the air") and the possibility of human flight, offers the evidence of objects floating in water as proof of man's ability to remain aloft in the air (pp. 213–15).

4. *Subtile* ("often written subtle"): "Thin; not dense; not gross" (sense 1 in *Dictionary*).

5. Wilkins also considers the problem of inevitable human weariness as a bar to flying both in "Daedalus" and, more elaborately, in the *Discovery of a New World* (1638; 4th ed., 1684). In the former, he concedes that "because the arms extended, are but weak and easily wearied, therefore the motions by them [in flying] are like to be but short and slow"; and he holds out the possibility of using the legs instead of the arms to effect the movement of the wings (pp. 208–09). In the *Discovery*, he admits "that man being not naturally

endowed with any such condition as may inable him for this motion [of flying] . . . must needs be slower than any fowl, and less able to hold out. Thus is it also in swiming [*sic*]. . . . So that though a man could fly, yet he would be so slow in it, and so quickly weary, that he could never think to reach so great a journey as it is to the moon" (p. 160).

6. Cf. Wilkins's remark in "Daedalus" that "the main difficulty and labour of [the flying chariot] will be in the raising of it from the ground; neer unto which, the earth's attractive vigor, is of greatest efficacy" (p. 217). On several occasions Wilkins compares human flight to the flying of "domestick fowls"; see, for example, "Daedalus," p. 208; *Discovery of a New World*, p. 160.

7. The following passages, among others, from "Daedalus" and the *Discovery of a New World* show that Wilkins's views on gravity match perfectly the "artist's" conception: "The motion of

Sir, whose curiosity is so extensive, will easily conceive with what pleasure a philosopher, furnished with wings, and hovering in the sky, would see the earth, and all its inhabitants, rolling beneath him, and presenting to him successively, by its diurnal motion, all the countries within the same parallel.[8] How must it amuse the pendent spectator to see the moving scene of land and ocean, cities and desarts! To survey with equal security the marts of trade, and the fields of battle; mountains infested by barbarians, and fruitful regions gladdened by plenty, and lulled by peace! How easily shall we then trace the Nile through all his passage; pass over to distant regions, and examine the face of nature from one extremity of the earth to the other!"

"All this," said the prince, "is much to be desired, but I am afraid that no man will be able to breathe[9] in these regions of speculation[1] and tranquility.[2] I have been told, that respiration is difficult upon lofty mountains,[3] yet from these

---

this chariot," he avers, "(though it may be difficult at the first) yet will still be easier as it ascends higher, till at length it shall become utterly devoid of gravity, when the least strength will be able to bestow upon it a swift motion" ("Daedalus," p. 218). In the *Discovery* he declares, "If a man were above the sphere of this magnetical vertue, which proceeds from the earth, he might there stand as firmly as in the open air, as he can now upon the ground: And not only so, but he may also move with a far greater swiftness, than any living creatures here below, because then he is without all gravity, being not attracted any way" (p. 169).

8. Discussing the various uses of the flying chariot, Wilkins observes that "it would be serviceable also for the conveyance of a man to any remote place of this earth. . . . For when once it was elevated for some few miles, so as to be above that orb of magnetick virtue, which is carried about by the earth's diurnall revolution, it might then be

very easily and speedily directed to any particular place of this great globe. If the place which we intended," he adds, "were under the same parallel, why then the earth's revolution once in 24 howers, would bring it to be under us, so that it would be but descending in a straight line, and wee might presently be there" ("Daedalus," p. 220).

9. In the *Discovery of a New World*, Wilkins recognizes as one of the problems of a flight to the moon the "extream thinness" of the air which might make it "unfit for expiration" (p. 180).

1. *Speculation:* "Examination by the eye; view" (sense 1 in *Dictionary*).

2. In "Daedalus" Wilkins asserts that the "upper parts of the world are always quiet and serene" (p. 221).

3. Like Rasselas, Wilkins, in the *Discovery of a New World* (p. 180), adduces the difficulty of breathing at great heights as an indication of what a flier can expect on his way through the empyrean. Also cf. William Derham's *Physico-Theology*, p. 6.

precipices, though so high as to produce great tenuity of the air, it is very easy to fall: therefore[c] I suspect, that from any height, where life can be supported, there may be danger of too quick descent."

"Nothing," replied the artist, "will ever be attempted, if all possible objections must be first overcome.[4] If you will favour my project I will try the first flight at my own hazard. I have considered the structure of all volant[5] animals, and find the folding continuity of the bat's wings[6] most easily accommodated to the human form. Upon this model I shall begin my task to morrow, and in a year expect to tower into the air beyond the malice or pursuit of man. But I will work only on this condition, that the art shall not be divulged, and that you shall not require me to make wings for any but ourselves."

"Why," said Rasselas, "should you envy[7] others so great an advantage? All skill ought to be exerted for universal good;[8] every man has owed much to others, and ought to repay the kindness that he has received."[9]

"If men were all virtuous," returned the artist, "I should

c. therefore *59b*] and *59a*

---

4. SJ himself echoed the artist on at least one occasion: "So many objections might be made to everything," he observed, "that nothing could overcome them but the necessity of doing something" (*Life*, II.128).

5. Under *volant* ("Flying; passing through the air") in his *Dictionary*, SJ quotes a passage from Chapter VI of Book II ("Daedalus," p. 191) of Wilkins's *Mathematical Magick*.

6. Cf. Wilkins's recommendation to prospective fliers in "Daedalus": "He that would regularly attempt any thing to this purpose, . . . should first make enquiry what kind of wings would bee most usefull to this end; those of a bat being most easily imitable, and perhaps nature did by them purposely intend some intimation to direct us in such experiments; that creature being not properly a bird, because not amongst the *ovipara*, to imply that other kind of creatures are capable of flying as well as birds, and if any should attempt it, that would be the best pattern for imitation" (p. 223).

7. *To envy:* "To grudge; to impart unwillingly; to withold [*sic*] maliciously" (sense 3 in *Dictionary*).

8. Cf. SJ's assertion in a letter to Richard Farmer (*Letters* 227): "no man ought to keep wholly to himself any possession that may be useful to the publick."

9. Cf. *Rambler* 56 (par. 1): "The great end of society is mutual beneficence."

with great alacrity teach them all to fly. But what would be
the security of the good, if the bad could at pleasure invade
them from the sky? Against an army sailing through the
clouds neither walls, nor mountains, nor seas, could afford
any security. A flight of northern savages might hover in
the wind, and light at once with irresistible violence upon
the capital of a fruitful region that was rolling under them.
Even this valley, the retreat of princes, the abode of happiness, might be violated by the sudden descent of some of
the naked nations that swarm on the coast of the southern
sea."

The prince promised secrecy, and waited for the performance, not wholly hopeless of success. He visited the work
from time to time, observed its progress, and remarked
many[d] ingenious contrivances to facilitate motion, and
unite levity with strength.[1] The artist was every day more
certain that he should leave vultures and eagles behind
him, and the contagion of his confidence seized upon the
prince.

In a year the wings were finished, and, on a morning
appointed, the maker appeared furnished for flight on a
little promontory:[2] he waved his pinions a while to gather
air, then leaped from his stand, and in an instant dropped
into the lake. His wings, which were of no use in the air,
sustained him in the water, and the prince drew him to
land, half dead with terrour and vexation.[3]

d. many *59b*] the *59a*

---

1. Near the conclusion of Chapter
VIII of "Daedalus," Wilkins mentions
"those speciall contrivances, whereby
the strength of these wings may be sev-
erally applyed either to ascent, descent,
progressive, or a turning motion" (p.
222).
2. As a means of surmounting the
initial difficulty of an aerial flight, Wilkins suggests in "Daedalus" that the flying chariot take "its first rise from some
mountain or other high place" (p. 217).
In his choice of a "stand" overlooking

the lake, the "artist" is following the
practice of early would-be aeronauts
(including Domingo in Francis God-
win's *Man in the Moone* [1638]), who
realized that falling into water would
be much less injurious than falling
onto mother earth.
3. In his discussion of flight by wings,
Wilkins, after mentioning several attempts by previous "artists," general-
izes thus in "Daedalus": "Though the
truth is, most of these artists did un-
fo[r]tunately miscarry by falling down

Chap. VII.

The prince finds a man of learning.

The prince was not much afflicted by this disaster, having suffered himself to hope for a happier event, only because he had no other means of escape in view. He still persisted in his design to leave the Happy Valley by the first opportunity.

His imagination was now at a stand; he had no prospect of entering into the world; and, notwithstanding all his endeavours to support[1] himself, discontent by degrees preyed upon him, and he began again to lose his thoughts in sadness, when the rainy season, which in these countries is periodical,[2] made it inconvenient to wander in the woods.

The rain continued longer and with more violence than had been ever known: the clouds broke on the surrounding mountains, and the torrents streamed into the plain on every side, till the cavern was too narrow to discharge the water. The lake overflowed its banks, and all the level of the valley was covered with the inundation.[3] The eminence, on which the palace was built, and some other spots of rising

---

and breaking their arms or legs, yet that may be imputed to their want of experience, and too much fear, which must needs possesse men in such dangerous and strange attempts" (p. 204). In the letter making up *Rambler* 199 (par. 3), SJ has the "natural philosopher" Hermeticus confess that "I have twice dislocated my limbs, and once fractured my skull in essaying to fly"; and in *Adventurer* 45 (par. 1) SJ comments: "A voyage to the moon, however romantic and absurd the scheme may now appear, since the properties of air have been better understood, seemed highly probable to many of the aspiring wits in the last century, who began to doat upon their glossy plumes, and fluttered with impatience for the hour of their departure."

1. *To support:* "To endure any thing painful without being overcome" (sense 2 in *Dictionary*).

2. A passage in *Voyage to Abyssinia*, pointing out that "from the beginning of June to that of September, it rains more or less every day," describes the discomforts of this "dreadful season," the "Abyssinian winter"—a time when it is "impossible to go far from home" (pp. 55–56).

3. As a result of the "rains that are almost continually falling in this [winter] season," according to *Voyage to Abyssinia*, "the rivers overflow their banks, and therefore in a place like this, where there are neither bridges nor boats, are, if they are not fordable, utterly impassable" (p. 55).

ground, were all that the eye could now discover. The herds and flocks left the pastures, and both the wild beasts and the tame retreated to the mountains.

This inundation confined all the princes to domestick[4] amusements, and the attention of Rasselas was particularly seized by a poem, which Imlac[5] rehearsed,[a] upon the various conditions of humanity.[6] He commanded the poet to attend him in his apartment, and recite his verses a second time; then entering into familiar talk, he thought himself happy in having found a man who knew the world so well, and could so skilfully paint the scenes of life. He asked a thousand questions about things, to which, though common to all other mortals, his confinement from childhood had kept him a stranger. The poet pitied his ignorance, and loved his curiosity,[7] and entertained him from day to day with novelty and instruction, so that the prince regretted the necessity of sleep, and longed till the morning should renew his pleasure.

As they were sitting together, the prince commanded Imlac to relate his history, and to tell by what accident he was forced, or by what motive induced, to close his life in the Happy Valley. As he was going to begin his narrative, Rasselas was called to a concert,[8] and obliged to restrain his curiosity till the evening.

a. rehearsed 59*b*] recited 59*a*

---

4. *Domestick:* "Private; done at home; not open" (sense 2 in *Dictionary*).

5. In the *Life* (iv.31), SJ is reported as saying: "Imlac in 'Rasselas,' I spelt with a *c* at the end, because it is less like English, which should always have the Saxon *k* added to the *c*." In his "Grammar" he declares that "*c* . . . , according to English orthography, never ends a word." For the probable source (Hiob Ludolf's *New History of Ethiopia*) of the name *Imlac*, see Introduction, p. xxviii above.

6. Emerson has pointed out that this topic was "such a subject as Johnson chose over and over again in his essays"

(p. 150) and, one may add, in *The Vanity of Human Wishes* and indeed in *Rasselas* itself.

7. SJ repeatedly extolled the "passion" of curiosity. In the dedication at the beginning of his *Voyage to Abyssinia*, he writes: "A generous and elevated mind is distinguish'd by nothing more certainly than an eminent degree of curiosity, nor is that curiosity ever more agreeably or usefully employ'd, than in examining the laws and customs of foreign nations" (p. 2). Also see *Rambler* 5 (par. 17), 103 (par. 1), 105 (pars. 1–2), 150 (par. 6); Introduction, p. xxxviii.

8. One early traveller records being

Chap. VIII.

The history of Imlac.

The close of the day is, in the regions of the torrid zone, the only season of diversion and entertainment, and it was therefore mid-night before the musick ceased, and the princesses retired. Rasselas then called for his companion and required him to begin the story of his life.

"Sir," said Imlac, "my history will not be long: the life that is devoted to knowledge passes silently away, and is very little diversified by events. To talk in publick, to think in solitude, to read and to hear, to inquire, and answer inquiries, is the business of a scholar.[1] He wanders about the world without pomp or terrour, and is neither known nor valued but by men like himself.

"I was born in the kingdom of Goiama, at no great distance from the fountain of the Nile.[2] My father was a wealthy merchant,[3] who traded between the inland countries of Africk[4] and the ports of the Red Sea. He was honest, frugal and diligent, but of mean sentiments, and narrow comprehension: he desired only to be rich, and to

---

"entertain'd with consorts of the harp and a kind of violin" while visiting an Abyssinian city (Charles Jacques Poncet, *Voyage to Aethiopia* [cited in the Introduction, p. xxix above], p. 143).

1. As Charles G. Osgood has noted (*MLN*, LXIX [1954], 246), Imlac's characterization of a scholar resembles this passage from Macrobius (*Saturnalia* 1.2.4): "*Neque enim recte institutus animus requiescere aut utilius aut honestius usquam potest, quam in aliqua opportunitate docte ac liberaliter colloquendi, interrogandique et respondendi comitate*" ["for nowhere can the educated mind find more useful or more seemly relaxation than in taking some opportunity for learned and polite conversation and friendly discussion," trans. P. V. Davies, 1969, pp. 31–32]. Cf. SJ's re-

marks in *Adventurer* 85 (par. 18): "To read, write, and converse in due proportions, is . . . the business of a man of letters"; and in Sermon 8 (par. 14): "The business of the life of a scholar is to accumulate, and to diffuse, knowledge; to learn, in order that he may teach." Cf. p. 37, n. 7, below. During at least one period in his life, SJ himself "seemed to [William Maxwell] to be considered as a kind of publick oracle, whom every body thought they had a right to visit and consult" (*Life*, II.118–19).

2. See p. 7, n. 5, above.

3. *Merchant:* "One who trafficks to remote countries" (*Dictionary*).

4. Hill points out that in *Voyage to Abyssinia* "*Africa* or *Africk*" appears "indifferently" (p. 166).

conceal his riches, lest he should be spoiled[5] by the gover-
nours of the province."[6]

"Surely," said the prince, "my father must be negligent of
his charge, if any man in his dominions dares take that
which belongs to another. Does he not know that kings are
accountable for injustice permitted as well as done? If I
were emperour, not the meanest of my subjects should be
oppressed with impunity. My blood boils when I am told
that a merchant durst not enjoy his honest gains for fear of
losing them[a] by the rapacity of power. Name the governour
who robbed the people, that I may declare his crimes to the
emperour."

"Sir," said Imlac, "your ardour is the natural effect of
virtue animated by youth: the time will come when you will
acquit your father, and perhaps hear with less impatience
of the governour. Oppression is, in the Abissinian dominions, neither frequent nor tolerated; but no form of government has been yet discovered, by which cruelty can be
wholly prevented.[7] Subordination[8] supposes power on one
part and subjection on the other; and if power be in the
hands of men, it will sometimes be abused. The vigilance of
the supreme magistrate may do much, but much will still
remain undone. He can never know all the crimes that are
committed, and can seldom punish all that he knows."

"This," said the prince, "I do not understand, but I had
rather hear thee than dispute. Continue thy narration."

a. them *added 59b*

---

5. *To spoil:* "To plunder; to strip of
goods" (sense 2 in *Dictionary*).

6. In Abyssinia, according to *Voyage
to Abyssinia,* "The governors purchase
their commissions, or to speak properly their privilege of pillaging the
provinces" (p. 214).

7. Cf. Sermon 24 (par. 25): "Daily
experience may convince us, that all
the avenues by which injury and oppression may break in upon life, cannot be guarded by positive prohibi-

tions. Every man sees, and may feel,
evils, which no law can punish."

8. Boswell, who dubs subordination
SJ's "favourite subject," records numerous instances of SJ's belief in the
multifaceted concept, which he once
espoused "as most conducive to the
happiness of society" (*Life,* II.13; I.408).
For additional references, see the entry
in the index to the *Life,* VI.368 and
Donald J. Greene's *The Politics of Samuel
Johnson* (1960), *passim.*

"My father," proceeded Imlac, "originally intended that I should have no other education, than such as might qualify me for commerce; and discovering in me great strength of memory, and quickness of apprehension, often declared his hope that I should be some time the richest man in Abissinia."

"Why," said the prince, "did thy father desire the increase of his wealth, when it was already greater than he durst discover or enjoy? I am unwilling to doubt thy veracity, yet inconsistencies cannot both be true."

"Inconsistencies," answered Imlac, "cannot both be right, but, imputed to man, they may both be true. Yet diversity is not inconsistency. My father might expect a time of greater security. However, some desire is necessary to keep life in motion,[9] and he, whose real wants are supplied, must admit those of fancy."

"This," said the prince, "I can in some measure conceive. I repent that I interrupted thee."

"With this hope," proceeded Imlac, "he sent me to school; but when I had once found the delight of knowledge, and felt the pleasure of intelligence and the pride of invention, I began silently to despise riches, and determined to disappoint the purpose of my father, whose grossness of conception raised my pity. I was twenty years old before his tenderness would expose me to the fatigue of travel, in which time I had been instructed, by successive masters, in all the literature[1] of my native country. As every hour taught me something new, I lived in a continual course of gratifications;[2] but, as I advanced towards manhood, I lost much of the reverence with which I had been used to look on my

---

9. Cf. SJ's response to Boswell's question about the "*reason* for taking so much trouble" in human "pursuits": "'Sir, (said he, in an animated tone) it is driving on the system of life'" (*Life*, IV.112).

1. *Literature:* "Learning; skill in letters" (*Dictionary*).

2. SJ repeatedly cited novelty as a principal cause of human pleasure and gratification. Cf. p. 16, n. 4, above; *Rambler* 121 (par. 7), 135 (par. 8); "Life of Prior" (*Lives*, II.206, par. 67); *Life*, II.123. He also praised *Spectator* 626, which presents similar notions, as "one of the finest pieces in the English language" (*Life*, III.33).

instructors; because, when the lesson was ended, I did not find them wiser or better than common men.

"At length my father resolved to initiate me in commerce, and, opening one of his subterranean treasuries, counted out ten thousand pieces of gold. 'This, young man,' said he, 'is the stock with which you must negociate.[3] I began with less than the fifth part, and you see how diligence and parsimony[4] have increased it. This is your own to waste or to improve. If you squander it by negligence or caprice, you must wait for my death before you will be rich: if, in four years, you double your stock, we will thenceforward let subordination cease, and live together as friends and partners; for he shall always be equal with me, who is equally skilled in the art of growing rich.'

"We laid our money upon camels, concealed in bales of cheap goods, and travelled to the shore of the Red Sea. When I cast my eye on the expanse of waters my heart bounded like that of a prisoner escaped. I felt an unextinguishable curiosity kindle in my mind, and resolved to snatch this opportunity of seeing the manners of other nations, and of learning sciences[5] unknown in Abissinia.

"I remembered that my father had obliged[6] me to the improvement of my stock, not by a promise which I ought not to violate, but by a penalty which I was at liberty to incur, and therefore determined to gratify my predominant desire, and by drinking at the fountains of knowledge, to quench the thirst of curiosity.

"As I was supposed to trade without connexion with my father, it was easy for me to become acquainted with the master of a ship, and procure a passage to some other country. I had no motives of choice to regulate my voyage; it was sufficient for me that, wherever I wandered, I should

---

3. *To negotiate:* "To have intercourse of business; to traffick; to treat: whether of publick affairs, or private matters" (*Dictionary*).

4. *Parsimony:* "Frugality; covetousness; niggardliness; saving temper" (*Dictionary*).

5. *Science:* "Any art or species of knowledge" (sense 4 in *Dictionary*).

6. *To oblige:* "To bind; to impose obligation; to compel to something" (sense 1 in *Dictionary*).

see a country which I had not seen before. I therefore entered a ship bound for Surat,[7] having left a letter for my father declaring my intention.

Chap. IX.

The history of Imlac continued.

"When I first entered upon the world of waters,[1] and lost sight of land, I looked round about me with pleasing terrour,[2] and thinking my soul enlarged by the boundless prospect, imagined that I could gaze round for ever without satiety; but, in a short time, I grew weary of looking on barren uniformity, where I could only see again what I had already seen. I then descended into the ship, and doubted for a while whether all my future pleasures would not end like this in disgust and disappointment. 'Yet, surely,' said I, 'the ocean and the land are very different; the only variety of water is rest and motion, but the earth has mountains and vallies, desarts and cities: it is inhabited by men of different customs and contrary opinions; and I may hope to find variety in life, though I should miss it in nature.'

"With this thought[a] I quieted my mind, and amused myself during the voyage; sometimes by learning from the sailors the art of navigation, which I have never practised, and sometimes by forming schemes for my conduct in different situations, in not one of which I have been ever placed.

"I was almost weary of my naval amusements when we landed safely at Surat. I secured my money, and purchasing

a. thought *59b*] hope *59a*

---

7. According to Bowen's *Geography,* "Surat [is] the greatest town for trade and commerce in all the Mogul's dominions" (II.328).

1. Cf. *Paradise Lost,* III.11: "The rising world of waters dark and deep."

2. Cf. Burke's *Philosophical Enquiry* into the Origin of our Ideas of the Sublime and Beautiful (ed. J. T. Boulton, 1958, p. 46): "terror is a passion which always produces delight when it does not press too close." See also p. 42, n. 5, below.

some commodities for show, joined myself to a caravan that was passing into the inland country.[3] My companions, for some reason or other, conjecturing that I was rich, and, by my inquiries and admiration,[4] finding that I was ignorant, considered me as a novice whom they had a right to cheat, and who was to learn at the usual expence the art of fraud. They exposed me to the theft of servants, and the exaction of officers, and saw me plundered upon false pretences, without any advantage to themselves, but that of rejoicing in the superiority of their own knowledge."

"Stop a moment," said the prince. "Is[b] there such depravity in man, as that he should injure another without benefit to himself? I can easily conceive that all are pleased with superiority; but your ignorance was merely accidental, which, being neither your crime nor your folly, could afford them no reason to applaud themselves; and the knowledge which they had, and which you wanted, they might as effectually have shewn by warning,[c] as betraying you."

"Pride," said Imlac, "is seldom delicate, it will please itself with very mean advantages; and envy feels not its own happiness, but when it may be compared with the misery of others. They were my enemies because they grieved to think[d] me rich, and my oppressors because they delighted to find me weak."

"Proceed," said the prince: "I doubt not of the facts which you relate, but imagine that you impute them to mistaken motives."

"In this company," said Imlac, "I arrived at Agra, the capital of Indostan, the city in which the great Mogul[5]

b. prince. Is *59b*] prince, is *59a*   c. warning, *59b*] warning you, *59a*
d. grieved to think *59b*] thought *59a*

---

3. In journeying from Surat inland toward Agra, Imlac traversed a route often followed by early travellers and trade caravans; see, for example, *Histoire Générale des Voyages* (1752), x.57ff., 92; *Sir Thomas Roe's Voyage to India* (Churchill's *Collection of Voyages and Travels* [1705], 1.769f.).

4. *Admiration:* "Wonder; the act of admiring or wondering" (sense 1 in *Dictionary*).

5. "Mogol, or Great Mogol, [is] a name given to the emperor of the continent of the Indies, on this side, and about the river Ganges" (*The Great Historical, Geographical, Genealogical, and Poetical Dictionary,* 2 vols.; 2d ed., ed. Jeremy Collier, 1701).

commonly resides.[6] I applied myself to the language of the country, and in a few months was able to converse with the learned men; some of whom I found morose and reserved, and others easy and communicative; some were unwilling to teach another what they had with difficulty learned themselves; and some shewed that the end of their studies was to gain the dignity of instructing.[7]

"To the tutor of the young princes I recommended myself so much, that I was presented to the emperour as a man of uncommon knowledge. The emperour asked me many questions concerning my country and my travels; and though I cannot now recollect any thing that he uttered above the power of a common man, he dismissed me astonished at his wisdom, and enamoured of his goodness.

"My credit was now so high, that the merchants, with whom I had travelled, applied to me for recommendations to the ladies of the court. I was surprised at their confidence of solicitation, and gently reproached them with their practices on the road. They heard me with cold indifference, and shewed no tokens of shame or sorrow.

"They then urged their request with the offer of a bribe; but what I would not do for kindness I would not do for money; and refused them, not because they had injured me, but because I would not enable them to injure others; for I knew they would have made use of my credit to cheat those who should buy their wares.

"Having resided at Agra, till there was no more to be learned, I travelled into Persia, where I saw many remains of ancient magnificence,[8] and observed many new accommodations[9] of life. The Persians are a nation eminently

---

6. "Agra the ordinary residence of the king" (*Sir Thomas Roe's Voyage to India* [Churchill's *Collection of Voyages and Travels*, 1.803]) is situated "about 700 miles north-east of Surat, a journey which the caravans generally perform in nine weeks" (Bowen's *Geography*, II.315).

7. Cf. *Adventurer* 126 (par. 9): "Though learning may be conferred by solitude, its application must be attained by general conversation. He has

learned to no purpose, that is not able to teach."

8. Numerous early travellers to Persia mention, if they do not actually describe, the ruins of ancient temples and palaces; see, for example, John Harris, *Navigantium atque Itinerantium Bibliotheca* (1748), II.888–89.

9. *Accommodations:* "Conveniences, things requisite to ease or refreshment" (*Dictionary*).

social,[1] and their assemblies afforded me daily opportunities of remarking characters and manners, and of tracing
human nature through all its variations.

"From Persia I passed into Arabia, where I saw a nation at
once pastoral and warlike;[2] who live without any settled
habitation; whose only wealth is their flocks and herds; and
who have yet carried on, through all ages, an hereditary
war with all mankind, though they neither covet nor envy
their possessions.

Chap. X.

Imlac's history continued. A dissertation upon poetry.[1]

"Wherever I went, I found that poetry was considered as
the highest learning,[2] and regarded with a veneration

---

1. The sociability of the Persians is often stressed in seventeenth- and eighteenth-century writings on Persia. Bowen (*Geography*, II.173) is only repeating the comment of many reporters when he says, "One of the most commendable qualities of the Persians," who are "courtly, civil, complaisant, and well-bred," "is their kindness to strangers, the reception, and protection they afford them."

2. Imlac's estimate of the Arabs coincides with the views of numerous early observers and commentators, to whom it appeared—in the words of one of them—that "the Arabs concern themselves with nothing but their cattle, following their princes, going to war, and robbing passengers" (*The Travels of the Chevalier d'Arvieux in Arabia the Desart* [2d ed., 1732], p. 189). See also Bowen's *Geography*, II.125–26.

1. Two different interpretations have marked discussions of this famous chapter. The first—possibly still dominant—hypothesis equates Imlac's "dissertation" with SJ's personal beliefs and

thus treats the pronouncements as a partial exposition of SJ's own poetic theory. The second—more recent—interpretation distinguishes Imlac the character from SJ the author and concludes that in their totality the character's statements, some of which, it is argued, run counter to SJ's opinions, decidedly deflate Imlac's profession of poetry. In an essay entitled "The Reader, the General, and the Particular: Johnson and Imlac in Chapter Ten of *Rasselas*" (*Eighteenth-Century Studies*, v [1971], 80–96), Howard D. Weinbrot undertakes an analysis of the likenesses and differences between Imlac's and SJ's notions, and he also mentions a number of earlier discussions of the subject.

2. In the spurious *Travels and Adventures of Edward Brown, Esq.* (1739), John Campbell (for SJ's assessment of him and his writings, see *Life*, 1.417–18) makes remarks that are similar to Imlac's observation. After saying that "poetry seems to have been in esteem with all the Oriental nations from the ear-

somewhat approaching to that which man would pay to the angelick nature. And it yet fills me with wonder, that, in almost all countries, the most ancient poets are considered as the best:[3] whether it be that every other kind of knowledge is an acquisition gradually attained, and poetry is a gift conferred at once; or that the first poetry of every nation surprised them as a novelty, and retained the credit by consent which it received by accident at first: or whether, as[a] the province of poetry is to describe nature and passion,[4]

---

a. whether, as 59b] whether 59a

---

liest point of time," Campbell treats the enthusiasm for it as the leading Oriental intellectual "passion" (pp. 390–91). Restricting his comment to one eastern nation, Thomas Rymer, in his *Preface to the Translation of Rapin's "Reflections on Aristotle's Treatise of Poesie"* (1674), notes that the "Persians . . . glory in their poets and poetry more than all the world besides" (*Critical Essays of the Seventeenth Century,* ed. J. E. Spingarn [1908], II.165).

Extremely high praise of poetry—labelled the "queen of the arts," for example—occurs frequently, of course, in early English criticism. SJ himself declares that rhetoric and poetry "supply life with its highest intellectual pleasures" (Preface to *The Preceptor* [1748], par. 21) and that "the chief glory of every people arises from its authors" (Preface to the *Dictionary* [third from last paragraph]). Moreover, according to Mrs. Piozzi, "His idea of poetry was magnificent indeed, and very fully was he persuaded of its superiority over every other talent bestowed by heaven on man. His chapter upon that particular subject in his *Rasselas,* is really written from the fulness of his heart" (*Anecdotes,* 1.284–85). See also *Life,* II.125.

3. Cf. Sir William Temple's remark that "What honour and request the

antient poetry has lived in may not only be observed from the universal reception and use in all nations from China to Peru, from Scythia to Arabia, but from the esteem of the best and the greatest men as well as the vulgar." Later he says that "the great heighths and excellency both of poetry and musick fell with the Roman learning and empire, and have never since recovered the admiration and applauses that before attended them" (*Of Poetry* [1690] in *Critical Essays of the Seventeenth Century,* ed. J. E. Spingarn [1908], III.107, 108). In his *Preface to Shakespeare* (par. 3), SJ declares that "to works . . . appealing wholly to observation and experience, no other test can be applied than length of duration and continuance of esteem. What mankind have long possessed they have often examined and compared, and if they persist to value the possession, it is because frequent comparisons have confirmed opinion in its favour."

4. *Nature:* "The constitution and appearances of things" (sense 7 in *Dictionary*); illustrated by this quotation from Sir Joshua Reynolds's fourth *Discourse* on art (1771; final par.): "The works, whether of poets, painters, moralists, or historians, which are built upon general nature, live for ever; while those which depend for their existence

which are always the same,[5] the[b] first writers took possession of the most striking objects for description, and the
most probable occurrences for fiction, and left nothing to
those that followed them, but transcription of the same
events, and new combinations of the same images.[6] Whatever be the reason, it is commonly observed that the early
writers are in possession of nature, and their followers of
art: that the first excel in strength and invention, and the
latter in elegance and refinement.[7]

"I was desirous to add my name to this illustrious frater-

b. the *59b*] and the *59a*

---

on particular customs and habits, a
partial view of nature, or the fluctua-
tion of fashion, can only be coeval with
that which first raised them from obscurity." *Passion:* "Violent commotion
of the mind" (sense 3 in *Dictionary*).
With the notion expressed, cf. John
Dennis's assertion, in his *Advancement
and Reformation of Modern Poetry*, that
poetry is "an imitation of nature, by a
pathetick and numerous speech" and
that "passion . . . is the characteristical
mark of poetry, and, consequently,
must be every where" (*Critical Works*,
ed. E. N. Hooker [1939], 1.215).

5. In *Adventurer* 99 (par. 8), SJ states
that "human nature is always the
same." In No. 95 (pars. 2, 8), he observes, "Writers of all ages have had the
same sentiments, because they have in
all ages had the same objects of speculation; the interests and passions, the
virtues and vices of mankind, have
been diversified in different times, only
by unessential and casual varieties";
and later, the "influence" of the passions "is uniform, and their effects
nearly the same in every human breast:
a man loves and hates, desires and
avoids, exactly like his neighbour."

6. On several different occasions, SJ

mentions the primacy of early writers
when compared to their successors.
For example, pondering the causes of
the ancients' superior compositions, he
says (*Rambler* 169, par. 6), "Some advantage they might gain merely by pri-
ority, which put them in possession of
the most natural sentiments, and left
us nothing but servile repetition or
forced conceits." See also *Rambler* 86
(par. 2), 143 (par. 2); *Preface to Shakespeare* (par. 3); *Life*, III.333.

7. The contrast between early, natural poetic genius (frequently exemplified by Homer) and later, refined, "correct" genius (often exemplified by
Virgil) long formed a commonplace of
literary criticism, which occurs, for example, in Sir William Temple's essay *Of
Poetry* and *Spectator* 160 (par. 4). SJ
once observed that "the dispute as to
the comparative excellence of Homer
or Virgil was inaccurate. We must consider . . . whether Homer was not the
greatest poet, though Virgil may have
produced the finest poem. Virgil was
indebted to Homer for the whole invention of the structure of an epick
poem, and for many of his beauties"
(*Life*, III.193–94). See also "Life of Dryden" (*Lives*, 1.447–48, par. 304).

nity. I read all the poets of Persia and Arabia,[8] and was able to repeat by memory the volumes that are suspended in the mosque of Mecca.[9] But I soon found that no man was ever great by imitation.[1] My desire of excellence impelled me to transfer my attention to nature and to life.[2] Nature was to be my subject, and men to be my auditors: I could never describe what I had not seen: I could not hope to move those with delight or terrour, whose interests and opinions I did not understand.

"Being now resolved to be a poet, I saw every thing with a new purpose; my sphere of attention was suddenly magni-

---

8. For indications of the reputed popularity of poetry in these countries and the high esteem with which it was regarded, see Bowen's *Geography*, II.175; Campbell's *Travels and Adventures of Edward Brown, Esq.*, pp. 390–91.

9. In his essay "On the Poetry of the Eastern Nations" (a part of his volume entitled *Poems Consisting Chiefly of Translations from the Asiatick Languages* [1772]), Sir William Jones details the circumstances which led to the suspension of the poetic works in the mosque at Mecca. "At the beginning of the seventh century," he writes, "the Arabick language was brought to a high degree of perfection by a sort of poetical academy, that used to assemble at stated times, in a place called Ocadh, where every poet produced his best composition . . . : the most excellent of these poems were transcribed in characters of gold upon Egyptian paper, and hung up in the temple, whence they were named Modhahebat, or Golden, and Moallakat, or Suspended" (p. 183). Jones later published an edition (including an English translation) of some of these poems under the title of *The Moallakát, or Seven Arabian Poems, Which Were Suspended on the Temple at Mecca* (1782). For somewhat different ac-

counts of the origin of the "suspended" poems, see the correspondent's letter in the *Gentleman's Magazine*, XXIII (1753), 272; Gibbon's *Decline and Fall of the Roman Empire*, ed. J. B. Bury, V.325. In a note (44), Bury points out that "the legend of the seven poems hung in the Kaaba has no foundation."

1. In *Rambler* 154 (par. 14), SJ makes the same statement: "No man ever yet became great by imitation." Cf. *Rambler* 86 (par. 2). Similar remarks about imitation often occur, of course, in early literary criticism.

2. Like many of his predecessors and contemporaries, SJ repeatedly invokes the representation of "life" and "nature" as the chief criterion of literary merit. In *Rambler* 4 (par. 12), for example, he declares, "It is justly considered as the greatest excellency of art, to imitate nature." In his *Proposals for Printing, by Subscription, the Dramatick Works of William Shakespeare*, he remarks, "It is the great excellence of Shakespeare, that he drew his scenes from nature, and from life" (Vol. VII, Yale Edition of the Works of Samuel Johnson, ed. Arthur Sherbo, 1968, p. 53). See also his "Life of Cowley" (*Lives*, I.19, par. 52), Dedication to Charlotte Lennox's *Shakespeare Illustrated* (*Works*, VII.49),

fied: no kind of knowledge was to be overlooked.[3] I ranged mountains and deserts for images and resemblances, and pictured upon my mind every tree of the forest and flower of the valley. I observed with equal care the crags of the rock and the pinnacles of the palace. Sometimes I wandered along the mazes of the rivulet, and sometimes watched the changes of the summer clouds.[4] To a poet nothing can be useless. Whatever is beautiful, and whatever is dreadful, must be familiar to his imagination: he must be conversant with all that is awfully vast or elegantly little.[5] The plants of the garden, the animals of the wood, the minerals of the earth, and meteors of the sky, must all concur to store his

---

review (par. 10) of Joseph Warton's *Essay on the Writings and Genius of Pope* (in the *Literary Magazine* for 1756, 1.35–38), and *Preface to Shakespeare* (*Works*, VII.62, 89, *et passim*).

3. Imlac's expansive conception of the knowledge requisite for a poet may be compared to SJ's comment in the "Life of Milton" (*Lives*, 1.170–71, par. 208) on the "powers" ("all . . . which are singly sufficient for other compositions") required for an epic poet, who must be conversant with "history," "morality," "policy and the practice of life," "physiology" (defined in SJ's *Dictionary* as "The doctrine of the constitution of the works of nature"), the subtleties of language, and "all the varieties of metrical modulation." Previously Dryden had observed that a good epic poet must possess, "besides an universal genius, . . . universal learning" (*A Discourse concerning the Original and Progress of Satire* [*Essays*, ed. W. P. Ker, 1900], 11.43). Cf. similar remarks by Charles Gildon (*The Complete Art of Poetry* [1718], 1.71) and John Dennis (*The Causes of the Decay and Defects of Dramatick Poetry* [*Critical Works*, ed. E. N. Hooker (1939), 11.297]).

4. With Imlac's extensive scrutiny of natural and man-made ("pinnacles of

the palace") objects, cf. this comment by Addison in *Spectator* 417 (pars. 3–4): "A poet should take as much pains in forming his imagination, as a philosopher in cultivating his understanding. He must gain a due relish of the works of nature, and be thoroughly conversant in the various scenary of a country life.

"When he is stored with country images, if he would go beyond pastoral, and the lower kinds of poetry, he ought to acquaint himself with the pomp and magnificence of courts. He should be very well versed in every thing that is noble and stately in the productions of art, whether it appear in painting or statuary, in the great works of architecture which are in their present glory, or in the ruins of those which flourished in former ages."

5. As a number of commentators have pointed out, the distinction made in this sentence between "beautiful," "elegantly little" objects and "dreadful," "awfully vast"—hence sublime— objects seems to be indebted to Burke's *Philosophical Enquiry into the Origin of our Ideas of the Sublime and Beautiful* (1757); see Part 2, Section VII ("Vastness"); Part 3, Section XIII ("Beautiful objects small").

mind with inexhaustible variety: for every idea is useful for the inforcement or decoration of moral or religious truth;[6] and he, who knows most, will have most power of diversifying his scenes, and of gratifying his reader with remote allusions and unexpected instruction.

"All the appearances of nature I was therefore careful to study, and every country which I have surveyed has contributed something to my poetical powers."

"In so wide a survey," said the prince, "you must surely have left much unobserved. I have lived, till now, within the circuit of these mountains, and yet cannot walk abroad without the sight of something which I had never beheld before, or never heeded."

"The business of a poet," said Imlac, "is to examine, not the individual, but the species;[7] to remark general properties and large appearances: he does not number the streaks of the tulip,[8] or describe the different shades in the verdure of the forest.[9] He is to exhibit in his portraits of nature such

---

6. "The task of an author," says SJ in *Rambler* 3 (par. 1), "is, either to teach what is not known, or to recommend known truths, by his manner of adorning them; either to let new light in upon the mind, and open new scenes to the prospect, or to vary the dress and situation of common objects, so as to give them fresh grace and more powerful attractions." Cf. Dryden's comment, in *A Defense of "An Essay of Dramatic Poesy"* (*Essays*, ed. Ker, I.121), that "moral truth is the mistress of the poet as much as of the philosopher; poesy must resemble natural truth, but it must *be* ethical. Indeed, the poet dresses truth, and adorns nature, but does not alter them."

7. Cf. these comments by SJ: (1) "In the writings of other poets a character is too often an individual; in those of Shakespeare it is commonly a species" (*Preface to Shakespeare*, par. 8); (2) "[Samuel Foote's 'talent of exhibiting character'] is not comedy, which exhib-

its the character of a species, as that of a miser gathered from many misers: it is farce, which exhibits individuals" (*Life*, II.95).

8. Long before 1759, partly owing to the "tulipomania" of the seventeenth century, the tulip had become famous for its great variety in size, shape, color, striping, etc. For additional information about the background of Imlac's remark, see Robert Folkenflik, "The Tulip and its Streaks: Contexts of *Rasselas* X," *Ariel,* IX (1978), 57–71; esp. 62–67.

9. "Poetry," says SJ in *Rambler* 36 (par. 6), "cannot dwell upon the minuter distinctions, by which one species differs from another, without departing from that simplicity of grandeur which fills the imagination; nor dissect the latent qualities of things, without losing its general power of gratifying every mind by recalling its conceptions." Also cf. the "Life of Cowley" (*Lives*, I.45, par. 133), where SJ, noting

prominent and striking features, as recal the original to every mind; and must neglect the minuter discriminations, which one may have remarked, and another have neglected, for those characteristicks which are alike obvious to vigilance and carelesness.

"But the knowledge of nature is only half the task of a poet; he must be acquainted likewise with all the modes of life.[1] His character requires that he estimate the happiness and misery of every condition; observe the power of all the passions in all their combinations, and trace the changes of the human mind as they are modified by various institutions and accidental influences of climate or custom,[2] from the spriteliness of infancy to the despondence of decrepitude.[3] He must divest himself of the prejudices of his age or country; he must consider right and wrong in their abstracted and invariable state; he must disregard present laws and opinions, and rise to general and transcendental truths, which will always be the same:[4] he must therefore

---

the absence in Cowley's poems of the "grandeur of generality," remarks that "all the power of description is destroyed by a scrupulous enumeration; and the force of metaphors is lost when the mind by the mention of particulars is turned more upon the original than the secondary sense."

1. In this context, "knowledge of nature" obviously means knowledge of external nature. For the knowledge of nature *and* life which the poet must possess, see p. 41, n. 2, above. Earlier John Dennis had included "a knowledge of mankind and the world" in the "generous education" he considered requisite for a poet (*A Large Account of Taste* [*Critical Works,* ed. Hooker, 1.290]); and among the means by which, according to Leonard Welsted, "a person" gifted with a "genius" for poetry may improve his talent is "carrying his enquiries closely and carefully into men, manners, human nature" (*Critical Essays of the Eighteenth Century,*

1700–1725, ed. W. H. Durham [1915], p. 373).

2. On the "alterations" in the "modes of life" and in the operations of the "passions" which "writers of the present and future ages" must observe and record, see *Adventurer* 95 (pars. 11–13). Also cf. the "Life of Savage" (*Lives,* II.358, par. 101).

3. *Decrepitude:* "The last stage of decay; the last effects of old age" (*Dictionary*).

4. *Transcendental:* "General; pervading many particulars" (sense 1 in *Dictionary*). With the notions expressed in this passage, cf. SJ's implied intention in the *Rambler* essays: after saying that he has largely ignored transient topics, he adds that "they only were expected to peruse [the essays], whose passions left them leisure for abstracted truth, and whom virtue could please by its naked dignity" (208, par. 3). In his Preface to *Valentinian,* Robert Wolseley specifies "general notions and ab-

content himself with the slow progress of his name; contemn the applause of his own time, and commit his claims to the justice of posterity. He must write as the interpreter of nature, and the legislator of mankind,[5] and consider himself as presiding over the thoughts and manners of future[c] generations; as a being superiour to time and place.

"His[d] labour is not yet at an end: he must know many languages and many sciences;[6] and, that his stile may be worthy of his thoughts, must, by incessant practice, familiarize to himself every delicacy of speech and grace of harmony."[7]

---

c. future *59b*] successive *59a*   d. *New paragraph:* "His *59b*] place. His *59a*

---

stracted truths" among the aspects of "nature" which "poetical wit" should express (*Critical Essays of the Seventeenth Century*, ed. Spingarn, III.21).

5. Cf. Joseph Warton's remark, in his *Essay on the Writings and Genius of Pope* (which SJ reviewed in the *Literary Magazine*), about Orpheus: "I have lately seen a manuscript ode, entitled, 'On the Use and Abuse of Poetry,' in which Orpheus is considered . . . as the first legislator and civilizer of mankind" (3d ed., 1772, p. 59). For this reference, I am indebted to Hardy, p. 139.

6. In his "Life of Milton" (*Lives*, I.124, par. 92), SJ remarks: "[Milton] had done what he knew to be necessarily previous to poetical excellence: he had made himself acquainted with 'seemly arts and affairs' ["insight into all seemly and generous arts and affaires," Milton, *The Reason of Church-Government Urg'd Against Prelaty* (Spingarn, I.199)], his comprehension was extended by various knowledge, and his memory stored with intellectual treasures. He was skilful in many lan-

guages, and had by reading and composition attained the full mastery of his own. He would have wanted little help from books, had he retained the power of perusing them." Cf. Thomas Rymer's Preface to the translation of Rapin's *Reflections on Aristotle's Treatise of Poesie* ("Although a [heroic] poet is oblig'd to know all arts and sciences, yet he ought discreetly to manage this knowledge" [Spingarn, II.169]); Edward Phillips's Preface to *Theatrum Poetarum* ("Heroic poesie ought to be the result of all that can be contrived of profit, delight, or ornament, either from experience in human affairs or from knowledge of all arts and sciences" [Spingarn, II.268]).

7. Cf. SJ's comment in his "Life of Milton": "Nor is he yet a [epic] poet till he has attained the whole extension of his language, distinguished all the delicacies of phrase, and all the colours of words, and learned to adjust their different sounds to all the varieties of metrical modulation" (*Lives*, I.170–71, par. 208).

Chap. XI.

Imlac's narrative continued. A hint on pilgrimage.

Imlac now felt the enthusiastic[1] fit, and was proceeding to aggrandize his own profession, when the prince cried out, "Enough! Thou hast convinced me, that no human being can ever be a poet. Proceed[a] with thy narration."

"To be a poet," said Imlac, "is indeed very difficult."[2] "So difficult," returned the prince, "that I will at present hear no more of his labours. Tell me whither you went when you had seen Persia."

"From Persia," said the poet, "I travelled through Syria, and for three years resided in Palestine, where I conversed with great numbers of the northern and western nations of Europe; the nations which are now in possession of all power and all knowledge; whose armies are irresistible, and whose fleets command the remotest parts of the globe. When I compared these men with the natives of our own kingdom, and those that surround us, they appeared almost another order of beings. In their countries it is difficult to wish for any thing that may not be obtained: a thousand arts, of which we never heard, are continually labouring for their convenience and pleasure; and whatever their own climate has denied them is supplied by their commerce."

"By what means," said the prince, "are the Europeans thus powerful? or why, since they can so easily visit Asia and

a. Proceed 59b] Proceed now 59a

---

1. *Enthusiastick:* "Vehemently hot in any cause" (sense 2 in *Dictionary*).

2. With Imlac's assertion, cf. the following passage in Sir William Temple's essay *Of Poetry* (Spingarn, iii.80–81): "But tho' invention be the mother of poetry, yet this child is like all others born naked, and must be nourished with care, cloathed with exactness and elegance, educated with industry, instructed with art, improved by application, corrected with severity, and accomplished with labour and with time, before it arrives at any great perfection or growth. 'Tis certain that no composition requires so many several ingredients, or of more different sorts than this, nor that to excel in any qualities there are necessary so many gifts of nature and so many improvements of learning and of art." This passage is part of a longer excerpt from Temple's essay which appears under the section entitled "On Poetry" in Part 1 of *The Preceptor* (3d ed., 1758, I.14–15).

Africa for trade or conquest, cannot the Asiaticks and Africans invade their coasts, plant colonies in their ports, and give laws to their natural princes? The same wind that carries them back would bring[b] us thither."

"They are more powerful, Sir, than we," answered Imlac, "because they are wiser; knowledge will always predominate over ignorance, as man governs the other animals. But why their knowledge is more than ours, I know not what reason can be given, but the unsearchable will of the Supreme Being."[3]

"When," said the prince with a sigh, "shall I be able to visit Palestine, and mingle with this mighty confluence of nations? Till that happy moment shall arrive, let me fill up the time with such representations as thou canst give me. I am not ignorant of the motive that assembles such numbers in that place, and cannot but consider it as the center of wisdom and piety, to which the best and wisest men of every land must be continually resorting."[4]

"There are some nations," said Imlac, "that send few visitants[5] to Palestine; for many numerous and learned sects in Europe, concur to censure pilgrimage as superstitious, or deride it as ridiculous."

"You know," said the prince, "how little my life has made me acquainted with diversity of opinions: it will be too long to hear the arguments on both sides; you, that have considered them, tell me the result."

"Pilgrimage," said Imlac, "like many other acts of piety,

b. bring *59a, 59b*] *changed to* convey *in the YC.*

---

3. In June of 1781, while riding in a carriage with Boswell, SJ, who remarked that "he had not looked at" the book "since it was first published," eagerly "seized" upon a copy of *Rasselas* belonging to Boswell and commenced reading it. He pointed out to Boswell the two paragraphs beginning with "By what means" and concluding with "Supreme Being" and said: "'This, Sir, no man can explain otherwise'" (*Life*, IV.119).

4. "The Abyssins," according to *Voyage to Abyssinia*, "were much addicted to pilgrimages into the Holy-Land" (p. 207).

5. *Visitant:* "One who goes to see another" (*Dictionary*). Another sense— "One who visits a place, shrine, etc. from religious motives"—distinguished by the *OED* is closer to the meaning of the word in the present context.

may be reasonable or superstitious, according to the principles upon which it is performed. Long journies in search of
truth are not commanded. Truth, such as is necessary to the
regulation of life, is always found where it is honestly
sought. Change of place is no natural cause of the increase
of piety, for it inevitably produces dissipation of mind. Yet,
since men go every day to view the fields^c where great
actions have been performed, and return with stronger
impressions of the event, curiosity of the same kind may
naturally dispose us to view that country whence our religion had its beginning; and I believe no man surveys those
awful scenes without some confirmation of holy resolutions. That the Supreme Being may be more easily propiti-
ated in one place than in another, is the dream of idle
superstition; but that some places may operate upon our
own minds in an uncommon manner, is an opinion which
hourly experience will justify. He who supposes that his
vices may be more successfully combated in Palestine, will,
perhaps, find himself mistaken, yet he may go thither without folly: he who thinks they will be more freely pardoned,
dishonours at once his reason and religion."[6]

"These," said the prince, "are European distinctions. I

c. fields 59b] places 59a

---

6. On at least two other occasions, SJ
discussed visits to holy places. In his
Journey to the Western Islands of Scotland,
recording his and Boswell's trip to the
island of Iona, he writes: "Whatever
withdraws us from the power of our
senses; whatever makes the past, the
distant, or the future predominate
over the present, advances us in the
dignity of thinking beings. Far from
me and from my friends, be such frigid
philosophy as may conduct us indifferent and unmoved over any ground
which has been dignified by wisdom,
bravery, or virtue. That man is little to
be envied, whose patriotism would not
gain force upon the plain of Marathon,
or whose piety would not grow warmer

among the ruins of Iona?" (Mary Lascelles, ed., Vol. IX, Yale Edition of the
Works of Samuel Johnson, 1971, p.
148). Later in 1774, responding to Boswell's avowal of "a peculiar satisfaction"
in attending Easter service at St. Paul's
Cathedral, he comments: "It may be
dangerous to receive too readily, and
indulge too fondly, opinions, from
which, perhaps, no pious mind is
wholly disengaged, of local sanctity and
local devotion. You know what strange
effects they have produced over a great
part of the Christian world. . . . To
what degree fancy is to be admitted
into religious offices, it would require
much deliberation to determine. I am
far from intending totally to exclude

will consider them another time. What have you found to be the effect of knowledge? Are those nations happier than we?"

"There is so much infelicity," said the poet, "in the world, that scarce any man has leisure from his own distresses to estimate the comparative happiness of others. Knowledge is certainly one of the means of pleasure, as is confessed by the natural desire which every mind feels of increasing its ideas.[7] Ignorance is mere privation, by which nothing can be produced: it is a vacuity in which the soul sits motionless and torpid for want of attraction; and, without knowing why, we always rejoice when we learn, and grieve when we forget. I am therefore inclined to conclude, that, if nothing counteracts the natural consequence of learning, we grow more happy as our minds take a wider range.[8]

---

it. . . . Fancy is always to act in subordination to Reason. We may take Fancy for a companion, but must follow Reason as our guide. . . . When we enter a church we habitually recall to mind the duty of adoration, but we must not omit adoration for want of a temple; because we know, and ought to remember, that the Universal Lord is every where present; and that, therefore, to come to Iona, or to Jerusalem, though it may be useful, cannot be necessary" (Life, II.276–77).

7. SJ was a staunch believer in man's natural wish for, and satisfaction in the attainment of, knowledge. His pleased reaction (Life, I.458) to the inquisitive Thames boatboy (who "would give what I have" for knowledge of the Argonauts) is well known: "Sir (said he), a desire of knowledge is the natural feeling of mankind; and every human being, whose mind is not debauched, will be willing to give all that he has to get knowledge." Speaking again to Boswell in 1775, he remarked (Life, II.357): "All knowledge is of itself of some value. There is nothing so min-

ute or inconsiderable, that I would not rather know it than not." See also his comments to Susannah Thrale in Letters 944, and on curiosity, on p. 30, n. 7, above. And cf. Addison's statement in Spectator 413 (par. 4) that God "has annexed a secret pleasure to the idea of anything that is new or uncommon, that he might encourage us in the pursuit after knowledge, and engage us to search into the wonders of his creation; for every new idea brings such a pleasure along with it, as rewards any pains we have taken in its acquisition, and consequently serves as a motive to put us upon fresh discoveries." For SJ's views on "idea" as "image," see p. 173, n. 5, below.

8. Cf. SJ's observation in 1766: " 'Sir, that all who are happy, are equally happy, is not true. A peasant and a philosopher may be equally satisfied, but not equally happy. Happiness consists in the multiplicity of agreeable consciousness. A peasant has not capacity for having equal happiness with a philosopher' " (Life, II.9).

"In enumerating the particular comforts of life we shall find many advantages on the side of the Europeans. They cure wounds and diseases with which we languish and perish. We suffer inclemencies of weather which they can obviate. They have engines for the despatch of many laborious works, which we must perform by manual industry. There is such communication between distant places, that one friend can hardly be said to be absent from another. Their policy⁹ removes all publick inconveniencies: they have roads cut through their mountains, and bridges laid upon their rivers. And, if we descend to the privacies of life, their habitations are more commodious, and their possessions are more secure."

"They are surely happy," said the prince, "who have all these conveniencies, of which I envy none so much as the facility with which separated friends interchange their thoughts."

"The Europeans," answered Imlac, "are less unhappy than we,¹ but they are not happy. Human life is every where a state in which much is to be endured, and little to be enjoyed."²

---

9. In SJ's *Dictionary,* sense 1 of *policy* is "The art of government, chiefly with respect to foreign powers"; sense 2 is "Art; prudence; management of affairs; stratagem."

1. In his life of Sir Francis Drake, SJ considers the relative happiness of people in "civilized" and "savage" countries. "It is, perhaps, a just observation," he says, "that, with regard to outward circumstances, happiness and misery are equally diffused through all states of human life." Later, however, he declares that "some skepticks have made, very unnecessarily, a difficulty of determining" "whether more enlightened nations ought to look upon [uncivilized nations] with pity, as less happy than themselves." And he goes on to remark that "the question is not, whether a good Indian or bad Englishman be most happy; but, which state is

most desirable, supposing virtue and reason the same in both" (*Works of Samuel Johnson* [1825], VI.356, 366–67).

2. SJ, of course, voices Imlac's estimate of life in many other writings and conversations. He often declared, so William Maxwell reported, "that there was more to be endured than enjoyed, in the general condition of human life" (*Life,* II.124). In *Rambler* 165 (par. 3), he says that "the utmost felicity which we can ever attain, will be little better than alleviation of misery, and we shall always feel more pain from our wants than pleasures from our enjoyments." Cf. also *Rambler* 32 (par. 6), 204–05, 207 (par. 1); *Adventurer* 69 (par. 12), 111 (pars. 1, 3), 120; "Life of Collins" (*Lives,* III.337, par. 6); *Letters* 329; *Idler* 89 (par. 1); *Johnsonian Miscellanies,* ed. G. B. Hill (2 vols., 1897), II.256–57; *Life,* IV.300–02.

Chap. XII.

The story of Imlac continued.

"I am not yet willing," said the prince, "to suppose that happiness is so parsimoniously distributed to mortals; nor can believe but that, if I had the choice of life,[1] I should be able to fill every day with pleasure. I would injure no man, and should provoke no resentment: I would relieve every distress, and should enjoy the benedictions of gratitude. I would choose my friends among the wise, and my wife among the virtuous; and therefore should be in no danger from treachery, or unkindness. My children should, by my care, be learned and pious, and would repay to my age what their childhood had received. What would dare to molest him who might call on every side to thousands enriched by his bounty, or assisted by his power? And why should not

---

1. In his letter to William Strahan of 20 Jan 1759, SJ says that "the title" of *Rasselas* "will be The choice of Life or The History of ——— Prince of Abissinia" (see Introduction, p. xix above). In his edition of *Rasselas*, Hardy points out that "the 'choice of life'. . . was, in one context or another, a frequent topos in classical literature" (pp. 141–42). He quotes a passage from Cicero's *De Officiis*, i.32–33 (115, 117, 119), a part of which reads in translation: "What role we ourselves may choose to sustain is decided by our own free choice. . . . Above all we must decide who and what manner of men we wish to be and what calling in life we would follow; and this is the most difficult problem in the world. For it is in the years of early youth, when our judgment is most immature, that each of us decides that his calling in life shall be that to which he has taken a special liking. . . . There is one class of people that is very rarely met with: it is composed of those who are endowed with marked natural ability, or exceptional

advantages of education and culture, or both, and who also have time to consider carefully what career in life they prefer to follow" (Loeb edition, trans. Walter Miller, 1913, pp. 119, 121). And Hardy cites a number of other references, including Plato's *Republic*, ix.7 (581C), x.15 (617D); Aristotle's *Ethics*, i.5; Cicero's *Tusculanae Disputationes*, v.3 (8–9); Macrobius's *Commentariorum in Somnium Scipionis*, ii.17. In an essay entitled "Johnson's *Rasselas:* Implicit Contexts" (*Journal of English and Germanic Philology*, LXXIV [1975], 1–25, esp. 6–16), Earl R. Wasserman relates the "choice of life" theme in *Rasselas* to two classical allegories, Prodicus's "Choice of Hercules" and Cebes's "Tablet" or "Picture of Human Life," and argues that SJ's tale "implicitly mocks" the "journey pattern" (p. 14) of the amalgamated allegories. The "choice" theme also figures importantly in SJ's allegorical "Vision of Theodore" and his fairy tale "The Fountains." For additional details, see Introduction, p. xliv above; pp. 183–90, 226–27 below.

life glide quietly away in the soft reciprocation of protection and reverence?[2] All this may be done without the help of European refinements, which appear by their effects to be rather specious than useful. Let us leave them and persue our journey."

"From Palestine," said Imlac, "I passed through many regions of Asia; in the more civilized kingdoms as a trader, and among the barbarians of the mountains as a pilgrim. At last I began to long for my native country, that I might repose after my travels, and fatigues, in the places where I had spent my earliest years, and gladden my old companions with the recital of my adventures. Often did I figure to myself those, with whom I had sported away the gay hours of dawning life, sitting round me in its evening, wondering at my tales, and listening to my counsels.[3]

"When this thought had taken possession of my mind, I considered every moment as wasted which did not bring me nearer to Abissinia. I hastened into Egypt, and, notwithstanding my impatience, was detained ten months in the contemplation of its ancient magnificence, and in enquiries after the remains of its ancient learning.[4] I found in Cairo a

---

2. Cf. *The Vanity of Human Wishes*, ll. 291–98, esp. 293–94: "An age that melts with unperceiv'd decay, / And glides in modest innocence away"; Dryden's *State of Innocence* (1677): "Still quitting ground, by unperceived decay, / And steal myself from life, and melt away" (p. 42).

3. "Every man," SJ remarks in a letter to Sir Joshua Reynolds (*Letters* 261), "has a lurking wish to appear considerable in his native place." In *Idler* 43 (par. 9), he contrasts the difference between the returning traveller's expectations and what he actually finds after a long absence: "We leave the beauty in her bloom, and, after an absence of twenty years, wonder, at our return, to find her faded. We meet those whom we left children, and can scarcely persuade ourselves to treat them as men.

. . . The man of business, wearied with unsatisfactory prosperity, retires to the town of his nativity, and expects to play away the last years with the companions of his childhood, and recover youth in the fields where he once was young."

4. "Arts and sciences flourish'd among [the Egyptians] very early, as we may amongst other authours, learn from Diodorus Siculus. This historian informs us that Homer, Lycurgus, Solon, Plato, Pythagoras, Democritus, and many other great men travell'd into Egypt for improvement and information, and particularly to converse with the Egyptian priests, who were the only masters of the contemplative sciences. These priests, beside matters of religion, taught arithmetick and geometry. . . . Musick, likewise astronomy

mixture of all nations; some brought thither by the love of knowledge, some by the hope of gain, and many by the desire of living after their own manner without observation, and of lying hid in the obscurity of multitudes: for, in a city, populous as Cairo, it is possible to obtain at the same time the gratifications of society, and the secrecy of solitude.[5]

"From Cairo I travelled to Suez,[6] and embarked on the Red Sea, passing along the coast till I arrived at the port from which I had departed twenty years before. Here I joined myself to a caravan and re-entered my native country.

"I now expected the caresses of my kinsmen, and the congratulations of my friends, and was not without hope that my father, whatever value he had set upon riches, would own with gladness and pride a son who was able to add to the felicity and honour of the nation. But I was soon convinced that my thoughts were vain. My father had been dead fourteen years, having divided his wealth among my brothers, who were removed to some other provinces. Of my companions the greater part was in the grave, of the rest some could with difficulty remember me, and some considered me as one corrupted by foreign manners.[7]

---

and astrology, was part of the Egyptians talent" (s.v. "Egypt" in *The Great Historical, Geographical, Genealogical, and Poetical Dictionary;* 2 vols., 2d ed., ed. Jeremy Collier [1701]). In his *Dictionary* under sense 11 of *master,* SJ quotes this passage from South's *Sermons* ([1859], 1.32): "To the Jews join the Egyptians, the first masters of learning."

5. With this description of Cairo, cf. the opinions of London expressed by SJ, Boswell, and others in the *Life,* iii.378–79.

6. "Suez, . . . a sea-port town of Egypt, in the bottom of the Red Sea. . . . It is a great rendezvous of the Ethiopians" (s.v. "Suez" in *Dictionary,* Collier

[1701]).

7. Three years after the publication of *Rasselas,* SJ, describing to his friend Giuseppe Baretti his first visit back home to Lichfield in many years, observes: "Last winter I went down to my native town, where I found the streets much narrower and shorter than I thought I had left them, inhabited by a new race of people, to whom I was very little known. My play-fellows were grown old, and forced me to suspect, that I was no longer young. My only remaining friend has changed his principles, and was become the tool of the predominant faction" (*Letters* 142). Cf. *Idler* 58 (par. 6).

"A man used to vicissitudes is not easily dejected. I forgot, after a time, my disappointment, and endeavoured to recommend myself to the nobles of the kingdom: they admitted me to their tables, heard my story, and dismissed me. I opened a school, and was prohibited to teach. I then resolved to sit down in the quiet of domestick life, and addressed a lady that was fond of my conversation, but rejected my suit, because my father was a merchant.

"Wearied at last with solicitation and repulses, I resolved to hide myself for ever from the world, and depend no longer on the opinion or caprice of others. I waited for the time when the gate of the Happy Valley should open, that I might bid farewell to hope and fear: the day came; my performance[a] was distinguished with favour, and I resigned myself with joy to perpetual confinement."

"Hast thou here found happiness at last?" said Rasselas. "Tell me without reserve; art thou content with thy condition? or, dost thou wish to be again wandering and inquiring? All the inhabitants of this valley celebrate their lot, and, at the annual visit of the emperour, invite others to partake of their felicity."

"Great prince," said Imlac, "I shall speak the truth: I know not one of all your attendants who does not lament the hour when he entered this retreat. I am less unhappy than the rest, because I have a mind replete with images, which I can vary and combine at pleasure.[8] I can amuse my solitude by the renovation of the knowledge which begins to fade from my memory, and by[b] recollection of the accidents of my past life.[9] Yet all this ends in the sorrowful

---

a. performance *is underlined in the YC.*   b. by *59b*] with the *59a*

---

8. Some "understandings," says SJ in *Rambler* 135 (par. 10), are "so fertile and comprehensive, that they can always feed reflection with new supplies, and suffer nothing from the preclusion of adventitious amusements. . . . But others live only from day to day, and must be constantly enabled, by foreign supplies, to keep out the encroach-

ments of languor and stupidity." In *Idler* 101 (par. 4), the aged Omar recounts his youthful—but unrealized—plan to "store my mind with images, which I shall be busy through the rest of my life in combining and comparing."

9. Cf. SJ's remarks about knowledge in a letter to Mrs. Piozzi (*Letters* 429):

consideration, that my acquirements are now useless, and that none of my pleasures can be again enjoyed. The rest, whose minds have no impression but of the present moment, are either corroded by malignant passions, or sit stupid in the gloom of perpetual vacancy."

"What passions can infest those," said the prince, "who have no rivals? We are in a place where impotence precludes malice, and where all envy is repressed by community of enjoyments."

"There may be community," said Imlac, "of material possessions, but there can never be community of love or of esteem. It must happen that one will please more than another; he that knows himself despised will always be envious; and still more envious and malevolent, if he is condemned to live in the presence of those who despise him. The invitations, by which they allure others to a state which they feel to be wretched, proceed from the natural malignity of hopeless misery. They are weary of themselves, and of each other, and expect to find relief in new companions. They envy the liberty which their folly has forfeited, and would gladly see all mankind imprisoned like themselves.

"From this crime, however, I am wholly free. No man can say that he is wretched by my persuasion. I look with pity on the crowds who are annually soliciting admission to captivity, and wish that it were lawful for me to warn them of their danger."

"My dear Imlac," said the prince, "I will open to thee my whole heart. I^c have long meditated an escape from the Happy Valley. I have examined the mountains on every side, but find myself insuperably barred: teach me the way

---

c. heart. I *59b*] heart, that I *59a*

"He that has early learned much, perhaps seldom makes with regard to life and manners much addition to his knowledge, not only because as more is known there is less to learn, but because a mind stored with images and principles, turns inwards for its own entertainment, and is employed in sorting those ideas which run into confusion, and in recollecting those which are stealing away, practices by which wisdom may be kept but not gained."

to break my prison; thou shalt be the companion of my flight, the guide of my rambles, the partner of my fortune, and my sole director in the *choice of life.*"

"Sir," answered the poet, "your escape will be difficult, and, perhaps, you may soon repent your curiosity. The world, which you figure to yourself smooth and quiet as the lake in the valley, you will find a sea foaming with tempests, and boiling with whirlpools: you will be sometimes over-whelmed by the waves of violence, and sometimes dashed against the rocks of treachery. Amidst wrongs and frauds, competitions and anxieties, you will wish a thousand times for these seats of quiet, and willingly quit hope to be free from fear."[1]

"Do not seek to deter me from my purpose," said the prince: "I am impatient to see what thou hast seen; and, since thou art thyself weary of the valley, it is evident, that thy former state was better than this. Whatever be the consequence of my experiment, I am resolved to judge with my own eyes of the various conditions of men, and then to make deliberately my *choice of life.*"

"I am afraid," said Imlac, "you are hindered by stronger restraints than my persuasions; yet, if your determination is fixed, I do not counsel you to despair. Few things are impossible to diligence and skill."

Chap. XIII.

Rasselas discovers the means of escape.

The prince now dismissed his favourite to rest, but the narrative of wonders and novelties filled his mind with

---

1. In *Rambler* 63 (par. 6), SJ remarks: "We often change a lighter for a great-er evil, and wish ourselves restored again to the state from which we thought it desirable to be delivered." Cf. also Matthew Hale's specific asser-tion in *The Primitive Origination of Man-kind* (1677) that "the anticipations of fear are ever more vigorous than the anticipations of hope." He continues: "The objects, means, and occasions of our fears in relation to sensuals, are ever more and greater than the objects of our hope; because we are obnoxious more to dangers, and those of divers kinds, than we are to deliverances and recoveries from sensible evils" (pp. 375–76).

perturbation.[1] He revolved all that he had heard, and prepared innumerable questions for the morning.

Much of his uneasiness was now removed. He had a
friend to whom he could impart his thoughts, and whose
experience could assist him in his designs. His heart was
no longer condemned to swell with silent vexation. He
thought that even the Happy Valley might be endured with
such a companion, and that, if they could range the world
together, he should have nothing further to desire.

In a few days the water was discharged, and the ground
dried. The prince and Imlac then walked out together to
converse without the notice of the rest. The prince, whose
thoughts were always on the wing, as he passed by the gate,
said, with a countenance of sorrow, "Why art thou so
strong, and why is man so weak?"

"Man is not weak," answered his companion; "knowledge
is more than equivalent to force.[2] The master of mechan-
icks laughs at strength. I can burst the gate, but cannot do it
secretly. Some other expedient must be tried."

As they were walking on the side of the mountain, they
observed that the conies,[3] which the rain had driven from
their burrows, had taken shelter among the bushes, and
formed holes behind them, tending upwards in an oblique
line. "It has been the opinion of antiquity," said Imlac, "that
human reason borrowed many arts from the instinct of
animals;[4] let us, therefore, not think ourselves degraded by

---

1. *Perturbation:* "Commotion of passions" (sense 5 in *Dictionary*).

2. Cf. Ecclesiastes ix.16: "Then said I,
wisdom is better than strength." For
this reference, I am indebted to Hardy
(p. 143).

3. *Cony:* "A rabbit; an animal that
burroughs in the ground" (*Dictionary*).

4. Numerous writers, from classical
to modern times, have asserted man's
indebtedness in various areas to the instinct of animals. In the *Essay on Man*,
Pope expresses the borrowings thus:

See him from nature rising slow to art!
To copy instinct then was reason's
    part;

Thus then to man the voice of Nature
    spake—
"Go, from the creatures thy
    instructions take:
Learn from the birds what food the
    thickets yield;
Learn from the beasts the physic of
    the field;
Thy arts of building from the bees
    receive;
Learn of the mole to plow, the worm to
    weave;
Learn of the little nautilus to sail,
Spread the thin oar, and catch the
    driving gale." [iii.169–78]

learning from the coney. We may escape by piercing the mountain in the same direction. We will begin where the summit hangs over the middle part, and labour upward till we shall issue out beyond the prominence."

The eyes of the prince, when he heard this proposal, sparkled with joy. The execution was easy, and the success certain.

No time was now lost. They hastened early in the morning to chuse a place proper for their mine.[5] They clambered with great fatigue among crags and brambles, and returned without having discovered any part that favoured their design. The second and the third day were spent in the same manner, and with the same frustration. But, on the fourth, they found a small cavern, concealed by a thicket, where they resolved to make their experiment.

Imlac procured instruments proper to hew stone and remove earth, and they fell to their work on the next day with more eagerness than vigour. They were presently exhausted by their efforts, and sat down to pant upon the grass. The prince, for a moment, appeared to be discouraged. "Sir," said his companion, "practice will enable us to continue our labour for a longer time; mark, however, how far we have advanced, and you will find that our toil will some time have an end. Great works are performed, not by strength, but perseverance:[6] yonder palace was raised by single stones, yet you see its height and spaciousness. He that shall walk with vigour three hours a day will pass in seven years a space equal to the circumference of the globe."[7]

---

5. *Mine:* "a subterranean cavity" (OED).

6. George L. Barnett has pointed out (*Notes & Queries,* CCI [1956], 485–86) that Imlac's maxim echoes a remark in Cicero's *De Senectute.* VI.17: "*Non viribus aut velocitate aut celeritate corporum res magnae geruntur, sed consilio, auctoritate, sententia*" ("Great works are performed, not by strength or speed or physical dexterity, but by reflection, force of character, and determination"). Cf. SJ's similar comment in *Rambler* 43 (par. 10): "All the performances of human art, at which we look with praise or wonder, are instances of the resistless force of perseverance: it is by this that the quarry becomes a pyramid, and that distant countries are united with canals."

7. In *Adventurer* 69 (par. 7), SJ remarks that "the effects of human in-

They returned to their work[a] day after day, and, in a short time, found a fissure in the rock, which enabled them to pass far with very little obstruction. This Rasselas considered as a good omen. "Do not disturb your mind," said Imlac, "with other hopes or fears than reason may suggest: if you are pleased with prognosticks of good, you will be terrified likewise with tokens of evil, and your whole life will be a prey to superstition.[8] Whatever facilitates our work is more than an omen, it is a cause of success. This is one of those pleasing surprises which often happen to active resolution.[9] Many things difficult to design prove easy to performance."

Chap. XIV.

Rasselas and Imlac receive an unexpected visit.

They had now wrought their way to the middle, and solaced their toil[a] with the approach of liberty, when the prince, coming down to refresh himself with air, found his sister Nekayah standing before the mouth of the cavity. He started and stood confused, afraid to tell his design, and yet

a. work 59*b*] labour 59*a*   a. toil 59*b*] labour 59*a*

dustry and skill are more easily subjected to calculation [than is "the work of chance"]; whatever can be completed in a year, is divisible into parts, of which each may be performed in the compass of a day." Hill, who performed the necessary calculations with Imlac's figures, has noted that SJ "must have reckoned vigorous walking at the rate of a little over three miles an hour" (p. 174). Both Boswell and Mrs. Piozzi (*Anecdotes*, 1.200–01) comment on SJ's frequent use of computation as a means, in Boswell's words (*Life*, 1.72), of preventing "his mind from preying upon itself."

8. In a similar statement in *Rambler* 29 (pars. 13, 14), SJ warns against giving way either to hope or fear, which are "both equally fallacious; as hope enlarges happiness, fear aggravates calamity. . . . All fear is in itself painful, and when it conduces not to safety is painful without use." Cf. No. 43 (par. 13). SJ himself, so Boswell observes, "was prone to superstition, but not to credulity. Though his imagination might incline him to a belief of the marvellous and the mysterious, his vigorous reason examined the evidence with jealousy" (*Life*, IV.426; V.17–18).

9. Cf. *Adventurer* 69 (par. 7): "Of every great and complicated event, part depends upon causes out of our power, and part must be effected by vigour and perseverance."

hopeless to conceal it. A few moments determined him to repose on her fidelity, and secure her secrecy by a declaration without reserve.

"Do not imagine," said the princess, "that I came hither as a spy: I had long[b] observed from my window, that you and Imlac directed your walk every day towards the same point, but I did not suppose you had any better reason for the preference than a cooler shade, or more fragrant bank; nor followed you with any other design than to partake of your conversation. Since then not suspicion but fondness has detected you, let me not lose the advantage of my discovery. I am equally weary of confinement with yourself, and not less desirous of knowing what is done or suffered in the world. Permit me to fly with you from this tasteless tranquility, which will yet grow more loathsome when you have left me. You may deny me to accompany you, but cannot hinder me from following."

The prince, who loved Nekayah above his other sisters, had no inclination to refuse her request, and grieved that he had lost an opportunity of shewing his confidence by a voluntary communication. It was therefore agreed that she should leave the valley with them; and that, in the mean time, she should watch, lest any other straggler[1] should, by chance or curiosity, follow them to the mountain.

At length their labour was at an end; they saw light beyond the prominence, and, issuing to the top of the mountain, beheld the Nile, yet a narrow current, wandering beneath them.

The prince looked round with rapture, anticipated all the pleasures of travel, and in thought was already transported beyond his father's dominions. Imlac, though very joyful at his escape, had less expectation of pleasure in the world, which he had before tried, and of which he had been weary.

Rasselas was so much delighted with a wider horizon,

b. long *59b*] often *59a*

---

1. *Straggler:* "A wanderer; a rover; one who forsakes his company; one who rambles without any settled direction" (sense 1 in *Dictionary*).

that he could not soon be persuaded to return into the valley. He informed his sister that the way was open, and that nothing now remained but to prepare for their departure.

Chap. XV.

The prince and princess leave the valley, and see many wonders.

The prince and princess had jewels sufficient to make them rich whenever they came into a place of commerce, which, by Imlac's direction, they hid in their cloaths, and, on the night of the next full moon, all left the valley. The princess was followed only by a single favourite,[1] who did not know whither she was going.

They clambered through the cavity, and began to go down on the other side. The princess and her maid turned their eyes towards every part, and, seeing nothing to bound their prospect, considered themselves as in danger of being lost in a dreary vacuity. They stopped and trembled. "I am almost afraid," said the princess, "to begin a journey of which I cannot perceive an end, and to venture into this immense plain where I may be approached on every side by men whom I never saw." The prince felt nearly the same emotions, though he thought it more manly to conceal them.

Imlac smiled at their terrours,[2] and encouraged them to proceed; but the princess continued irresolute till she had been imperceptibly drawn forward too far to return.

In the morning they found some shepherds in the field, who set milk and fruits before them.[3] The princess won-

---

1. In her *Memoirs* (1824), Laetitia-Matilda Hawkins remarks (1.57) that Mary, eldest daughter of Saunders Welch, who married Nollekens the sculptor, is the "original of Johnson's Pekuah in *Rasselas*."

2. *Terrour:* "Fear received" (sense 2 in *Dictionary*).

3. *Voyage to Abyssinia* dwells at length on the Abyssinian custom which "obliges" the country people to feed and entertain all strangers who visit them. "This practise is so well established, that a stranger goes into a house of one he never saw, with the same familiarity, and assurance of welcome, as into that of an intimate friend, or near relation" (p. 50).

dered that she did not see a palace ready for her reception, and a table spread with delicacies; but, being faint and hungry, she drank the milk and eat[4] the fruits, and thought them of a higher flavour than the products of the valley.

They travelled forward by easy journeys, being all unaccustomed to toil or difficulty, and knowing, that though they might be missed, they could not be persued. In a few days they came into a more populous region, where Imlac was diverted with the admiration[5] which his companions expressed at the diversity of manners, stations and employments.

Their dress was such as might not bring upon them the suspicion of having any thing to conceal, yet the prince, wherever he came, expected to be obeyed, and the princess was frighted,[6] because those that came into her presence did not prostrate themselves before her. Imlac was forced to observe them with great vigilance, lest they should betray their rank by their unusual behaviour, and detained them several weeks in the first village to accustom them to the sight of common mortals.

By degrees the royal wanderers were taught to understand that they had for a time laid aside their dignity,[7] and were to expect only such regard as liberality and courtesy could procure. And Imlac, having, by many admonitions, prepared them to endure the tumults of a port, and the ruggedness of the commercial race,[8] brought them down to the sea-coast.

The prince and his sister, to whom every thing was new, were gratified equally at all places, and therefore remained

---

4. According to SJ's *Dictionary*, the "preterite" of *to eat* is "*ate*, or *eat*." Cf. use on p. 133 below.

5. See p. 36, n. 4, above.

6. Both *to fright* and *to frighten* appear in SJ's *Dictionary*.

7. *Dignity:* "Rank of elevation" (sense 1 in *Dictionary*).

8. *Ruggedness:* "Roughness; asperity" (sense 2 in *Dictionary*). With the entire

phrase, cf. SJ's comment in his life of Dryden that "the general conduct of [book] traders was much less liberal in those times than in our own; their views were narrower, and their manners grosser. To the mercantile ruggedness of that race the delicacy of the poet was sometimes exposed" (*Lives*, 1.407, par. 187).

for some months at the port without any inclination to pass further. Imlac was content with their stay, because he did not think it safe to expose them, unpractised in the world, to the hazards of a foreign country.

At last he began to fear lest they should be discovered, and proposed to fix a day for their departure. They had no pretensions to judge for themselves, and referred the whole scheme to his direction. He therefore took passage in a ship to Suez; and, when the time came, with great difficulty prevailed on the princess to enter the vessel. They had a quick and prosperous voyage, and from Suez travelled by land to Cairo.

Chap. XVI.

They enter Cairo, and find every man happy.

As they approached the city, which filled the strangers with astonishment, "This," said Imlac to the prince, "is the place where travellers and merchants assemble from all the corners of the earth. You will here find men of every character, and every occupation. Commerce is here honourable:[1] I will act as a merchant, and you shall live as strangers, who have no other end of travel than curiosity; it will soon be observed that we are rich; our reputation will procure us access to all whom we shall desire to know; you will see all the conditions of humanity, and enable yourself at leisure to make your *choice of life*."

---

1. Cairo's size as a metropolis was sufficient to elicit from Henry Blount, a seventeenth-century visitor, the bold declaration that it is "clearly the greatest concourse of mankinde in these times, and perhaps that ever was" (*A Voyage into the Levant* [2d ed., 1636], p. 3). And a century later, Richard Pococke in his *Description of the East* (2 vols., 1743–45), while admitting that "Grand Cairo has been much magnified as to its extent, and the number of its inhabitants" (1.26), mentions the "great mixture of people" in the city and the "conveniency of water carriage" which makes it a "place of [such] great trade ... that probably near a quarter of the souls in the city [are not] fix'd inhabitants" (1.38–39). Cf. also William Lithgow's *Travels* (1692 ed., pp. 291, 293), a passage from which Hill quotes (p. 175).

They now entered the town, stunned by the noise,[2] and offended[3] by the crowds. Instruction had not yet so prevailed over habit, but that they wondered to see themselves pass undistinguished along the street, and met by the lowest of the people without reverence or notice. The princess could not at first bear the thought of being levelled with the vulgar, and, for some days, continued in her chamber, where she was served by her favourite Pekuah[a] as in the palace of the valley.

Imlac, who understood traffick, sold part of the jewels the next day, and hired a house, which he adorned with such magnificence, that he was immediately considered as a merchant of great wealth. His politeness attracted many acquaintance,[4] and his generosity made him courted by many dependants. His table was crowded by men of every nation, who all admired his knowledge, and solicited his favour. His companions, not being able to mix in the conversation, could make no discovery[5] of their ignorance or surprise, and were gradually initiated in the world as they gained knowledge of the language.

The prince had, by frequent lectures, been taught the use and nature of money;[6] but the ladies could not, for a long time, comprehend what the merchants did with small

a. Pekuah *added* 59b

2. "The attention of a new-comer" to London, says SJ in *Adventurer* 67 (par. 3), "is generally first struck by the multiplicity of cries that stun him in the streets, and the variety of merchandise and manufactures which the shopkeepers expose on every hand." Cf. *Spectator* 250 (par. 1): "There is nothing which more astonishes a foreigner and frights a country squire, than the cries of London."

3. *To offend:* "To assail; to attack" (sense 2 in *Dictionary*).

4. Under sense 4 ("The person with whom we are acquainted; him of whom we have some knowledge, without the intimacy of friendship") of *acquaintance* in his *Dictionary*, SJ adds: "In this sense, the plural is, in some authours, *acquaintance*, in others *acquaintances*." Cf. pp. 97, 154 below.

5. *Discovery:* "The act of revealing or disclosing any secret" (sense 2 in *Dictionary*).

6. Money obviously did not circulate in the Happy Valley. Moreover, according to *Voyage to Abyssinia*, "There is no money in Abyssinia, except in the eastern provinces, where they have iron coin" (p. 50).

pieces of gold and silver, or why things of so little use should be received as equivalent to the necessaries of life.

They studied the language two years, while Imlac was preparing to set before them the various ranks and conditions of mankind. He grew acquainted with all who had any thing uncommon in their fortune or conduct. He frequented the voluptuous[7] and the frugal, the idle and the busy, the merchants and the men of learning.

The prince, being now able to converse with fluency, and having learned the caution necessary to be observed in his intercourse with strangers, began to accompany Imlac to places of resort, and to enter into all assemblies, that he might make his *choice of life*.

For some time he thought choice needless, because all appeared to him equally happy.[8] Wherever he went he met gayety and kindness, and heard the song of joy, or the laugh of carelesness. He began to believe that the world overflowed with universal plenty, and that nothing was withheld either from want or merit; that every hand showered liberality, and every heart melted with benevolence: "and who then," says he, "will be suffered to be wretched?"

Imlac permitted the pleasing delusion, and was unwilling to crush the hope of inexperience, till one day, having sat a while silent, "I know not," said the prince, "what can be the reason that I am more unhappy than any of our friends. I see them perpetually and unalterably chearful, but feel my own mind restless and uneasy.[9] I am unsatisfied with those pleasures which I seem most to court; I live in the crowds of

---

7. *Voluptuous:* "Given to excess of pleasure; luxurious" (*Dictionary*).

8. Cf. *Rambler* 196 (par. 5): "He who has seen only the superficies of life believes every thing to be what it appears, and rarely suspects that external splendor conceals any latent sorrow or vexation."

9. "If the general disposition of things be estimated by the representation which every one makes of his own state," says SJ in *Rambler* 128 (par. 3), "the world must be considered as the abode of sorrow and misery. . . . If we judge by the account which may be obtained of every man's fortune from others, it may be concluded, that we all are placed in an elysian region, overspread with the luxuriance of plenty, and fanned by the breezes of felicity."

jollity, not so much to enjoy company as to shun myself,[1] and am only loud and merry to conceal my sadness."[2]

"Every man," said Imlac, "may, by examining his own mind, guess what passes in the minds of others:[3] when you feel that your own gaiety is counterfeit, it may justly lead you to suspect that of your companions not to be sincere. Envy is commonly reciprocal.[4] We are long before we are convinced that happiness is never to be found, and each believes it possessed by others, to keep alive the hope of obtaining it for himself. In the assembly, where you passed the last night, there appeared such spriteliness of air, and volatility of fancy, as might have suited beings of an higher order, formed to inhabit serener regions inaccessible to care or sorrow: yet, believe me, prince, there was not one who did not dread the moment when solitude should deliver him to the tyranny of reflection."[5]

---

1. SJ himself, of course, much preferred company to solitariness, which promoted his melancholia. "I am very unwilling to be left alone, Sir," he once remarked, "and therefore I go with my company down the first pair of stairs, in some hopes that they may, perhaps, return again" (*Life*, 1.490).

2. In Sermon 16 (par. 29), SJ declares: "Men are often driven, by reflection and remorse, into the hurries of business, or of pleasure, and fly from the terrifying suggestions of their own thoughts to banquets and to courts."

3. Cf. *Adventurer* 138 (par. 2): "In estimating the pain or pleasure of any particular state, every man, indeed, draws his decisions from his own breast, and cannot with certainty determine, whether other minds are affected by the same causes in the same manner. Yet by this criterion we must be content to judge, because no other can be obtained; and, indeed, we have no reason to think it very fallacious." See also *Adventurer* 95 (par. 8).

4. Commenting on envy in *Idler* 32

(par. 9), SJ remarks: "All envy would be extinguished if it were universally known that there are none to be envied."

5. With this whole sentence, cf. *Adventurer* 120 (pars. 5, 6): "He that enters a gay assembly, beholds the chearfulness displayed in every countenance, and finds all sitting vacant and disengaged, with no other attention than to give or to receive pleasure; would naturally imagine, that he had reached at last the metropolis of felicity, the place sacred to gladness of heart, from whence all fear and anxiety were irreversibly excluded. Such, indeed, we may often find to be the opinion of those, who from a lower station look up to the pomp and gayety which they cannot reach; but who is there of those who frequent these luxurious assemblies, that will not confess his own uneasiness, or cannot recount the vexations and distresses that prey upon the lives of his gay companions?

"The world, in its best state, is nothing more than a larger assembly of beings, combining to counterfeit hap-

"This," said the prince, "may be true of others, since it is true of me; yet, whatever be the general infelicity of man, one condition is more happy than another, and wisdom surely directs us to take the least evil in the *choice of life.*"

"The causes of good and evil," answered Imlac, "are so various and uncertain, so often entangled with each other,[6] so diversified by various relations, and so much subject to accidents which cannot be foreseen, that he who would fix his condition upon incontestable reasons of preference, must live and die enquiring and deliberating."[7]

"But surely," said Rasselas, "the wise men, to whom we listen with reverence and wonder, chose that mode of life for themselves which they thought most likely to make them happy."

"Very few," said the poet, "live by choice. Every man is placed in his present condition by causes which acted without his foresight, and with which he did not always willingly co-operate;[8] and therefore you will rarely meet one who does not think the lot of his neighbour better than his own."

---

piness which they do not feel, employing every art and contrivance to embellish life, and to hide their real condition from the eyes of one another." Cf. *Idler* 18 (pars. 4, 8).

6. Cf. *Adventurer* 108 (par. 9): "good and evil are in real life inseparably united."

7. In *Rambler* 63, SJ emphasizes the difficulty of making a totally wise and reasonable choice of life. "The good and evil of different modes of life," he says (par. 10), "are sometimes so equally opposed, that perhaps no man ever yet made his choice between them upon a full conviction, and adequate knowledge. . . . The mind no sooner imagines itself determined by some prevalent advantage, than some convenience of equal weight is discovered on the other side." Also cf. *Rambler* 19, which recounts the variety of choices made by the brilliant but changeable

Polyphilus. With the thought of the sentence, cf. *Spectator* 162 (par. 3), part of which is quoted in SJ's *Dictionary* under *inconstancy:* "Irresolution on the schemes of life which offer themselves to our choice, and inconstancy in pursuing them, are the greatest and most universal causes of all our disquiet and unhappiness." In a letter to Boswell, SJ observes: "Life is not long, and too much of it must not pass in idle deliberation how it shall be spent; deliberation, which those who begin it by prudence, and continue it with subtilty, must, after long expense of thought, conclude by chance. To prefer one future mode of life to another, upon just reasons, requires faculties which it has not pleased our Creator to give us" (*Life*, II.22).

8. SJ expresses similar doubts about the efficacy of choice in various other writings. In *Rambler* 184 (par. 4), he

"I am pleased to think," said the prince, "that my birth has given me at least one advantage over others, by enabling me to determine for myself. I have here the world before me; I will review it at leisure: surely happiness is somewhere to be found."

Chap. XVII.

The prince associates with young men of spirit and gaiety.[1]

Rasselas rose next day, and resolved to begin his experiments upon life. "Youth," cried he, "is the time of gladness: I will join myself to the young men, whose only business is to gratify their desires, and whose time is all spent in a succession of enjoyments."

To such societies he was readily admitted,[2] but a few days brought him back weary and disgusted. Their mirth was without images,[3] their laughter without motive; their pleasures were gross and sensual, in which the mind had no part;[4] their conduct was at once wild and mean; they

---

says: "It is not commonly observed, how much, even of actions considered as particularly subject to choice, is to be attributed to accident, or some cause out of our own power, by whatever name it be distinguished." If a person will review his life, he continues, "he will find that of the good or ill which he has experienced, a great part came unexpected . . . ; that every event has been influenced by causes acting without his intervention; and that whenever he pretended to the prerogative of foresight, he was mortified with new conviction of the shortness of his views." Cf. also *Idler* 55 (par. 2), 101; p. 67, n. 7, above.

1. In Sermon 14 (par. 4), SJ declares: "The young and the gay imagine happiness to consist in shew, in merriment and noise, or in a constant succession

of amusements, or in the gratification of their appetites, and the frequent repetition of sensual pleasures." Cf. *Adventurer* 34, which contains a description of the dissolute youth of Misargyrus.

2. In Sermon 20 (par. 40), SJ remarks that "man is so far formed for society, that even solitary wickedness quickly disgusts; and debauchery requires its combinations and confederacies, which, as intemperance diminishes their numbers, must be filled up with new proselytes."

3. *Image:* "An idea; a representation of any thing to the mind; a picture drawn in the fancy" (sense 5 in *Dictionary*).

4. "The young and the gay," SJ asserts in Sermon 14 (par. 4), "please themselves, not with thinking justly,

laughed at order and at law, but the frown of power dejected, and the eye of wisdom abashed them.

The prince soon concluded, that he should never be
happy in a course of life of which he was ashamed. He
thought it unsuitable to a reasonable being to act without a
plan, and to be sad or chearful only by chance. "Happiness," said he, "must be something solid and permanent,
without fear and without uncertainty."[5]

But his young companions had gained so much of his
regard by their frankness and courtesy, that he could
not leave them without warning and remonstrance. "My
friends," said he, "I have seriously considered our manners
and our prospects, and find that we have mistaken our own
interest. The first years of man must make provision for the
last.[6] He that never thinks never can be wise. Perpetual
levity must end in ignorance; and intemperance, though it
may fire the spirits for an hour, will make life short or
miserable.[7] Let us consider that youth is of no long duration, and that in maturer age, when the enchantments of
fancy shall cease, and phantoms of delight dance no more
about us, we shall have no comforts but the esteem of wise
men, and the means of doing good.[8] Let us, therefore, stop,

---

but with avoiding to think at all, with a
suspense of all the operations of their
intellectual faculties, which defends
them from remembrance of the past,
or anticipation of the future. They lull
themselves in an enervate, and cow-
ardly dissipation, and, instead of being
happy, are only indolent."

5. Cf. *Rambler* 53 (par. 12): "To make
any happiness sincere, it is necessary
that we believe it to be lasting; since
whatever we suppose ourselves in danger of losing, must be enjoyed with solicitude and uneasiness."

6. Cf. Ecclesiastes xii.1: "Remember
now thy Creator in the days of thy
youth, while the evil days come not,
nor the years draw nigh, when thou
shalt say, I have no pleasure in them."

7. In "The Vision of Theodore" (pp.
210–11 below), SJ devotes a paragraph
to the unfortunate beings who suc-
cumb to Intemperance and who "lose
all regard but for the present moment."

8. With the prince's admonitions, cf.
Sir William Temple's comments in his
essay "Of Health and Long Life": "As
they are only the clean beasts which
chew the cud, when they have fed
enough; so they must be clean and virtuous men, that can reflect with pleasure upon the past accidents or courses
of their lives. Besides, men who grow
old with good sense, or good fortunes,
and good nature, cannot want the pleasure of pleasing others, by assisting
with their gifts, their credit, their advice, such as deserve it; as well as their

while to stop is in our power: let us live as men who are sometime to grow old,[9] and to whom it will be the most dreadful of all evils not to count their past years but by follies, and to be reminded of their former luxuriance of health only by the maladies which riot has produced."

They stared a while in silence one upon another, and, at last, drove him away by a general chorus of continued laughter.

The consciousness that his sentiments were just, and his intentions kind, was scarcely sufficient to support him against the horrour of derision.[1] But he recovered his tranquility, and persued his search.

Chap. XVIII.

The prince finds a wise and happy man.[1]

As he was one day walking in the street, he saw a spacious building which all were, by the open doors, invited to enter: he followed the stream of people, and found it a hall or school of declamation, in which professors read lectures to their auditory.[2] He fixed his eye upon a sage raised above the rest, who discoursed with great energy on the government of the passions.[3] His look was venerable, his action

---

care of children, kindness to friends, and bounty to servants" (*Works*, 1720, II [*Miscellanea*].288).

9. Cf. SJ's dictum in *Rambler* 50 (final par.) that a man who "would pass the latter part of life with honour and decency, must, when he is young, consider that he shall one day be old; and remember, when he is old, that he has once been young."

1. In a conversation with Boswell on the relative happiness of a boy and a man, SJ remarked: "Ah! Sir, a boy's being flogged is not so severe as a man's having the hiss of the world against him" (*Life*, 1.451).

1. As the following notes make clear, numerous ideas expressed in this chapter closely resemble concepts set forth in seventeenth- and eighteenth-century English versions of stoicism and neo-stoicism. For a detailed treatment of the background of the chapter, see Gwin J. Kolb, "The Use of Stoical Doctrines in *Rasselas*, Chapter XVIII," *Modern Language Notes*, LXVIII (1953), 439–47.

2. *Auditory:* "An audience; a collection of persons assembled to hear" (sense 1 in *Dictionary*).

3. Cf. the title ("Of the Government of Passions") of the third treatise in J. F. Senault's *Use of Passions* (1649) and the reference to the "steddy government of the passions" in the Dedication to George Stanhope's *Epictetus his Morals, with Simplicius his Comment* (1700).

graceful, his pronunciation clear, and his diction elegant. He shewed, with great strength of sentiment, and variety of illustration, that human nature is degraded and debased, when the lower faculties predominate over the higher; that when fancy, the parent of passion, usurps the dominion of the mind, nothing ensues but the natural effect of unlawful government, perturbation and confusion; that she betrays the fortresses of the intellect to rebels, and excites her children to sedition against reason their lawful sovereign.[4] He compared reason to the sun, of which the light is constant, uniform, and lasting;[5] and fancy to a meteor, of bright but transitory lustre, irregular in its motion, and delusive in its direction.[6]

---

4. Views of human nature (also employing the "government" and "rebellion" figure) similar to those of the sage commonly appear in earlier stoical and neo-stoical works. J. F. Senault, for example, in the Dedication to *The Use of Passions*, purposes to "bring all men to observe, how passions are raised in them, how they rebel against reason, how they seduce the understanding, and what sleights they use to enslave the will." Later he declares that the passions "are become disloyal, and no longer acknowledging the voyce of their soveraign [reason]" (p. 133); and elsewhere he explains that "the senses are seduced by objects, these help to abuse imagination, which excites disorders in the inferior part of the soul, and raiseth passions, so as they are no longer in that obedience, wherein original justice kept them; and though they be subject to the empire of reason, yet they so mutiny, as they are not to be brought within the compass of their duty, but by force or cunning" (p. 103). In *Man without Passion: or, the Wise Stoick* (1675), Anthony Le Grand voices a still more negative opinion of the passions: once the "soul" has admitted them, he says, "she is no longer able to set them bounds, they contemn her government, ... they become obsti-

nate in rebellion; and ... they oblige their soveraign to take laws of them" (pp. 99–100). Also cf. Guillaume Du Vair's *The True Way to Vertue and Happiness* (1623), pp. 10–12, and his *Morall Philosophy of the Stoicks* (1677), pp. 17–19; Stanhope's *Epictetus his Morals*, p. 228.

5. In at least three earlier works—Lipsius's *Two Books of Constancy* (translated by Sir John Stradling [1594] and edited by Rudolf Kirk and Clayton M. Hall [1939]), Le Grand's *Man without Passion*, and George Bennet's *New Translation of the Morals of Seneca* (1745 [p. 126])—reason is also compared to the sun. Lipsius calls it a "cleere sunne" (p. 161) with "bright beames" (p. 159), "resolute and immoveable in a good purpose, not variable in iudgment" (p. 81); and Le Grand visions "the Sun of Reason" as beginning "to dart forth his lights" (p. 140).

6. Cf. Stanhope's remark that Epictetus warns against "apprehensions" of the imagination, which is "but a fancy of our own, and no more," because they "embitter ones life with a world of terrors and troubles, by the excess of irregularity of their motions" (*Epictetus his Morals*, p. 52); and Le Grand's assertion that the passions persuade "the mind" and "the will" to "follow their

He then communicated the various precepts given from time to time for the conquest of passion,[7] and displayed the happiness of those who had obtained the important victory,[8] after which man is no longer the slave of fear, nor the fool of hope; is no more emaciated by envy, inflamed by anger, emasculated by tenderness, or depressed by grief;[9] but walks on calmly through the tumults or the privacies of life, as the sun persues alike his course through the calm or the stormy sky.[1]

He enumerated many examples of heroes immovable by

---

irregular motions" (*Man without Passion*, pp. 71–72). In *Rambler* 125 (par. 2), SJ describes "imagination" as "a licentious and vagrant faculty, unsusceptible of limitations, and impatient of restraint."

7. "Precepts" for the conduct of life are emphasized in such works as Du Vair's *Morall Philosophy of the Stoicks* and Bennet's translation of Seneca's *Morals.* To "sheild [*sic*] our reason," says Du Vair, "let us have some fair precepts, and short sentences concerning every passion . . . and stop . . . the first precipitate motions of the soul, that would storm it" (p. 27). Seneca declares that "precepts are of great weight, and a few useful ones . . . do more towards a happy life, than whole volumes of cautions which we know not where to find; these . . . precepts . . . are the rules by which we ought to square our lives" (p. 114). Also cf. Sir Roger L'Estrange's *Seneca's Morals by Way of Abstract* (13th ed., 1729), pp. 117–20; Elizabeth Carter's translation of Epictetus (2 vols., 1758), II.295.

8. Cf. L'Estrange's assertion, in his *Abstract* of Seneca's *Morals,* that "A wise man . . . will be still happy, . . . because he submits himself to reason, and governs his actions by counsel, not by passion" (p. 96). Similarly, Epictetus, according to Stanhope, remarks that the man whose life "is untainted with perturbation and sensual pleasure, must needs be above all grief, and all fear,

absolutely free, and exquisitely happy" (p. 45). In the introduction to her translation of Epictetus, Carter says that the stoics' "favourite doctrine" was their insistence "that a wise man must always be happy" (I.xxv).

9. Du Vair's *Morall Philosophy of the Stoicks,* Le Grand's *Man without Passion,* and L'Estrange's *Abstract* of Seneca's *Morals* describe specific passions in terms similar to those employed by SJ's sage. Cf. "Hope and fear treat their guests as slaves," "Grief deals with us as a tyrant," "Love . . . treat[s] us with oppression" (Le Grand, p. 258); "Envy . . . gnaws the heart to our continual torment" (Du Vair, p. 53); "Anger is a turbulent humour . . . transporting a man into misbecoming violences" (L'Estrange, p. 282).

1. The figures in this passage are paralleled by imagery in Bennet's translation of Seneca's *Morals* and Le Grand's *Man without Passion.* According to Seneca, "a wise man . . . walks without stumbling and is never surprized, he lives always true and steady to himself" (p. 93). "Good men," he says later, "suffer many inconveniences; but virtue like the sun, still goes on with her work, and finishes her course, let the air be never so cloudy" (p. 100). And Le Grand declares: "A wise man ought to imitate the stars . . . in the firmament, he ought to consider the sublunary revolutions without alteration, and the evil that assaults him ought no more to

pain or pleasure,[2] who looked with indifference on those modes or accidents to which the vulgar give the names of good and evil.[3] He exhorted his hearers to lay aside their prejudices, and arm themselves against the shafts of malice or misfortune, by invulnerable patience;[a] concluding, that this state only was happiness, and that this happiness was in every one's power.[4]

a. patience 59*b*] patienc 59*a*

---

discompose him, then [*sic*] the splendid favors of fortune to swell his mind" (p. 132).

2. In his *Morall Philosophy of the Stoicks*, Du Vair suggests that in order "to render [the] precepts [for proper behavior] more strong, and hard to undermine," men should "garrison them with the beautiful examples of such as have generously behaved themselves in the like occasions" (p. 27). In *Epictetus his Morals*, Stanhope singles out Hercules, Theseus, Diogenes, and Socrates as "illustrious heroes," whose steadfastness in various crises "recommend[s] their examples to posterity" (p. 108). Also cf. Carter's translation of Epictetus, II.175, 176, 179; Bennet's translation of Seneca's *Morals*, pp. 184, 194.

3. The "indifferent" attitude of the heroes invoked by SJ's sage is the same as that imputed to "wise men" or "philosophers" by numerous stoical and neo-stoical writers. For example, the wise man, suggests Le Grand in *Man without Passion*, rejects "the noise of a biassed and interressed multitude" (p. 94) and views both "ill accident" and good fortune with "indifference" (p. 9). According to Bennet's translation of Seneca's *Morals*, Seneca asserts that "a truly great mind . . . despises what the vulgar admire" (p. 189) and that "a brave man . . . tramples indifferently upon the glories and terrors of fortune" (p. 371). Also cf. L'Estrange's *Seneca's Morals by Way of Abstract*, pp.

197–98; Carter's translation of Epictetus, I.iii; II.194; Stanhope's *Epictetus his Morals*, pp. 53, 139, 354. In *Rambler* 66 (par. 2), SJ clearly has the stoics in mind when he remarks of some "instructors of mankind": "They have employed their reason and eloquence to persuade us, that nothing is worth the wish of a wise man, have represented all earthly good and evil as indifferent, and counted among vulgar errors the dread of pain, and the love of life."

4. The sage's final exhortation resembles comments in several stoical works. "It is only philosophy," declares Seneca in Bennet's translation of the *Morals*, "that makes the mind invincible and places us out of the reach of fortune, so that all her arrows fall short of us" (p. 142). Furthermore, he, Epictetus, and Le Grand warmly praise the virtue of "invincible patience" (Bennet, p. 98) or "fortitude" as the *sine qua non* of happiness. In the words of Epictetus as rendered by Stanhope's *Epictetus his Morals*, "the escaping afflictions is only a piece of good fortune . . . ; but the bearing them with fortitude and decency is a happiness of the soul, and what the man is properly the better for" (p. 388). Also cf. Carter's translation of Epictetus, I.226; II.195, 332; Le Grand's *Man without Passion*, p. 120. In *Idler* 41 (final par.), SJ, almost certainly reflecting on his mother's recent death, asserts that "philosophy may infuse stubbornness, but religion only can give patience."

Rasselas listened to him with the veneration due to the instructions of a superiour being, and, waiting for him at the door, humbly implored the liberty of visiting so great a master of true wisdom. The lecturer hesitated a moment, when Rasselas put a purse of gold into his hand, which he received with a mixture of joy and wonder.

"I have found," said the prince, at his return to Imlac, "a man who can teach all that is necessary to be known, who, from the unshaken throne of rational fortitude, looks down on the scenes of life changing beneath him.[5] He speaks, and attention watches his lips. He reasons, and conviction closes his periods. This man shall be my future guide: I will learn his doctrines, and imitate his life."

"Be not too hasty," said Imlac, "to trust, or to admire, the teachers of morality: they discourse like angels, but they live like men."[6]

Rasselas, who could not conceive how any man could reason so forcibly without feeling the cogency of his own arguments, paid his visit in a few days, and was denied admission. He had now learned the power of money, and made his way by a piece of gold to the inner apartment, where he found the philosopher in a room half darkened,

---

5. "Tranquillity," says Seneca in Bennet's translation of the *Morals*, "raises us to the summit, and makes every man his own supporter . . . ; he, whose judgment is right and constant enjoys a perpetual calm" (p. 88). Similarly, according to Stanhope's *Epictetus his Morals*, Epictetus speaks of those superior men who "imitate the divine excellencies" and who "sit enthroned on high, and look down, and order all things, with . . . undisturbed security" (p. 152). In *Rambler* 32 (par. 2), SJ remarks that the stoics "proclaimed themselves exalted, by the doctrines of their sect, above the reach of those miseries, which embitter life to the rest of the world."

6. With Imlac's use of *angels* in his comparison, cf. (1) Senault's observation in *The Use of Passions* that stoical doctrine "promiseth to change men into angels, to raise them above a mortal condition, and to put storms and thunder under their feet"; this promise, Senault adds, has "brought forth none [sic] effects" (pp. 123–24); (2) Le Grand's statement in *Man without Passion* that the disciples of the stoics "are accounted but asses, only because they would approach too near the perfections of angels" (p. 5). In *Rambler* 54 (par. 3), SJ draws a sharp contrast between the lectures and the actions of a "speculatist," who, though he "may see and shew the folly of terrestrial hopes, fears, and desires, every hour will give proofs that he never felt it."

with his eyes misty, and his face pale. "Sir," said he, "you are come at a time when all human friendship is useless; what I suffer cannot be remedied, what I have lost cannot be supplied. My daughter, my only daughter, from whose tenderness I expected all the comforts of my age, died last night of a fever. My views, my purposes, my hopes are at an end: I am now a lonely being disunited from society."

"Sir," said the prince, "mortality is an event by which a wise man can never be surprised: we know that death is always near, and it should therefore always be expected."[7] "Young man," answered the philosopher, "you speak like one that has never felt the pangs of separation." "Have you then forgot the precepts," said Rasselas, "which you so powerfully enforced? Has wisdom no strength to arm the heart against calamity? Consider, that external things[8] are naturally variable, but truth and reason are always the same."[9] "What comfort," said the mourner, "can truth and

---

7. The phenomenon of death affords possibly the supreme test of fidelity to stoical principles, whose proponents often express opinions on the subject very similar to those voiced by Rasselas. For example, Epictetus, as interpreted by Stanhope's *Epictetus his Morals*, classifies under "external things" (p. 65) our "natural tenderness" for "our wives and children, our kindred, our friends, and our countrymen" (p. 66). He then goes on to say that a man must learn "to encounter his affection for a child" and must seek to make "all the dispositions of his mind . . . carry the impression of this . . . reflection, That what he thus dotes upon, is but a man; if a man, consequently a brittle and frail creature, and what he is in a continual possibility of losing. And when his mind is once thoroughly possess'd with this consideration, and confirmed with an habitual recollection of it, whenever that child is snatch'd away from him, he is prepared for the stroke, and cannot be surprised and confounded with pas-

sion, as if some strange or new thing had happened to him" (p. 68). Also cf. Carter's translation of Epictetus, II.34, 125, 264, 335; Bennet's translation of Seneca's *Morals*, pp. 135, 236; Du Vair's *Morall Philosophy of the Stoicks*, p. 65; Le Grand's *Man without Passion*, pp. 241, 266–67.

8. "That man should never suffer his happiness to depend upon external circumstances, is one of the chief precepts of the Stoical philosophy," says SJ in *Rambler* 6; but, he continues, "such extravagance of philosophy . . . is overthrown by the experience of every hour, and the powers of nature rise up against it" (pars. 1, 2). In *Idler* 41 (final par.), he comments that "the dictates of Zeno, who commands us to look with indifference on external things, may dispose us to conceal our sorrow, but cannot assuage it."

9. In the "Life of Cowley," SJ declares: "Truth indeed is always truth, and reason is always reason; they have an intrinsick and unalterable value,

reason afford me? of what effect are they now, but to tell
me, that my daughter will not be restored?"[1]

The prince, whose humanity would not suffer him to
insult misery with reproof, went away convinced of the
emptiness of rhetorical sound, and the inefficacy of pol-
ished periods and studied sentences.

Chap. XIX.

A glimpse of pastoral life.

He was still eager upon the same enquiry; and, having
heard of a hermit, that lived near the lowest cataract of the
Nile, and filled the whole country with the fame of his
sanctity, resolved to visit his retreat, and enquire whether
that felicity, which publick life could not afford, was to be
found in solitude; and whether a man, whose age and
virtue made him venerable, could teach any peculiar art of
shunning evils, or enduring them.

Imlac and the princess agreed to accompany him, and,
after the necessary preparations, they began their journey.
Their way lay through fields, where shepherds tended their
flocks, and the lambs were playing upon the pasture.
"This," said the poet, "is the life which has been often
celebrated for its innocence and quiet: let us pass the heat
of the day among the shepherds' tents, and know whether
all our searches are not to terminate in pastoral simplicity."[1]

The proposal pleased them, and they induced the shep-

---

and constitute that intellectual gold
which defies destruction" (*Lives*, 1.59,
par. 182).

1. As Hill notes (pp. 177–78), the
sage's grief over his daughter's death is
comparable to an incident involving
Parson Adams in Book IV, chap. 8, of
Fielding's *Joseph Andrews*, which, however, Hill points out, SJ apparently
never read (*Life*, II.174).

1. With Imlac's remarks, cf. the following passage from SJ's "Life of Sav-

age": "[Savage] had planned out a
scheme of life for the country, of which
he had no knowledge but from pas-
torals and songs. He imagined that he
should be transported to scenes of
flowery felicity, like those which one
poet has reflected to another; and had
projected a perpetual round of innocent pleasures, of which he suspected
no interruption from pride, or ignorance, or brutality" (*Lives*, II.410, par.
262).

herds, by small presents and familiar questions, to tell their opinion of their own state: they were so rude and ignorant, so little able to compare the good with the evil of the occupation, and so indistinct in their narratives and descriptions, that very little could be learned from them.[2] But it was evident that their hearts were cankered with discontent; that they considered themselves as condemned to labour for the luxury of the rich, and looked up with stupid malevolence toward those that were placed above them.

The princess pronounced with vehemence, that she would never suffer these envious savages to be her companions, and that she should not soon be desirous of seeing any more specimens of rustick happiness;[3] but could not believe that all the accounts of primeval pleasures were fabulous, and was yet in doubt whether life had any thing that could be justly preferred to the placid gratifications of fields and woods. She hoped that the time would come, when, with a few virtuous and elegant companions, she should gather flowers planted by her own hand, fondle the lambs of her own ewe, and listen, without care, among brooks and breezes, to one of her maidens reading in the shade.[4]

Chap. XX.

The danger of prosperity.

On the next day they continued their journey, till the heat

---

2. The shepherds resemble the Scottish Highlanders of whom SJ writes in *A Journey to the Western Islands of Scotland:* "They have inquired and considered little, and do not always feel their own ignorance. They are not much accustomed to be interrogated by others; and seem never to have thought upon interrogating themselves" (Mary Lascelles, ed., Vol. IX, Yale Edition of the Works of Samuel Johnson, 1971, p. 117).

3. Cf. *Idler* 71, in which Dick Shifter, who has dreamed of "pastoral delights

and rural innocence," is quickly disabused of his fancies by the "coarse" "manners" and "mischievous" "disposition" of actual "rustics."

4. In the "Life of Gay," SJ attacks extended poetic depictions of the kinds of pastoral delights anticipated by the princess: "There is something in the poetical Arcadia so remote from known reality and speculative possibility, that we can never support its representation through a long work. A pastoral of an hundred lines may be endured; but who will hear of sheep

compelled them to look round for shelter. At a small distance they saw a thick wood, which they no sooner entered than they perceived that they were approaching the habitations of men. The shrubs were diligently cut away to open walks where the shades were darkest; the boughs of opposite trees were artificially interwoven; seats of flowery turf were raised in vacant spaces, and a rivulet, that wantoned along the side of a winding path, had its banks sometimes opened into small basons,[1] and its stream sometimes obstructed by little mounds of stone heaped together to increase its murmurs.[2]

They passed slowly through the wood, delighted with such unexpected accommodations,[3] and entertained each other with conjecturing what, or who, he could be, that, in those rude and unfrequented regions, had leisure and art for such harmless luxury.[4]

As they advanced, they heard the sound of musick, and saw youths and virgins dancing in the grove; and, going still further, beheld a stately palace built upon a hill surrounded with woods. The laws of eastern hospitality[5] allowed them to enter, and the master welcomed them like a man liberal and wealthy.

He was skilful enough in appearances soon to discern that they were no common guests, and spread his table with magnificence. The eloquence of Imlac caught his attention,

---

and goats, and myrtle bowers and purling rivulets, through five acts? Such scenes please barbarians in the dawn of literature, and children in the dawn of life; but will be for the most part thrown away as men grow wise, and nations grow learned" (*Lives*, II.284–85, par. 32).

1. Under *basin* in his *Dictionary*, SJ observes: "It is often written *bason*, but not according to etymology."

2. As Hill points out, in this passage SJ is "describing the landscape-gardening that was in fashion in his time" (p. 179). In the "Life of Shenstone," after noting that Shenstone "began . . . to point his prospects, to diversify his

surface, to entangle his walks, and to wind his waters," SJ remarks: "I will not enquire" whether "any great powers of mind" are required "to plant a walk in undulating curves . . . ; to make water run where it will be heard, and to stagnate where it will be seen; to leave intervals where the eye will be pleased" (*Lives*, III.350, par. 10).

3. See p. 37, n. 9, above.

4. Cf. SJ's comment in the "Life of Shenstone": "it must be . . . confessed that to embellish the form of nature is an innocent amusement" (*Lives*, III.351, par. 10).

5. See p. 61, n. 3, above.

and the lofty courtesy of the princess excited his respect. When they offered to depart he entreated their stay, and was the next day still more unwilling to dismiss them than before. They were easily persuaded to stop, and civility grew up in time to freedom and confidence.

The prince now saw all the domesticks chearful, and all the face of nature smiling round the place, and could not forbear to hope that he should find here what he was seeking; but when he was congratulating the master upon his possessions, he answered with a sigh, "My condition has indeed the appearance of happiness, but appearances are delusive. My prosperity puts my life in danger; the Bassa[6] of Egypt is my enemy, incensed only by my wealth and popularity. I have been hitherto protected against him by the princes of the country; but, as the favour of the great is uncertain, I know not how soon my defenders may be persuaded to share the plunder with the Bassa.[7] I have sent my treasures into a distant country,[8] and, upon the first alarm, am prepared to follow them. Then will my enemies riot[9] in my mansion, and enjoy the gardens which I have planted."

---

6. In his *Dictionary,* SJ defines *bashaw* ("sometimes written *bassa*") as "A title of honour and command among the Turks, the viceroy of a province; the general of an army."

7. Richard Pococke's *Description of the East* contains three chapters (Vol. I, Book IV, 161ff.) describing the confused, corrupt government of Egypt by the Turks—a government which, it is pointed out, consisted, on the one hand, of a "Pasha" representing the "Grand Seignor" and having "but very little power"; and, on the other, of a group of independent favorites and military leaders whom, as the political winds shifted, the Pasha was forced to caress or try to destroy. Pococke also refers to the almost universal practice of "squeezing" whereby the "little officers oppress the people; the great officers squeeze them," and so on until the "Grand Seignor at last seizes the riches of the great officers about him" (1.162, 171). Cf., too, the following passage from Campbell's *Travels and Adventures of Edward Brown:* "The Beys and the Cheiks live magnificently, and amass fortunes by plundering the country people. . . . The Bassa hath vast demands to satisfy, and in order to have wherewith to satisfy them, it is most evident that he must plunder too; a disposition to do this puts him upon a par with his neighbours, and as many of them may want his assistance, they are glad to afford him theirs" (p. 368).

8. Cf. the unrealized intention of Nouradin, the enormously rich man who dies in *Rambler* 120, of withdrawing his "wealth to a safer country" (par. 3).

9. *To riot:* "To revel; to be dissipated in luxurious enjoyment" (sense 1 in *Dictionary*).

They all joined in lamenting his danger, and deprecating his exile; and the princess was so much disturbed with the tumult of grief and indignation, that she retired to her apartment. They continued with their kind inviter a few days longer, and then went forward to find the hermit.

Chap. XXI.

The happiness of solitude.[1] The hermit's history.

They came on the third day,[2] by the direction of the peasants, to the hermit's cell:[3] it was a cavern in the side of a mountain, over-shadowed with palm-trees; at such a distance from the cataract, that nothing more was heard than a gentle uniform murmur,[4] such as composed the mind to pensive meditation,[5] especially when it was assisted by the wind whistling among the branches. The first rude essay of nature had been so much improved by human labour, that the cave contained several apartments, appropriated to different uses, and often afforded lodging to travellers, whom darkness or tempests happened to overtake.

The hermit sat on a bench at the door, to enjoy the coolness of the evening. On one side lay a book with pens and papers, on the other mechanical instruments of various

---

1. For expressions of SJ's generally unfavorable opinion of the solitary life, see *Adventurer* 126; Sermon 1 (par. 1); *Anecdotes* ("Solitude . . . is dangerous to reason, without being favourable to virtue. . . . Solitude is the surest nurse of all prurient passions" [1.219–20]); *Life*, 1.144, n. 2; IV.427.

2. The third day after leaving the country gentleman's residence, not after leaving Cairo.

3. Cf. the retirement to a cell of Theodore, Hermit of Teneriffe (p. 195 below).

4. SJ is apparently glancing at the persistent tradition which attributed to the cataracts of the Nile such a tremendous roar as to produce deafness in t!

nearby dwellers (see, for example, *Description of the East* by Pococke [1.122], who went up the river to the lowest cataract and who labelled the report "fabulous"; *Voyage to Abyssinia*, pp. 83–84). In his Preface (p. 3) to the *Voyage to Abyssinia*, SJ commends Father Lobo because "his cataracts fall from the rock without deafening the neighbouring inhabitants."

5. Under sense 1 ("Deep thought; close attention; contrivance; contemplation") of *meditation* in his *Dictionary*, SJ quotes ll.385–87 of Milton's *Comus*: "'Tis most true, / That musing meditation most affects / The pensive secrecy of desert cell."

kinds. As they approached him unregarded, the princess observed that he had not the countenance of a man that had found, or could teach, the way to happiness.

They saluted him with great respect, which he repaid like a man not unaccustomed to the forms of courts. "My children," said he, "if you have lost your way, you shall be willingly supplied with such conveniencies for the night as this cavern will afford. I have all that nature requires, and you will not expect delicacies in a hermit's cell."

They thanked him, and, entering, were pleased with the neatness and regularity of the place. The hermit set flesh and wine before them, though he fed only upon fruits and water.[6] His discourse was chearful without levity, and pious without enthusiasm.[7] He soon gained the esteem of his guests, and the princess repented of her hasty censure.

At last Imlac began thus: "I do not now wonder that your reputation is so far extended; we have heard at Cairo of your wisdom, and came hither to implore your direction for this young man and maiden in the *choice of life*."

"To him that lives well," answered the hermit, "every form of life is good; nor can I give any other rule for choice, than to remove from all apparent evil."[8]

"He will remove most certainly from evil," said the prince, "who shall devote himself to that solitude which you have recommended by your example."

"I have indeed lived fifteen years in solitude," said the hermit, "but have no desire that my example should gain any imitators. In my youth I professed arms, and was raised by degrees to the highest military rank. I have traversed wide countries at the head of my troops, and seen many battles and sieges. At last, being disgusted by the prefer-

---

6. Cf. the diet—"fruits and herbs and water"—of Theodore, the Hermit of Teneriffe (p. 195 below).

7. *Enthusiasm:* "A vain belief of private revelation; a vain confidence of divine favour or communication" (sense 1 in *Dictionary*).

8. "Socrates," remarks SJ approvingly in the "Life of Milton," "was . . . of opinion that what we had to learn was, how to do good and avoid evil" (*Lives*, 1.100, par. 41). Cf. 1 Thessalonians 5.22: "Abstain from all appearance of evil."

ment[a] of a younger officer, and feeling that my vigour was[b] beginning to decay, I resolved to close my life in peace, having found the world full of snares, discord, and misery. I had once escaped from the persuit of the enemy by the shelter of this cavern, and therefore chose it for my final residence. I employed artificers to form it into chambers, and stored it with all that I was likely to want.

"For some time after my retreat, I rejoiced like a tempest-beaten sailor at his entrance into the harbour, being delighted with the sudden change of the noise and hurry of war, to stillness and repose.[9] When the pleasure of novelty went away,[1] I employed my hours in examining the plants which grow in the valley, and the minerals which I collected from the rocks.[2] But that enquiry is now grown tasteless and irksome. I have been for some time unsettled and distracted: my mind is disturbed with a thousand perplexities of doubt, and vanities of imagination, which hourly prevail upon me, because I have no opportunities of relaxation or diversion. I am sometimes ashamed to think that I could not secure myself from vice, but by retiring from the exercise[c] of virtue,[3] and begin to suspect that I was rather impelled by resentment, than led by devotion, into solitude.

a. preferments 59b   b. feeling . . . was 59b] finding my vigour 59a
c. exercise 59b] practice 59a

---

9. Cf. SJ's comment on Cowley in *Rambler* 6 (par. 14): "He forgot, in the vehemence of desire, that solitude and quiet owe their pleasures to those miseries, which he was so studious to obviate; for such are the vicissitudes of the world, through all its parts, that day and night, labour and rest, hurry and retirement, endear each other; such are the changes that keep the mind in action; we desire, we pursue, we obtain, we are satiated; we desire something else, and begin a new persuit."

1. See p. 33, n. 2, above.

2. Sir George MacKenzie's essay extolling solitude mentions researches into "flowers, anatomy," and other "sci-

ences" as examples of the "employment or divertisement" offered by the solitary life (*Essays upon Several Moral Subjects* [1713], p. 139).

3. In *Rambler* 44 (par. 9), SJ's friend Elizabeth Carter declares that "society is the true sphere of human virtue. In social, active life, difficulties will perpetually be met with; restraints of many kinds will be necessary; and studying to behave right in respect of these is a discipline of the human heart, useful to others, and improving to itself." Cf. SJ's later remarks on religious orders, virtue, and vice: "It is as unreasonable for a man to go into a Carthusian convent for fear of being

My fancy riots[4] in scenes of folly,[5] and I lament that I have lost so much, and have gained so little. In solitude, if I escape the example of bad men, I want likewise the counsel and conversation of the good. I have been long comparing the evils with the advantages of society,[6] and resolve to return into the world to morrow.[7] The life of a solitary man will be certainly miserable, but not certainly devout."

They heard his resolution with surprise, but, after a short pause, offered to conduct him to Cairo. He dug up a considerable treasure which he had hid[8] among the rocks, and accompanied them to the city, on which, as he approached it, he gazed with rapture.[9]

Chap. XXII.

The happiness of a life led according to nature.[1]

---

immoral, as for a man to cut off his hands for fear he should steal. . . . I said to the Lady Abbess of a convent, 'Madam, you are here, not for the love of virtue, but the fear of vice.' She said, 'She should remember this as long as she lived'" (*Life*, II.434–35).

4. See p. 79, n. 9, above.

5. Cf. *Idler* 32 (par. 12): "Many have no happier moments than those that they pass in solitude, abandoned to their own imagination, which sometimes puts sceptres in their hands or mitres on their heads, shifts the scene of pleasure with endless variety, bids all the forms of beauty sparkle before them, and gluts them with every change of visionary luxury."

6. Cf. *Rambler* 104 (par. 1): "The apparent insufficiency of every individual to his own happiness or safety, compels us to seek from one another assistance and support."

7. See p. 13, n. 8, above.

8. In SJ's *Dictionary*, both *hid* and *hidden* are listed as "*part. pass.* of *hide.*"

9. The hermit's delight exemplifies SJ's contention in *Rambler* 207 (par. 7)

that "every man . . . consoles himself with the hope of change; if . . . he is secluded from the world, he listens with a beating heart to distant noises, longs to mingle with living beings, and resolves to take hereafter his fill of diversions."

1. The latter part of this chapter, as the following notes to specific passages make clear, contains a satiric pastiche of notions regarding the law of nature and associated religious-philosophical concepts. Donald Greene has pointed out that "a life led according to nature" is a translation of the Stoic catchword invented by Zeno of Citium (as reported by Diogenes Laertius in his *Lives of the Philosophers*) and latinized as *secundum naturam vivere* by Lipsius. SJ owned copies of both Laertius and Lipsius. Assertions that Rousseau (in his *Discourses*) was the object of SJ's ridicule are examined by Gwin J. Kolb in "Rousseau and the Background of the 'Life Led according to Nature' in Chapter 22 of *Rasselas*," *Modern Philology*, LXXIII, No. 4, Pt. 2 (1976), S66–S73.

Rasselas[a] went often to an assembly of learned men,[2] who met at stated times to unbend their minds, and compare their opinions. Their manners were somewhat coarse, but their conversation was instructive, and their disputations acute, though sometimes too violent, and often continued till neither controvertist[3] remembered upon what question they began. Some faults were almost general among them: every one was desirous to dictate to the rest, and every one was pleased to hear the genius or knowledge of another depreciated.

In this assembly Rasselas was relating his interview with the hermit, and the wonder with which he heard him censure a course of life which he had so deliberately chosen, and so laudably followed. The sentiments of the hearers were various. Some were of opinion, that the folly of his choice had been justly punished by condemnation to perpetual perseverance.[4] One of the youngest among them, with great vehemence, pronounced him an hypocrite.[5] Some talked of the right of society to the labour of individuals, and considered retirement as a desertion of duty.[6]

a. Rasselas 59b] Rassselas 59a

---

2. Emerson points out that "literary clubs were a characteristic feature of eighteenth-century life in London" (p. 162).

3. *Controvertist:* "Disputant; a man versed or engaged in literary wars or disputations" (*Dictionary*). Jeremy Collier, SJ writes in the "Life of Congreve," "was formed for a controvertist; with sufficient learning; with diction vehement and pointed, though often vulgar and incorrect; with unconquerable pertinacity; with wit in the highest degree keen and sarcastick; and with all those powers exalted and invigorated by just confidence in his cause" (*Lives*, II.220–21, par. 19).

4. *Perseverance:* "Persistence in any design or attempt; steadiness in pursuits; constancy in progress. It is applied alike to good and ill" (sense 1 in *Dictionary*).

5. Cf. *Idler* 27 (par. 8): "It is not uncommon to charge the difference between promise and performance, between profession and reality, upon deep design and studied deceit; but the truth is, that there is very little hypocrisy in the world; we do not so often endeavour or wish to impose on others as on ourselves."

6. In *Idler* 19 (par. 2), SJ comments that "mankind is one vast republick, where every individual receives many benefits from the labours of others, which, by labouring in his turn for others, he is obliged to repay; and . . . where the united efforts of all are not able to exempt all from misery, none have a right to withdraw from their task of vigilance, or to be indulged in idle wisdom or solitary pleasures." Cf. *Life*, IV.223.

Others readily allowed, that there was a time when the claims of the publick were satisfied, and when a man might properly sequester himself, to review his life, and purify his heart.[7]

One, who appeared more affected with the narrative than the rest, thought it likely, that the hermit would, in a few years, go back to his retreat, and, perhaps, if shame did not restrain, or death intercept him, return once more from his retreat into the world: "For the hope of happiness," said[b] he, "is so strongly impressed, that the longest experience is not able to efface it. Of the present state, whatever it be, we feel, and are forced to confess, the misery,[8] yet, when the same state is again at a distance, imagination paints it as desirable. But the time will surely come, when desire will be no longer our torment, and no man shall be wretched but by his own fault."[9]

"This," said a philosopher, who had heard him with tokens of great impatience, "is the present condition of a wise man. The time is already come, when none are wretched but by their own fault.[1] Nothing is more idle, than to enquire after happiness, which nature has kindly placed within our reach.[2] The way to be happy is to live according

b. said _59b_] says _59a_

---

7. In _Idler_ 38 (par. 11), SJ says that "perhaps retirement ought rarely to be permitted, except to those whose employment is consistent with abstraction, and who, tho' solitary, will not be idle; to those whom infirmity makes useless to the commonwealth, or to those who have paid their due proportion to society, and who, having lived for others, may be honourably dismissed to live for themselves." Cf. his remarks on retirement in _Life_, v.62–63.

8. Cf. _Adventurer_ 120 (par. 2): "There is . . . no topic on which it is more superfluous to accumulate authorities, nor any assertion of which our own eyes will more easily discover, or our sensations more frequently impress the truth, than, that misery is the lot of man, that our present state is a state of danger and infelicity."

9. Declaring in _Adventurer_ 120 (par. 13) that "the miseries of life, may, perhaps, afford some proof of a future state," SJ concludes: "there will surely come a time, when every capacity of happiness shall be filled, and none shall be wretched but by his own fault."

1. Cf. Le Grand's statement, in his _Man without Passion_, that he "wonder[s] not that man should be so miserable since he himself is a conspirator against his own felicity, . . . since he takes pride in his own miseries, and emploies all [nature's] benefits to make himself unhappy or guilty" (p. 115).

2. Le Grand expresses a similar view: "Nature is too liberal to deny us our desires," he says. "She is too noble to

to nature, in obedience to that universal and unalterable law with which every heart is originally impressed;[3] which is not written on it by precept, but engraven by destiny, not instilled by education, but infused at our nativity.[4] He that lives according to nature will suffer nothing from the delusions of hope, or importunities of desire: he will receive and reject with equability of temper; and act or suffer as the reason of things shall alternately prescribe.[5] Other men may amuse themselves with subtle definitions, or intricate

---

refuse us a gift [happiness] which she preserves for us in the cabinet of our soul: and her guide is too faithful to carry us astray from that good to which we aspire" (p. 16).

3. In his *Christianity as Old as the Creation* (1731), the deist Matthew Tindal posits human happiness as the end of natural religion, which has always been "universal, unchangeable, & indelibly implanted in human-nature." "It can't be deny'd," he says, "that the end for which God implanted this religion in human nature, was to make men happy here as well as hereafter; (God's will in relation to man & human happiness being equivalent terms) & therefore, he cou'd not, at any time, leave them destitute of the most proper means to answer this end" (p. 257). Also cf. Samuel Clarke's assertion—drawn from Cicero's *De re publica* (3.22.33) and *De legibus* (1.6.19; 2.4.8; 2.4.10)—that the "law of nature . . . is of universal extent, and everlasting duration; . . . can neither be wholly abrogated, nor repealed in any part of it . . . : Which being founded in the nature and reason of things . . . is of the same original with the eternal reasons or proportions of things" (*A Discourse concerning the Unchangeable Obligations of Natural Religion, and the Truth and Certainty of the Christian Revelation*, 6th ed. [1724], p. 65).

4. As first noted by the reviewer

(Owen Ruffhead; see Introduction, pp. xlvii–xlix above) in the *Monthly Review* for May 1759 (xx.433), this passage seems to be a translation of Cicero's description of the law of nature contained in his oration for Milo, section 10: "*ad quam non docti, sed facti, non instituti, sed imbuti sumus*" ("which comes to us not by education but by constitution, not by training but by intuition," *Cicero: The Speeches*, ed. N. H. Watts [Loeb Library, 1931], pp. 16, 17). Also cf. Tindal's insistence, in *Christianity as Old as the Creation*, that "there's a religion of nature & reason written in the hearts of every one of us from the first creation, by which all mankind must judge of the truth of any instituted religion whatever" (p. 52); the assertion by a speaker in Philip Skelton's *Ophiomaches; or Deism Revealed* (2 vols., 1749) that the "law of nature" is "implanted in the breasts of all men, and adequate to all their moral purposes. As every one must acknowledge there is such a law within him, independent of all instruction, there can be no need of a revelation" (i.51).

5. Cf. Clarke's comment that the "same reason of things" which causes God "to act in constant conformity . . . to justice, equity, goodness and truth; *ought* also" to make men "govern all their actions by the same rules" (*A Discourse concerning the Unchangeable Obligations of Natural Religion*, p. 39).

raciocination. Let them learn to be wise by easier means: let them observe the hind of the forest, and the linnet of the grove: let them consider the life of animals, whose motions are regulated by instinct; they obey their guide and are happy.[6] Let us therefore, at length, cease to dispute, and learn to live; throw away the incumbrance of precepts,[7] which they who utter them with so much pride and pomp do not understand, and carry with us this simple and intelligible maxim, That deviation from nature is deviation from happiness."[8]

When he had spoken, he looked round him with a placid air, and enjoyed the consciousness of his own beneficence. "Sir," said the prince, with great modesty, "as I, like all the rest of mankind, am desirous of felicity, my closest attention has been fixed upon your discourse: I doubt not the truth of a position which a man so learned has so confidently advanced. Let me only know what it is to live according to nature."

---

6. With the philosopher's counsel, cf. this passage from Tindal's *Christianity as Old as the Creation:* "When we see with what skill & contrivance, birds, without being taught by any, but the God of Nature, build their nests; and how artfully the spiders frame their webs . . . and the beasts avoid all noxious herbs: And not to multiply instances, how all animals are endow'd with sufficient sagacity, for preserving themselves & species; must we not own, that what we call *instinct*, is a certain & infallible guide for inferior animals? and can we doubt, whether man, the Lord of the Creation, has not from his superior reason, sufficient notices of whatever makes for his greatest, his eternal happiness" (p. 252). In his *Sermons* (1729), Joseph Butler paraphrases a similar argument and then brands it "licentious talk"; the words "following Nature," he declares, have quite another sense than that of "bare-

ly acting as we please" (pp. 29–30, 31–32).

7. Cf. Le Grand's remark in *Man without Passion* that those who "observe nature" have no need for the "precepts of morality [which] have yet produced but paper vertues" (p. 16).

8. According to Tindal in *Christianity as Old as the Creation,* "if the highest internal excellence, the greatest plainness & simplicity, unanimity, universality, antiquity . . . can recommend a law; all these, 'tis own'd do, in an eminent degree, belong to the law of nature" (pp. 55–56). Tindal is also sure that "every deviation from the rules of right reason being an imperfection, must carry with it a proportionable unhappiness" (p. 19); and that "happy is the man, who is so far, at least, directed by the law of reason, and the religion of nature, as to suffer no mysteries or unintelligible propositions . . . to confound his understanding" (p. 209).

"When I find young men so humble and so docile," said the philosopher, "I can deny them no information which my studies have enabled me to afford. To live according to nature, is to act always with due regard to the fitness arising from the relations and qualities of causes and effects;[9] to concur with the great and unchangeable scheme of universal felicity; to co-operate with the general disposition and tendency of the present system of things."

The prince soon found that this was one of the sages whom he should understand less as he heard him longer.[1] He therefore bowed and was silent, and the philosopher, supposing him satisfied, and the rest vanquished, rose up

---

9. Samuel Clarke was probably the best known English expounder of the concept of "fitness." Regarding the basis of moral obligation, he declares, for example: "The same necessary and eternal 'different relations,' that different things bear one to another; and the same consequent 'fitness or unfitness' of the application of different things or different relations one to another, with regard to which the will of God always and necessarily *does* determine it self . . . *ought* likewise constantly to determine the wills of all subordinate rational beings, to govern all their actions by the same rules, for the good of the publick in their respective stations" (*A Discourse* , p. 4). Also cf. the description of Fielding's "philosopher" Square, who "measured all actions by the 'unalterable rule of right' and the 'eternal fitness of things'" (*Tom Jones*, book 3, chapter 3). At the end of Part IX, "On Moral Philosophy," of *The Preceptor* (3d ed., 1758, II.380), "A Life according to Nature" is defined as acting "'in a conformity to our original constitution, and in a subordination to the eternal order of things.'"

1. Like Rasselas, some eighteenth-century commentators were puzzled by the explication of such concepts as the

fitness of things, moral obligation, virtue, etc. "'Tis very observable," complains Thomas Johnson in *An Essay on Moral Obligation* (1731), "that the maintainers ["Dr. Clark and his followers"] of this 'natural, necessary, or independent fitness' of things and actions, have constantly declined letting us know what they mean by 'moral obligation' (except a synonomous term can be called a definition) and when they are called upon for a reason, why these fitnesses or relations *must* be obeyed, or our actions regulated by them, their answer is, that 'tis self-evident, that all men must perceive it as such" (p. 25). Again, in his *Essays on the Characteristics* (1751), John Brown asks, "What is 'right reason,' and what these 'eternal Relations' which are affirmed [by Clarke] to be the test or criterion of virtue?" "'Tis observable," he continues, "that when [Clarke] comes to prove the truth and reality of these 'Relations,' he is forced to resolve into a 'self-evident' proposition. . . . And as the 'sublime' and 'beautiful' give us no more determinate ideas than the 'virtuous,' so neither can we obtain any additional information from the 'fit' and 'reasonable'" (5th ed., 1764, pp. 118–19).

and departed with the air of a man that had co-operated with the present system.

Chap. XXIII.

The prince and his sister divide between them the work of observation.

Rasselas returned home full of reflexions, doubtful how to direct his future steps. Of the way to happiness he found the learned and simple equally ignorant; but, as he was yet young,[1] he flattered himself that he had time remaining for more experiments, and further enquiries. He communicated to Imlac his observations and his doubts, but was answered by him with new doubts, and remarks that gave him no comfort. He therefore discoursed more frequently and freely with his sister, who had yet the same hope with himself, and always assisted him to give some reason why, though he had been hitherto frustrated, he might succeed at last.

"We have hitherto," said she, "known but little of the world: we have never yet been either great or mean. In our own country, though we had royalty, we had no power, and in this we have not yet seen the private recesses of domestick peace. Imlac favours not our search, lest we should in time find him mistaken. We will divide the task between us: you shall try what is to be found in the splendour of courts, and I will range the shades of humbler life. Perhaps command and authority may be the supreme blessings, as they

---

1. Hill has pointed out that "Rasselas by this time was about thirty-two. He is in his twenty-sixth year at the opening of the story . . . ; he passes twenty months 'in visionary bustle' . . . ; and four months 'in resolving to lose no more time in idle resolves'. . . . Ten months he spent in 'fruitless researches' for a means of escape . . . ; and a year with the inventor of the wings. . . . Some months, perhaps a year, must be given to his conversations with Imlac, to digging the outlet, and to the journey to Cairo. In that town they studied the language two years . . . before they began their 'experiments upon life.' That Shakespeare makes Hamlet thirty years old often raises wonder. It is more surprising that Rasselas should be represented as thirty-two" (pp. 181–82).

afford most opportunities of doing good: or, perhaps, what this world can give may be found in the modest habitations of middle fortune; too low for great designs, and too high for penury and distress."

Chap. XXIV.

The prince examines the happiness of high stations.

Rasselas applauded the design, and appeared next day with a splendid retinue at the court of the Bassa. He was soon distinguished for his magnificence, and admitted, as a prince whose curiosity had brought him from distant countries, to an intimacy with the great officers, and frequent conversation with the Bassa himself.

He was at first inclined to believe, that the man must be pleased with his own condition, whom all approached with reverence, and heard with obedience, and who had the power to extend his edicts to a whole kingdom. "There can be no pleasure," said he, "equal to that of feeling at once the joy of thousands all made happy by wise administration. Yet, since, by the law of subordination, this sublime delight can be in one nation but the lot of one, it is surely reasonable to think that[a] there is some satisfaction more popular[1] and accessible,[2] and that millions can hardly be subjected to the will of a single man, only to fill his particular breast with incommunicable content."

These thoughts were often in his mind, and he found no solution of the difficulty. But as presents and civilities gained him more familiarity, he found that almost every man who[b] stood high in employment hated all the rest, and

a. that *added* 59b   b. who 59b] that 59a

1. Hardy glosses (p. 155) *popular* as "belonging to the people."
2. Cf. SJ's comment in the *Life:* "I agree with Mr. Boswell that there must be a high satisfaction in being a feudal lord; but we are to consider, that we ought not to wish to have a number of men unhappy for the satisfaction of one" (II.178; see also v.106).

was hated by them, and that their lives were a continual succession of plots and detections, stratagems and escapes, faction and treachery. Many of those, who surrounded the Bassa, were sent only to watch and report his conduct; every tongue was muttering censure, and every eye was searching for a fault.

At last the letters of revocation arrived,[3] the Bassa was carried in chains to Constantinople,[4] and his name was mentioned no more.

"What are we now to think of the prerogatives of power," said Rasselas to his sister; "is it without any efficacy to good? or, is the subordinate degree only dangerous, and the supreme safe and glorious? Is the Sultan the only happy man in his dominions? or, is the Sultan himself subject to the torments of suspicion, and the dread of enemies?"

In a short time the second Bassa was deposed.[5] The Sultan, that had advanced him, was murdered by the Janisaries,[6] and his successor had other views and different favourites.

Chap. XXV.

The princess persues her enquiry with more diligence than success.

The princess, in the mean time, insinuated[1] herself into

---

3. *Revocation:* "Act of recalling" (sense 1 in *Dictionary*). The *OED* notes: "In 17–18th cent. esp. the recall of a representative or ambassador from abroad; also in 'letters of revocation.'"

4. The section of *The Preceptor* on Egypt points out that "Egypt is at present a province of the Turkish empire; and is govern'd by a particular Bassa, . . . whose post is generally esteem'd the most honourable government of any belonging to the Turkish empire" (3d ed., 1758, 1.267). Egypt had become a province in 1517.

5. After citing the unwillingness of a

particular Bassa of Suaquem to act upon certain "proposals of traffick," *Voyage to Abyssinia* observes that "the condition of a Turkish officer is too uncertain to allow him to entertain prospects of future advantages" (p. 127).

6. *Janizary:* "One of the guards of the Turkish king" (*Dictionary*). In the section of *The Preceptor* on Turkey, we are told that the janizaries, "esteem'd the best soldiers in the Turkish armies," "frequently grow mutinous, and have proceeded so far sometimes as to depose the sultan" (3d ed., 1758, 1.230).

1. *To insinuate:* "To push gently into

many families; for there are few doors, through which
liberality, joined with good humour, cannot find its way.
The daughters of many houses were airy[2] and chearful, but
Nekayah had been too long accustomed to the conversation
of Imlac and her brother to be much pleased with childish
levity and prattle which had no meaning. She found their
thoughts narrow, their wishes low, and their merriment
often artificial. Their pleasures, poor as they were, could
not be preserved pure, but were embittered by petty competitions and worthless emulation. They were always jealous of the beauty of each other; of a quality to which
solicitude can add nothing, and from which detraction can
take nothing away. Many were in love with triflers like
themselves, and many fancied that they were in love when
in truth they were only idle. Their affection was seldom
fixed on sense or virtue, and therefore seldom ended but in
vexation. Their grief, however, like their joy, was transient;
every thing floated in their mind unconnected with the past
or future, so that one desire easily gave way to another, as a
second stone cast into the water effaces and confounds the
circles of the first.

With these girls she played as with inoffensive animals,
and found them proud of her countenance,[3] and weary of
her company.

But her purpose was to examine more deeply, and her
affability easily persuaded the hearts that were swelling
with sorrow to discharge their secrets in her ear: and
those whom hope flattered, or prosperity delighted, often
courted her to partake their pleasures.

The princess and her brother commonly met in the evening in a private summer-house on the bank of the Nile,
and related to each other the occurrences of the day. As

---

favour or regard: commonly with the
reciprocal pronoun" (sense 2 in *Dictionary*).

2. *Airy:* "Gay; sprightly; full of mirth;
vivacious; lively; spirited; light of
heart" (sense 8 in *Dictionary*). SJ once

called Mrs. Cholmondeley "a very airy
lady" (*Life*, v.248).

3. *Countenance:* "Patronage; appearance of favour; appearance on any
side; support" (sense 6 in *Dictionary*).

they were sitting together, the princess cast her eyes upon the river that flowed before her. "Answer," said she, "great father of waters,[4] thou that rollest thy floods through eighty nations, to the invocations of the daughter of thy native king. Tell me if thou waterest, through all thy course, a single habitation from which thou dost not hear the murmurs of complaint?"

"You are then," said Rasselas, "not more successful in private houses than I have been in courts." "I have, since the last partition of our provinces,"[5] said the princess, "enabled myself to enter familiarly into many families, where there was the fairest show of prosperity and peace, and know not one house that is not haunted by some fury[a] that destroys its quiet.

"I did not seek ease among the poor, because I concluded that there it could not be found.[6] But I saw many poor whom I had supposed to live in affluence. Poverty has, in large cities, very different appearances: it is often concealed in splendour,[7] and often in extravagance. It is the care of a very great part of mankind to conceal their indigence from

a. fury 59b] fiend 59a

---

4. In the "Life of Gray," SJ severely criticized the poet's use of a similar apostrophe in the *Ode on a Distant Prospect of Eton College:* "His supplication to father Thames, to tell him who drives the hoop or tosses the ball, is useless and puerile. Father Thames has no better means of knowing than himself" (*Lives,* III.434–35, par. 30). See also p. 7, n. 5, above.

5. *Province:* "The proper office or business of any one" (sense 2 in *Dictionary*).

6. SJ repeatedly asserted the absence of felicity among the poor. In *Rambler* 57 (par. 5), he says that "mankind seem unanimous . . . in abhorring [poverty] as destructive to happiness." In *Rambler* 53 (par. 2), he declares that "in the prospect of poverty, there is nothing

but gloom and melancholy; the mind and body suffer together; its miseries bring no alleviations; it is a state in which every virtue is obscured, and in which no conduct can avoid reproach: a state in which cheerfulness is insensibility, and dejection sullenness, of which the hardships are without honour, and the labours without reward." Also cf. his comments about poverty in the review (*Literary Magazine* [1757], pp. 171–75, 251–53, 301–06) of Soame Jenyns's *Free Enquiry into the Nature and Origin of Evil* (1757); *Life,* IV.149, 152, 157.

7. Cf. the following anecdote reported by Mrs. Piozzi in *Thraliana,* ed. Katharine C. Balderston (2d ed., 1951), I.199: "We drank tea at a house where the plate was splendid, & the china

the rest: they support themselves by temporary expedients, and every day is lost in contriving for the morrow.[8]

"This, however, was an evil, which, though frequent, I saw with less pain, because I could relieve it. Yet some have refused my bounties; more offended with my quickness to detect their wants, than pleased with my readiness to succour them:[9] and others, whose exigencies compelled them to admit my kindness, have never been able to forgive their benefactress.[1] Many, however, have been sincerely grateful without the ostentation of gratitude, or the hope of other favours."

END of the FIRST VOLUME.

Chap. XXVI.

The princess continues her remarks upon private life.

Nekayah perceiving her brother's attention fixed, proceeded in her narrative.

---

elegant—the footman waited however in a ragged livery: as we came home I mentioned it: why ay says [SJ] you may shut poverty out of the door if you please; but the jade will poke her pale face in at the window." Declaring that "there is no place where œconomy can be so well practised as in London," SJ also observed: "You cannot play tricks with your fortune in a small place; you must make an uniform appearance. Here a lady may have well-furnished apartments, and elegant dress, without any meat in her kitchen" (*Life*, III.378). Also cf. *Anecdotes* (1.317).

8. Cf. SJ's comment in *Adventurer* 120 (par. 7) that "there is in the world more poverty than is generally imagined" and that "great numbers," "pressed by real necessities which it is their chief ambition to conceal," "are forced to purchase the appearance of competence and cheerfulness at the expense of many comforts and conveniencies of

life" (*Idler* 17, par. 2). Cf. SJ's observations on poverty in Sermons 4, 5, 19 (*Sermons*, ed. Jean H. Hagstrum and James Gray, Vol. XIV, Yale Edition of the Works of Samuel Johnson, 1978, pp. 46–48 and n. 2, 58–59 and n. 6, 207 and n. 6).

9. While a poor student at Oxford University, SJ himself, as is well known, "threw . . . away with indignation" "a pair of new shoes" which someone had placed "at his door" (*Life*, 1.77).

1. In *Rambler* 87 (par. 9), SJ remarks that "there are minds so impatient ["not able to endure" (*Dictionary*)] of inferiority, that their gratitude is a species of revenge, and they return benefits, not because recompence is a pleasure, but because obligation is a pain." In *Rambler* 166 (par. 8), he comments that "to be obliged, is to be in some respect inferior to another." Cf. *Life*, 1.246.

"In families, where there is or is not poverty, there is commonly discord: if a kingdom be, as Imlac tells us, a great family, a family likewise is a little kingdom,[1] torn with factions and exposed to revolutions. An unpractised observer expects the love of parents[2] and children to be constant and equal; but this kindness seldom continues beyond the years of infancy: in a short time the children become rivals to their parents.[3] Benefits are allayed[4] by reproaches, and gratitude debased by envy.

"Parents and children seldom act in concert: each child endeavours to appropriate the esteem or fondness of the parents,[5] and the parents, with yet less temptation, betray each other to their children; thus some place their confidence in the father, and some in the mother, and, by degrees, the house is filled with artifices and feuds.

"The opinions of children and parents, of the young and the old, are naturally opposite,[6] by the contrary effects of

---

1. In *Rambler* 148 (par. 7), SJ quotes approvingly Aristotle's observation (*Politics*, I.2.21 [A7.1255^{b}19]) that "the government of a family is naturally monarchical."

2. Cf. the following exchange between Boswell and SJ: "BOSWELL. 'Do you think, Sir, that what is called natural affection is born with us?'... JOHNSON. 'Why, Sir, I think there is an instinctive natural affection in parents towards their children'" (*Life*, II.101). Later, however, SJ declared that "'natural affection is nothing: but affection from principle and established duty is sometimes wonderfully strong'" (*Life*, IV.210).

3. Cf. *Rambler* 55, written by a supposed correspondent, "unhappily a woman before my mother can willingly cease to be a girl," who says that the Rambler "would contribute to the happiness of many families, if, by any arguments or persuasions, you could make mothers ashamed of rivalling their children" (final par.). In the *Life* (I.427), SJ remarks that "there must al-

ways be a struggle between a father and son, while one aims at power and the other at independence."

4. *To allay:* "To join any thing to another, so as to abate its predominant qualities. It is used commonly in a sense contrary to its original meaning, and is, to make something bad, less bad. To obtund; to repress; to abate" (sense 2 in *Dictionary*). In the *Life*, SJ seemingly uses the term *unalloyed*, which, unlike *unallayed*, is not listed in his *Dictionary* (III.388; see p. 166, n. 4, below); however, Hill may be correct in saying that "probably [Boswell] uses the form of the word to which he himself was accustomed" (p. 185).

5. In her *Anecdotes*, Mrs. Piozzi comments that SJ and his brother Nathaniel "did not . . . much delight in each other's company, being always rivals for the mother's fondness; and many of the severe reflections on domestic life in *Rasselas* took their source from its author's keen recollections of the time passed in his early years" (I.150–51).

6. Cf. *Rambler* 196 (par. 3), which de-

hope and despondence, of expectation and experience, without crime or folly on either side. The colours of life in youth and age appear different, as the face of nature in spring and winter.⁷ And how can children credit the assertions of parents, which their own eyes show them to be false?⁸

"Few parents act in such a manner as much to enforce their maxims by the credit of their lives.⁹ The old man trusts wholly to slow contrivance and gradual progression: the youth expects to force his way by genius, vigour, and precipitance.¹ The old man pays regard to riches,² and the youth reverences virtue.³ The old man deifies prudence:⁴

---

scribes the "revolution of sentiments" that causes "a perpetual contest between the old and young."

7. Cf. *Rambler* 69 (par. 7): "So different are the colours of life, as we look forward to the future, or backward to the past; and so different the opinions and sentiments which this contrariety of appearance naturally produces, that the conversation of the old and young ends generally with contempt or pity on either side"; *Rambler* 50 (par. 11): "It is a hopeless endeavour to unite the contrarieties of spring and winter; it is unjust to claim the privileges of age, and retain the play-things of childhood."

8. SJ asks a similar question in *Rambler* 50 (par. 9). "Can it raise much wonder," he inquires, if the old "see their posterity rather willing to trust their own eyes in their progress into life, than enlist themselves under guides who have lost their way?"

9. Cf. *Rambler* 50 (par. 10): "The teacher gains few proselytes by instruction which his own behavior contradicts."

1. With this sentence, cf. the following passage from *Rambler* 111 (par. 3): "At our entrance into the world, when health and vigour give us fair promises of time sufficient for the regular matu-

ration of our schemes, and a long enjoyment of our acquisitions, we are eager to seize the present moment; we pluck every gratification within our reach . . . , and croud all the varieties of delight into a narrow compass: but age seldom fails to change our conduct; we grow negligent of time in proportion as we have less remaining, and suffer the last part of life to steal from us in languid preparations for future undertakings, or slow approaches to remote advantages."

2. Cf. *Rambler* 69 (par. 4): "The most usual support of old age is wealth. He whose possessions are large, and whose chests are full, imagines himself always fortified against invasions on his authority."

3. In the *Life,* SJ declares that "young men have more virtue than old men; they have more generous sentiments in every respect" (1.445). According to Mrs. Piozzi, he "was always on the side of the children against the old folks— old people says he have no honour, no delicacy; the world has blunted their sensibility & appetite or avarice governs the last stage" (*Thraliana,* ed. Katharine Balderston, 1.181).

4. *Prudence:* "Wisdom applied to practice" (*Dictionary*).

the youth commits himself to magnanimity and chance. The young man, who intends no ill, believes that none is intended, and therefore acts with openness and candour:[5] but his father, having suffered the injuries of fraud, is impelled to suspect, and too often allured to practice it. Age looks with anger on the temerity of youth, and youth with contempt on the scrupulosity of age.[6] Thus parents and children, for the greatest part, live on to love less and less: and, if those whom nature has thus closely united are the torments of each other, where shall we look for tenderness and consolation?"

"Surely," said the prince, "you must have been unfortunate in your choice of acquaintance:[7] I am unwilling to believe, that the most tender of all relations is thus impeded in its effects by natural necessity."

"Domestick discord," answered she, "is not inevitably and fatally[8] necessary; but yet is not easily avoided. We seldom see that a whole family is virtuous: the good and evil[9]

---

5. *Candour:* "Sweetness of temper; purity of mind; openness; ingenuity; kindness" (*Dictionary*). Describing the traits of youth in notes for what became *Rambler* 196, SJ characterizes the young man as "confident of others . . . , never imagines they will venture to treat him ill. Ready to trust; expecting to be trusted"—but "convinced by time of the selfishness . . . , the treachery of men" (*Life,* ii.206).

6. As Hill points out (p. 185), *scrupulosity* "was a favorite word with Johnson" (cf. its use on p. 161 below). In *Rambler* 69 (par. 7), SJ observes that "to a young man entering the world, with fulness of hope, and ardor of persuit, nothing is so unpleasing as the cold caution, the faint expectations, the scrupulous diffidence which experience and disappointments certainly infuse; and the old man wonders in his turn that the world never can grow wiser, that neither precepts, nor testimonies, can cure boys of their credulity

and sufficiency; and that not one can be convinced that snares are laid for him, till he finds himself entangled."

Nekayah's description of the antithetical characters of youth and age resembles earlier versions of a commonplace extending back as far as Aristotle's *Rhetoric* (ii.xii–xiii [1389^a–1390^b]), which mentions most of the individual traits specified by the princess. Also cf. Bacon's essay "Of Youth and Age."

7. See p. 64, n. 4, above.

8. *Fatally:* "By the decree of fate; by inevitable and invincible determination" (sense 2 in *Dictionary*). Cf. the meaning of *fatal,* p. 18, n. 7, above.

9. In his edition (1895) of *Rasselas,* O. F. Emerson records (p. 71) the *59a* reading as "the good and the evil" (see also his article on "The Text of Johnson's *Rasselas*" [*Anglia,* xxii (Dec 1899), 504]); like *RWC* (p. 225), I have not found a copy of *59a* with this reading.

cannot well agree; and the evil can yet less agree with one another: even the virtuous fall sometimes to variance, when their virtues are of different kinds, and tending to extremes.[1] In general, those parents have most reverence who most deserve it: for he that lives well cannot be despised.

"Many other evils infest private life. Some are the slaves of servants whom they have trusted with their affairs. Some are kept in continual anxiety to the caprice of rich relations, whom they cannot please, and dare not offend. Some husbands are imperious, and some wives perverse: and, as it is always more easy to do evil than good, though the wisdom or virtue of one can very rarely make many happy, the folly or vice of one may often make many miserable."[2]

"If such be the general effect of marriage," said the prince, "I shall, for the future, think it dangerous to connect my interest with that of another, lest I should be unhappy by my partner's fault."

"I have met," said the princess, "with many who live single for that reason; but I never found that their prudence ought to raise envy. They dream away their time without friendship, without fondness, and are driven to rid themselves of the day, for which they have no use, by childish amusements, or vicious delights. They act as beings under the constant sense of some known inferiority, that fills their minds with rancour, and their tongues with censure. They are peevish at home, and malevolent abroad; and, as the out-laws of human nature, make it their business and their pleasure to disturb that society which debars them from its privileges. To live without feeling or exciting sympathy, to be fortunate without adding to the felicity of others, or afflicted without tasting the balm of pity, is a state

---

1. Cf. SJ's comment that "virtue almost never produces freindship [sic]. . . . Enmity takes place between men who are good different ways" (*Life*, IV.530).

2. Cf. Sermon 1 (par. 7): "Every man may injure a family, and produce domestic disorders and distresses; almost every one has opportunities, and perhaps sometimes temptations, to rebel as a wife, or tyrannize as a husband."

more gloomy than solitude: it is not retreat but exclusion from mankind. Marriage has many pains, but celibacy has no pleasures."[3]

"What then is to be done?" said Rasselas; "the more we enquire, the less we can resolve. Surely he is most likely to please himself that has no other inclination to regard."

Chap. XXVII.

Disquisition upon greatness.

The conversation had a short pause. The prince, having considered his sister's observations, told her, that she had surveyed life with prejudice, and supposed misery where she did not find it. "Your narrative," says he, "throws yet a darker gloom upon the prospects of futurity: the predictions of Imlac were but faint sketches of the evils painted by Nekayah. I have been lately convinced that quiet is not the daughter of grandeur, or of power: that her presence is not to be bought by wealth, nor enforced by conquest. It is evident, that as any man acts in a wider compass, he must be more exposed to opposition from enmity[1] or miscarriage from chance; whoever has many to please or to govern,

---

3. At the beginning of *Rambler* 18 (par. 1), which is largely devoted to a recital of unhappy marriages, SJ says: "There is no observation more frequently made by such as employ themselves in surveying the conduct of mankind, than that marriage, though the dictate of nature, and the institution of providence, is yet very often the cause of misery, and that those who enter into that state can seldom forbear to express their repentance, and their envy of those whom either chance or caution has witheld [*sic*] from it." On the other hand, in *Rambler* 115 (final par.), he states, via the character Hymenaeus, that "I believe [marriage] able to afford the highest happiness decreed to our present state." And on other occasions he expressed the opinion that "marriage is the best state for man in general" and that "even ill assorted marriages were preferable to cheerless celibacy" (*Life*, II.457, 128). Cf. *Letters* 147.

1. Cf. *Adventurer* 120 (par. 8): "The highest of mankind can promise themselves no exemption from that discord or suspicion, by which the sweetness of domestic retirement is destroyed; and must always be even more exposed, in the same degree as they are elevated above others, to the treachery of dependants, the calumny of defamers, and the violence of opponents."

must use the ministry of many agents, some of whom will be wicked, and some ignorant; by some he will be misled, and by others betrayed.[2] If he gratifies one he will offend another: those that are not favoured will think themselves injured; and, since favours can be conferred but upon few, the greater number will be always discontented."[3]

"The discontent," said the princess, "which is thus unreasonable, I hope that I shall always have spirit to despise, and you, power to repress."

"Discontent," answered Rasselas, "will not always be without reason under the most just or vigilant administration of publick affairs. None, however attentive, can always discover that merit which indigence[4] or faction may happen to obscure; and none, however powerful, can always reward it. Yet, he that sees inferiour desert advanced above him, will naturally impute that preference to partiality or caprice; and, indeed, it can scarcely be hoped that any man, however magnanimous by nature, or exalted by condition, will be able to persist for ever in fixed and inexorable justice of distribution: he will sometimes indulge his own affections, and sometimes those of his favourites; he will permit some to please him who can never serve him; he will discover in those whom he loves qualities which in reality they do not possess; and to those, from whom he receives pleasure, he will in his turn endeavour to give it. Thus will recommendations sometimes prevail which were purchased

---

2. In the *Life*, SJ is reported as saying: "'The inseparable imperfection annexed to all human governments, consisted . . . in not being able to create a sufficient fund of virtue and principle to carry the laws into due and effectual execution. Wisdom might plan, but virtue alone could execute. And where could sufficient virtue be found?'" (II.118).

3. Cf. SJ's similar remark in his "Life of Swift" (*Lives*, III.21, par. 51): "Every man of known influence has so many

petitions which he cannot grant, that he must necessarily offend more than he gratifies, because the preference given to one affords all the rest a reason for complaint. 'When I give away a place,' said Lewis XIV., 'I make an hundred discontented, and one ungrateful'" [Voltaire, *Le Siècle de Louis XIV* (1751), chap. 26].

4. Cf. *London*, ll. 176–77: "This mournful truth is ev'ry where confess'd, / SLOW RISES WORTH, BY POVERTY DEPRESS'D."

by money, or by the more destructive bribery of flattery[5] and servility.

"He that has much to do will do something wrong, and of that wrong must suffer the consequences; and, if it were possible that he should always act rightly, yet when such numbers are to judge of his conduct, the bad will censure and obstruct him by malevolence, and the good sometimes by mistake.

"The highest stations cannot therefore hope to be the abodes of happiness, which I would willingly believe to have fled from thrones and palaces to seats of humble privacy and placid obscurity. For what can hinder the satisfaction, or intercept the expectations, of him whose abilities are adequate to his employments, who sees with his own eyes the whole circuit of his influence, who chooses by his own knowledge all whom he trusts, and whom none are tempted to deceive by hope or fear? Surely he has nothing to do but to love and to be loved, to be virtuous and to be happy."

"Whether perfect happiness would be procured by perfect goodness," said Nekayah, "this world will never afford an opportunity of deciding. But this, at least, may be maintained, that we do not always find visible happiness in proportion to visible virtue.[6] All natural and almost all political evils, are incident alike to the bad and good:[7] they are

---

5. While in the Hebrides, Boswell "boasted . . . of my independency of spirit" and said that "I could not be bribed"; to which SJ replied: "Yes, you may be bribed by flattery" (*Life*, v.305–06). Cf. Gay's *Fables*, 1.7–8: "Learn to contemn all praise betimes, / For flattery's the nurse of crimes."

6. Cf. *Adventurer* 120 (par. 9): "the quiver of Omnipotence is stored with arrows, against which the shield of human virtue, however adamantine it has been boasted, is held up in vain: we do not always suffer by our crimes; we are not always protected by our inno-cence."

7. SJ writes in *Adventurer* 120 (pars. 10–11), "A good man is by no means exempt from the danger of suffering by the crimes of others. . . . A good man is subject, like other mortals, to all the influences of natural evil." In Sermon 15 (par. 30), he declares that "under the dispensation of the gospel we are no where taught, that the good shall have any exemption from the common accidents of life, or that natural and civil evil shall not be equally shared by the righteous and the wicked." Cf. Ecclesiastes ix.11.

confounded in the misery of a famine, and not much distinguished in the fury of a faction; they sink together in a
tempest, and are driven together from their country by
invaders. All that virtue can afford is quietness of conscience, a steady prospect of a happier state;[8] this may
enable us to endure calamity with patience; but remember
that patience must suppose pain."

Chap. XXVIII.

Rasselas and Nekayah continue their conversation.

"Dear princess," said Rasselas, "you fall into the common
errours of exaggeratory declamation, by producing, in a
familiar[1] disquisition, examples of national calamities, and
scenes of extensive misery, which are found in books rather
than in the world, and which, as they are horrid,[2] are or-
dained to be rare. Let us not imagine evils which we do not
feel, nor injure life by misrepresentations. I cannot bear
that querelous eloquence which threatens every city with a
siege like that of Jerusalem,[3] that makes famine attend on
every flight of locusts, and suspends pestilence on the wing
of every blast that issues from the south.

"On necessary and inevitable evils, which overwhelm
kingdoms at once, all disputation is vain: when they happen
they must be endured. But it is evident, that these bursts of

---

8. Discussing the benefits gained
from "the relation of other men's infelicity," SJ asserts in *Rambler* 52 (final
par.) that to some people "it is an act of
the highest charity to represent the calamities which not only virtue has suffered, but virtue has incurred; to inform them that one evidence of a
future state is the uncertainty of any
present reward for goodness; and to
remind them . . . of the distresses and
penury of men 'of whom the world was
not worthy.'" And he later wrote Boswell: "There is but one solid basis of
happiness; and that is, the reasonable

hope of a happy futurity" (*Letters* 578).
Cf. *Rambler* 203 (final par.); Locke's last
words to Anthony Collins (William
Warburton, *The Divine Legation of Moses
Demonstrated* [2 vols., 1738], I.xxiii):
"This world . . . affords no solid satisfaction but the consciousness of well
doing, and the hopes of another life."
  1. *Familiar:* "Unceremonious; free,
as among persons long acquainted"
(sense 3 in *Dictionary*).
  2. *Horrid:* "Hideous; dreadful;
shocking" (sense 1 in *Dictionary*).
  3. In A.D. 70 Jerusalem was besieged
and laid in ruins by the emperor Titus.

universal distress are more dreaded than felt: thousands and ten thousands flourish in youth, and wither in age, without the knowledge of any other than domestick evils, and share the same pleasures and vexations whether their kings are mild or cruel,[4] whether the armies of their country persue their enemies, or retreat before them.[5] While courts are disturbed with intestine competitions, and ambassadours are negotiating in foreign countries,[6] the smith still plies his anvil, and the husbandman drives his plow forward; the necessaries of life are required and obtained, and the successive business of the seasons continues to make its wonted revolutions.

"Let us cease to consider what, perhaps, may never happen, and what, when it shall happen, will laugh at human speculation. We will not endeavour to modify the motions of the elements, or to fix the destiny of kingdoms. It is our business to consider what beings like us may perform; each labouring for his own happiness, by promoting within his circle, however narrow, the happiness of others.[7]

"Marriage is evidently the dictate of nature; men and women were made to be companions of each other,[8] and

---

4. In Sermon 1 (par. 7), SJ remarks: "Very few men have it in their power to injure society in a large extent; the general happiness of the world can be very little interrupted by the wickedness of any single man, and the number is not large of those by whom the peace of any particular nation can be disturbed." Elsewhere he declared: "'I would not give half a guinea to live under one form of government rather than another. It is of no moment to the happiness of an individual. . . . The danger of the abuse of power is nothing to a private man'" (*Life*, II.170). Cf. also this couplet (ll. 429–30) which he contributed to Goldsmith's *The Traveller* (1764): "How small, of all that human hearts endure, / That part which laws or kings can cause or cure."

5. According to Mrs. Piozzi, SJ observed: "Historians magnify events expected, or calamities endured. . . . Among all your lamentations, who eats the less? Who sleeps the worse, for one general's ill success, or another's capitulation?" (*Anecdotes*, 1.203–04).

6. With the prince's remarks on armies and ambassadors, cf. SJ's comment in a letter to Giuseppe Baretti: "The good or ill success of battles and embassies extends itself to a very small part of domestic life: we all have good and evil, which we feel more sensibly than our petty part of public miscarriage or prosperity" (*Letters* 147).

7. See pp. 18, n. 4, 82, n. 3, above.

8. At least once SJ strongly expressed an opinion of marriage contrary to the prince's view: "It is so far from being

therefore I cannot be persuaded but that marriage is one of the means of happiness."[9]

"I know not," said the princess, "whether marriage be more than one of the innumerable modes of human misery.[1] When I see and reckon the various forms of connubial infelicity,[2] the unexpected causes of lasting discord, the diversities of temper, the oppositions of opinion, the rude collisions of contrary desire where both are urged by violent impulses, the obstinate contests of disagreeing virtues, where both are supported by consciousness of good intention, I am sometimes disposed to think with the severer casuists of most nations, that marriage is rather permitted than approved, and that none, but by the instigation of a passion too much indulged, entangle themselves with indissoluble compacts."[3]

"You seem to forget," replied Rasselas, "that you have, even now, represented celibacy as less happy than marriage. Both conditions may be bad, but they cannot both be worst. Thus it happens when wrong opinions are entertained, that they mutually destroy each other, and leave the mind open to truth."

"I did not expect," answered the princess, "to hear that

---

natural for a man and woman to live in a state of marriage, that we find all the motives which they have for remaining in that connection, and the restraints which civilized society imposes to prevent separation, are hardly sufficient to keep them together" (*Life*, II.165).

9. SJ's "general and constant advice," Mrs. Piozzi reports, "when consulted about the choice of a wife, a profession, or whatever influences a man's particular and immediate happiness, was always to reject no positive good from fears of its contrary consequences" (*Anecdotes*, 1.314). See also p. 99, n. 3, above.

1. See SJ's remark about marriage as a cause of misery, p. 99, n. 3, above. Cf. Sermon 1 (par. 10): "That mar-

riage . . . , an institution designed only for the promotion of happiness, and for the relief of the disappointments, anxieties, and distresses to which we are subject in our present state, does not always produce the effects, for which it was appointed; that it sometimes condenses the gloom, which it was intended to dispel, and encreases the weight, which was expected to be made lighter by it, must, however unwillingly, be yet acknowledged."

2. For SJ's instances of "connubial infelicity," see *Rambler* 18.

3. Cf. SJ's comment that "it is not from reason and prudence that people marry, but from inclination" (*Life*, II.101).

imputed to falshood which is the consequence only of frailty. To the mind, as to the eye, it is difficult to compare with exactness objects vast in their extent, and various in their parts. Where we see or conceive the whole at once we readily note the discriminations and decide the preference: but of two systems, of which neither can be surveyed by any human being in its full compass of magnitude and multiplicity of complication,[4] where is the wonder, that judging of the whole by parts, I am alternately affected by one and[a] the other as either presses on my memory or fancy?[5] We differ from ourselves just as we differ from each other, when we see only part of the question, as in the multifarious relations of politicks and morality: but when we perceive the whole at once, as in numerical computations,[6] all agree in one judgment, and none ever varies his opinion."[7]

"Let us not add," said the prince, "to the other evils of life, the bitterness of controversy, nor endeavour to vie with each other in subtilties of argument. We are employed in a search, of which both are equally to enjoy the success, or

a. alternately affected . . . and *59b*] affected . . . or *59a*

---

4. Cf. SJ's following comments in *Rambler* 125 (par. 1) and *Life* (1.444): "It is impossible to impress upon our minds an adequate and just representation of an object so great that we can never take it into our view"; "The human mind is so limited, that it cannot take in all the parts of a subject, so that there may be objections raised against any thing." Cf. Locke's *Of the Conduct of the Understanding* (3.3); Isaac Watts's *Logick* ([1725], 10th ed., 1755, p. 124).

5. In *Adventurer* 107 (par. 3), SJ observes: "we are finite beings, furnished with different kinds of knowledge, exerting different degrees of attention, one discovering consequences which escape another, none taking in the whole concatenation of causes and effects, and most comprehending but a very small part; each comparing what

he observes with a different criterion, and each referring it to a different purpose."

6. Cf. the remark in *The Preceptor* (3d ed., 1758), under the section on "The Elements of Logick" (11.28), that "our ideas of numbers are of all others the most accurate and distinct, nor does the multitude of units assembled together, in the least puzzle or confound the understanding."

7. Cf. SJ's observation in *Adventurer* 107 (par. 2): "With regard to simple propositions, where the terms are understood, and the whole subject is comprehended at once, there is such an uniformity of sentiment among all human beings, that, for many ages, a very numerous set of notions were supposed to be innate, or necessarily coexistent with the faculty of reason."

suffer by the miscarriage. It is therefore fit that we assist each other. You surely conclude too hastily from the infelicity of marriage against its institution; will[b] not the misery of life[8] prove equally that life cannot be the gift of heaven? The world must be peopled by marriage, or peopled without it."

"How the world is to be peopled," returned Nekayah, "is not my care, and needs not be yours. I see no danger that the present generation should omit to leave successors behind them: we are not now enquiring for the world, but for ourselves."

Chap. XXIX.[a]

The debate on marriage continued.

"The good of the whole," says Rasselas, "is the same with the good of all its parts. If marriage be best for mankind it must be evidently best for individuals, or a permanent and necessary duty must be the cause of evil, and some must be inevitably sacrificed to the convenience of others. In the estimate which you have made of the two states, it appears that the incommodities of a single life are, in a great measure, necessary and certain, but those of the conjugal state accidental and avoidable.

"I cannot forbear to flatter myself that prudence and benevolence will make marriage happy. The general folly

b. institution; will 59b] institution. Will 59a
a. XXIX 60] XXVIII 59a, 59b *The misnumbering—by one—of the chapters continues throughout the remainder of 59a and 59b (with the exception in the latter of chapter* XXX, *which is misnumbered* XXXIX, *and* XLVII, *which is misnumbered* LXVI).

---

8. "An accurate view of the world," SJ writes in *Rambler* 45 (pars. 2–3), "will confirm, that marriage is not commonly unhappy, otherwise than as life is unhappy; and that most of those who complain of connubial miseries, have as much satisfaction as their nature would have admitted, or their conduct procured in any other condition." Later he observes, "I am afraid that whether married or unmarried, we shall find the vesture of terrestrial existence more heavy and cumbrous, the longer it is worn."

of mankind is the cause of general complaint.[1] What can be expected but disappointment and repentance from a choice made in the immaturity of youth, in the ardour of desire, without judgment, without foresight, without enquiry after conformity of opinions, similarity of manners,[2] rectitude of judgment, or purity of sentiment.

"Such is the common process of marriage. A youth and maiden meeting by chance, or brought together by artifice, exchange glances, reciprocate civilities, go home, and dream of one another. Having little to divert attention, or diversify thought, they find themselves uneasy when they are apart, and therefore conclude that they shall be happy together. They marry, and discover what nothing but voluntary blindness had before concealed; they wear out life in altercations, and charge nature with cruelty.

"From those early marriages proceeds likewise the rivalry of parents and children: the son is eager to enjoy the world before the father is willing to forsake it, and there is hardly room at once for two generations. The daughter begins to bloom before the mother can be content to fade,[3] and neither can forbear to wish for the absence of the other.

---

1. For examples of folly in marriage, see *Rambler* 18, 45 (par. 8). In the *Rambler* 45, SJ goes on (pars. 9, 10) to mention the "ancient" Russian "custom" whereby "men and women never saw each other till they were joined beyond the power of parting" and to say that "if we observe the manner in which those converse, who have singled out each other for marriage, we shall, perhaps, not think that the Russians lost much by their restraint." Also cf. the following exchange between SJ and Boswell: "BOSWELL. '... Sir, you are not of opinion with some who imagine that certain men and certain women are made for each other; and that they cannot be happy if they miss their counterparts.' JOHNSON. 'To be sure not, Sir. I believe marriages would in general be as happy, and often more so, if they were all made by the Lord Chancellor, upon a due consideration of characters and circumstances, without the parties having any choice in the matter'" (*Life*, II.461).

2. Arguing in Sermon 1 the similarities between friendship and marriage, SJ quotes Catiline's observation that "strict friendship 'is to have the same desires and the same aversions'" (*Nam idem velle atque idem nolle, ea demum firma amicitia est.* Sallust, *Bellum Catilinae*, XX.4–5) and then remarks: "Whoever is to chuse a friend is to consider first the resemblance, or the dissimilitude of tempers. How necessary this caution is to be urged as preparatory to marriage, the misery of those who neglect it sufficiently evinces" (*Sermons*, p. 11 and n. 4).

3. See p. 95, n. 3, above.

"Surely all these evils may be avoided by that deliberation and delay which prudence prescribes to irrevocable choice. In the variety and jollity of youthful pleasures life may be well enough supported without the help of a partner. Longer time will increase experience, and wider views will allow better opportunities of enquiry and selection: one advantage, at least, will be certain; the parents will be visibly older than their children."

"What reason cannot collect,"[4] said Nekayah, "and what experiment has not yet taught, can be known only from the report of others. I have been told that late marriages are not eminently happy. This is a question too important to be neglected, and I have often proposed it to those, whose accuracy of remark, and comprehensiveness of knowledge, made their suffrages[5] worthy of regard. They have generally determined, that it is dangerous for a man and woman to suspend their fate upon each other, at a time when opinions are fixed, and habits are established; when friendships have been contracted on both sides, when life has been planned into method, and the mind has long enjoyed the contemplation of its own prospects.[6]

"It is scarcely possible that two travelling through the world under the conduct of chance, should have been both directed to the same path, and it will not often happen that either will quit the track which custom has made pleasing. When the desultory levity of youth has settled into regularity, it is soon succeeded by pride ashamed to yield, or obstinacy delighting to contend. And even though mutual esteem produces mutual desire to please, time itself, as it modifies unchangeably the external mien, determines likewise the direction of the passions, and gives an inflexible rigidity to the manners. Long customs are not easily bro-

---

4. *To collect:* "To infer as a consequence; to gather from premises" (sense 4 in *Dictionary*).

5. *Suffrage:* "Vote; voice given in a controverted point" (*Dictionary*).

6. According to William Maxwell, SJ "did not approve of late marriages, observing, that more was lost in point of time, than compensated for by any possible advantages" (*Life,* II.128).

ken:[7] he that attempts to change the course of his own life, very often labours in vain; and how shall we do that for others which we are seldom able to do for ourselves?"

"But surely," interposed the prince, "you suppose the chief motive of choice forgotten or neglected. Whenever I shall seek a wife, it shall be my first question, whether she be willing to be led by reason?"

"Thus it is," said Nekayah, "that philosophers are deceived. There are a thousand familiar disputes which reason never can decide; questions that elude investigation, and make logick ridiculous; cases where something must be done, and where little can be said. Consider the state of mankind, and enquire how few can be supposed to act upon any occasions, whether small or great, with all the reasons of action present to their minds. Wretched would be the pair above all names of wretchedness, who should be doomed to adjust by reason every morning all the minute detail of a domestick day.

"Those who marry at an advanced age, will probably escape the encroachments of their children; but, in diminution of this advantage, they will be likely to leave them, ignorant and helpless, to a guardian's mercy: or, if that should not happen, they must at least go out of the world before they see those whom they love best either wise or great.

"From their children, if they have less to fear, they have less also to hope, and they lose, without equivalent, the joys of early love, and the convenience of uniting with manners pliant, and minds susceptible of new impressions, which might wear away their dissimilitudes by long cohabitation, as soft bodies, by continual attrition, conform their surfaces to each other.

"I believe it will be found that those who marry late are best pleased with their children, and those who marry early with their partners."

---

7. Cf. Sermon 15 (par. 19): "Habits are formed by repeated acts, and there- fore old habits are always strongest." Cf. p. 202, ll. 7–10 below.

"The union of these two affections," said Rasselas, "would produce all that could be wished. Perhaps there is a time when marriage might unite them, a time neither too early for the father, nor too late for the husband."

"Every hour," answered the princess, "confirms my prejudice in favour of the position so often uttered by the mouth of Imlac, 'That nature sets her gifts on the right hand and on the left.' Those conditions, which flatter hope and attract desire, are so constituted, that, as we approach one, we recede from another. There are goods so opposed that we cannot seize both, but, by too much prudence, may pass between them at too great a distance to reach either. This is often the fate of long consideration; he does nothing who endeavours to do more than is allowed to humanity. Flatter not yourself with contrarieties of pleasure. Of the blessings set before you make your choice, and be content. No man can taste the fruits of autumn while he is delighting his scent with the flowers of the spring: no man can, at the same time, fill his cup from the source and from the mouth of the Nile."[8]

Chap. XXX.

Imlac enters, and changes the conversation.

Here Imlac entered, and interrupted them. "Imlac,"[a] said Rasselas, "I have been taking from the princess the dismal history of private life, and am almost discouraged from further search."

a. them. "Imlac, *59b*] them. His look was clouded with thought. "Imlac, *59a*

---

8. With the whole of Nekayah's reply, cf. *Rambler* 178 (pars. 3–4), in which SJ observes: "Providence has fixed the limits of human enjoyment by immoveable boundaries, and has set different gratifications at such a distance from each other, that no art or power can bring them together. This great law it is the business of every rational being to understand, that life may not pass away in an attempt to make contradictions consistent. . . . Of two objects tempting at a distance on contrary sides it is impossible to approach one but by receding from the other; by long deliberation and dilatory projects, they may be both lost, but can never be both gained."

"It seems to me," said Imlac, "that while you are making the choice of life, you neglect to live. You wander about a single city, which, however large and diversified, can now afford few novelties, and forget that you are in a country, famous among the earliest monarchies for the power and wisdom of its inhabitants; a country where the sciences first dawned that illuminate the world, and beyond which the arts cannot be traced of civil[1] society or domestick life.[2]

"The old Egyptians have left behind them monuments of industry and power before which all European magnificence is confessed to fade away. The ruins of their architecture are the schools of modern builders, and from the wonders which time has spared we may conjecture, though uncertainly, what it has destroyed."

"My curiosity," said Rasselas, "does not very strongly lead me to survey piles of stone, or mounds of earth; my business is with man.[3] I came hither not to measure fragments of temples, or trace choaked aqueducts, but to look upon the various scenes of the present world."

"The things that are now before us," said the princess, "require attention, and deserve[b] it.[4] What have I to do with

b. require . . . deserve 59b] necessarily require . . . sufficiently deserve 59a

---

1. *Civil:* "Civilized; not barbarous" (sense 9 in *Dictionary*). Cf. p. 134, l. 17 below. *Civilized* is not listed separately in the *Dictionary* but it appears in two quotations illustrating the meaning of *to civilize.* SJ "would not admit *civilization,* but only *civility*" in the fourth edition of the *Dictionary* (*Life,* 11.155).

2. With this comment about Egypt, cf. the statement in the section on "Trade and Commerce" of *The Preceptor* (3d ed., 1758, 11.393) that "we find in the records of antiquity, no nation celebrated more early for carrying all arts to perfection than the inhabitants of Egypt."

3. Cf. *Idler* 97 (par. 8): "He that would travel for the entertainment of others, should remember that the

great object of remark is human life." Mrs. Piozzi also reports that when travelling with her and Mr. Thrale SJ would say: "'A blade of grass is always a blade of grass, whether in one country or another: let us if we *do* talk, talk about something; men and women are my subjects of enquiry; let us see how these differ from those we have left behind'" (*Anecdotes,* 1.215).

4. With the princess's observation, cf. *Paradise Lost,* VIII. 192–94: "to know / That which before us lies in daily life, / Is the prime wisdom." These lines are cited by Hardy (p. 163), who points out that "as a moralist [SJ] took this sentiment very seriously (v. esp. *Rambler* 24, 180)." Mrs. Piozzi remarks that "all [SJ's] conversation precepts tended to-

the heroes or the monuments of ancient times? with times which never can return, and heroes, whose form of life was different from all that the present condition of mankind requires or allows."

"To know any thing," returned the poet, "we must know its effects; to see men we must see their works, that we may learn what reason has dictated, or passion has incited, and find what are the most powerful motives of action. To judge rightly of the present we must oppose it to the past; for all judgment is comparative,[5] and of the future nothing can be known. The truth is, that no mind is much employed upon the present: recollection and anticipation fill up almost all our moments.[6] Our passions are joy and grief, love and hatred, hope and fear. Of joy and grief the past is the object, and the future of hope and fear; even love and hatred respect the past, for the cause must have been before the effect.

"The present state of things is the consequence of the former, and it is natural to inquire what were the sources of the good that we enjoy, or of the evil that we suffer.[7] If we act only for ourselves, to neglect the study of history is not

---

wards the dispersion of romantic ideas, and were chiefly intended to promote the cultivation of 'That which before thee lies in daily life.' . . . And when he talked of authors, his praise went spontaneously to such passages as are sure in his own phrase to leave something behind them useful on common occasions, or observant of common manners" (*Anecdotes*, 1.282).

5. Cf. Sermon 16 (par. 29): "One general method of judging, and determining upon the value, or excellence of things, is by comparing one with another."

6. "So few of the hours of life," says SJ in *Rambler* 41 (par. 1), "are filled up with objects adequate to the mind of man, and so frequently are we in want of present pleasure or employment, that we are forced to have recourse every moment to the past and future

for supplemental satisfactions, and relieve the vacuities of our being, by recollection of former passages, or anticipation of events to come." Also cf. *Rambler* 203 (par. 1): "The time present is seldom able to fill desire or imagination with immediate enjoyment, and we are forced to supply its deficiencies by recollection or anticipation."

7. With Imlac's remark, cf. SJ's statement in the Preface to *The Preceptor* (3d ed., 1758, 1.xx–xxi): "The study of *chronology* and *history* seems to be one of the most natural delights of the human mind. It is not easy to live without enquiring by what means every thing was brought into the state in which we now behold it, or without finding in the mind some desire of being informed concerning the generations of mankind, that have been in possession of the world before us, whether they were

prudent: if we are entrusted with the care of others, it is not just. Ignorance, when it is voluntary, is criminal; and he may properly be charged with evil who refused to learn how he might prevent it.

"There is no part of history so generally useful as that which relates the progress of the human mind, the gradual improvement of reason, the successive advances of science,[8] the vicissitudes of learning and ignorance, which are the light and darkness of thinking beings, the extinction and resuscitation of arts, and the[c] revolutions of the intellectual world.[9] If accounts of battles and invasions are peculiarly the business of princes, the useful or elegant arts are not to be neglected; those who have kingdoms to govern have understandings to cultivate.

"Example is always more efficacious than precept.[1] A soldier is formed in war, and a painter must copy pictures. In this, contemplative life has the advantage: great actions are seldom seen, but the labours of art are always at hand for those who desire to know what art has been able to perform.

"When the eye or the imagination is struck with any uncommon work the next transition of an active mind is to the means by which it was performed.[2] Here begins the

c. and the *59b*] and all the *59a*

---

better or worse than ourselves; or what good or evil has been derived to us from their schemes, practices, and institutions."

8. *Science:* "Knowledge" (sense 1 in *Dictionary*). Cf. the same meaning on p. 141, l. 35, below.

9. In "An Account of the Harleian Library" ([1742], par. 12), SJ expresses a comparable regard for intellectual history. Catalogues of books, he says, are of great importance to "those whom curiosity has engaged in the study of literary history, and who think the intellectual revolutions of the world more worthy of their attention, than the ravages of tyrants." Elsewhere, of

course, he expresses a high opinion of the "history of manners" and biography; see, e.g., *Rambler* 60; *Life*, 1.425; III.333; v.79; *Johnsonian Miscellanies*, ed. G. B. Hill (2 vols., 1897), II.8.

1. Cf. Seneca's similar maxim (*Epistles*, vi.5): *Longum iter est per praecepta, breve et efficax per exempla* ("the way is long if one follows precepts, but short and helpful, if one follows patterns" [Loeb Classical Library trans.]).

2. Cf. SJ's remark in the "Life of Butler": "When any work has been viewed and admired the first question of intelligent curiosity is, how was it performed?" (*Lives*, 1.213, par. 40).

true use of such contemplation; we enlarge our comprehension by new ideas, and perhaps recover some art lost to mankind, or learn what is less perfectly known in our own country. At least we compare our own with former times, and either rejoice at our improvements, or, what is the first motion towards good, discover our defects."

"I am willing," said the prince, "to see all that can deserve my search." "And I," said the princess, "shall rejoice to learn something of the manners of antiquity."

"The most pompous[3] monument of Egyptian greatness, and one of the most bulky works of manual industry," said Imlac, "are the pyramids;[4] fabricks raised before the time of history, and of which the earliest narratives afford us only uncertain traditions.[5] Of these the greatest is still standing, very little injured by time."

"Let us visit them to morrow," said Nekayah. "I have often heard of the pyramids, and shall not rest, till I have seen them within and without with my own eyes."

Chap. XXXI.

They visit the pyramids.

The resolution being thus taken, they set out the next day. They laid tents upon their camels, being resolved to stay among the pyramids till their curiosity was fully satisfied. They travelled gently, turned aside to every thing remarkable, stopped from time to time and conversed with the inhabitants, and observed the various appearances of towns ruined and inhabited, of wild and cultivated nature. When they came to the Great Pyramid[1] they were as-

---

3. *Pompous:* "Splendid; magnificent; grand" (*Dictionary*).

4. For a discussion of the probable sources of SJ's treatment of the pyramids in the following chapters, see Introduction, pp. xxxii–xxxiii above.

5. Among the earliest commentaries on the pyramids are passages by Herodotus, Diodorus Siculus, Strabo, and Pliny the Elder (editions of the last two of which were in SJ's library); for additional details about these commentaries, see pp. 45–46 of Weitzman's essay cited on p. xxiii, n. 7, above.

1. For early English descriptions of the Great Pyramid of Cheops, see Introduction, p. xxxii above.

tonished at the extent of the base, and the height of the top. Imlac explained to them the principles upon which the pyramidal form was chosen for a fabrick intended to co-extend its duration with that of the world: he showed that its gradual diminution gave it such stability, as defeated all the common attacks of the elements,[2] and could scarcely be overthrown by earthquakes themselves, the least resistible of natural violence. A concussion that should shatter the pyramid would threaten the dissolution of the continent.

They measured all its dimensions, and pitched their tents at its foot.[3] Next day they prepared to enter its interiour apartments, and having hired the common guides[4] climbed up to the first passage, when the favourite of the princess, looking into the cavity, stepped back and trembled. "Pekuah," said the princess, "of what art thou afraid?" "Of the narrow entrance," answered the lady, "and of the dreadful gloom. I dare not enter a place which must surely be inhabited by unquiet souls. The original possessors of these dreadful vaults will start up before us, and, perhaps, shut us in[a] for ever." She spoke, and threw her arms round the neck of her mistress.

a. in 59*b*] up 59*a*

---

2. In his remarks on the stability of the "pyramidal form," Imlac voices widespread "rules of architecture, which," as Sir William Temple has noted in his "Essay upon the Original and Nature of Government," "teach us that the *pyramid* is of all figures the firmest, and least subject to be shaken or overthrown by any concussions or accidents from the earth or air; and it grows still so much the firmer, by how much broader the bottom and sharper the top" (*Works*, 1.105). Cf. also John Greaves's similar comment in his *Pyramidographia* (Churchill's *Collection of Voyages and Travels* [1732], II.712).

3. Measuring, in one way or another, the pyramids (especially the largest of them) was an accepted part of the early visitor's sightseeing trip to the tombs. In his *Description of the East* (1.42–43), Pococke reviews some of the measurements of previous writers and then presents his own findings. Like Rasselas's party, he, too, while on a second visit to the monuments, "pitch'd a tent in the plain, about half a mile" from the pyramids (p. 48). Cf., also, the allusion to pyramid-measuring in *Spectator* 1 (par. 4).

4. In his *Account . . . of the Ottoman Empire* (1709), Aaron Hill refers to the "guides, who undertook our conduct thro' this dismal passage" into the Great Pyramid (p. 250).

"If all your fear be of apparitions," said the prince, "I will promise you safety: there is no danger from the dead; he that is once buried will be seen no more."

"That the dead are seen no more," said Imlac, "I will not undertake to maintain against the concurrent and unvaried testimony of all ages, and of all nations. There is no people, rude or learned, among whom apparitions of the dead are not related and believed.[5] This opinion, which, perhaps, prevails as far as human nature is diffused, could become universal only by its truth: those, that never heard of one another, would not have agreed in a tale which nothing but experience can make credible. That it is doubted by single cavillers can very little weaken the general evidence, and some who deny it with their tongues confess it by their fears.

"Yet I do not mean to add new terrours to those which have already seized upon Pekuah. There can be no reason why spectres should haunt the pyramid more than other places, or why they should have power or will to hurt innocence and purity. Our entrance is no violation[b] of their privileges;[c] we can take nothing from them, how then can we offend them?"

"My dear Pekuah," said the princess, "I will always go

b. violation *emend.*] violution 59*a*, violtion 59*b*   c. priviledges 59*b*

---

5. In *Spectator* 110 (par. 6), Addison expresses an opinion (cited in part in SJ's *Dictionary* under *appearance* and *fabulous*) similar to Imlac's: "I think a person who is ... terrify'd with the imagination of ghosts and spectres much more reasonable, than one who contrary to the reports of all historians sacred and prophane, ancient and modern, and to the traditions of all nations, thinks the appearance of spirits fabulous and groundless." On the same subject, SJ later remarked: (1) "'It is wonderful that five thousand years have now elapsed since the creation of the world, and still it is undecided whether or not there has ever been an instance of the spirit of any person appearing after death. All argument is against it; but all belief is for it'"; (2) "'A total disbelief of [apparitions] is adverse to the opinion of the existence of the soul between death and the last day; the question simply is, whether departed spirits ever have the power of making themselves perceptible to us'" (*Life*, III.230; IV.94). Cf. also his prayer in 1752 on his wife's death (*Life*, I.235). See, too, Ralph Cudworth, *The True Intellectual System of the Universe* (2d ed. [1743], II.700, 834–35).

before you, and Imlac shall follow you. Remember that you are the companion of the princess of Abissinia."

"If the princess is pleased that her servant should die," returned the lady, "let her command some death less dreadful than enclosure in this horrid cavern. You know I dare not disobey you: I must go if you command me; but, if I once enter, I never shall come back."

The princess saw that her fear was too strong for expostulation or reproof, and embracing her, told her that she should stay in the tent till their return. Pekuah was yet not satisfied, but entreated the princess not to persue so dreadful a purpose as that of entering the recesses of the pyramid. "Though I cannot teach courage," said Nekayah, "I must not learn cowardice; nor leave at last undone what I came hither only to do."

Chap. XXXII.

They enter the pyramid.

Pekuah descended to the tents, and the rest entered the pyramid: they passed through the galleries, surveyed the vaults of marble, and examined the chest in which the body of the founder is supposed to have been reposited.[1] They then sat down in one of the most spacious chambers to rest a while before they attempted to return.

"We have now," said Imlac, "gratified our minds with an exact view of the greatest work of man, except the wall of China.[2]

---

1. Numerous seventeenth- and eighteenth-century travel books contain either first- or second-hand descriptions of the interior of the Great Pyramid. Specific features mentioned include the marble chambers and the sarcophagus or "chest" which, it was believed, once held the body of the monarch. The likeliest sources of SJ's depiction are Greaves's *Pyramidographia*, Hill's *Account of the . . . Ottoman Empire*, and Pococke's *A Description of the East*. For

further details, see Introduction, p. xxxii above.

2. Cf. Père J. B. Du Halde's remark in his *Description of China* (2 vols., 1738, I.20) that "no work in the world is equal to" the Great Wall; SJ's "Essay" on Du Halde's book in the *Gentleman's Magazine*, XII (1742), 322. In a conversation with Boswell, SJ "expressed a particular enthusiasm with respect to visiting the wall of China," and said that "'there would be a lustre reflected upon'" Bos-

"Of the wall it is very easy to assign the motives. It secured a wealthy and timorous nation from the incursions of barbarians,[3] whose unskilfulness in arts made it easier for them to supply their wants by rapine than by industry, and who from time to time poured in upon the habitations of peaceful commerce, as vultures descend upon domestick fowl.[a] Their celerity and fierceness made the wall necessary, and their ignorance made it efficacious.

"But for the pyramids no reason has ever been given adequate to the cost and labour of the work. The narrowness of the chambers proves that it could afford no retreat from enemies, and treasures might have been reposited at far less expence with equal security. It seems to have been erected only in compliance with that hunger of imagination which preys incessantly upon life,[4] and must be always appeased by some employment. Those who have already all that they can enjoy, must enlarge their desires.[5] He that has built for use, till use is supplied, must begin to build for vanity,[6] and extend his plan to the utmost power of human performance, that he may not be soon reduced to form another wish.

a. fowl 59a, 59b] changed to fowls in the YC.

---

well's children from his "'spirit and curiosity'" in going to view the Great Wall (*Life*, III.269).

3. Du Halde describes the construction of the Great Wall, built "to defend three great provinces against the irruptions of the Tartars," in his *General History of China* (2 vols., 1741), II.76–77; see also his *Description of China*, I.20–22.

4. Cf. *Rambler* 104 (par. 3): "The desires of mankind are much more numerous than their attainments, and the capacity of the imagination much larger than actual enjoyment."

5. In *Adventurer* 119 (par. 4), SJ observes that "it seems to be the great business of life, to create wants as fast as they are satisfied"; in *Idler* 30 (par.

1), he says: "The desires of man encrease with his acquisitions; every step which he advances brings something within his view, which he did not see before, and which, as soon as he sees it, he begins to want. Where necessity ends curiosity begins, and no sooner are we supplied with every thing that nature can demand, than we sit down to contrive artificial appetites."

6. This criticism of the pyramids is at least as old as Pliny the Elder, who in his *Natural History* calls them "a superfluous and foolish display of wealth," in the construction of which "much vanity" was displayed by the kings of Egypt (Book XXXVI. xvi.75–76, Loeb Classical Library trans.).

"I consider this mighty structure as a monument of the insufficiency of human enjoyments.[7] A king, whose power is unlimited, and whose treasures surmount all real and imaginary wants, is compelled to solace, by the erection of a pyramid, the satiety of dominion and tastelessness of pleasures,[8] and to amuse the tediousness of declining life, by seeing thousands labouring without end, and one stone, for no purpose, laid upon another. Whoever thou art, that, not content with a moderate condition, imaginest happiness in royal magnificence, and dreamest that command or riches can feed the appetite of novelty with perpetual[b] gratifications, survey the pyramids, and confess thy folly!"[9]

Chap. XXXIII.

The princess meets with an unexpected misfortune.

They rose up, and returned through the cavity at which they had entered, and the princess prepared for her favourite a long narrative of dark labyrinths, and costly rooms, and of the different impressions which the varieties of the way had made upon her. But, when they came to their train, they found every one silent and dejected: the men discovered shame and fear in their countenances, and the women were weeping in the tents.

What had happened they did not try to conjecture, but immediately enquired. "You had scarcely entered into the

b. perpetual 59*b*] successive 59*a*

---

7. Cf. *Rambler* 207 (par. 1): "Such is the emptiness of human enjoyment, that we are always impatient of the present. Attainment is followed by neglect, and possession by disgust; and the malicious remark of the Greek epigrammatist on marriage [Palladas, *Greek Anthology*, XI.381] may be applied to every other course of life, that its two days of happiness are the first and the last."

8. SJ once observed that the building of "grand houses," the construction of "fine gardens," and the creation of "splendid places of public amusement" were "'all only struggles for happiness'" (*Life*, III.198–99).

9. Cf. William Warburton's labelling the pyramids "works of human pride, and folly" in *The Divine Legation of Moses Demonstrated*, I.xv–xvi.

pyramid," said one of the attendants, "when a troop of Arabs rushed upon us: we were too few to resist them, and too slow to escape. They were about to search the tents, set us on our camels, and drive us along before them, when the approach of some Turkish horsemen put them to flight; but they seized the lady Pekuah with her two maids, and carried them away: the Turks are now persuing them by our instigation, but I fear they will not be able to overtake them."[1]

The princess was overpowered with surprise and grief. Rasselas, in the first heat of his resentment, ordered his servants to follow him, and prepared to persue the robbers with his sabre in his hand. "Sir," said Imlac, "what can you hope from violence or valour? the Arabs are mounted on horses trained to battle and retreat; we have only beasts of burthen. By leaving our present station we may lose the princess, but cannot hope to regain Pekuah."

In a short time the Turks returned, having not been able to reach the enemy. The princess burst out into new lamentations, and Rasselas could scarcely forbear to reproach them with cowardice; but Imlac was of opinion, that the escape of the Arabs was no addition to their misfortune, for, perhaps, they would have killed their captives rather than have resigned them.

Chap. XXXIV.

They return to Cairo without Pekuah.

There was nothing to be hoped from longer stay. They returned to Cairo repenting of their curiosity, censuring the negligence of the government, lamenting their own rashness which had neglected to procure a guard, imagining many expedients by which the loss of Pekuah might

---

1. On pp. 44–45 of the essay cited on p. xxiii, n. 7, above, Weitzman notes several similarities between the abduction of Pekuah and an episode (also involving Arab robbers and Turkish pursuers) in Hill's *Account of the . . . Ottoman Empire* (pp. 265–66), and he concludes that Hill's work is the probable source of the incident in *Rasselas*.

have been prevented, and resolving to do something for her recovery, though none could find any thing proper to be done.

Nekayah retired to her chamber, where her women attempted to comfort her, by telling her that all had their troubles, and that lady Pekuah had enjoyed much happiness in the world for a long time, and might reasonably expect a change of fortune. They hoped that some good would befal her wheresoever she was, and that their mistress would find another friend who might supply her place.

The princess made them no answer, and they continued the form of condolence, not much grieved in their hearts that the favourite was lost.

Next day the prince presented to the Bassa a memorial of the wrong which he had suffered, and a petition for redress.[1] The Bassa threatened to punish the robbers, but did not attempt to catch them, nor, indeed, could any account or description be given by which he might direct the persuit.

It soon appeared that nothing would be done by authority. Governors, being accustomed to hear of more crimes than they can punish, and more wrongs than they can redress, set themselves at ease by indiscriminate negligence, and presently forget the request when they lose sight of the petitioner.

Imlac then endeavoured to gain some intelligence by private agents. He found many who pretended to an exact knowledge of all the haunts of the Arabs, and to regular correspondence with their chiefs, and who readily undertook the recovery of Pekuah. Of these, some were furnished with money for their journey, and came back no more; some were liberally paid for accounts which a few

---

1. In a passage describing the efforts of a group of Frenchmen to punish certain Ethiopians for the murder of a compatriot, *Voyage to Abyssinia* says that "a memorial was likewise given to the Bassa" (who was about to assume command of part of Ethiopia) "entreating him to lend his assistance in the punishment" of the guilty persons (p. 148).

days discovered to be false. But the princess would not suffer any means, however improbable, to be left untried. While she was doing something she kept her hope alive. As one expedient failed, another was suggested; when one messenger returned unsuccessful, another was despatched to a different quarter.

Two months had now passed, and of Pekuah nothing had been heard; the hopes which they had endeavoured to raise in each other grew more languid, and the princess, when she saw nothing more to be tried, sunk[2] down inconsolable in hopeless dejection. A thousand times she reproached herself with the easy compliance by which she permitted her favourite to stay behind her. "Had not my fondness," said she, "lessened my authority, Pekuah had not dared to talk of her terrours. She ought to have feared me more than spectres. A severe look would have overpowered her; a peremptory command would have compelled obedience. Why did foolish indulgence prevail upon me? Why did I not speak and refuse to hear?"

"Great princess," said Imlac, "do not reproach yourself for your virtue, or consider that as blameable by which evil has accidentally been caused. Your tenderness for the timidity of Pekuah was generous and kind. When we act according to our duty, we commit the event to him by whose laws our actions are governed, and who will suffer none to be finally punished for obedience.[3] When, in prospect of some good, whether natural or moral, we break the rules prescribed us, we withdraw from the direction of superiour wisdom, and take all consequences upon ourselves. Man cannot so far know the connexion of causes and events, as that he may venture to do wrong in order to do right. When

---

2. In his *Dictionary*, SJ defines *sunk* as "the preterite and participle passive of *sink*." But he also defines *sank* as "the preterite of *sink*." See p. 18, n. 6, above.

3. Cf. SJ's declaration in *Rambler* 185 (par. 13): "The utmost excellence at which humanity can arrive, is a con-

stant and determinate pursuit of virtue, without regard to present dangers or advantage; a continual reference of every action to the divine will; an habitual appeal to everlasting justice; and an unvaried elevation of the intellectual eye to the reward which perseverance only can obtain."

we persue our end by lawful means, we may always console our miscarriage by the hope of future recompense. When we consult only our own policy, and attempt to find a nearer way to good, by overleaping the settled boundaries of right and wrong, we cannot be happy even by success, because we cannot escape the consciousness of our fault; but, if we miscarry, the disappointment is irremediably embittered. How comfortless is the sorrow of him, who feels at once the pangs of guilt, and the vexation of calamity which guilt has brought upon him?[4]

"Consider, princess, what would have been your condition, if the lady Pekuah had intreated to accompany you, and, being compelled to stay in the tents, had been carried away; or how would you have born the thought, if you had forced her into the pyramid, and she had died before you in agonies of terrour."

"Had either happened," said Nekayah, "I could not have endured life till now: I should have been tortured to madness by the remembrance of such cruelty, or must have pined away in abhorrence of myself."

"This at least," said Imlac, "is the present reward of virtuous conduct, that no unlucky consequence can oblige us to repent it."

Chap. XXXV.

The princess languishes for want of[a] Pekuah.

Nekayah, being thus reconciled to herself, found that no evil is insupportable but that which is accompanied with consciousness of wrong. She was, from that time, delivered from the violence of tempestuous sorrow,[1] and sunk into

---

a. languishes . . . of 59b] continues to lament 59a

---

4. Cf. SJ's remark in the *Life:* "'If . . . the cause of our grief is occasioned by our own misconduct, if grief is mingled with remorse of conscience, it should be lasting'" (III.136–37).

1. In *Rambler* 47, which is devoted to a discussion of this particular "passion," SJ describes sorrow as "that state

silent pensiveness and gloomy tranquillity. She sat from morning to evening recollecting all that had been done or said by her Pekuah,[2] treasured up with care every trifle on which Pekuah had set an accidental value, and which might recal to mind any little incident or careless conversation. The sentiments of her, whom she now expected to see no more, were treasured[b] in her memory as rules of life, and she deliberated to no other end than to conjecture on any occasion what would have been the opinion and counsel of Pekuah.

The women, by whom she was attended, knew nothing of her real condition,[3] and therefore she could not talk to them but with caution and reserve. She began to remit her curiosity, having no great care to collect notions which she had no convenience[4] of uttering. Rasselas endeavoured first to comfort and afterwards to divert her; he hired musicians, to whom she seemed to listen, but did not hear them, and procured masters to instruct her in various arts, whose lectures, when they visited her again, were again to be repeated. She had lost her taste of pleasure and her ambition of excellence. And her mind, though forced into short excursions,[5] always recurred to the image of her friend.

Imlac was every morning earnestly enjoined[6] to renew

b. treasured 59b] treasured up 59a

of the mind in which our desires are fixed upon the past, without looking forward to the future, an incessant wish that something were otherwise than it has been, a tormenting and harrassing want of some enjoyment or possession which we have lost, and which no endeavours can possibly regain" (par. 3). In his *Dictionary*, he observes that "sorrow is not commonly understood as the effect of present evil, but of lost good."

2. Cf. SJ's recommendation in a letter of condolence to James Elphinston on the death of his mother that he

"write down" his recollections of her, which, SJ says, "you will read . . . with great pleasure" (*Life*, 1.212).

3. In SJ's *Dictionary*, sense 6 of *condition* is "rank." The illustrative quotations include two lines from *The Tempest* (III.i.59–60): "I am in my condition / A prince, Miranda."

4. *Convenience:* "Fitness of time or place" (sense 4 in *Dictionary*).

5. *Excursion:* "Digression; ramble from a subject" (sense 4 in *Dictionary*).

6. In his *Dictionary*, SJ remarks that to *enjoin* "is more authoritative than *direct*, and less imperious than *command*."

his enquiries, and was asked every night whether he had yet heard of Pekuah, till not being able to return the princess the answer that she desired, he was less and less willing to come into her presence. She observed his backwardness, and commanded him to attend her. "You are not," said she, "to confound impatience with resentment, or to suppose that I charge you with negligence, because I repine at your unsuccessfulness. I do not much wonder at your absence; I know that the unhappy are never pleasing, and that all naturally avoid the contagion of misery. To hear complaints is wearisome alike to the wretched and the happy; for who would cloud by adventitious grief the short gleams of gaiety which life allows us? or who, that is struggling under his own evils, will add to them the miseries of another?

"The time is at hand, when none shall be disturbed any longer by the sighs of Nekayah: my search after happiness is now at an end. I am resolved to retire from the world[7] with all its flatteries and deceits, and will hide myself in solitude, without any other care than to compose my thoughts, and regulate my hours by a constant succession of innocent occupations, till, with a mind purified from all earthly desires, I shall enter into that state, to which all are hastening, and in which I hope again to enjoy the friendship of Pekuah."

"Do not entangle your mind," said Imlac, "by irrevocable determinations,[8] nor increase the burthen of life by a vol-

---

7. See pp. 80, n. 1, and 85, n. 7, above.

8. SJ consistently opposed the making of most vows. In a note on *Love's Labour's Lost* he comments on the "folly of vows": "They are made without sufficient regard to the variations of life, and are therefore broken by some unforeseen necessity. They proceed commonly from a presumptuous confidence, and a false estimate of human power" (*Johnson on Shakespeare*, ed. Arthur Sherbo [Yale Edition of the Works of Samuel Johnson, 1968],

VII.267); cf. the note on King Lear in VIII.663. In the "Life of Cowley," commending the "just and noble thoughts" in the passage, he quotes the following lines (95–99) from Cowley's "Ode: Upon Liberty": "Where honour or where conscience *does* not bind, / No other law shall shackle me; / Slave to myself I ne'er will be; / Nor shall my future actions be confin'd / By my own present mind" (*Lives*, I.60, par. 189). He declares, too, in a letter to Mrs. Piozzi: "All unnecessary vows are folly, because they suppose a prescience of

untary accumulation of misery: the weariness of retirement[9] will continue or increase when the loss of Pekuah is
forgotten. That you have been deprived of one pleasure is
no very good reason for rejection of the rest."

"Since Pekuah was taken from me," said the princess, "I
have no pleasure to reject or to retain. She that has no one
to love or trust has little to hope. She wants the radical
principle of happiness. We may, perhaps, allow that what
satisfaction this world can afford, must arise from the conjunction of wealth, knowledge and goodness: wealth is
nothing but as it is bestowed, and knowledge nothing but as
it is communicated:[1] they must therefore be imparted to
others, and to whom could I now delight to impart them?
Goodness[c] affords the only comfort which can be enjoyed
without a partner, and goodness may be practised in retirement."

"How far solitude may admit goodness, or advance it, I
shall not," replied Imlac, "dispute at present. Remember
the confession of the pious hermit. You will wish to return
into the world, when the image of your companion has left
your thoughts." "That time," said Nekayah, "will never
come. The generous frankness, the modest obsequiousness,[2] and the faithful secrecy of my dear Pekuah, will
always be more missed, as I shall live longer to see vice and
folly."

"The state of a mind oppressed with a sudden calamity,"
said Imlac, "is like that of the fabulous inhabitants of the
new created earth, who, when the first night came upon

---

c. communicated: . . . Goodness 59*b*] communicated. Goodness 59*a*

---

the future which has not been given us.
They are, I think, a crime because they
resign that life to chance which God
has given us to be regulated by reason;
and superinduce a kind of fatality,
from which it is the great privilege of
our nature to be free" (*Letters* 308).
Also cf. *Life*, II.21; III.357; *Anecdotes*
(I.299).

9. Cf. *Adventurer* 102, which describes Mercator's discontent in retirement.

1. See pp. 31, n. 1, 37, n. 7, above.

2. In SJ's *Dictionary*, *obsequiousness* is
defined as "Obedience; compliance";
and in the *OED* as "Ready compliance
or obedience; eagerness to serve or
please; dutiful service."

them, supposed that day never would return.[3] When the clouds of sorrow gather over us, we see nothing beyond them, nor can imagine how they will be dispelled: yet a new day succeeded to the night, and sorrow is never long without a dawn of ease. But they who restrain themselves from receiving comfort, do as the savages would have done, had they put out their eyes when it was dark. Our minds, like our bodies, are in continual flux; something is hourly lost, and something acquired. To lose much at once is inconvenient to either, but while the vital powers remain uninjured, nature will find the means of reparation. Distance has the same effect on the mind as on the eye, and while we glide along the stream of time, whatever we leave behind us is always lessening, and that which we approach increasing in magnitude. Do not suffer life to stagnate; it will grow muddy for want of motion:[4] commit yourself again to the current of the world;[5] Pekuah will vanish by degrees; you will meet in your way some other favourite, or learn to diffuse[6] yourself in general conversation."

"At least," said the prince, "do not despair before all remedies have been tried: the enquiry after the unfortunate lady is still continued, and shall be carried on with yet greater diligence, on condition that you will promise to wait a year for the event, without any unalterable resolution."

Nekayah thought this a reasonable demand, and made

---

3. The grief produced in "fabulous" men by the initial darkness on earth is mentioned or glanced at, as E. E. Duncan-Jones has noted (*TLS*, 3 April 1959, p. 193), in Manilius's *Astronomicon*, i.66–70 ("The sun, when night came on, withdrawn, they griev'd, / As dead, and joy'd next morn when he reviv'd" [*The Five Books of M. Manilius*, trans. Thomas Creech (1697), p. 5]); Statius's *Thebaid*, iv.282–84; Lucretius's *De rerum natura*, v. 973–76; and Marvell's *The First Anniversary of the Government under O.C.*, ll.337–40.

4. Cf. *Rambler* 47 (final par.): "[Sorrow] is the putrefaction of stagnant life, and is remedied by exercise and motion"; 165 (par. 3): "The stream of life, if it is not ruffled by obstructions, will grow putrid by stagnation."

5. In *Rambler* 47 (par. 12), SJ says: "The safe and general antidote against sorrow, is employment." In letters to Mrs. Piozzi on her first husband's death, he remarked: "A mind occupied by lawful business, has little room for useless regret"; "I think business the best remedy for grief as soon as it can be admitted" (*Letters* 717, 721). Cf. *Anecdotes* (1.252).

6. *To diffuse:* "To spread; to scatter; to disperse" (sense 2 in *Dictionary*).

the promise to her brother, who had been advised by Imlac to require it. Imlac had, indeed, no great hope of regaining Pekuah, but he supposed, that if he could secure the interval of a year, the princess would be then in no danger of a cloister.

Chap. XXXVI.

Pekuah is still remembered. The progress of sorrow.[a]

Nekayah, seeing that nothing was omitted for the recovery of her favourite, and having, by her promise, set her intention of retirement at a distance, began imperceptibly to return to common cares and common pleasures.[1] She rejoiced without her own consent at the suspension of her sorrows, and sometimes caught herself with indignation in the act of turning away her mind from the remembrance of her, whom yet she resolved never to forget.[2]

She then appointed a certain hour of the day for meditation on the merits and fondness of Pekuah, and for some weeks retired constantly at the time fixed, and returned with her eyes swollen and her countenance clouded. By degrees she grew less scrupulous, and suffered any important and pressing avocation to delay the tribute of daily tears.[3] She then yielded to less occasions; sometimes forgot

a. remembered. . . . sorrow. *59b*] remembered by the princess. *59a*

---

1. In *Rambler* 47 (par. 13), SJ comments: "Time is observed generally to wear out sorrow, and its effects might doubtless be accelerated by quickening the succession, and enlarging the variety of objects."

2. Cf. the following incident in the *Life:* "Dr. Taylor mentioned a gentleman . . . who had endeavoured to *retain* grief. He told Dr. Taylor, that after his Lady's death . . . , he *resolved* that the grief . . . should be lasting; but that he found he could not keep it long.

JOHNSON. 'All grief for what cannot in the course of nature be helped, soon wears away; in some sooner . . . , in some later; but it never continues very long'" (III.136).

3. In *Rambler* 47 (par. 5), SJ observes: "It seems determined, by the general suffrage of mankind, that sorrow . . . must give way, after a stated time, to social duties, and the common avocations of life." In *Dictionary*, sense 2 of *avocation* is "The business that calls; or the call that summons away."

what she was indeed afraid to remember, and, at last, wholly released herself from the duty of periodical affliction.

Her real love of Pekuah was yet not diminished. A thousand occurrences brought her back to memory, and a thousand wants, which nothing but the confidence of friendship can supply, made her frequently regretted. She, therefore, solicited Imlac never to desist from enquiry, and to leave no art of intelligence untried, that, at least, she might have the comfort of knowing that she did not suffer by negligence or sluggishness. "Yet what," said she, "is to be expected from our persuit of happiness, when we find the state of life to be such, that happiness itself is the cause of misery? Why should we endeavour to attain that, of which the possession cannot be secured? I shall henceforward fear to yield my heart to excellence, however bright, or to fondness, however tender, lest I should lose again what I have lost in Pekuah."[4]

Chap. XXXVII.

The princess hears news of Pekuah.

In seven months, one of the messengers, who had been sent away upon the day when the promise was drawn from the princess, returned, after many unsuccessful rambles, from the borders of Nubia,[1] with an account that Pekuah was in the hands of an Arab chief, who possessed a castle or fortress on the extremity of Egypt. The Arab, whose revenue was plunder, was willing to restore her, with her two attendants, for two hundred ounces of gold.

---

4. In *Rambler* 47 (par. 7), SJ mentions those "rules of intellectual health" which "teach us not to trust ourselves with favourite enjoyments, not to indulge the luxury of fondness, but to keep our minds always suspended in such indifference, that we may change the objects about us without emotion." He goes on to assert (par. 9), however, that "an attempt to preserve life in a state of neutrality and indifference, is unreasonable and vain."

1. "Nubia is bounded on the north by Upper Egypt . . . on the east by the Red Sea, on the south by Aethiopia" (Bowen, *Geography*, II.396).

The price was no subject of debate. The princess was in extasies when she heard that her favourite was alive, and might so cheaply be ransomed. She could not think of delaying for a moment Pekuah's happiness or her own, but entreated her brother to send back the messenger with the sum required. Imlac, being consulted, was not very confident of the veracity of the relator, and was still more doubtful of the Arab's faith, who might, if he were too liberally trusted, detain at once the money and the captives. He thought it dangerous to put themselves in the power of the Arab, by going into his district, and could not expect that the Rover[a] would so much expose himself as to come into the lower country,[2] where he might be seized by the forces of the Bassa.

It is difficult to negotiate where neither will trust. But Imlac, after some deliberation, directed the messenger to propose that Pekuah should be conducted by ten horsemen to the monastry of St. Anthony, which is situated in the deserts of Upper-Egypt,[3] where she should be met by the same number, and her ransome should be paid.

a. Rover 59b] Arab 59a

---

2. According to Bowen's *Geography*, "Egypt is commonly divided into Upper, Lower, and Middle, with respect to the course of the river Nile, which runs through the middle of it. . . . LOWER EGYPT" is "the last of the three thro' which that river runs, and from which it discharges itself into the sea" (II.381, 387).

3. Describing Upper Egypt in his *Geography*, Bowen says that "the greatest curiosity" in the deserts of "Thebais" "is the monastery of St. Antony, near some of the high mountains, where that famed ascetic lived and died" (II.394). During his trip to Upper Egypt, Pococke actually visited the "convent of St. Antony"; he remarks that "the country is very little inhabited" above the convent and that the people "on the east side are mostly Arabs, who submit to no government" (*A Description of the East*, I.70, 71; see also p. 128). According to the *Encyclopaedia Britannica* (1947), Saint Anthony, "the first Christian monk, was born in middle Egypt. At the age of 20 he began to practise an ascetic life, and after 15 years of this life, he withdrew for solitude to a mountain by the Nile, called Pispir. . . . In the early years of the 4th century, he emerged from his retreat to organize the monastic life of the monks who imitated him. After a time, he again withdrew to the mountain by the Red sea, where now stands the monastery that bears his name (Der Mar Antonios)." *Voyage to Abyssinia* mentions him (pp. 312, 314).

That no time might be lost, as they expected that the proposal would not be refused, they immediately began their journey to the monastry; and, when they arrived, Imlac went forward with the former messenger to the Arab's fortress. Rasselas was desirous to go with them, but neither his sister nor Imlac would consent. The Arab, according to the custom of his nation, observed the laws of hospitality with great exactness to those who put themselves into his power,[4] and, in a few days, brought Pekuah with her maids, by easy journeys, to their place[b] appointed, where receiving the stipulated price, he restored her with great respect[c] to liberty and her friends, and undertook to conduct them back towards Cairo beyond all danger of robbery or violence.

The princess and her favourite embraced each other with transport too violent to be expressed, and went out together to pour the tears of tenderness in secret, and exchange professions of kindness and gratitude. After a few hours they returned into the refectory of the convent, where, in the presence of the prior and his brethren, the prince required of Pekuah the history of her adventures.

Chap. XXXVIII.

The adventures of the lady Pekuah.

"At what time, and in what manner, I was forced away," said Pekuah, "your servants have told you. The suddenness of the event struck me with surprise, and I was at first rather

---

b. "their place *should perhaps be* the place" (*RWC*)   c. receiving . . . respect 59*b*]
he received the stipulated price, and, with great respect, restored her 59*a*

---

4. Cf. Gibbon's comment in the *Decline and Fall of the Roman Empire*, ed. J. B. Bury, v.326: "The same hospitality which was practised by Abraham and celebrated by Homer is still renewed in the camps of the Arabs. The ferocious Bedoweens, the terror of the desert, embrace, without inquiry or hesitation, the stranger who dares to confide in their honour and to enter their tent. His treatment is kind and respectful; he shares the wealth or the poverty of his host; and, after a needful repose, he is dismissed on his way, with thanks, with blessings, and perhaps with gifts."

stupified than agitated with any passion of either fear or sorrow. My confusion was encreased by the speed and tumult of our flight while we were followed by the Turks, who, as it seemed, soon despaired to overtake us, or were afraid of those whom they made a shew of menacing.

"When the Arabs saw themselves out of danger they slackened their course, and, as I was less harrassed by external violence, I began to feel more uneasiness in my mind. After some time we stopped near a spring shaded with trees in a pleasant meadow,[1] where we were set upon the ground, and offered such refreshments as our masters were partaking. I was suffered to sit with my maids apart from the rest, and none attempted to comfort or insult us. Here I first began to feel the full weight of my misery. The girls sat weeping in silence, and from time to time looked on[a] me for succour. I knew not to what condition we were doomed, nor could conjecture where would be the place of our captivity, or whence to draw any hope of deliverance. I was in the hands of robbers and savages, and had no reason to suppose that their pity was more than their justice, or that they would forbear the gratification of any ardour of desire, or caprice of cruelty. I, however, kissed my maids, and endeavoured to pacify them by remarking, that we were yet treated with decency, and that, since we were now carried beyond pursuit, there was no danger of violence to our lives.

"When we were to be set again on horseback, my maids clung round me, and refused to be parted, but I commanded them not to irritate those who had us in their power. We travelled the remaining part of the day through an unfrequented and pathless country, and came by moonlight to the side of a hill, where the rest of the troop was stationed. Their tents were pitched, and their fires kindled, and our chief was welcomed as a man much beloved by his dependants.

a. on 59b] up to 59a

1. Hill comments that "Johnson was thinking of English not of Egyptian scenery" (p. 191).

"We were received into a large tent, where we found women who had attended their husbands in the expedition. They set before us the supper which they had provided, and I eat[2] it rather to encourage my maids than to comply with any appetite of my own. When the meat[3] was taken away they spread the carpets for repose. I was weary, and hoped to find in sleep that remission of distress which nature seldom denies. Ordering myself therefore to be undrest, I observed that the women looked very earnestly upon me, not expecting, I suppose,[b] to see me so submissively attended. When my upper vest was taken off, they were apparently struck with the splendour of my cloaths, and one of them timorously laid her hand upon the embroidery.[4] She then went out, and, in a short time, came back with another woman, who seemed to be of higher rank, and greater authority. She did, at her entrance, the usual act of reverence, and, taking me by the hand, placed me in a smaller tent, spread with finer carpets, where I spent the night quietly with my maids.

"In the morning, as I was sitting on the grass, the chief of the troop came towards me.[c] I rose up to receive him, and he bowed with great respect. 'Illustrious lady,' said he, 'my fortune is better than I had presumed to hope; I am told by my women, that I have a princess in my camp.' 'Sir,' answered I, 'your women have deceived themselves and you; I am not a princess, but an unhappy stranger who intended soon to have left this country, in which I am now to be imprisoned for ever.' 'Whoever, or whencesoever, you are,' returned the Arab, 'your dress, and that of your servants, show your rank to be high, and your wealth to be great. Why should you, who can so easily procure your ransome, think yourself in danger of perpetual captivity? The pur-

---

b. suppose *59b*] supposed *59a*   c. me. *59b*] me: *59a*

2. See p. 62, n. 4, above.
3. *Meat:* "Food in general" (sense 2 in *Dictionary*).
4. Abyssinian "people of quality," *Voyage to Abyssinia* remarks (p. 49), "love

bright and glaring colours, and dress themselves much in the Turkish manner. . . . Their robes are always full of gold and silver embroidery."

pose of my incursions is to encrease my riches, or more properly to gather tribute. The sons of Ishmael[5] are the natural and hereditary lords of this part of the continent, which is usurped by late invaders, and low-born tyrants, from whom we are compelled to take by the sword what is denied to justice.[6] The violence of war admits no distinction; the lance that is lifted at guilt and power will sometimes fall on innocence and gentleness.'

" 'How little,' said I, 'did I expect that yesterday it should have fallen upon me.'

" 'Misfortunes,' answered the Arab, 'should always be expected. If the eye of hostility could learn reverence or pity,[d] excellence like yours had been exempt from injury. But the angels of affliction spread their toils alike for the virtuous and the wicked, for the mighty and the mean. Do not be disconsolate; I am not one of the lawless and cruel rovers of the desert; I know the rules of civil[7] life; I will fix your ransome, give a pasport to your messenger, and perform my stipulation with nice punctuality.'[8]

d. learn . . . pity *59b*] have learned to spare *59a*

---

5. For an account of Ishmael, the outcast son of Abraham and Hagar and the traditional ancestor of the Arab peoples, see Genesis xvi.11–15, xxi.9–21.

6. Describing the "character" of the Arabs in his *Geography,* Bowen says that, "as to their living altogether upon plunder, they, especially the Ishmaelites, are so far from disowning it, or being asham'd of it, that they think themselves the only nation that is entitled to that way of living; because Abraham, the father of their progenitor, is recorded to have sent him away without any portion, from which they infer that he left him the whole world to range in at pleasure" (11.126). Gibbon's comparable remarks in the *Decline and Fall of the Roman Empire* (ed. J. B. Bury, v.322) present a rather different hypothesis regarding the Arabs'

actions: "The separation of the Arabs from the rest of mankind has accustomed them to confound the ideas of stranger and enemy; and the poverty of the land has introduced a maxim of jurisprudence which they believe and practise to the present hour. They pretend that, in the division of the earth, the rich and fertile climates were assigned to the other branches of the human family; and that the posterity of the outlaw Ismael might recover, by fraud or force, the portion of inheritance of which he had been unjustly deprived."

7. See p. 111, n. 1, above.

8. *Punctuality:* "Nicety; scrupulous exactness" (*Dictionary*). Cf. *Rambler* 201 (par. 5): "The chief praise to which a trader aspires is that of punctuality, or an exact and rigorous observance of commercial engagements."

"You will easily believe that I was pleased with his courtesy; and finding that his predominant passion was desire of money, I began now to think my danger less, for I knew that no sum would be thought too great for the release of Pekuah. I told him that he should have no reason to charge me with ingratitude, if I was used with kindness, and that any ransome, which could be expected for a maid of common rank, would be paid, but that he must not persist to rate me as a princess. He said, he would consider what he should demand, and then, smiling, bowed and retired.

"Soon after the women came about me, each contending to be more officious[9] than the other, and my maids themselves were served with reverence. We travelled onward by short journeys. On the fourth day the chief told me, that my ransome must be two hundred ounces of gold; which I not only promised him, but told him, that I would add fifty more, if I and my maids were honourably treated.

"I never knew the power of gold before. From that time I was the leader of the troop. The march of every day was longer or shorter as I commanded, and the tents were pitched where I chose to rest. We now had camels and other conveniencies for travel, my own women were always at my side, and I amused myself with observing the manners of the vagrant nations, and with viewing remains of ancient edifices with which these deserted countries appear to have been, in some distant age, lavishly embellished.

"The chief of the band was a man far from illiterate: he was able to travel by the stars or the compass, and had marked in his erratick[1] expeditions such places as are most worthy the notice of a passenger.[2] He observed to me, that buildings are always best preserved in places little frequented, and difficult of access: for, when once a country declines from its primitive splendour, the more inhabitants are left, the quicker ruin will be made. Walls supply stones

---

9. *Officious:* "Kind; doing good offices" (sense 1 in *Dictionary*). See also p. 12, n. 4, above.

1. *Erratick:* "Wandering; uncertain; keeping no certain order; holding no

established course" (sense 1 in *Dictionary*).

2. *Passenger:* "A traveller; one who is upon the road; a wayfarer" (sense 1 in *Dictionary*).

more easily than quarries, and palaces and temples will be demolished to make stables of granate, and cottages of porphyry."

Chap. XXXIX.

The adventures of Pekuah continued.

"We wandered about in this manner for some weeks, whether, as our chief pretended, for my gratification, or, as I rather suspected, for some convenience of his own. I endeavoured to appear contented where sullenness and resentment would have been of no use, and that endeavour conduced much to the calmness of my mind; but my heart was always with Nekayah, and the troubles of the night much overbalanced the amusements of the day. My women, who threw all their cares upon their mistress, set their minds at ease from the time when they saw me treated with respect, and gave themselves up to the incidental alleviations of our fatigue without solicitude or sorrow. I was pleased with their pleasure, and animated with their confidence. My condition had lost much of its terrour, since I found that the Arab ranged the country merely to get riches. Avarice is an uniform and tractable vice: other intellectual distempers are different in different constitutions of mind; that which sooths the pride of one will offend the pride of another; but to the favour of the covetous there is a ready way, bring money and nothing is denied.

"At last we came to the dwelling of our chief, a strong and spacious house built with stone[1] in an island of the Nile, which lies, as I was told, under the tropick. 'Lady,' said the Arab, 'you shall rest after your journey a few weeks[a] in this

a. after . . . weeks 59b] a few weeks after your journey 59a

---

1. In his essay cited on p. xxiii, n. 7, above, Weitzman suggests that SJ's depiction of the Arab's dwelling is modelled on the seraglio of "a rich Turk or bey, perhaps the Ottoman Sultan" (p. 51) as presented in such works as Greaves's *Description of the Grand Seignor's Seraglio* and Hill's *Present State of the . . . Ottoman Empire*.

place, where you are to consider yourself as sovereign. My occupation is war: I have therefore chosen this obscure residence, from which I can issue unexpected, and to which I can retire unpersued. You may now repose in security: here are few pleasures, but here is no danger.' He then led me into the inner apartments, and seating me on the richest couch,[b] bowed to the ground. His women, who considered me as a rival, looked on me with malignity; but being soon informed that I was a great lady detained only for my ransome, they began to vie with each other in obsequiousness[2] and reverence.

"Being again comforted with new assurances of speedy liberty, I was for some days diverted from impatience by the novelty of the place. The turrets overlooked the country to a great distance, and afforded a view of many windings of the stream. In the day I wandered from one place to another as the course of the sun varied the splendour of the prospect, and saw many things which I had never seen before. The crocodiles and river-horses[3] are[c] common in this unpeopled region, and I often looked upon them with terrour, though I knew that they could not hurt me. For some time I expected to see mermaids and tritons, which, as Imlac has told me, the European travellers have stationed in the Nile, but no such beings ever appeared, and the Arab, when I enquired after them, laughed at my credulity.[4]

b. on . . . couch *59b*] in the place of honour *59a*   c. are *59b*] were *59a*

---

2. See p. 126, n. 2, above.

3. According to *Voyage to Abyssinia*, "The Nile has at least as great numbers of each [crocodiles and river-horses] as any river in the world" (p. 85, cf. p. 80). In his *Dictionary*, SJ defines *hippopotamus* as "The river horse. An animal found in the Nile."

4. In his *Travels of the Jesuits in Ethiopia* (1710), Balthazar Telles denies the existence of tritons and sirens or mermaids in the Sea of Dambea, through

which the Nile flows. "It is most certain," he says, "there are no tritons nor sirens in this lake, as Johnson was inform'd, and he tells us in his map of Ethiopia, in his *Atlas*, publish'd *An.* 1653" (p. 15). "Johnson" was "Jan Jansson, the seventeenth-century Dutch mapmaker and publisher," and the "map of Ethiopia" (containing the notation "*Tritones et syrenes in hoc lacu esse dicuntur*") appears "in the 1653 translation into Spanish of Jansson's *Novus*

"At night the Arab always attended me to a tower set apart for celestial observations, where he endeavoured to teach me the names and courses of the stars. I had no great inclination to this study, but an appearance of attention was necessary to please my instructor, who valued himself for his skill, and, in a little while, I found some employment requisite to beguile the tediousness of time, which was to be passed always amidst the same objects. I was weary of looking in the morning on things from which I had turned away weary in the evening: I therefore was at last willing to observe the stars rather than do nothing, but could not always compose my thoughts, and was very often thinking on Nekayah when others imagined me contemplating the sky. Soon after the Arab went upon another expedition, and then my only pleasure was to talk with my maids about the accident by which we were carried away, and the happiness that we should all enjoy at the end of our captivity."

"There were women in your Arab's fortress," said the princess, "why did you not make them your companions, enjoy their conversation, and partake their diversions? In a place where they found business or amusement, why should you alone sit corroded with idle melancholy? or why could not you bear for a few months that condition to which they were condemned for life?"

"The diversions of the women," answered Pekuah, "were only childish play, by which the mind accustomed to stronger operations could not be kept busy. I could do all which they delighted in doing by powers merely sensitive,[5] while my intellectual faculties were flown to Cairo. They ran from room to room as a bird hops from wire to wire in his cage. They danced for the sake of motion, as lambs frisk in a meadow. One sometimes pretended to be hurt that the rest

atlas, sive theatrum orbis terrarum (Amsterdam, 1640–50)." For this information about Jansson and his map, I am indebted to the essay cited on p. xxiii, n. 7, above by Donald M. Lockhart, who argues (p. 524) that SJ probably drew on Telles's *Travels* for the allusions to the crocodiles, river-horses, mermaids, and tritons in this paragraph.

5. *Sensitive:* "Having sense or perception, but not reason" (*Dictionary*).

might be alarmed, or hid herself that another might seek her. Part of their time passed in watching the progress of light bodies that floated on the river, and part in marking the various forms into which clouds broke in the sky.

"Their business was only needlework,[6] in which I and my maids sometimes helped them; but you know that the mind will easily straggle from the fingers, nor will you suspect that captivity and absence from Nekayah could receive solace from[d] silken flowers.

"Nor was much satisfaction to be hoped from their conversation: for of what could they be expected to talk? They had seen nothing; for they had lived from early youth in that narrow spot: of what they had not seen they could have no knowledge, for they could not read. They had no ideas but of the few things that were within their view, and had hardly names for any thing but their cloaths and their food. As I bore a superiour character, I was often called to terminate their quarrels, which I decided as equitably as I could. If it could have amused me to hear the complaints of each against the rest, I might have been often detained by long stories, but the motives of their animosity were so small that I could not listen[e] without intercepting the tale."[7]

"How," said Rasselas, "can the Arab, whom you represented as a man of more than common accomplishments, take any pleasure in his seraglio, when it is filled only with women like these. Are they exquisitely beautiful?"

"They do not," said Pekuah, "want that unaffecting and ignoble beauty which may subsist without spriteliness or

d. receive . . . from 59*b*] be much solaced by 59*a*   e. listen 59*b*] listen long 59*a*

---

6. In the essay cited on p. xxiii, n. 7, above, Weitzman points out (p. 53) that Hill's *Present State of the . . . Ottoman Empire* mentions "making 'embroidery in various colours'" (p. 162) as the principal activity of the women in the sultan's seraglio.

7. In his *Dictionary,* SJ illustrates

sense 2 of *to intercept* ("To obstruct; to cut off; to stop from being communicated; to stop in the progress. It is used of the thing or person passing") with a passage from *Titus Andronicus* (III.i.38–40) which concludes: "For that they will not intercept my tale."

sublimity, without energy of thought or dignity of virtue. But to a man like the Arab such beauty was only a flower casually plucked and carelesly thrown away. Whatever pleasures he might find among them, they were not those of friendship or society. When they were playing about him he looked on them with inattentive superiority: when they vied for his regard he sometimes turned away disgusted. As they had no knowledge, their talk could take nothing from the tediousness of life:[8] as they had no choice, their fondness, or appearance of fondness, excited in him neither pride nor gratitude; he was not exalted in his own esteem by the smiles of a woman who saw no other man, nor was much obliged by that regard, of which he could never know the sincerity, and which he might often perceive to be exerted not so much to delight him as to pain a rival. That which he gave, and they received, as love, was only a careless distribution of superfluous time, such love as man can bestow upon that which he despises, such as has neither hope nor fear, neither joy nor sorrow."

"You have reason, lady, to think yourself happy," said Imlac, "that you have been thus easily dismissed. How could a mind, hungry for knowledge, be willing, in an intellectual famine, to lose such a banquet as Pekuah's conversation?"

"I am inclined to believe," answered Pekuah, "that he was for some time in suspense; for, notwithstanding his promise, whenever I proposed to dispatch a messenger to Cairo, he found some excuse for delay. While I was detained in his house he made many incursions into the neighbouring countries, and, perhaps, he would have refused to discharge me, had his plunder been equal to his wishes. He returned always courteous, related his adventures, de-

---

8. Cf. Aspasia's warning to Irene in SJ's *Irene* (III.viii.85) that, once admitted to the Sultan's seraglio, she will "wear the tedious hours of life away." SJ himself, Hardy observes (p. 169), "was always ready to acknowledge 'the *taedium vitae*' (cf. *Life*, 1.394), and for this reason sought 'novelty' in both life and literature." Hardy also compares Pekuah's remark with that by Imlac on p. 49 above: "Ignorance is mere privation, by which nothing can be produced: it is a vacuity in which the soul sits motionless and torpid for want of attraction."

lighted to hear my observations, and endeavoured to advance my acquaintance with the stars. When I importuned him to send away my letters, he soothed me with professions of honour and sincerity; and, when I could be no longer decently denied, put his troop again in motion, and left me to govern in his absence. I was much afflicted by this studied procrastination, and was sometimes afraid that I should be forgotten; that you would leave Cairo, and I must end my days in an island of the Nile.

"I grew at last hopeless and dejected, and cared so little to entertain him, that he for a while more frequently talked with my maids. That he should fall in love with them, or with me, might have been equally fatal, and I was not much pleased with the growing friendship. My anxiety was not long; for, as I recovered some degree of chearfulness, he returned to me, and I could not forbear to despise my former uneasiness.

"He still delayed to send for my ransome, and would, perhaps, never have determined, had not your agent found his way to him. The gold, which he would not fetch, he could not reject when it was offered. He hastened to prepare for our journey hither, like a man delivered from the pain of an intestine conflict. I took leave of my companions in the house, who dismissed me with cold indifference."

Nekayah, having heard her favourite's relation, rose and embraced her, and Rasselas gave her an hundred ounces of gold, which she presented to the Arab for the fifty that were promised.

Chap. XL.

The history of a man of learning.

They returned to Cairo, and were so well pleased at finding themselves together, that none of them went much abroad. The prince began to love learning, and one day declared to Imlac, that he intended to devote himself to science,[1] and pass the rest of his days in literary solitude.

---

1. See p. 113, n. 8, above.

"Before you make your final choice," answered Imlac, "you ought to examine its hazards, and converse with some of those who are grown old in the company of themselves. I have just left the observatory of one of the most learned astronomers in the world,[2] who has spent forty years in unwearied attention to the motions and appearances of the celestial bodies, and has drawn out his soul in endless calculations. He admits a few friends once a month to hear his deductions and enjoy his discoveries. I was introduced as a man of knowledge worthy of his notice. Men of various ideas and fluent conversation are commonly welcome to those whose thoughts have been long fixed upon a single point, and who find the images of other things stealing away. I delighted him with my remarks, he smiled at the narrative of my travels, and was glad to forget the constellations, and descend for a moment into the lower world.

"On the next day of vacation[3] I renewed my visit, and was so fortunate as to please him again. He relaxed from that time the severity of his rule, and permitted me to enter at my own choice. I found him always busy, and always glad to be relieved. As each knew much which the other was desirous of learning, we exchanged our notions with great delight. I perceived that I had every day more of his confidence, and always found new cause of admiration in the profundity of his mind. His comprehension is vast, his memory capacious and retentive, his discourse is methodical, and his expression clear.

"His integrity and benevolence are equal to his learning. His deepest researches and most favourite studies are willingly interrupted for any opportunity of doing good by his counsel or his riches. To his closest retreat, at his most busy

---

2. Under the entry for *astronomy* in his *Dictionary*, SJ quotes the following passage from Ephraim Chambers's *Cyclopaedia:* "The origin of astronomy is uncertain; but from Egypt it travelled into Greece, where Pythagoras was the first European who taught that the earth and planets turn round the sun . . . ; as he himself had been instructed by the Egyptian priests. From the time of Pythagoras, astronomy sunk into neglect, till it was revived by the Ptolemys, kings of Egypt."

3. *Vacation:* "Leisure; freedom from trouble or perplexity" (sense 2 in *Dictionary*).

moments, all are admitted that want his assistance:[4] 'For though I exclude idleness and pleasure, I will never,' says he, 'bar my doors against charity. To man is permitted the contemplation of the skies, but the practice of virtue is commanded.'"[5]

"Surely," said the princess, "this man is happy."

"I visited him," said Imlac, "with more and more frequency, and was every time more enamoured of his conversation: he was sublime[6] without haughtiness, courteous without formality, and communicative without ostentation. I was at first, great princess,[a] of your opinion, thought him the happiest of mankind, and often congratulated him on the blessing that he enjoyed. He seemed to hear nothing with indifference but the praises of his condition, to which he always returned a general answer, and diverted the conversation to some other topic.

"Amidst this willingness to be pleased, and labour to please, I had quickly[b] reason to imagine that some painful sentiment pressed upon his mind. He often looked up earnestly towards the sun, and let his voice fall in the midst of

a. great princess *59b*] Madam *59a*   b. quickly *59b*] always *59a*

---

4. In Lady Knight's opinion, Imlac's description of the astronomer "summed up" SJ's own character; see *Johnsonian Miscellanies*, ed. G. B. Hill (2 vols., 1897), II.175–76.

5. With the astronomer's assertion, cf. *Rambler* 180 (pars. 4–5): "Raphael, in return to Adam's enquiries into the courses of the stars and the revolutions of heaven, counsels him to withdraw his mind from idle speculations, and employ his faculties upon nearer and more interesting objects, the survey of his own life, the subjection of his passions, the knowledge of duties which must daily be performed, and the detection of dangers which must daily be incurred [*Paradise Lost*, VIII.15–197].

"This angelic counsel every man of letters should have before him." Like-

wise, in the "Life of Milton," SJ declares: "The knowledge of external nature, and the sciences which that knowledge requires or includes, are not the great or the frequent business of the human mind. Whether we provide for action or conversation . . . , the first requisite is the religious and moral knowledge of right and wrong. . . . We are perpetually moralists, but we are geometricians only by chance. . . . One man may know another half his life without being able to estimate his skill in hydrostaticks or astronomy, but his moral and prudential character immediately appears" (*Lives*, I.99, 100, par. 39).

6. *Sublime*: "Lofty of mien; elevated in manner" (sense 5 in *Dictionary*).

his discourse. He would sometimes, when we were alone, gaze upon me in silence with the air of a man who longed to speak what he was yet resolved to suppress. He would often[c] send for me with vehement injunctions of haste, though, when I came to him, he had nothing extraordinary to say. And sometimes, when I was leaving him, would call me back, pause a few moments and then dismiss me.

Chap. XLI.

The astronomer discovers[1] the cause of his uneasiness.

"At last the time came when the secret burst his reserve. We were sitting together last night in the turret of his house, watching the emersion[2] of a satellite of Jupiter. A sudden tempest clouded the sky, and disappointed our observation. We sat a while silent in the dark, and then he addressed himself to me in these words: 'Imlac, I have long considered thy friendship as the greatest blessing of my life. Integrity without knowledge is weak and useless, and knowledge without integrity is dangerous and dreadful. I have found in thee all the qualities requisite for trust, benevolence, experience, and fortitude. I have long discharged an office which I must soon quit at the call of nature, and shall rejoice in the hour of imbecility[3] and pain to devolve it upon thee.'

"I thought myself honoured by this testimony, and protested that whatever could conduce to his happiness would add likewise to mine.

"'Hear, Imlac, what thou wilt not without difficulty credit. I have possessed for five years the regulation of weather, and the distribution of the seasons:[4] the sun has

c. often 59b] sometimes 59a

---

1. To discover: "To make known; not to disguise; to reveal" (sense 4 in Dictionary).

2. Emersion: "The time when a star, having been obscured by its too near approach to the sun, appears again" (Dictionary).

3. See p. 19, n. 1, above.

4. Discussing "Notional Insanity" in his Observations on the Nature, Kinds, Causes, and Prevention of Insanity ([1782–86] 2d ed., 2 vols., 1806), Dr. Thomas Arnold instances the person who "imagines that he has the power of . . . directing the action of the elements, regulating the weather, and dis-

listened to my dictates, and passed from tropick to tropick by my direction; the clouds, at my call, have poured their waters, and the Nile has overflowed at my command; I have restrained the rage of the dog-star,[5] and mitigated the fervours of the crab.[6] The winds alone, of all the elemental[7] powers, have hitherto refused my authority, and multitudes have perished by equinoctial tempests which I found myself unable to prohibit or restrain. I have administered this great office with exact justice, and made to the different nations of the earth an impartial dividend of rain and sunshine. What must have been the misery of half the globe, if I had limited the clouds to particular regions, or confined the sun to either side of the equator?' "

---

tributing the seasons" (1.135, 136). In a footnote to this passage, he writes: "Though I can produce nothing better than poetical authority for this instance, yet as it is perfectly consonant to what I myself have experienced to be fact, I have ventured to set it down as such. The authority I allude to, is that of Dr. JOHNSON, in his *Rasselas;* where he has beautifully illustrated this variety, in the character of an astronomer, who fancied he had such a power. The whole story, and the observations upon insanity which accompany it, are as just, and philosophical, as they are elegant; and are worthy of the pen from which they proceeded." Then, saying that he will "only make a short extract" (1.136–37), Arnold quotes the section of chap. XLII below beginning with "About ten years ago" (p. 146) and ending with "every day exerted it" (p. 147). For evidence of other physicians' admiration for SJ's depiction of the astronomer, see Kathleen M. Grange, "Dr. Samuel Johnson's Account of a Schizophrenic Illness in *Rasselas,*" *Medical History,* VI (1962), 162–68, 291.

5. Cf. "The Dog-star rages!" in Pope's *Epistle to Dr. Arbuthnot,* l.3, which is quoted in *Dictionary* under *to madden.* Under *dogstar* (defined as "The star which gives the name to the dogdays") in the *Dictionary,* SJ quotes this couplet—"All shun the raging dogstar's sultry heat, / And from the half-unpeopled town retreat"—and attributes it to Addison (but I have not found it in his poetry). In his discussion of dog-days in *Pseudodoxia Epidemica,* Sir Thomas Browne notes that the Egyptians were the "primitive and leading magnifiers" of the dog-star and that they connected its "rising and setting" with the "inundation of the river Nylus" (*Works,* ed. Geoffrey Keynes, 2d ed. [1964], II.325).

6. *Crab:* "The sign in the zodiack" (sense 5 in *Dictionary*). For the illustrative quotation ("Then parts the Twins and Crab, the dog divides, / and Argo's keel, that broke the frothy tides"), SJ draws upon Creech's translation (Book I, p. 26) of *The Five Books of M. Manilius,* which contains a description of the various heavenly bodies (including the dog-star which causes "powers" that "vex the world with opposite extremes" [Book I, p. 17] and the crab with its "unruly fires" [Book I, p. 56]) and the influence they presumably exert on the earth and its inhabitants.

7. *Elemental:* "Produced by some of the four elements" (sense 1 in *Dictionary*).

Chap. XLII.

The opinion of the astronomer is explained and justified.[a]

"I suppose he discovered in me, through the obscurity of the room, some tokens of amazement and doubt, for, after a short pause, he proceeded thus:

"'Not to be easily credited will neither surprise nor offend me; for I am, probably, the first of human beings to whom this trust has been imparted. Nor do I know whether to deem this distinction a reward or punishment; since I have possessed it I have been far less happy than before, and nothing but the consciousness of good intention could have enabled me to support the weariness of unremitted vigilance.'

"'How long, Sir,' said I, 'has this great office been in your hands?'

"'About ten years ago,' said he, 'my daily observations of the changes of the sky led me to consider, whether, if I had the power of the seasons, I could confer greater plenty upon the inhabitants of the earth. This contemplation fastened on my mind, and I sat days and nights in imaginary dominion, pouring upon this country and that the showers of fertility, and seconding every fall of rain with a due proportion of sunshine. I had yet only the will to do good, and did not imagine that I should ever have the power.

"'One day as I was looking on the fields withering with heat, I felt in my mind a sudden wish that I could send rain on the southern mountains, and raise the Nile to an inundation.[1] In the hurry of my imagination I commanded rain to fall, and, by comparing the time of my command,

a. opinion . . . justified 59b] astronomer justifies his account of himself 59a

_____

1. After a passage noting and rejecting other possible causes of the Nile's annual overflow, *Voyage to Abyssinia* states (p. 89) that constant rains on the mountains of Abyssinia (which "in its natural situation [is] much higher than Egypt"), falling "from June to September" and transmitted by "rivers, brooks and torrents," "necessarily swell" the Nile "above the banks, and fill the plains of Egypt with the inundation."

with that of the inundation, I found that the clouds had listned to my lips.'

"'Might not some other cause,' said I, 'produce this concurrence? the Nile does not always rise on the same day.'[2]

"'Do not believe,' said he with impatience, 'that such objections could escape me: I reasoned long against my own conviction, and laboured against truth with the utmost obstinacy. I sometimes suspected myself of madness, and should not have dared to impart this secret but to a man like you, capable of distinguishing the wonderful from the impossible, and the incredible from the false.'

"'Why, Sir,' said I, 'do you call that incredible, which you know, or think you know, to be true.'

"'Because,' said he, 'I cannot prove it by any external evidence; and I know too well the laws of demonstration to think that my conviction ought to influence another, who cannot, like me, be conscious of its force.[3] I, therefore, shall not attempt to gain credit by disputation. It is sufficient that I feel this power, that I have long possessed, and every day exerted it. But the life of man is short, the infirmities of age increase upon me, and the time will soon come when the regulator of the year must mingle with the dust. The care of appointing a successor has long disturbed me; the night and the day have been spent in comparisons of all the characters which have come to my knowledge, and I have yet found none so worthy as thyself.'"

Chap. XLIII.

The astronomer leaves Imlac his directions.

"'Hear therefore, what I shall impart, with attention,

---

2. Under sense 1 of *to weigh* in his *Dictionary*, SJ quotes a passage from Bacon's *Natural History* (VIII.743) which asserts that the Nile "beginneth to rise" on "the seventeenth of June." On the other hand, the river's actual flooding, according to *Voyage to Abyssinia* (p. 89), "comes regularly about the month of July, or three weeks after the beginning of a rainy season in Aethiopia." Cf. also Pococke's *Description of the East*, 1.199, 201.

3. Commenting later on "apparitions," SJ expresses an opinion similar to the astronomer's: "A man who thinks he has seen an apparition, can only be convinced himself; his authority will not convince another" (*Life*, IV.94).

such as the welfare of a world requires. If the task of a king be considered as difficult, who has the care only of a few millions, to whom he cannot do much good or harm,[1] what must be the anxiety of him, on whom depend the action of the elements, and the great gifts of light and heat!—Hear me therefore with attention.

"'I have diligently considered the position of the earth and sun, and formed innumerable schemes in which I changed their situation.[2] I have sometimes turned aside the axis of the earth, and sometimes varied the ecliptick of the sun: but I have found it impossible to make a disposition by which the world may be advantaged;[3] what one region gains, another loses by any imaginable alteration, even without considering the distant parts of the solar system with which we are unacquainted. Do not, therefore, in thy administration of the year, indulge thy pride by innovation; do not please thyself with thinking that thou canst make thyself renowned to all future ages, by disordering the seasons. The memory of mischief is no desirable fame. Much less will it become thee to let kindness or interest prevail. Never rob other countries of rain to pour it on thine own. For us the Nile is sufficient.'[4]

"I promised that when I possessed the power, I would use

---

1. See p. 103, n. 4, above.

2. In *Adventurer* 45 (par. 12), SJ comments that "some philosophers have been foolish enough to imagine, that improvements might be made in the system of the universe, by a different arrangement of the orbs of heaven."

3. Cf. SJ's remark about the "position of the earth" in *Idler* 43 (par. 1): "The natural advantages which arise from the position of the earth which we inhabit with respect to the other planets, afford much employment to mathematical speculation; by which it has been discovered, that no other conformation of the system could have given such commodious distributions of light

and heat, or imparted fertility and pleasure to so great a part of a revolving sphere."

4. Under *bountifully* in his *Dictionary*, SJ quotes a shortened version of this passage from Sir Thomas Browne's *Pseudodoxia Epidemica*: "It is affirmed by many, and received by most, that it never raineth in Egypt, the [Nile] supplying that defect, and bountifully requiting it in its inundation"; Browne immediately adds, however, that this belief "must . . . be received in a qualified sense, that is, that it rains but seldom at any time in the summer, and very rarely in the winter" (*Works*, ed. Keynes, 2d ed., II.455).

it with inflexible integrity, and he dismissed me, pressing my hand. 'My heart,' said he, 'will be now at rest, and my benevolence will no more destroy my quiet: I have found a man of wisdom and virtue, to whom I can chearfully bequeath the inheritance of the sun.'"

The prince heard this narration with very serious regard, but the princess smiled, and Pekuah convulsed herself with laughter. "Ladies," said Imlac, "to mock the heaviest of human afflictions is neither charitable nor wise. Few can attain this man's knowledge, and few practise his virtues; but all may suffer his calamity. Of the uncertainties of our present state, the most dreadful and alarming is the uncertain continuance of reason."[5]

The princess was recollected,[6] and the favourite was abashed. Rasselas, more deeply affected, enquired of Imlac,

---

5. Writing of William Collins in a letter to Joseph Warton, SJ comes close to an expression of Imlac's opinion: "The moralists all talk of the uncertainty of fortune, and the transitoriness of beauty; but it is yet more dreadful to consider that the powers of the mind are equally liable to change, that understanding may make its appearance and depart, that it may blaze and expire" (*Letters* 96). SJ's well known fear of insanity is evidenced by the comments of Mrs. Piozzi, Sir John Hawkins, and Boswell. In her *Anecdotes* (1.199), Mrs. Piozzi says: "Mr. Johnson's health had been always bad since I first knew him, and his over-anxious care to retain without blemish the perfect sanity of his mind, contributed much to disturb it. He had studied medicine diligently in all its branches; but had given particular attention to the diseases of the imagination, which he watched in himself with a solicitude destructive of his own peace, and intolerable to those he trusted." Referring in his *Life of Johnson* (pp. 369–70; cf. p. 288) to the chapter in *Rasselas* on the "danger of insanity," Hawkins remarks: "It cannot but excite the pity of all those who gratefully accept and enjoy Johnson's endeavours to reform and instruct, to reflect that the peril he describes he believed impending over him." And Boswell observes (*Life*, 1.66): "To Johnson, whose supreme enjoyment was the exercise of his reason, the disturbance or obscuration of that faculty was the evil most to be dreaded. Insanity, therefore, was the object of his most dismal apprehension; and he fancied himself seized by it, or approaching to it, at the very time when he was giving proofs of a more than ordinary soundness and vigour of judgement."

6. *To recollect:* "To recover reason or resolution" (sense 2 in *Dictionary*). "Recollected" thus means, as Hardy says (p. 172), "brought back to a state of composure." Emerson suggests (p. xlviii) that SJ's practice of balancing constructions may have produced "was recollected" (rather than the usual "recollected herself") as a parallel to "was abashed."

whether he thought such maladies of the mind frequent, and how they were contracted.

Chap. XLIV.

The dangerous prevalence[1] of imagination.

"Disorders of intellect," answered Imlac, "happen much more often than superficial observers will easily believe.[2] Perhaps, if we speak with rigorous exactness, no human mind is in its right state.[3] There is no man whose imagination does not sometimes predominate over his reason, who can regulate his attention wholly by his will, and whose ideas will come and go at his command. No man will be found in whose mind airy[4] notions do not sometimes tyrannise, and force him to hope or fear beyond the limits of sober probability. All power of fancy over reason is a degree of insanity;[5] but while this power is such as we can controll

---

1. *Prevalence:* "Superiority; influence; predominance; efficacy; force; validity" (*Dictionary*). As the contents of this chapter make clear and as Donald J. Greene has pointed out (*Johnson, Boswell, and Their Circle: Essays Presented to L. F. Powell* [1965], p. 157), SJ "is talking about . . . the danger ensuing when an individual's fantasy prevails over his contact with reality."

2. According to Boswell, "When [SJ] talked of madness, he was to be understood as speaking of those who were in any great degree disturbed, or as it is commonly expressed, 'troubled in mind'" (*Life*, III.175).

3. Cf. Locke's remark in his *Essay concerning Human Understanding* that "madness" is "a weakness to which all men are . . . liable" and "a taint which . . . universally infects mankind" (II.xxxiii.4); also see n. 5 below. In his *Observations on Insanity*, Thomas Arnold, after quoting Boileau's *Satire* IV, ll. 39–40 ("Tous les hommes sont fous,

et malgré tous leurs soins, / Ne diffèrent entre eux que du plus ou du moins"), states that "*notional delirium . . .* seems to be peculiar to madness; and I am sorry to find myself under the necessity of so far agreeing with the satirist, as to assert, that the bulk of mankind, morally, at least, I will not say medically speaking, are more or less affected by it" (I.67).

4. In SJ's *Dictionary*, sense 6 of *airy* is "Wanting reality; having no steady foundation in truth or nature; vain; trifling"—a sense which is illustrated by the Earl of Roscommon's translation (1680) of Horace's *Art of Poetry*, ll. 268–69; "Nor (to avoid such meanness) soaring high, / With empty sound, and airy notions, fly." Cf. the phrases "amuse ourselves with the dance of airy images" and "a temporary recession from the realities of life to airy fictions" in *Idler* 32 (pars. 11, 13).

5. SJ once remarked that madness "is occasioned by too much indulgence of

and repress, it is not visible to others, nor considered as any depravation of the mental faculties: it is not pronounced madness but when it comes ungovernable, and apparently influences speech or action.[6]

"To indulge the power of fiction, and send imagination out upon the wing, is often the sport of those who delight too much in silent speculation.[7] When we are alone we are not always busy; the labour of excogitation is too violent to last long; the ardour of enquiry will sometimes give way to idleness or satiety.[8] He who has nothing external that can divert him, must find pleasure in his own thoughts, and

---

imagination" (*Life*, IV.208). With Imlac's statement, cf. Locke's assertion in his *Essay concerning Human Understanding* that "opposition to reason deserves [the name of madness], and is really madness; and there is scarce a man so free from it, but that if he should always, on all occasions, argue or do as in some cases he constantly does, would not be thought fitter for Bedlam than civil conversation" (II.xxxiii.4). Earlier Locke says that madmen, "by the violence of their imaginations, having taken their fancies for realities, . . . make right deductions from them" (II.xi.13). Hardy presents (p. 173) for comparison the following passage from Swift's *A Tale of a Tub* (sect. IX: "A Digression concerning . . . Madness"): "But when a man's fancy gets astride on his reason, when imagination is at cuffs with the senses, and common understanding, as well as common sense, is kickt out of doors; the first proselyte he makes, is himself (ed. A. C. Guthkelch and D. Nichol Smith, 2d ed., 1958, p. 171)." In his *Observations on Insanity*, Thomas Arnold lists and discusses (II.263–68) "Too great activity of imagination" as one of the causes of insanity, and under the section "Of the Prevention of Insanity," he says: "In short, the imagination should so be subdued, and kept under, that the mind may be able

to attend to reality, and the nature of things, and not suffer itself to be seduced by fancy" (II.331). *Insane* but not *insanity* appears in the first and fourth editions of *Dictionary*.

6. Cf. SJ's comment that "many a man is mad in certain instances, and goes through life without having it perceived:—for example, a madness has seized a person of supposing himself obliged literally to pray continually—had the madness turned the opposite way and the person thought it a crime ever to pray, it might not improbably have continued unobserved" (*Life*, IV.31).

7. See p. 83, n. 5, above.

8. In *Rambler* 89, discussing the necessity of "hours for relaxation and amusement" amid "profound study and intense meditation" (par. 1), SJ says: "It is certain, that, with or without our consent, many of the few moments allotted us will slide imperceptibly away, and that the mind will break, from confinement to its stated tasks, into sudden excursions. Severe and connected attention is preserved but for a short time; and when a man shuts himself up in his closet, and bends his thoughts to the discussion of any abstruse question, he will find his faculties continually stealing away to more pleasing entertainments" (par. 2).

must conceive himself what he is not; for who is pleased with what he is?[9] He then expatiates in boundless futurity, and culls from all imaginable conditions that which for the present moment he should most desire, amuses his desires with impossible enjoyments, and confers upon his pride unattainable dominion. The mind dances from scene to scene, unites all pleasures in all combinations, and riots in delights which nature and fortune, with all their bounty, cannot bestow.[1]

"In time some particular train of ideas fixes the attention, all other intellectual gratifications are rejected, the mind, in weariness or leisure, recurs constantly to the favourite conception,[2] and feasts on the luscious[3] falsehood whenever she is offended with the bitterness of truth.[4] By degrees the reign of fancy is confirmed; she grows first imperious, and in time despotick. Then fictions begin to operate as realities, false opinions fasten upon the mind, and life passes in dreams of rapture or of anguish.[5]

---

9. Cf. *Rambler* 5 (par. 1): "Every man is sufficiently discontented with some circumstances of his present state, to suffer his imagination to range more or less in quest of future happiness, and to fix upon some point of time, in which, by the removal of the inconvenience which now perplexes him, or acquisition of the advantage which he at present wants, he shall find the condition of his life very much improved."

1. Cf. *Idler* 32 (par. 13), in which SJ says that "it is easy in" the "semi-slumbers" of solitude "to collect all the possibilities of happiness, to alter the course of the sun, to bring back the past, and anticipate the future, to unite all the beauties of all seasons, and all the blessings of all climates, to receive and bestow felicity, and forget that misery is the lot of man"; see also *Rambler* 89 (par. 4).

2. According to Francis Pearson Walesby, editor of the 1825 edition of SJ's *Works*, Dr. Francis Willis, physician to George III, "defined, in remarkable accordance with this case in *Rasselas*, insanity to be the tendency of a mind to cherish one idea, or one set of ideas, to the exclusion of others" (1.293 n.).

3. *Luscious:* "Pleasing; delightful" (sense 3 in *Dictionary*).

4. Cf. SJ's *Preface to Shakespeare* (par. 67): "The mind, which has feasted on the luxurious wonders of fiction, has no taste of the insipidity of truth."

5. Cf. Addison's comment at the end of his series of essays on the pleasures of the imagination: God "can transport the imagination with such beautiful and glorious visions, as cannot possibly enter into our present conceptions, or haunt it with such ghastly spectres and apparitions, as would make us hope for annihilation, and think existence no better than a curse. In short, he can so exquisitely ravish or torture the soul through this single faculty, as might suffice to make up the whole Heaven or Hell of any finite being" (*Spectator* 421, penultimate par.).

"This, Sir, is one of the dangers of solitude, which the hermit has confessed not always to promote goodness, and the astronomer's misery has proved to be not always propitious to wisdom."

"I will no more," said the favourite, "imagine myself the queen of Abissinia. I have often spent the hours, which the princess gave to my own disposal, in adjusting ceremonies and regulating the court; I have repressed the pride of the powerful, and granted the petitions of the poor; I have built new palaces in more happy situations, planted groves upon the tops of mountains, and have exulted in the beneficence of royalty, till, when the princess entered, I had almost forgotten to bow down before her."

"And I," said the princess, "will not allow myself any more to play the shepherdess in my waking dreams. I have often soothed my thoughts with the quiet and innocence of pastoral employments, till I have in my chamber heard the winds whistle, and the sheep bleat; sometimes freed the lamb entangled in the thicket, and sometimes with my crook encountered the wolf. I have a dress like that of the village maids, which I put on to help my imagination, and a pipe on which I play softly, and suppose myself followed by my flocks."

"I will confess," said the prince, "an indulgence of fantastick delight more dangerous than yours. I have frequently endeavoured to image the possibility of a perfect government, by which all wrong should be restrained, all vice reformed, and all the subjects preserved in tranquility and innocence.[6] This thought produced innumerable schemes of reformation, and dictated many useful regulations and salutary edicts. This has been the sport and sometimes the labour of my solitude; and I start, when I think with how little anguish I once supposed the death of my father and my brothers."

"Such," says Imlac, "are the effects of visionary schemes: when we first form them we know them to be absurd, but familiarise them by degrees, and in time lose sight of their folly."[7]

---

6. See p. 32, ll. 17–19, above and n. 7.   7. With the "visionary schemes" (in-

Chap. XLV.

They discourse with an old man.

The evening was now far past, and they rose to return home. As they walked along the bank of the Nile, delighted with the beams of the moon quivering on the water, they saw at a small distance an old man, whom the prince had often heard in the assembly of the sages. "Yonder," said he, "is one whose years have calmed his passions, but not clouded his reason: let us close the disquisitions of the night, by enquiring what are his sentiments of his own state, that we may know whether youth alone is to struggle with vexation, and whether any better hope remains for the latter part of life."

Here the sage approached and saluted them. They invited him to join their walk, and prattled[1] a while as acquaintance[2] that had unexpectedly met one another. The old man was chearful and talkative, and the way seemed short in his company. He was pleased to find himself not disregarded, accompanied them to their house, and, at the prince's request, entered with them. They placed him in the seat of honour, and set wine and conserves[3] before him.

"Sir," said the princess, "an evening walk must give to a man of learning, like you, pleasures which ignorance and youth can hardly conceive. You know the qualities[4] and the

---

cluding those of Pekuah, Nekayah, and Rasselas) mentioned or described in this chapter, cf. the following passage in *Rambler* 2 (par. 7): "When the knight of La Mancha gravely recounts to his companions the adventures by which he is to signalize himself in such a manner that he shall be summoned to the support of empires, solicited to accept the heiress of the crown which he has preserved, have honours and riches to scatter about him, and an island to bestow on his worthy squire, very few readers, amidst their mirth or pity, can

deny that they have admitted visions of the same kind."

1. *To prattle:* "To talk lightly; to chatter; to be trivially loquacious" (*Dictionary*).

2. See p. 64, n. 4, above.

3. Under *conserve* in his *Dictionary*, SJ quotes a passage from Bacon's *Natural History* (VIII.705) noting that "in Turkey and the East certain confections, . . . which are like to candied conserves, . . . are made of sugar and lemons."

4. *Quality:* "Property; accidental adjunct" (sense 2 in *Dictionary*).

causes of all that you behold, the laws by which the river flows, the periods in which the planets perform their revolutions. Every thing must supply you with contemplation, and renew the consciousness of your own dignity."[5]

"Lady," answered he, "let the gay and the vigorous expect pleasure in their excursions, it is enough that age can obtain ease.[6] To me the world has lost its novelty: I look round, and see what I remember to have seen in happier days.[7] I rest against a tree, and consider, that in the same shade I once disputed upon the annual overflow of the Nile[8] with a friend who is now silent in the grave. I cast my eyes upwards, fix them on the changing moon, and think with pain on the vicissitudes of life. I have ceased to take much delight in physical truth;[9] for what have I to do with those things which I am soon to leave?"

"You may at least recreate yourself," said Imlac, "with the recollection of an honourable and useful life, and enjoy the praise which all agree to give you."

"Praise," said the sage, with a sigh, "is to an old man an empty sound. I have neither mother to be delighted with the reputation of her son, nor wife to partake the honours of her husband.[1] I have outlived my friends and my rivals.

---

5. Emerson notes (p. 174) that *dignity* "means not 'worthiness' but advancement, high place in knowledge."

6. Cf. *Rambler* 85 (par. 4): "Ease is the utmost that can be hoped from a sedentary and unactive habit; ease, a neutral state between pain and pleasure." In his essay "Of Health and Long Life," Sir William Temple remarks: "One comfort of age may be, that whereas younger men are usually in pain, when they are not in pleasure; old men find a sort of pleasure, whenever they are out of pain" (*Works*, II [Miscellanea].288).

7. Cf. *Idler* 44 (par. 8): "Every revived idea reminds us of a time when something was enjoyed that is now lost, when some hope was not yet blasted,

when some purpose had yet not languished into sluggishness or indifference."

8. See p. 146, n. 1, above.

9. *Physical:* "Relating to nature or to natural philosophy; not moral" (sense 1 in *Dictionary*). The sage differs sharply from SJ, who, as Hill points out (p. 194), "never lost his ardent curiosity." When he was almost sixty-nine, he declared: "It is a man's own fault, it is from want of use, if his mind grows torpid in old age" (*Life*, III.254).

1. SJ's mother died on 20 Jan 1759 (see Introduction, pp. xx–xxiii above, for a discussion of the connection between her final illness and death and the composition of *Rasselas*), his wife seven years earlier, on 28 March 1752.

Nothing is now of much importance; for I cannot extend my interest beyond myself. Youth is delighted with applause, because it is considered as the earnest of some future good, and because the prospect of life is far extended: but to me, who am now declining to decrepitude,[2] there is little to be feared from the malevolence of men, and yet less to be hoped from their affection or esteem. Something they may yet take away, but they can give me nothing. Riches would now be useless, and high employment would be pain. My retrospect of life recalls to my view many opportunities of good neglected, much time squandered upon trifles, and more lost in idleness and vacancy.[3] I leave many great designs unattempted, and many great attempts unfinished.[4] My mind is burthened with no heavy crime, and therefore I compose myself to tranquility; endeavour to abstract my thoughts from hopes and cares, which, though reason knows them to be vain, still try to keep their old possession of the heart; expect, with serene humility, that hour which nature cannot long delay; and hope to possess in a better state that happiness which here I could not find,[5] and that virtue which here I have not attained."

He rose and went away, leaving his audience not much

In the Preface (last par.) to his *Dictionary*, he says that he has "protracted my work till most of those whom I wished to please have sunk into the grave, and success and miscarriage are empty sounds: I therefore dismiss it with frigid tranquillity, having little to fear or hope from censure or from praise." In *Idler* 41 (par. 9), which appeared on 27 Jan 1759, he asks: "What is success to him that has none to enjoy it[?] Happiness is not found in self-contemplation; it is perceived only when it is reflected from another." Also cf. *Rambler* 203 (par. 5).

2. See p. 44, n. 3, above.

3. According to SJ in *Idler* 44 (par. 9), "few can review the time past without heaviness of heart. He remembers many calamities incurred by folly, many opportunities lost by negli-

gence." In *Idler* 88 (par. 4), he says: "He that in the latter part of his life too strictly enquires what he has done, can very seldom receive from his own heart such an account as will give him satisfaction." Cf. *Rambler* 203 (par. 7).

4. Cf. *Idler* 88 (par. 6): "He that compares what he has done with what he has left undone, will feel the effect which must always follow the comparison of imagination with reality; he will look with contempt on his own unimportance, and wonder to what purpose he came into the world."

5. Cf. SJ's statement in *Adventurer* 107 (last par.) that, because of the uncertainties of human life, "the only thought . . . on which we can repose with comfort, is that which presents to us the care of Providence, whose eye takes in the whole of things, and under

elated with the hope of long life.[6] The prince consoled himself with remarking, that it was not reasonable to be disappointed by this account; for age had never been considered as the season of felicity, and, if it was possible to be easy in decline and weakness, it was likely that the days of vigour and alacrity might be happy; that the noon of life might be bright, if the evening could be calm.

The princess suspected that age was querulous[7] and malignant, and delighted to repress the expectations of those who had newly entered the world. She had seen the possessors of estates look with envy on their heirs, and known many who enjoy pleasure no longer than they can confine it to themselves.

Pekuah conjectured, that the man was older than he appeared, and was willing to impute his complaints to delirious dejection; or else supposed that he had been unfortunate, and was therefore discontented: "For nothing," said she, "is more common than to call our own condition, the condition of life."

Imlac, who had no desire to see them depressed, smiled at the comforts which they could so readily procure to themselves, and remembered, that at the same age, he was equally confident of unmingled prosperity, and equally fertile of consolatory expedients. He forbore to force upon them unwelcome knowledge, which time itself would too soon impress. The princess and her lady retired; the madness of the astronomer hung upon their minds, and they desired Imlac to enter upon his office, and delay next morning the rising of the sun.

---

whose direction all involuntary errors will terminate in happiness." Cf. *The Vanity of Human Wishes*, ll.367–68: "With these [goods] celestial wisdom calms the mind, / And makes the happiness she does not find."

6. "Life is not the object of science," SJ declares in *Adventurer* 107 (last par.);

"we see a little, very little; and what is beyond we only can conjecture. If we enquire of those who have gone before us, we receive small satisfaction."

7. In *Rambler* 50 (par. 7), SJ mentions "the querulousness and indignation which is observed so often to disfigure the last scene of life."

Chap. XLVI.

The princess and Pekuah visit the astronomer.

The princess and Pekuah having talked in private of Imlac's astronomer, thought his character at once so amiable and so strange, that they could not be satisfied without a nearer knowledge, and Imlac was requested to find the means of bringing them together.

This was somewhat difficult; the philosopher had never received any visits from women, though he lived in a city that had in it many Europeans who followed the manners of their own countries, and many from other parts of the world that lived there with European liberty. The ladies would not be refused, and several schemes were proposed for the accomplishment of their design. It was proposed to introduce them as strangers in distress, to whom the sage was always accessible; but, after some deliberation, it appeared, that by this artifice, no acquaintance could be formed, for their conversation would be short, and they could not decently importune him often. "This," said Rasselas, "is true; but I have yet a stronger objection against the misrepresentation of your state. I have always considered it as treason against the great republick of human nature, to make any man's virtues the means of deceiving him, whether on great or little occasions. All imposture weakens confidence and chills benevolence.[1] When the sage finds

---

1. Both in his writings and in his conversation, SJ stressed the virtue of truthfulness and the avoidance of deception. At the beginning of *Adventurer* 50, on the "Lye of Vanity," he wrote: "When Aristotle was once asked, what a man could gain by uttering falsehoods; he replied, 'not to be credited when he shall tell the truth' [Diogenes Laertius, *Lives*, "Aristotle," xi]. . . . The liar, and only the liar, is invariably and universally despised, abandoned, and disowned." At the end, he said: "I cannot but think, that they who destroy the confidence of society, weaken the credit of intelligence, and interrupt the security of life . . . might very properly be awakened to a sense of their crimes, by denunciations of a whipping post or pillory." He later remarked: (1) "Without truth there must be a dissolution of society. . . . Society is held together by communication and information; and I remember this remark of Sir Thomas Brown's, 'Do the devils lie? No; for then Hell could not subsist'"; (2) "The general rule is, that truth should never be violated, because it is of the utmost importance to the comfort of life, that we should have a full security by mutual faith; and occasional inconveniencies should be willingly suffered

that you are not what you seemed, he will feel the resentment natural to a man who, conscious of great abilities, discovers that he has been tricked by understandings meaner
than his own, and, perhaps, the distrust, which he can
never afterwards wholly lay aside, may stop the voice of
counsel, and close the hand of charity; and where will you
find the power of restoring his benefactions to mankind, or
his peace to himself?"

To this no reply was attempted, and Imlac began to hope
that their curiosity would subside; but, next day, Pekuah
told him, she had now found an honest pretence for a visit
to the astronomer, for she would solicite permission to
continue under him the studies in which she had been
initiated by the Arab, and the princess might go with her
either as a fellow-student, or because a woman could not
decently come alone. "I am afraid," said Imlac, "that he will
be soon weary of your company: men advanced far in
knowledge do not love to repeat the elements of their art,
and I am not certain, that even of the elements, as he will
deliver them connected with inferences, and mingled with
reflections, you are a very capable auditress." "That," said
Pekuah, "must be my care: I ask of you only to take me
thither. My knowledge is, perhaps, more than you imagine
it, and by concurring always with his opinions I shall make
him think it greater than it is."

The astronomer, in pursuance of this resolution, was
told, that a foreign lady, travelling in search of knowledge,
had heard of his reputation, and was desirous to become his
scholar. The uncommonness of the proposal raised at once
his surprise and curiosity, and when, after a short deliberation, he consented to admit her, he could not stay[2] without
impatience till the next day.

The ladies dressed themselves magnificently, and were
attended by Imlac to the astronomer, who was pleased to
see himself approached with respect by persons of so splendid an appearance. In the exchange of the first civilities he
was timorous and bashful; but, when the talk became regu-

---

that we may preserve it" (*Life*, III.293;
IV.305).

2. *To stay:* "To wait; to attend; to forbear to act" (sense 3 in *Dictionary*).

lar, he recollected[3] his powers, and justified the character which Imlac had given. Enquiring of Pekuah what could have turned her inclination towards astronomy, he received from her a history of her adventure at the pyramid, and of the time passed in the Arab's island. She told her tale with ease and elegance, and her conversation took possession of his heart. The discourse was then turned to astronomy: Pekuah displayed what she knew: he looked upon her as a prodigy of genius, and intreated her not to desist from a study which she had so happily begun.

They came again and again, and were every time more welcome than before. The sage endeavoured to amuse them, that they might prolong their visits, for he found his thoughts grow brighter in their company; the clouds of solicitude vanished by degrees, as he forced himself to entertain them, and he grieved when he was left at their departure to his old employment of regulating the seasons.

The princess and her favourite had now watched his lips for several months, and could not catch a single word from which they could judge whether he continued, or not, in the opinion of his preternatural commission. They often contrived to bring him to an open declaration, but he easily eluded all their attacks, and on which side soever they pressed him escaped from them to some other topick.

As their familiarity increased they invited him often to the house of Imlac, where they distinguished him by extraordinary respect. He began gradually to delight in sublunary pleasures. He came early and departed late; laboured to recommend himself by assiduity and compliance; excited their curiosity after new arts, that they might still want his assistance; and when they made any excursion of pleasure or enquiry, entreated to attend them.

By long experience of his integrity and wisdom, the prince and his sister were convinced that he might be trusted without danger; and, lest he should draw any false hopes from the civilities which he received, discovered to

---

3. *To recollect:* "To gather what is scattered; to gather again" (sense 3 in *Dictionary*).

him their condition, with the motives of their journey, and required his opinion on the choice of life.

"Of the various conditions which the world spreads before you, which you shall prefer," said the sage, "I am not able to instruct you. I can only tell that I have chosen wrong. I have passed my time in study without experience; in the attainment of sciences which can, for the most part, be but remotely useful to mankind.[4] I have purchased knowledge at the expence of all the common comforts of life: I have missed the endearing elegance of female friendship, and the happy commerce of domestick tenderness. If I have obtained any prerogatives above other students, they have been accompanied with fear, disquiet, and scrupulosity; but even of these prerogatives, whatever they were, I have, since my thoughts have been diversified by more intercourse with the world, begun to question the reality. When I have been for a few days lost in pleasing dissipation, I am always tempted to think that my enquiries have ended in errour, and that I have suffered much, and suffered it in vain."

Imlac was delighted to find that the sage's understanding was breaking through its mists, and resolved to detain him from the planets till he should forget his task of ruling them, and reason should recover its original influence.

From this time the astronomer was received into familiar friendship, and partook of all their projects and pleasures: his respect kept him attentive, and the activity of Rasselas did not leave much time unengaged. Something was always to be done; the day was spent in making observations which furnished talk for the evening, and the evening was closed with a scheme for the morrow.

The sage confessed to Imlac, that since he had mingled in the gay tumults of life, and divided his hours by a succes-

---

4. In *Rambler* 24 (par. 7), SJ remarks: "The great praise of Socrates is, that he drew the wits of Greece, by his instruction and example, from the vain pursuit of natural philosophy to moral inquiries, and turned their thoughts from stars and tides, and matter and motion, upon the various modes of virtue, and relations of life." See also p. 143, n. 5, above.

sion of amusements, he found the conviction of his authority over the skies fade gradually from his mind, and began
to trust less to an opinion which he never could prove to
others, and which he now found subject to variation from
causes in which reason had no part. "If I am accidentally
left alone for a few hours," said he, "my inveterate persuasion rushes upon my soul, and my thoughts are chained
down by some irresistible violence, but they are soon disen-
tangled by the prince's conversation, and instantaneously
released at the entrance of Pekuah. I am like a man habitually afraid of spectres, who is set at ease by a lamp, and
wonders at the dread which harrassed him in the dark, yet,
if his lamp be extinguished, feels again the terrours which
he knows that when it is light he shall feel no more. But I
am sometimes afraid lest I indulge my quiet by criminal
negligence, and voluntarily forget the great charge with
which I am intrusted. If I favour myself in a known errour,
or am determined by my own ease in a doubtful question of
this importance, how dreadful is my crime!"

"No disease of the imagination," answered Imlac, "is so
difficult of cure, as that which is complicated with the dread
of guilt: fancy and conscience then act interchangeably
upon us, and so often shift their places, that the illusions of
one are not distinguished from the dictates of the other. If
fancy presents images not moral or religious, the mind
drives them away when they give it pain, but when melan-
cholick notions take the form of duty, they lay hold on the
faculties without opposition, because we are afraid to exclude or banish them. For this reason the superstitious are
often melancholy, and the melancholy almost always superstitious.

"But do not let the suggestions of timidity overpower
your better reason: the danger of neglect can be but as the
probability of the obligation, which, when you consider it
with freedom, you find very little, and that little growing
every day less. Open your heart to the influence of the light,
which, from time to time, breaks in upon you: when scru-

ples[5] importune you, which you in your lucid moments know to be vain, do not stand to parley, but fly to business or to Pekuah,[6] and keep this thought always prevalent, that you are only one atom of the mass of humanity, and have neither such virtue nor vice, as that you should be singled out for supernatural favours or afflictions."

Chap. XLVII.

The prince enters and brings a new topick.

"All this," said the astronomer, "I have often thought, but my reason has been so long subjugated by an uncontrolable and overwhelming idea, that it durst not confide in its own decisions. I now see how fatally I betrayed my quiet, by suffering chimeras to prey upon me in secret; but melancholy shrinks from communication, and I never found a man before, to whom I could impart my troubles, though I had been certain of relief. I rejoice to find my own sentiments confirmed by yours, who are not easily deceived, and can have no motive or purpose to deceive. I hope that time

---

5. SJ repeatedly expressed a distaste for scruples, which he defined (in the singular) as "Doubt; difficulty of determination; perplexity: generally about minute things." He wrote to Boswell: "I am afraid of scruples" and "Let me warn you very earnestly against scruples" (*Life*, II.421, 423; see also 421–22, n. 3). And Mrs. Piozzi observed that "those teachers had more of his blame than praise, I think, who seek to oppress life with unnecessary scruples: 'Scruples would (as he observed) certainly make men miserable, and seldom make them good. Let us ever (he said) studiously fly from those instructors against whom our Saviour denounces heavy judgments, for having

bound up burdens grievous to be borne, and laid them on the shoulders of mortal men'" (*Anecdotes*, I.223).

6. Responding to Boswell's complaint of melancholy, SJ counselled: "Fix your thoughts upon your business, fill your intervals with company, and sunshine will again break in upon your mind" (*Life*, II.423). In his note on this passage, Hill cites (pp. 197–98) the conclusion of Burton's *Anatomy of Melancholy*: "Only take this for a corollary and conclusion; as thou tenderest thine own welfare in this and all other melancholy, thy good health of body and mind, observe this short precept, give not way to solitariness and idleness. 'Be not solitary, be not idle.'"

and variety will dissipate the gloom that has so long surrounded me,[1] and the latter part of my days will be spent in
peace."

"Your learning and virtue," said Imlac, "may justly give
you hopes."

Rasselas then entered with the princess and Pekuah, and
enquired whether they had contrived any new diversion for
the next day. "Such," said Nekayah, "is the state of life, that
none are happy but by the anticipation of change: the
change itself is nothing; when we have made it, the next
wish is to change again.[2] The world is not yet exhausted; let
me see something to morrow which I never saw before."

"Variety," said Rasselas, "is so necessary to content,[3] that
even the Happy Valley disgusted me by the recurrence of its
luxuries; yet I could not forbear to reproach myself with
impatience, when I saw the monks of St. Anthony support
without complaint, a life, not of uniform delight, but uniform hardship."

"Those men," answered Imlac, "are less wretched in their
silent convent than the Abissinian princes in their prison of
pleasure. Whatever is done by the monks is incited by an
adequate and reasonable motive. Their labour supplies
them with necessaries; it therefore cannot be omitted, and
is certainly rewarded. Their devotion prepares them for
another state, and reminds them of its approach, while it
fits them for it.[4] Their time is regularly distributed; one

---

1. Cf. SJ's comment that because of
melancholy he "had been obliged to fly
from study and meditation, to the dis-
sipating variety of life" (Life, 1.446).

2. Cf. Rambler 207 (par. 7): "So certainly is weariness the concomitant of
our undertakings, that every man, in
whatever he is engaged, consoles himself with the hope of change." See also
p. 82, n. 9, above.

3. "Upon the whole," says SJ in the
Preface to Shakespeare (par. 21), "all pleasure consists in variety." And again in
the "Life of Butler," he declares: "The
great source of pleasure is variety. Uni-

formity must tire at last, though it be
uniformity of excellence" (Lives, 1.212,
par. 35).

4. Cf. SJ's assertion at the end of
Rambler 124: "The duties of religion,
sincerely and regularly performed, will
always be sufficient to exalt the meanest, and to exercise the highest understanding. That mind will never be vacant, which is frequently recalled by
stated duties to meditations on eternal
interests; nor can any hour be long,
which is spent in obtaining some new
qualification for celestial happiness."

duty succeeds another, so that they are not left open to the distraction of unguided choice, nor lost in the shades of listless inactivity.[5] There is a certain task to be performed at an appropriated hour; and their toils are cheerful, because they consider them as acts of piety, by which they are always advancing towards endless felicity."

"Do you think," said Nekayah, "that the monastick rule is a more holy and less imperfect state than any other? May not he equally hope for future happiness who converses[6] openly with mankind, who succours the distressed by his charity, instructs the ignorant by his learning, and contributes by his industry to the general system of life; even though he should omit some of the mortifications which are practised in the cloister, and allow himself such harmless delights as his condition may place within his reach?"

"This," said Imlac, "is a question which has long divided the wise, and perplexed the good. I am afraid to decide on either part. He that lives well in the world is better than he that lives well in a monastery.[7] But, perhaps, every one is not able to stem the temptations of publick life; and, if he cannot conquer, he may properly retreat.[8] Some have little

---

5. Cf. SJ's comment in a letter to Giuseppe Baretti: "I do not wonder that, where the monastick life is permitted, every order finds votaries, and every monastery inhabitants. Men will submit to any rule, by which they may be exempted from the tyranny of caprice and of chance. They are glad to supply by external authority their own want of constancy and resolution, and court the government of others, when long experience has convinced them of their own inability to govern themselves. If I were to visit Italy, my curiosity would be more attracted by convents than by palaces" (*Letters* 138).

6. *To converse:* "To cohabit with; to hold intercourse with; to be a companion to: followed by *with*" (sense 1 in *Dictionary*).

7. In Sermon 3 (par. 19), SJ says: "He

is happy that carries about with him in the world the temper of the cloister; and preserves the fear of doing evil, while he suffers himself to be impelled by the zeal of doing good." See also p. 81, n. 8, above.

8. Distinguishing various kinds of "recluses" in *Adventurer* 126, SJ says (par. 13): "Some are unable to resist the temptations of importunity, or the impetuosity of their own passions incited by the force of present temptations: of these it is undoubtedly the duty to fly from enemies which they cannot conquer, and to cultivate, in the calm of solitude, that virtue which is too tender to endure the tempests of public life." Later, while in Scotland, he also remarked that "those who cannot resist temptations, and find they make themselves worse by being in the world,

power to do good, and have likewise little strength to resist evil. Many are weary of their conflicts with adversity, and are willing to eject those passions which have long busied them in vain. And many are dismissed by age and diseases from the more laborious duties of society.[9] In monasteries the weak and timorous may be happily sheltered, the weary may repose, and the penitent may meditate. Those retreats of prayer and contemplation have something so congenial to the mind of man,[1] that, perhaps, there is scarcely one that does not purpose to close his life in pious abstraction with a few associates serious as himself."

"Such," said Pekuah, "has often been my wish, and I have heard the princess declare, that she should not willingly die in a croud."[2]

"The liberty of using[3] harmless pleasures,"[4] proceeded Imlac, "will not be disputed; but it is still to be examined what pleasures are harmless. The evil of any pleasure that Nekayah can image is not in the act itself, but in its consequences. Pleasure, in itself harmless, may become mischievous, by endearing to us a state which we know to be transient and probatory,[5] and withdrawing our thoughts from

---

without making it better, may retire" (*Life*, v.62).

9. See p. 85, n. 7, above. Cf. *Life*, II.10; *Anecdotes* (I.316).

1. Visiting St. Andrews in Scotland, SJ commented, "I never read of a hermit, but in imagination I kiss his feet; never of a monastery, but I could fall on my knee, and kiss the pavement. But I think putting young people there, who know nothing of life, nothing of retirement, is dangerous and wicked" (*Life*, v.62).

2. Speaking of death, SJ once remarked, "I know not . . . whether I should wish to have a friend by me, or have it all between GOD and myself" (*Life*, II.93). Cf. *Life*, III.498.

3. Hardy notes (p. 178) that "this word retains the sense 'enjoying' from Latin *utor*."

4. For SJ himself, "harmless pleasures" denoted very warm approbation. David Garrick's death (in 1779), he later wrote in the "Life of Edmund Smith," "has . . . impoverished the publick stock of harmless pleasure" (*Lives*, II.21, par. 76). When Boswell asked, "'Is not *harmless pleasure* very tame?'" SJ replied: "'Nay, Sir, harmless pleasure is the highest praise. Pleasure is a word of dubious import; pleasure is in general dangerous, and pernicious to virtue; to be able therefore to furnish pleasure that is harmless, pleasure pure and unalloyed, is as great a power as man can possess'" (*Life*, III.388).

5. *Probatory*: "Serving for trial" (*Dictionary*). In Sermon 22 (par. 10), SJ declares: "The whole life of man is a state of probation; he is always in danger, and may be always in hope."

that, of which every hour brings us nearer to the beginning, and of which no length of time will bring us to the end. Mortification is not virtuous in itself, nor has any other use, but that it disengages us from the allurements of sense.[6] In the state of future perfection, to which we all aspire, there will be pleasure without danger, and security without restraint."[7]

The princess was silent, and Rasselas, turning to the astronomer, asked him, whether he could not delay her retreat, by shewing her something which she had not seen before.

"Your curiosity," said the sage, "has been so general, and your pursuit of knowledge so vigorous, that novelties are not now very easily to be found: but what you can no longer procure from the living may be given by the dead. Among the wonders of this country are the catacombs,[8] or the ancient repositories, in which the bodies of the earliest generations were lodged, and where, by the virtue of the gums which embalmed them, they yet remain without corruption."[9]

"I know not," said Rasselas, "what pleasure the sight of the catacombs can afford; but, since nothing else is offered,

---

6. Cf. *Rambler* 110 (par. 11): "Austerities and mortifications are means by which the mind is invigorated and roused, by which the attractions of pleasure are interrupted, and the chains of sensuality are broken. . . . Austerity is the proper antidote to indulgence; the diseases of the mind as well as body are cured by contraries, and to contraries we should readily have recourse, if we dreaded guilt as we dread pain."

7. Cf. SJ's remark that "the happiness of Heaven will be, that pleasure and virtue will be perfectly consistent" (*Life*, iii.292).

8. The entry for *catacombs* in SJ's *Dictionary* contains allusions only to Italian catacombs. Emerson points out that "the term 'catacomb' was originally used only for the subterranean burial places of Christians at Rome, but was later extended, first to similar Christian cemeteries in other places and then to those of other people" (p. 176).

9. Cf. Hill's comment at the beginning of chap. xxxvii of his *Account of the . . . Ottoman Empire* (p. 264): "I shall now proceed to give a . . . true account of those vast catacombs, wherein the old Egyptians were embalm'd and buried, and whose black, horrid wombs do yet contain a formidable proof, how long our humane bodies may preserve their substance, when defended by the help of art, from the destructive power of a natural corruption." Also see Weitzman's article on p. xxiii, n. 7, above.

I am resolved to view them, and shall place this with many other things which I have done, because I would do something."

They hired a guard of horsemen, and the next day visited the catacombs.[1] When they were about to descend into the sepulchral caves, "Pekuah," said the princess, "we are now again invading[2] the habitations of the dead; I know that you will stay behind; let me find you safe when I return." "No, I will not be left," answered Pekuah; "I will go down between you and the prince."

They then all descended, and roved with wonder through the labyrinth of subterraneous passages, where the bodies were laid in rows on either side.[3]

Chap. XLVIII.

Imlac discourses on the nature of the soul.[1]

"What reason," said the prince, "can be given, why the Egyptians should thus expensively preserve those carcasses which some nations consume with fire, others lay to mingle with the earth, and all agree to remove from their sight, as soon as decent rites can be performed?"

---

1. "There are no catacombs in the immediate vicinity of Cairo," Emerson notes (pp. 176–77), "but Pococke, in describing the catacombs of Saccara about ten miles from Gizeh, says [*Description of the East*, 1.48] the common way of reaching them is from Cairo, so that this may account for Johnson's reference." See Weitzman's article on p. xxiii, n. 7, above.

2. *Invading* is used in a sense ("To intrude upon, infringe, encroach on," *OED*) not defined in SJ's *Dictionary*, but he defines "invader" as "Encroacher; intruder" (sense 3).

3. Weitzman points out (pp. 49–50; see p. xxiii, n. 7, above) that Hill in his description of the Egyptian catacombs mentions the passages, "a gloomy labyrinth of death and horror," "on either side" of which "lie rang'd in measur'd order, at near three foot distance from each other, promiscuous bodies of men, women and children" (*Account of the . . . Ottoman Empire*, p. 264). Also cf. Pococke, *Description of the East*, 1.53–54.

1. The notions expressed in this chapter closely parallel concepts regarding the soul set forth by a variety of seventeenth- and eighteenth-century English writers. For a detailed exposition of the similarities, see Gwin J. Kolb, "The Intellectual Background of the Discourse on the Soul in *Rasselas*," *Philological Quarterly*, LIV (1975), 357–69, which has provided the material for most of the notes on discrete parts of the chapter; and Robert G. Walker, *Eighteenth-Century Arguments for Immortality and Johnson's "Rasselas"* (1977).

"The original[2] of ancient customs," said Imlac, "is commonly unknown; for the practice often continues when the cause has ceased; and concerning superstitious ceremonies it is vain to conjecture; for what reason did not dictate reason cannot explain. I have long believed that the practice of embalming arose only from tenderness to the remains of relations or friends, and to this opinion I am more inclined, because it seems impossible that this care should have been general: had all the dead been embalmed, their repositories must in time have been more spacious than the dwellings of the living. I suppose only the rich or honourable were secured from corruption, and the rest left to the course of nature.

"But it is commonly supposed that the Egyptians believed the soul to live as long as the body continued undissolved, and therefore tried this method of eluding death."[3]

"Could the wise Egyptians," said Nekayah, "think so grosly of the soul?[4] If the soul could once survive its separation, what could it afterwards receive or suffer from the body?"

"The Egyptians would doubtless think erroneously," said the astronomer, "in the darkness of heathenism, and the first dawn of philosophy. The nature of the soul is still disputed amidst all our opportunities of clearer knowledge:[5] some yet say, that it may be material, who, nevertheless, believe it to be immortal."

---

2. In SJ's *Dictionary, original* and *origin* are synonymous terms.

3. This explanation of the Egyptians' embalming practices occurs frequently in seventeenth- and eighteenth-century writings about Egypt. Because of their belief that "as long as the body endured, so long the soul continued with it," the Egyptians, so Greaves observes, "do keep their dead imbalmed so much the longer, to the end that the soul may for a long while continue" (*Pyramidographia*, [II.706]). See also John Francis Gemelli's *Voyage round the World* ([1693], Churchill, IV.26).

4. In his "Fragment on Mummies," Sir Thomas Browne remarks: "In what original this practice of the Egyptians had root, divers authors dispute; while some place the origin hereof in the desire to prevent the separation of the soul, by keeping the body untabified, and alluring the spiritual part to remain by sweet and precious odours. But all this," Browne adds, "was but fond inconsideration. The soul . . . is not stayed by bands and cerecloths . . . but fleeth to the place of invisibles" (*Works*, ed. Keynes, 2d ed., III.469).

5. Robert Watt's *Bibliotheca Britan-*

"Some," answered Imlac, "have indeed said that the soul is material,[6] but I can scarcely believe that any man has thought it, who knew how to think; for all the conclusions of reason enforce the immateriality of mind,[a][7] and all the notices of sense and investigations of science concur to prove the unconsciousness of matter.[8]

"It was never supposed that cogitation is inherent in matter,[9] or that every particle is a thinking being. Yet, if any part of matter be devoid of thought, what part can we suppose to think?[1] Matter can differ from matter only in form, density, bulk, motion, and direction of motion: to which of these, however varied or combined, can consciousness be annexed?[2] To be round or square, to be solid or

a. mind 59b] the mind 59a

---

nica (1824) lists more than eighty publications on the nature of the soul for the period between 1700 and 1759.

6. In *A Collection of Papers, which Passed between . . . Mr. Leibnitz and Dr. [Samuel] Clarke . . .* (1717), Leibnitz anticipates Imlac's statement. "Natural religion . . . ," he says, "seems to decay [in England] very much. Many will have human souls to be material: Others make God himself a corporeal being" (p. 3).

7. *Soul:* "The immaterial and immortal spirit of man" (sense 1 in *Dictionary*).

8. With the latter half of Imlac's statement, cf. the following remark in Isaac Watts's *Logick*, which supplied many quotations for SJ's *Dictionary:* "When we have judged that matter cannot think, and that the mind of man doth think, we then infer and conclude, that therefore the mind of man is not matter" (10th ed., 1755), p. 5. Also cf. Peter Browne's *The Procedure, Extent, and Limits of Human Understanding* (2d ed., 1729), p. 166. *Unconscious* but not *unconsciousness* appears in the *Dictionary*.

9. Under sense 1 of *cogitation*

("Thought; the act of thinking") in his *Dictionary*, SJ quotes the following passage from a sermon by Richard Bentley entitled "Matter and Motion Cannot Think": "These powers of cogitation, and volition and sensation, are neither inherent in matter as such, nor producible in matter by any motion and modification of it" (*Works*, ed. Alexander Dyce, 1838, III.35).

1. Discussing the "knowledge of the existence of a God" in his *Essay concerning Human Understanding*, Locke asks almost the same question as Imlac. "If all matter does not think," he inquires of believers in a material Deity, is it "only one atom that does so?" Answering his own query, he passes judgment: "This has as many absurdities" as the idea that "every particle of matter" thinks (IV.x.14–15). Cf. Samuel Clarke's *Letter to Mr. Dodwell; Wherein All the Arguments in his "Epistolary Discourse" against the Immortality of the Soul are Particularly Answered . . .* (4th ed., 1711), pp. 31–32.

2. In his controversy with Henry Dodwell and other "materialists," Clarke repeatedly anticipated Imlac's

fluid, to be great or little, to be moved slowly or swiftly one way or another, are modes of material existence, all equally alien from the nature of cogitation.[3] If matter be once without thought, it can only be made to think by some new modification, but all the modifications which it can admit are equally unconnected with cogitative powers."[4]

"But the materialists,"[5] said the astronomer, "urge that matter may have qualities with which we are unacquainted."[6]

"He who will determine," returned Imlac, "against that which he knows, because there may be something which he knows not; he that can set hypothetical possibility against acknowledged certainty, is not to be admitted among reasonable beings. All that we know of matter is, that matter is inert, senseless and lifeless; and if this conviction cannot be opposed but by referring us to something that we know not, we have all the evidence that human intellect can admit.[7] If that which is known may be over-ruled by that which is

---

opposition of mind and matter. See his *A Defense of an Argument* (3d ed., 1712), p. 8; *Second Defense* (3d ed., 1715), p. 14.

3. Clarke's *Third and Fourth Defense* (2d ed., 1712) contains lengthy discussions (pp. 6–11, 20–23, 28–34, 87–94, *et passim*) of the "roundness," "squareness," and "motion" of material bodies which deny again and again that "consciousness" can be analogized to the first two "modes" or defined as a "mode" of the latter quality. For comparable remarks about material substance, see William Wollaston's *Religion of Nature Delineated* (6th ed., 1738), p. 189; *The Preceptor* (3d ed., 1758), II.20–22.

4. Cf. Ralph Cudworth's declaration in *The True Intellectual System of the Universe* (1743, II.763) that "life and cogitation, sense and understanding" are "entities really distinct from matter, and no modifications or accidents thereof, but either accidents and modi-

fications, or rather essential attributes of substance incorporeal."

5. *Materialist:* "One who denies spiritual substances" (*Dictionary*).

6. Although emphasizing that he is not a "materialist," Locke places a similar limit on human knowledge in his *Essay concerning Human Understanding.* It is impossible for us, he says, "by the contemplation of our own ideas, without revelation, to discover whether Omnipotency has not given to some systems of matter, fitly disposed, a power to perceive and think, or else joined and fixed to matter, so disposed, a thinking immaterial substance" (IV.iii.6). Cf. Clarke's *Second Defense* (3d ed., 1715), p. 7; *Third and Fourth Defense* (2d ed., 1712), pp. 105–06.

7. In *The Deist's Manual* (1705, pp. 170–71), Charles Gildon also discusses the known and unknown aspects of substances and, though arguing differently, reaches the same conclusion as Imlac.

unknown, no being, not omniscient, can arrive at certainty."

"Yet let us not," said the astronomer, "too arrogantly limit the Creator's power."[8]

"It is no limitation of omnipotence," replied the poet, "to suppose that one thing is not consistent with another, that the same proposition cannot be at once true and false, that the same number cannot be even and odd, that cogitation cannot be conferred on that which is created incapable of cogitation."[9]

"I know not," said Nekayah, "any great use of this question.[1] Does that immateriality, which, in my opinion, you have sufficiently proved, necessarily include eternal duration?"[2]

"Of immateriality," said Imlac, "our ideas are negative, and therefore obscure. Immateriality seems to imply a natural power of perpetual duration as a consequence of exemption from all causes of decay: whatever perishes, is destroyed by the solution of its contexture, and separation of its parts; nor can we conceive how that which has no parts, and therefore admits no solution, can be naturally corrupted or impaired."[3]

---

8. Cf. Locke's comment in his *Reply to the . . . Bishop of Worcester's* [Edward Stillingfleet's] *Answer to his Second Letter* (1699), in *Works*, 12th ed., 1824, III.460–61.

9. In his collection entitled *Sylva: Familiar Letters upon Occasional Subjects* (1701, p. 182), Samuel Parker makes a statement comparable to Imlac's as a part of his argument concerning the soul's immortality. Samuel Clarke recognizes the same boundary on Supreme Power in his sermon "Of the Omnipotence of God" (*Sermons*, 1730–31, I.216). On the other hand, Locke, although agreeing, in his controversy with Edward Stillingfleet, that "omnipotency cannot make a substance to be solid and not solid at the same time," steadfastly upholds the proposition that God *may* have "endued some par-

cels of matter . . . with a faculty of thinking" (*Reply to the . . . Bishop of Worcester's Answer, Works*, 12th ed., 1824, III.465–66).

1. Cf. Peter Browne's similar but more extreme remark in *The Procedure . . . of Human Understanding* (2d ed., 1729, pp. 165, 166).

2. Cf. Peter Browne's answer (pp. 366, 367) to the Princess's question: The "spirit of a man" (distinguished from the "inferior soul"), he affirms, "is that part of our frame which is immaterial, and consequently hath immortality in its natural frame and essence."

3. Imlac's reasoning represents a favorite "proof" of the soul's immortality offered by early writers. "Nothing is more evident," says Samuel Parker in *Sylva* (1701, p. 159), "than that an immaterial substance is not, in its own

"I know not," said Rasselas, "how to conceive any thing without extension: what is extended must have parts, and you allow, that whatever has parts may be destroyed."[4]

"Consider your own conceptions," replied Imlac, "and the difficulty will be less. You will find substance without extension. An ideal form is no less real than material bulk: yet an ideal form has no extension. It is no less certain, when you think on a pyramid, that your mind possesses the idea[5] of a pyramid, than that the pyramid itself is standing. What space does the idea of a pyramid occupy more than the idea of a grain of corn? or how can either idea suffer laceration?[6] As is the effect such is the cause; as thought is, such is the power that thinks; a power impassive[7] and indiscerpible."[8]

---

nature, lyable to mortality or dissolution." Similarly, the *British Apollo* (4th ed., 1740, III.780) lists as one of the evidences of the soul's immortality the fact that it "is of an immaterial substance, and therefore void of parts. But we have no other idea of perishing, than as it is a dissolution or separation of parts." In SJ's *Dictionary*, sense 1 of *solution* is "Disruption; breach; disjunction; separation"; the definition of *contexture* is "The disposition of parts one amongst others; the composition of any thing out of separate parts; the system; the constitution; the manner in which any thing is woven or formed."

4. Cf. Cudworth's summary in *The True Intellectual System of the Universe* (1.69) of the atheists' proof that "body" is the only "substance in the world."

5. *Idea:* "Mental image" (*Dictionary*). SJ, Boswell reports, "at all times jealous of infractions upon the genuine English language, . . ." "was particularly indignant against the almost universal use of the word *idea* in the sense of *notion* or *opinion*, when it is clear that *idea* can only signify something of which an image can be formed in the mind. We may have an *idea* or *image* of

a mountain, a tree, a building; but we cannot surely have an *idea* or *image* of an *argument* or *proposition*" (*Life*, III.196).

6. In his *True Intellectual System* (II.827), Cudworth, drawing on Plotinus and Aristotle, presents a similar argument regarding the unextended, indivisible nature of the soul. And he concludes by repeating Aristotle's question (*De Anima*, 1.3.407a) as to how the soul could "perceive, that which is indivisible by what is divisible."

7. *Impassive:* "Exempt from the agency of external causes" (*Dictionary*).

8. *Indiscerptible* (not *indiscerpible*): "Not to be separated; incapable of being broken or destroyed by dissolution of parts" (*Dictionary*). The term is frequently applied to the soul (and to God Himself) by eighteenth-century proponents of immateriality and natural immortality. "Whatever substance is wholly *indiscerpible*," says Samuel Clarke in *A Defense of an Argument* (3d ed., 1712, p. 16), "is plainly, by virtue of that property, not only it self incapable of being destroyed by any natural power, . . . but all its qualities and modes also, are utterly incapable of being af-

"But the Being," said Nekayah, "whom I fear to name, the Being which made the soul, can destroy it."

"He, surely, can destroy it," answered Imlac, "since, however unperishable,[b] it receives from a superiour[c] nature its power of duration.[9] That it will not perish by any inherent cause of decay,[d] or principle of corruption, may be shown by[e] philosophy; but philosophy can tell no more. That it will not be annihilated by him that made it, we must humbly learn from higher authority."[1]

The whole assembly stood a while silent and collected.[2] "Let us return," said Rasselas, "from this scene of mortality. How gloomy would be these mansions of the dead to him who did not know that he shall never die; that what now acts shall continue its agency, and what now thinks shall think on for ever. Those that lie here stretched before us, the wise and the powerful of antient times, warn us to remember the shortness of our present state:[3] they were, perhaps, snatched away while they were busy, like us, in the choice of life."

b. unperishable *59b*] unperishable in itself *59a*   c. superiour *59b*] higher
59a   d. of decay, *added 59b*   e. shown by *59b*] collected from *59a*

---

fected in any measure, or changed in any degree, by any power of nature."

9. In his *Letter to Mr. Dodwell* (4th ed., 1711, pp. 7–8), Samuel Clarke recognizes the identical limitation on the indefinite existence of the soul as does Imlac. Cf. William Wollaston's *Religion of Nature Delineated* (6th ed., 1738), p. 192; Philip Skelton's *Deism Revealed* (2d ed., 1751), I.138.

1. Like Imlac, some of the earlier discussants of the soul's immateriality and immortality were acutely aware of the difference between knowledge derived from reason and that based on revelation. See Locke's second reply to Stillingfleet (*Works,* 12th ed., 1824, III.476); Richard Boulton's *Theological Works of the Honourable Robert Boyle, Esq; Epitomiz'd* (1715, III.12–13, 14). Discussing death, SJ once remarked that "'no wise man will be contented to die, if he

thinks he is to fall into annihilation: for however unhappy any man's existence may be, he yet would rather have it, than not exist at all. No; there is no rational principle by which a man can die contented, but a trust in the mercy of God, through the merits of Jesus Christ'" (*Life,* v.180).

2. In SJ's *Dictionary,* sense 5 ("To collect *himself*") of *to collect* is "To recover from surprise; to gain command over his thoughts; to assemble his sentiments."

3. Cf. SJ's assertion in *Rambler* 78 (last par.) that since the "great incentive to virtue is the reflection that we must die," "it will . . . be useful to accustom ourselves, whenever we see a funeral, to consider how soon we may be added to the number of those whose probation is past."

"To me," said the princess, "the choice of life is become less important; I hope hereafter to think only on the choice of eternity."[4]

They then hastened out of the caverns, and, under the protection of their guard, returned to Cairo.

Chap. XLIX.

The conclusion, in which nothing is concluded.

It was now the time of the inundation of the Nile: a few days after their visit to the catacombs, the river began to rise.[1]

They were confined to their house. The whole region being under water gave them no invitation to any excursions, and, being well supplied with materials for talk, they diverted themselves with comparisons of the different forms of life which they had observed, and with various schemes of happiness which each of them had formed.

Pekuah was never so much charmed with any place as the convent of St. Anthony, where the Arab restored her to the princess, and wished only to fill it with pious maidens, and to be made prioress of the order: she was weary of expectation and disgust,[2] and would gladly be fixed in some unvariable state.

The princess thought, that of all sublunary things, knowledge was the best: She desired first to learn all sciences, and then purposed to found a college of learned women, in which she would preside, that, by conversing with the old, and educating the young, she might divide her time between the acquisition and communication of wisdom, and raise up for the next age models of prudence, and patterns of piety.

The prince desired a little kingdom, in which he might administer justice in his own person, and see all the parts of

---

4. SJ expresses opinions similar to Nekayah's in several other places. See *Rambler* 203 (last par.); *The Vanity of Human Wishes*, ll. 343–68; *Rambler* 7 (par. 7); Sermon 4 (par. 18).

1. See p. 147, n. 2, above.

2. See p. 19, n. 2, above.

government with his own eyes; but he could never fix the limits of his dominion, and was always adding to the number of his subjects.

Imlac and the astronomer were contented to be driven along the stream of life without directing their course to any particular port.[3]

Of these wishes that they had formed they well knew that none could be obtained. They deliberated a while what was to be done, and resolved, when the inundation should cease, to return to Abissinia.[4]

F I N I S.

---

3. With Imlac's and the astronomer's lack of plans for the future, cf. SJ's comment in *Rambler* 29 (par. 6): "Things to come, except when they approach very nearly, are equally hidden from men of all degrees of understanding; and if a wise man is not amazed at sudden occurrences, it is not that he has thought more, but less upon futurity. He never considered things not yet existing as the proper objects of his attention; he never indulged dreams till he was deceived by their phantoms, nor ever realized nonentities to his mind. He is not surprised because he is not disappointed, and he escapes disappointment because he never forms any expectations."

4. This final sentence, it should be noted, does not state (despite the contrary assumptions of numerous commentators) that the prince and his party return to the Happy Valley in Abyssinia. Whether the group, even if it wishes to do so, would be re-admitted to the valley remains uncertain. For an examination of the inconclusive evidence, see Gwin J. Kolb, "Textual Cruxes in *Rasselas*," in *Johnsonian Studies*, ed. Magdi Wahba (1962), pp. 257–60.

THE VISION OF THEODORE,

THE HERMIT OF TENERIFFE

EDITOR'S INTRODUCTION

Apparently Johnson's first piece of allegorical fiction, "The Vision of Theodore, the Hermit of Teneriffe," was composed, on the authority of Thomas Tyers, "in one night" after the author had finished "an evening in Holborn."[1] Such a statement is consonant with reports of Johnson's speed in writing the *Life of Savage, Rasselas,* and the fairy tale "The Fountains," among other works. "The Vision" was one of Johnson's contributions to Robert Dodsley's two-volume textbook *The Preceptor,* published on 7 April 1748, which was designed for the instruction of youthful readers and seemingly intended to compete with John Newbery's more extensive collection, *The Circle of the Sciences* (1745–46?).[2] *The Preceptor* contains a Dedication, a Preface (also by Johnson), and twelve parts, devoted, respectively, to Reading, Speaking, and Writing Letters; Arithmetic, Geometry, and Architecture; Geography and Astronomy; Chronology and History; Rhetoric and Poetry; Drawing; Logic; Natural History; Ethics, or Morality; Trade and Commerce; Laws and Government; and Human Life and Manners.[3]

Some of the materials making up the two volumes were original; some were borrowed from other works.[4] "The Vision" ap-

1. "A Biographical Sketch of Dr. Samuel Johnson," *Gentleman's Magazine,* LVI (1784), 901. Tyers's revised "Sketch" appeared as an independent pamphlet in 1785.

2. For a discussion of SJ's connection with *The Preceptor* and the evidence (a notice in the *General Advertiser*) for the publication date of the work, see Allen T. Hazen, *Samuel Johnson's Prefaces & Dedications* (1937), pp. 171–72. To support his inference regarding the relationship between *The Preceptor* and *The Circle of the Sciences,* Hazen quotes this passage from SJ's Preface to the former: "It must not be expected, that in the following pages should be found a complete Circle of the Sciences." The tentative publication dates of the first edition of *The Circle of the Sciences* are drawn from the General Catalogue of the British Library.

3. The headings of these twelve parts appear on the title page of Vol. I of the first, and later, editions of *The Preceptor.* Excepting passages from "The Vision of Theodore" (which are located by page references to the text below), subsequent quotations from *The Preceptor,* like those cited previously, are located by volume and page references to the third edition (1758).

4. For a list of the known borrowed materials, see Hazen, pp. 173–74.

pears as the second section of the final part, on Human Life and
Manners. In the initial section, the speaker, or preceptor, urges
his "dear pupil," who has been conducted during the course of
the two volumes "into the first entrance . . . of the Temple of
Science" (II.517), to "pause . . . at the Portal of Life" and add
wisdom to his "other acquirements" (II.518). Certain "precepts"
may facilitate the "attainment" of wisdom and the tutor therefore
advises the student "to divide the study of yourself into the three
distinct subdivisions of Habits, Sentiments, and Passions."

"By Habit," the teacher continues, "is meant such a custom of
doing any particular action, as to fall into it involuntarily and
without thinking, or to repeat it so frequently as to render it
almost a part of our nature, not to be subdued without the greatest difficulty." Swearing is an instance of the first sort of habit,
drinking of the second. Having commented on both instances,
the preceptor "mention[s] . . . Idleness and Sauntering." Indolence, he says, citing "an Eastern writer, is the daughter of Folly,
the sister of Vice, and the mother of Misfortune. Whoever suffers
himself to fall into this pernicious Habit, cannot hope to make
much progress in learning or knowledge of any kind. . . . Wisdom
is not to be won without great assiduity and constant application."
Thus he entreats his pupil "to take particular care how you con-
tract bad habits of any kind," for, "in spite of all your endeavours
to shake them off, they will hang upon you to your destruction."
"I will illustrate this subject," he concludes, "and close my advice
to you on this head, with a beautiful and instructive fable, communicated to me by a friend for this purpose" (II.519–20). Then
follow the title and text of "The Vision."

Related in the first person by the hermit himself and addressed
to "Son of Perseverance, whoever thou art" (p. 195), the narrative
tells how Theodore, having retired to the foot of Mount Teneriffe, decides to climb to the top of the peak in the forty-eighth
year of his retreat. Becoming weary on his ascent, he resigns
himself to sleep when a supernatural "protector" appears before
him and directs him to "survey" the allegorical Mountain of
Existence and "be wise" (pp. 197–98). Obeying, Theodore observes at the bottom of the mountain a multitude of men and
women attended by the "virgin" Innocence. As the group ad-

vances upward, Education replaces Innocence and later Reason (preceded by her mistress Religion) succeeds Education as the monitor. A "troop of pygmies"—human habits—also accompany the travellers, sometimes smoothing their progress but often binding them with chains of appetites and passions. Some of the pilgrims, guided by Religion, make their way up to the "temple of Happiness" at the summit of the mountain. Others fall into the clutches of vicious habits and are lost to Ambition, Avarice, Intemperance, Indolence, Despair, etc. While Theodore is "musing on this miserable scene," his protector calls out, "Remember, Theodore, and be wise, and let not Habit prevail against thee." "I started," the hermit concludes, "and beheld myself surrounded by the rocks of Teneriffe; the birds of light were singing in the trees, and the glances of the morning darted upon me" (pp. 210–11, 212).

After the presentation of Johnson's "Vision," the teacher turns to the second of the "three distinct subdivisions" into which he had previously distinguished the study of the pupil's "self." Limiting his treatment to "a few of the most useful or dangerous" passions "as they commonly appear in human nature," he briefly discusses Admiration or Wonder, Fear, Pride, Anger, and Love (II.530, 531–33). His conclusion resembles his introduction of "The Vision": "As I clos'd the last part with a modern allegory, so I chuse to finish and illustrate this with one of the most beautiful fables in all antiquity" (II.533). Then follows "The Choice of Hercules," "composed by Prodicus," the tutor remarks later, "and . . . related by Xenophon in his *Memorable Things* of Socrates"; "it is here cloath'd in a new dress by a very eminent hand, and retains all the native elegance and simplicity of the prose original, heighten'd with all the graces of poetical ornament" (II.533–44, 544).[5]

The tutor next proceeds "to the third rule, which I laid down for the attainment of human happiness, which you [the pupil] may remember was the acquisition of wise and prudent Sentiments and Opinions" (II.544). A paragraph of didactic observa-

---

5. The "very eminent hand" was Bishop Robert Lowth (Hazen, p. 173), whose version of "The Choice" is cited hereafter in the text of this Introduction.

tions ensues, and then the teacher says, "I will close the whole of
my instructions to you on this head, and finish your education in
general with the celebrated 'Picture of Human Life,' by Cebes the
Theban, a disciple of Socrates, and one of those who assisted him
in his last hours; which I earnestly recommend to your most
serious study and frequent perusal. It is translated into English,
by a person considerably distinguished in the Republic of Letters,
and is as follows" (II.545).[6] The text of "The Picture of Human
Life" (II.545–60) brings *The Preceptor* to an end.

Its title, contents, and immediate context all serve to identify
the generic classification and literary background of "The Vision
of Theodore." Like its companion pieces, and in the words of the
"preceptor," the work is a "fable" (defined, under sense 1, in
Johnson's *Dictionary* as "A feigned story intended to enforce some
moral precept") or "allegory" (defined in Johnson's *Dictionary* as
"A figurative discourse, in which something other is intended,
than is contained in the words literally taken; as, 'wealth is the
daughter of diligence, and the parent of authority'"). Unlike
these pieces, it is cast in the form of a vision. "The Choice of
Hercules," by Prodicus, and "The Picture of Human Life," attributed to Cebes the Theban, were its most significant classical
forebears, which—famous in ancient times, largely ignored during the Middle Ages, rediscovered by many writers and painters
during the Renaissance and employed frequently as school
texts—possibly attained the height of their enormous popularity
in the eighteenth century.[7] Besides their inclusion in *The Precep-*

6. The "person" was Joseph Spence (Hazen, p. 173), whose version of "The
Picture" is cited hereafter in the text of this Introduction.

7. Prodicus of Ceos was a contemporary of Socrates (469 B.C.–399 B.C.); "The
Choice" was transmitted through Xenophon's *Memorabilia*. Cebes of Thebes may
have lived in the fourth century B.C.; his supposed "Picture" or "Table" was
probably composed in the first century A.D. For other details, see *The Oxford
Classical Dictionary* (1970), pp. 218, 882.

The principal bases of my statement on the fortunes of "The Choice" and "The
Picture" are two illuminating studies by Edwin Christian Heinle ("The Eighteenth
Century Allegorical Essay" [Ph.D. diss., Columbia Univ., 1957], esp. chap. 4 ["The
'Choice Theme': Prodicus and Cebes"], pp. 78–106) and Earl R. Wasserman
("Johnson's *Rasselas:* Implicit Contexts," *Journal of English and Germanic Philology,*
LXXIV [1975], 1–25, esp. 6–9, 12–16). See also Wasserman's "The Inherent Values
of Eighteenth-Century Personification," *PMLA,* LXV (1950), 437–39; and Carey
McIntosh's revealing *The Choice of Life: Samuel Johnson and the World of Fiction*
(1973), pp. 110–11.

tor, another indication of their mid-century appeal was the appearance of "The Picture of Human Life" in Robert Dodsley's *Museum* (1747) and of "The Choice of Hercules" in both Joseph Spence's *Polymetis* (1747) and Dodsley's *Collection of Poems* (1748).[8] Furthermore, at the beginning of the century, Addison, who exerted a remarkable influence on his contemporaries and successors, had undertaken the "revival" of allegory as "practised by the finest authors among the ancients"—authors who certainly included Prodicus and Cebes.[9] Earlier, too, the Third Earl of Shaftesbury had composed a substantial essay on "A Notion of the Historical Draught or Tablature of the Judgment of Hercules," had commissioned a painting and engraving based on Prodicus's "fable," had translated the allegory by Cebes, and had planned for it a "literary and artistic treatment" similar to that accorded Prodicus.[1] In 1735, Johnson himself had placed "Cebes" and "Xenophon" (which contains Prodicus's "Choice") on the list of Greek writers recommended to his cousin Samuel Ford as pre-university reading,[2] and in his Preface to *The Preceptor* he remarked that the two "fables . . . were of the highest authority, in the ancient pagan world" (I.xxx). Last, shortly before the publication of *The Preceptor*, the Scots Professor David Fordyce, in the first volume of his *Dialogues Concerning Education* (1745; 2d ed. also 1745), had warmly praised the instructional virtues of the two pieces.[3]

The first of these embodies a theme which is also present in the second and was to loom large in numerous eighteenth-century allegorical essays.[4] "The Choice of Hercules" depicts the allurements proffered the youthful Greek hero (retired to a "lonely

8. Heinle, pp. 99–100. For other eighteenth-century translations of "The Choice" and "The Picture," see Wasserman, "Johnson's *Rasselas*," p. 7, n. 12; p. 13, n. 21.

9. See *Spectator* 501 (par. 1); *Guardian* 152 (par. 2). Addison provides an English version of "The Choice" in *Tatler* 97 and mentions it again in *Spectator* 183 (par. 2); he also mentions "The Picture" (which he calls "The Table of Cebes") in *Tatler* 161 (par. 1).

1. For more details, see Heinle, pp. 48–49, 90, 91–92.

2. *Letters* 3.3; *Life*, 1.99–100.

3. See pp. 368–69, 375, 376, 392, 410, 411.

4. Dividing them into four groups—"The Choice of Ladies," "The Forked Path," "The Allegorical Mountain," and "The Procession" (p. 107)—Heinle discusses many of these essays in his fifth and sixth chapters, pp. 107–60.

vale" [II.534]) through a succession of speeches by two beautiful women (personifying Virtue and Sloth, respectively) who interrupt his contemplation, and then represents the hero's choice—of Virtue naturally—between the two. At the end of the "glorious path" of Virtue is happiness, the product of "a life well-spent: / In which no hour flew unimprov'd away; / In which some generous deed distinguish'd every day." Among the concomitants of Sloth, on the other hand, belong riot, indolence, intemperance, grief, and shame (II.542, 540, 541, 539). The Path of Virtue is a "rough" "steep ascent" requiring arduous "toil" and dangerous acts for its traversal; the Way of Sloth is "fair, easy, smooth, and plain" (II.535, 536, 538, 539). Four features, then—the "pictorial setting,"[5] the "choice" theme, the association of happiness with self-discipline and of misery with sensual indulgence, and the metaphorical notion of the ascending "path" of "virtue" (although they are certainly not unique to the form)—suggest a significant generic connection between the fable by Prodicus and that by Johnson.

Cebes's "Picture of Human Life" exhibits still more—and more striking—resemblances to "The Vision of Theodore." Indeed, the similarities between the two pieces are so numerous as to cause a reader to wonder whether Johnson had Cebes's allegory in mind when he composed his own.[6] Both works feature a wise guide who informs and instructs stationary listeners-viewers (of an allegorical picture and an allegorical mountain, respectively). Both portray human life as a physical ascent and happiness as the ultimate goal of the individual's upward movement—in Cebes, from birth at the bottom of the picture to the Edifice of Happiness at the top (II.554); in "The Vision," from Innocence toward the foot of the Mountain of Existence to the Temple of Happiness at the summit

5. I borrow this phrase from Heinle, who points out (p. iv) that a pictorial setting is one of the three common elements—the other two being a dream and a guide—in many eighteenth-century allegorical essays.

6. In Heinle's opinion, "the model for [the] system of roadways [in "The Vision"] is undoubtedly the long road of Cebes" (p. 141). McIntosh states that "many of Johnson's allegories are modeled after Prodicus and Cebes" (p. 112). And in his study *Samuel Johnson's Allegory* (1971), Bernard L. Einbond concludes that "Johnson may well have taken the germ of his idea [for habits in 'The Vision'] from Cebes' *Table*" (p. 64).

(pp. 199, 208). Both specify intemperance, sensuality, avarice, and despair among the other psychological states—gathered under the general category of "opinions, desires, and pleasures" (II.547) for Cebes, "appetites" and "passions" for Johnson—which obstruct the traveller's progress on the road to happiness. Again, although the Greek work, unlike the English, spends only a few words on the topic, both fables stress the cultivation of good, and the avoidance of bad, habits: at the end of "The Picture," the wise interpreter says, "Get a habit of doing right, whatever pain it costs you" (II.560); at the end of "The Vision," the "protector" calls out, "'Remember, Theodore, and be wise, and let not Habit prevail against thee'" (p. 212). Moreover, although it, unlike "The Vision," does not explicitly apply the figures of "chains" and "captivity" to the formation and power of habits, "The Picture" mentions the plight of those unfortunate mortals who are "led along like captives, some by Intemperance, and others by Arrogance; here by Covetousness, and there by Vain-Glory, or any other of the Vices: whose chains they are in vain striving to get loose from" (II.555). Finally, the brief appearance of Repentance in "The Picture" resembles that of Conscience in "The Vision," for both personifications induce the restoration of aberrant persons on the upward path to happiness.

If we admit the probability of Johnson's indebtedness to Cebes, however, we must also immediately acknowledge the marked divergences between "The Picture" and "The Vision." For additional anticipations of assorted aspects of the latter, we may turn to examples of the long-lived, widely cultivated genre commonly called the dream vision. Its English members, exceedingly diverse, include the Middle English *Pearl*, various works by Chaucer, the *Vision of William Concerning Piers Plowman*, at least one version of Prodicus's "Choice of Hercules" (in Alexander Barclay's *Ship of Fools*), Bunyan's *Pilgrim's Progress* ("delivered under the similitude of a dream"), and a host of eighteenth-century allegorical prose pieces, the most famous of which is Addison's "Vision of Mirzah" (*Spectator* 159).

"The Vision of Theodore" clearly belongs to the same literary family. In his *Dictionary*, Johnson defined the fourth sense of *vision* as "a dream; something shewn in a dream" and then adds:

"A dream happens to a sleeping, a vision may happen to a waking man. A dream is supposed natural, a vision miraculous; but they are confounded."[7] With some of its medieval predecessors, "The Vision" shares a number of traits, notably a heavily didactic theme, the convention of a guide for the dreamer, and such personified figures as Reason, Religion, Avarice, etc.[8] Like *Pilgrim's Progress*—one of only three books, according to Johnson, readers ever "wished longer"[9]—it pictures human life as an upward "pilgrimage" (Johnson's term) and stresses the dreadful power of the "cruel tyrant" Despair (cf. Giant Despair in *Pilgrim's Progress*). Like Addison's Mirzah, a resident of "Bagdat," Johnson's Theodore, Hermit of Mount Teneriffe, having ascended a considerable distance up a peak (Mirzah actually climbs to the top of a mountain), composed himself to sleep (Mirzah begins to "muse"), and being "instructed" by a supernatural "protector" (called a "genius" by Addison), observes, on looking eastward, an allegorical vision of human life (represented as a mountain by Johnson; a combination of a vale, a tide, a bridge, and paradisial islands by Addison). Finally, Johnson's employment of an allegorical mountain continued a convention previously used in essay visions by such authors as Addison, Steele, Parnell, and Fielding—to quite different ends.[1]

Most of the separate ingredients forming "The Vision of Theodore" thus display likenesses to elements in the classical allego-

7. Most commentators have assumed that Theodore experiences his vision while he is asleep. What the Hermit says, however, is that "an irresistible heaviness suddenly surprized me; I laid my head upon the bank and resigned myself to sleep: when methought I heard a sound as of the flight of eagles, and a being of more than human dignity stood before me" (p. 197). At the end of "The Vision," he says, "While I was musing on this miserable scene, my protector called out to me.... I started, and beheld myself surrounded by the rocks of Teneriffe" (p. 212). One can thus conclude that Theodore's vision takes place while he is semi-conscious and that, strictly speaking, the distinction made in the *Dictionary* between a dream and a vision also obtains in the allegory.

8. It should be noted, however, that, as Heinle points out (pp. 1–8, 17–28), most eighteenth-century English allegorists imitated the classical works by Prodicus and Cebes rather than medieval and Renaissance allegories, which tended to be condemned or ignored.

9. *Life*, 1.71, n. 1. The other two books are *Don Quixote* and *Robinson Crusoe*.

1. See, for example, *Tatler* 81; *Spectator* 460, 514, 558, 559; *Champion* for 13 Dec 1739.

ries by Prodicus and Cebes and earlier English dream visions. Still
another part of Johnson's composition—the geographical setting—can also be connected to a limited kind of literary, or "allu-
sive," tradition. The "Peak" constituting a portion of Teneriffe,
largest of the Canary Islands, had not, apparently, provided the
locale of an allegorical vision before Johnson's Theodore retired
there. But the mountain, long renowned for its height (about
12,000 feet), which caused some commentators to rank it among
the tallest in the world, had become a symbol, a designation of
immense height for English writers as early, at least, as the seventeenth century. Milton, Marvell, Sir Thomas Browne, Abraham
Cowley, and numerous others refer to the towering "pike," as it
was sometimes spelled, in various works.[2] During the next century, similar allusions were equally, perhaps even more, common.
Only a year before the appearance of "The Vision," Thomas
Warton, Jr., published his poem *The Pleasures of Melancholy*, which
begins: "Mother of musings, Contemplation sage, / Whose grotto
stands upon the topmost rock / of Teneriff." Johnson himself
commented humorously in *Rambler* 117: "That a garret will make
every man a wit, I am very far from supposing; I know there are
some who would continue blockheads even on the summit of the
Andes, or on the peak of Teneriffe."[3] And a well-known passage
in Hume's "Of the Standard of Taste" (1757) declares that "whoever would assert an equality of genius and elegance between
Ogilby and Milton, or Bunyan and Addison, would be thought to
defend no less an extravagance, than if he had maintained a mole
hill to be as high as Teneriffe, or a pond as extensive as the ocean."

By his choice of a setting for "The Vision,"[4] Johnson initiated a

---

2. *Paradise Lost*, IV.985–87; Marvell's "On the Victory Obtained by Blake over
the Spaniards, in the Bay of Santa Cruze, in the Island of Tenerif" [1657], ll. 77–
80; Browne's *Pseudodoxia Epidemica*, *The Works of Sir Thomas Browne*, ed. Geoffrey
Keynes (4 vols., 1964), II.451; Cowley's essay "Of Greatness," *Essays, Plays, and
Sundry Verses*, ed. A. R. Waller (1906), p. 433.

3. SJ mentions the peak of Teneriffe at least twice again—in two letters in 1784
(*Letters* 929.2, 1020) which discuss a current ballooning experiment (cut short by
the burning of the balloon).

4. For other possible reasons for SJ's selection of the setting, see Lawrence
Lipking's suggestive essay, "Learning to Read Johnson: *The Vision of Theodore* and
The Vanity of Human Wishes," *ELH*, XLIII (1976), 524–25.

pattern he was to repeat with variations in his other extended
pieces of fiction, *Rasselas* and "The Fountains." For each, he selected a famous mountainous site, actual, not fictional: the Peak of
Teneriffe; the prison for royalty (an elevated valley surrounded
by mountains)[5] in Amhara, a kingdom of Abyssinia; the Welsh
Mount Plinlimmon. In or near this location he placed central
characters—an elderly hermit, a youngish prince, an unmarried
woman—whose experiences, active and observational (not all of
them occurring, of course, in the original setting)—dramatize the
choices human beings make as they pursue earthly happiness.
Supernatural personages—a "protector" and a fairy—are partly
responsible for the experiences of the first and third characters.
Pervading a sizable amount of Western art and literature,[6] this
"choice" theme can be traced back, as indicated above, to the
Greek works by Prodicus and Cebes for the purpose of ascertain-
ing the proximate background of "The Vision of Theodore."

   Since *The Preceptor,* of which Johnson's allegory makes up a
segment, was apparently designed to compete with a somewhat
similar collection, *The Circle of the Sciences,* one may well inquire
whether the latter includes anything which might further illuminate the contemporary context of "The Vision." The answer is no.
But Volume II of David Fordyce's *Dialogues Concerning Education,*
which appeared the same year (1748)[7] as *The Preceptor,* contains a
section that bears comparison with Johnson's composition. In
Dialogue xvi ("On Dreaming"), Sophron relates a dream vision—
prompted, as he says, by his "musing" on "the celebrated Picture
of Cebes, that eminent moral limmer" (p. 259).

   Moving over open country intersected by many roads on which
various persons are travelling, Sophron (a member of a group

   5. In its precise configuration, SJ's Happy Valley differs markedly, of course,
from the actual "mount" in Amhara where the Abyssinian princes were imprisoned.
   6. For specific studies of the artistic and literary manifestations of the "choice"
theme, see Heinle, p. 79n.; Wasserman, "Johnson's *Rasselas,*" pp. 6, n. 6; 7–8.
   7. Subsequent quotations from Vol. II of the *Dialogues* (which was published,
according to the *Gentleman's Magazine* [xviii, 144], in March of 1748) are located
by page numbers in the text of this Introduction. Heinle also describes (pp. 127–
30) the "vision" related in the *Dialogues;* in addition, he summarizes (pp. 143–45)
a supplementary "vision" in Fordyce's *The Temple of Virtue* (1757).

bound for "the abode of Happiness") meets the Genius of Education, who warns his auditors to follow his directions and take the route, known to him alone, which leads to the Temple of Virtue (p. 260). Instead, lured by the female figures of Credulity and Deceit, Sophron and his companions quickly move along the road to the Bower of Bliss. Soon left alone, Sophron encounters Lady Pleasure, who, together with Lady Admiration, guides him to her palace, where, she assures him, "no gloomy cares or corroding sorrows enter, where neither sullen rules nor stoical pride are admitted to damp the jocund humor of the inhabitants" (p. 265). In the palace, he observes a large assortment of allegorical individuals, including Vanity, Intemperance, Luxury, Cruelty, Incontinence, Indolence, Remorse, and Shame. "Various petitioners presented themselves before the throne, and humbly offered their suits to the jolly goddess [Pleasure]" (p. 272). After the last of these petitioners (none of them admirable) has appeared, Sophron asks Simplicius to interpret his dream. But Simplicius refuses, saying that he would not consider undertaking such a task. To which Sophron replies that Simplicius has heard the last of his dreams.

Striking dissimilarities obviously separate The Vision of the Palace of Pleasure, as it may be called, and "The Vision of Theodore." Yet certain features suggest a common bond between the two pieces. Both are heavily didactic allegories, cast in the mold of visions, which delineate the "choice" theme and contain several of the same characters. Both exhibit strong affiliations with the allegories by Prodicus and Cebes. Both form parts of educational works (whose contents are otherwise quite different) published at about the same time. Therefore, without implying a direct causal connection of any sort between the two compositions, we may remark that Johnson (assuming his responsibility for the presence of "The Vision" in The Preceptor) was not unique among his contemporaries in employing the exceedingly popular genre of the allegorical vision within the confines of an avowed educational work. Fordyce, indeed, we should note further, seems to have recommended the issuance of the kind of collection exemplified a little later by "The Vision," "The Choice," and "The Picture": in the first volume (1745) of Fordyce's Dialogues, one of the speakers comments that, since "fable, allegory, and similar pleasant dialogue" are "the best and most successful method we can use in the education of children . . . , it might be of considerable use in education, if the most beautiful and interesting of those allegories, whether ancient or modern, which have or might have been mentioned [including, of course, "The Choice" and "The Picture"], were collected into one volume, and exhibited to the youth, as so many philosophical pictures of human life" (pp. 406–07). What Fordyce proposed,[8] Johnson, or Dodsley, or both, actually realized in the final part of *The Preceptor*.

RECEPTION, 1748–1800

It is impossible to measure the real efficacy of *The Preceptor,* and of "The Vision" in particular, as an instrument of education. But at an unspecified date (presumably between 1756 and 12 March 1760), Johnson himself, so Thomas Percy reported, "attribute[d] the palm over all he ever wrote" to the "little allegorical piece." Although such an appraisal seems excessive today, the unusual esteem bestowed on the essayistic vision during the eighteenth century, the immense vogue of the genre, and the physical parity (at least) of "The Vision" with the admired productions of Prodicus and Cebes all help to explain the apparent eccentricity of Johnson's judgment.[9] Moreover, Percy concurred with Johnson's high estimate, adding that the work "far excells" the production of Cebes.[1] In addition, several of Johnson's contemporaries expressed unreserved commendations for the piece. For example,

8. The possibility of some kind of connection between Fordyce and SJ during this period should be mentioned briefly. As Hazen points out (p. 172), SJ's association with *The Preceptor* may have included editorial duties. Part IX ("On Ethics, or Morality") of the work contains the initial publication of Fordyce's *Elements of Moral Philosophy,* which came out separately in 1754. Thus SJ and Fordyce may have communicated with each other one or more times.

9. For additional suggestions regarding the reasons for SJ's high estimate of "The Vision," see Lipking, pp. 517–37.

1. *The Correspondence of Thomas Percy & William Shenstone,* ed. Cleanth Brooks (Vol. VII [1977] of *The Percy Letters*), pp. 57, 58. In his *Life,* Boswell remarks: "The Bishop of Dromore heard Dr. Johnson say, that he thought ["The Vision"] was the best thing he ever wrote" (1.192). Percy and SJ apparently met first in 1756 (*Life,* 1.48, n. 2). The date of Percy's letter to Shenstone is 12 March 1760.

Joseph Towers, in his *Essay on the Life, Character, and Writings of Dr. Samuel Johnson* (1786), labels it "a beautiful and instructive allegory." Another *Life of Dr. Samuel Johnson*, probably composed by James Harrison and also published in 1786, goes much further. "The Vision," we are informed,

> is one of the finest moral allegories, if not the very finest, that ever proceeded from the pen of man. This is a bold assertion, but it is not a hasty one: and those who peruse the Vision . . . with attention; consider its excellent adaptation to the work [i.e., *The Preceptor*]; and reflect on the valuable precepts it inculcates; if they are at all zealous for the virtue of the rising generation, and the consequent felicity of their fellow-creatures, will not deem any encomium too great for its deserts.[2]

Neither Mrs. Piozzi's *Anecdotes of Samuel Johnson* (1786) nor Sir John Hawkins's *Life* (1787) assesses "The Vision";[3] but Boswell, characteristically more evaluative than his rivals, calls the piece "a most beautiful allegory of human life."[4] And Robert Anderson, in his *Life of Samuel Johnson*, repeats Boswell's comment, remarking also that the work "is indeed truly excellent."[5]

The appearances of "The Vision" both within and outside *The Preceptor* during, roughly, the first half-century of its existence supplement the testimonials to its merit offered by Johnson's early biographers. Eight London editions of *The Preceptor* were issued at fairly regular intervals—in 1748, 1754, 1758, 1763, 1769, 1775, 1783, and 1793. Moreover, Dublin editions came out in 1749, 1761, 1778, and 1786, and a German translation in 1765–67.[6] As a small part of the two-volume collection, Johnson's

2. For the passages from these two lives of SJ, see *The Early Biographies of Samuel Johnson*, ed. O M Brack, Jr., and Robert E. Kelley (1974), pp. 215, 268.
3. Mrs. Piozzi does not mention "The Vision"; Hawkins (p. 381n.) instances it, "the work of one sitting," as a specimen of SJ's rapidity of composition.
4. *Life*, 1.192.
5. 3d ed. (1815), p. 122.
6. For information about the London and Dublin editions and the German translation of *The Preceptor*, I have relied on R. C. Alston, *A Bibliography of the English Language from the Invention of Printing to the Year 1800*, Vol. VII (*Logic, Philosophy, Epistemology, Universal Language* [1967]), pp. 38–40.

allegory surely exerted only a negligible influence on the sales of the complete work; nonetheless, it is noteworthy that the collection itself evidently remained available for at least fifty years.

The earliest separate reprinting of "The Vision" occurred in the April 1748 number of the *Gentleman's Magazine,* where a postscript calls the allegory "beautiful" and a specimen of the "crowning" part of *The Preceptor.*[7] Thereafter the piece appeared in the following places and possibly elsewhere: *Grand Magazine of Magazines* (August–September, 1750); *De Hollandsche Wysgeer,* Part I (1759; a Dutch translation); Thomas Davies (ed.), *Miscellaneous and Fugitive Pieces,* I (1773); *Lloyd's Evening Post* for 18 May 1774 (an extract); *Lady's Magazine* (September–October, 1777), which recommends "The Vision" to those "who superintend the education of youth"; *Weekly Miscellany, or Instructive Entertainer* (1781); Harrison's *New Novelist's Magazine or Entertaining Library,* I (1786); Hawkins's edition (1787) of Johnson's works; the 1792 edition (prefaced by Arthur Murphy's *Essay on the Life and Genius of Samuel Johnson*) of Johnson's works; and *Aberdeen Magazine, or Universal Repository* (1797).[8]

Surveying the various signs of its reception, one may say that "The Vision" enjoyed a steady if unspectacular existence between 1748 and 1800 largely because of its inclusion in successive editions of *The Preceptor.* At the same time, the allegory's independent appearances denote its own moderate appeal to a reading public whose appetite for prose "visions" was both settled and strong. Several members of that public united in applying the epithet of beautiful to the work. Altered literary tastes would probably prevent most critics from using the term today, but for

7. XVIII (1748), 159–63, 164.

8. For information about the appearance of "The Vision" in the *Grand Magazine of Magazines, Lloyd's Evening Post,* and *Lady's Magazine,* I have drawn on Helen Louise McGuffie, *Samuel Johnson in the British Press, 1749–1784: A Chronological Checklist* (1976), pp. 11, 127, 214; for information about its appearance in *De Hollandsche Wysgeer* and Harrison's *New Novelist's Magazine,* I have drawn on *NCBEL,* II. col. 1144; and for the information about its appearance in the *Weekly Miscellany* (XV.505–09, 532–38) and the *Aberdeen Magazine* (II.482–86, 536–40), I am indebted to Robert Mayo. The allegory appears on pp. 80–94 of Vol. I of Davies's *Miscellaneous and Fugitive Pieces,* pp. 145–62 of Vol. XI of the 1787 works, and pp. 398–415 of Vol. II of the 1792 works.

the reader, young or old, willing to be persuaded of the potency of human habits, "The Vision of Theodore" still provides vivid instruction and sage counsel.[9]

THE TEXT

No manuscripts of "The Vision of Theodore" are known to exist. As noted above (p. 179), the earliest text forms a part of the two-volume collection *The Preceptor,* published on 7 April 1748. As also noted above (p. 191), six more London editions (1754, 1758, 1763, 1769, 1775, and 1783) of the collection appeared through 1784, the date of Johnson's death. A collation of the relevant portions of four copies of the first edition (Bodleian Library, British Library, Hyde Collection, Yale University Library; all printed from the identical setting of type), of one copy of each of the next six editions, and of Hawkins's edition (1787) of Johnson's *Works* reveals no evidence of authorial changes in "The Vision." Most of the differences between the first and later editions are confined to spelling and punctuation; virtually all of the minor substantive differences illustrate the truism that corruption mounts after the first edition. The text presented here is therefore that of the first edition (Yale copy), modified by (1) the reduction to lower case of the initial letters of all nouns save those originally printed in italics (which are here printed in roman); "Perseverance" on p. 195, l. 4; "Hermit" on p. 195. l. 6; and "Habit" on p. 212, l. 13; (2) the regularization of quotation marks; and (3) the silent correction of six obvious errors or oversights, all accidentals.

---

9. In Lipking's opinion, "All that ["The Vision"] teaches us—the central importance of education, the view of life as a heroic journey, the Christian applications of Prodicus and Cebes, the power of habit in the author's mind, and the ambivalent attitude toward vision itself—informs [Johnson's] later work" (p. 527). For Einbond, "the omnipresent threat of Habit is the heart of Johnson's message," and the "figures of Habit [are] the most entertaining of allegorical beings" (p. 61).

THE VISION OF THEODORE,
THE HERMIT OF TENERIFFE,
FOUND IN HIS CELL.[1]

Son of Perseverance, whoever thou[2] art, whose curiosity has led thee hither, read and be wise. He that now calls upon thee is Theodore the Hermit of Teneriffe, who in the fifty-seventh year of his retreat left this instruction to mankind, lest his solitary hours should be spent in vain.

I was once what thou art now, a groveller[3] on the earth, and a gazer at the sky; I traffick'd and heaped wealth together, I loved and was favoured, I wore the robe of honour, and heard the musick of adulation; I was ambitious, and rose to greatness; I was unhappy, and retired. I sought for some time what I at length found here, a place where all real wants might be easily supplied,[4] and where I might not be under the necessity of purchasing the assistance of men by the toleration of their follies. Here I saw fruits and herbs and water,[5] and here determined to wait the hand of death, which I hope, when at last it comes, will fall lightly upon me.

Forty-eight years had I now passed in forgetfulness of all mortal cares, and without any inclination to wander farther than the necessity of procuring sustenance required; but as

---

1. For a discussion of (1) "The Vision" as an allegorical "dream vision" and (2) the use of the Peak of Teneriffe (situated on the largest of the Canary Islands) as a symbol of great height by seventeenth- and eighteenth-century British writers, see Introduction, pp. 185–87 above.

2. According to SJ's *Dictionary*, "[*thou*] is used only in very familiar or very solemn language. When we speak to equals or superiors, we say *you;* but in solemn language, and in addresses of worship, we say *thou.*"

3. *To grovel* ("1. To lie prone; to creep low on the ground." "2. To be mean; to be without dignity or elevation.")—but not *groveller*—appears in SJ's *Dictionary*.

4. Cf. the decision of the hermit in *Rasselas* to retire to his cell, "a cavern in the side of a mountain" (ch. XXI, p. 80 above).

5. Cf. the action of the hermit in *Rasselas:* "he fed only upon fruits and water" (ch. XXI, p. 81 above).

I stood one day beholding the rock that overhangs my cell, I found in myself a desire to climb it; and when I was on its top, was in the same manner determined to scale the next, till by degrees I conceived a wish to view the summit of the mountain, at the foot of which I had so long resided. This motion of my thoughts I endeavoured to suppress, not because it appeared criminal, but because it was new; and all change, not evidently for the better, alarms a mind taught by experience to distrust itself.[6] I was often afraid that my heart was deceiving me, that my impatience of confinement rose from some earthly passion, and that my ardour to survey the works of nature, was only a hidden longing to mingle once again in the scenes of life.[7] I therefore endeavoured to settle my thoughts into their former state, but found their distraction every day greater. I was always reproaching myself with the want of happiness within my reach; and at last began to question whether it was not laziness rather than caution, that restrained me from climbing to the summit of Teneriffe.

I rose therefore before the day, and began my journey up the steep of the mountain;[8] but I had not advanced far, old as I was and burthened with provisions, when the day began to shine upon me; the declivities grew more precipitous,[9] and the sand slided[1] from beneath my feet; at last,

---

6. Cf. *The Plan of a Dictionary of the English Language* (par. 18): "All change is of itself an evil, which ought not to be hazarded but for evident advantage." Later, in the Preface (par. 16) to his *Dictionary,* SJ remarks that "'Change,' says Hooker, 'is not made without inconvenience, even from worse to better'" (*Of the Laws of Ecclesiastical Polity,* IV.xiv.1). Also cf. Sermon 7 (par. 2); *Letters* 827.

7. The hermit in *Rasselas* (ch. XXI, p. 83 above) expresses his desire to mix again in society by leaving his cell and accompanying the prince's party back to Cairo.

8. In Addison's "Vision of Mirzah"

(*Spectator* 159, par. 2), Mirzah, having "ascended the high hills of Bagdat," was "airing [himself] on the tops of the mountains" just before experiencing his vision; for a discussion of the similarities between Addison's essay and SJ's "Vision," see Introduction, p. 186 above.

9. *Declivity:* "Inclination or obliquity reckoned downwards; gradual descent; not precipitous or perpendicular: the contrary to acclivity" (*Dictionary*). Did SJ err in writing *declivities* instead of *acclivities?*

1. *Slided* does not appear in SJ's *Dictionary; slid* is defined as "The preterite of *slide.*"

fainting with labour, I arrived at a small plain, almost in-
closed by rocks and open only to the east.[2] I sat down to rest
a while, in full persuasion that when I had recovered my
strength, I should proceed on my design; but when once I
had tasted ease, I found many reasons against disturbing it.
The branches spread a shade over my head, and the gales[3]
of spring wafted odours to my bosom.

As I sat thus forming alternately excuses for delay, and
resolutions to go forward, an irresistible heaviness suddenly surprized me; I laid my head upon the bank and
resigned myself to sleep:[4] when methought I heard a sound
as of the flight of eagles, and a being of more than human
dignity stood before me. While I was deliberating how to
address him, he took me by the hand with an air of kindness, and asked me solemnly, but without severity, "Theodore, whither art thou going?" "I am climbing," answered I, "to the top of the mountain, to enjoy a more
extensive prospect of the works of nature." "Attend first"
(said he) "to the prospect which this place affords, and what
thou dost not understand I will explain.[5] I am one of the

---

2. Communications to the Royal Society in 1715 and 1752 (the latter by
William Heberden, later one of SJ's
physicians) mention a rocky area of
Mount Teneriffe—open to the east—
where climbers rested and which was
called "La Extancis de los Ingleses, or
the English baiting-place" (*Philosophical Transactions of the Royal Society*, XXIX
[1715], 320–22; XLVII [1752], 354).
SJ's apparent allusion to the "English
baiting-place" suggests that he possessed precise information about
Mount Teneriffe. For this reference I
am indebted to Lipking, pp. 524, 536.

3. *Gale:* "A wind not tempestuous,
yet stronger than a breeze" (*Dictionary*).

4. See p. 186, n. 7, above. The description of Theodore's state indicates
that he is semi-conscious while experiencing his vision ("I started," he says at
the end [p. 212 below]).

5. In Addison's "Vision of Mirzah"
(*Spectator* 159, pars. 3, 4), a supernatural "Genius" also takes Mirzah "by the
hand" and directs him to "cast thy eyes
eastward," whereupon Mirzah sees "a
huge valley and a prodigious tide of
water rolling through it." In Cebes's
"Picture of Human Life," an "Old Citizen" (par. 3) explains the meaning of
the picture ("hung up before one of
the chapels" [par. 1]) to a group of
strangers. In the picture itself, a "Genius" located "by the entrance" to life
"directs all that are going in, what they
should do after they are enter'd into
life; and shews them which way they
ought to take in order to be happy in it"
(par. 13). For a discussion of the similarities between Cebes's "Picture" and
SJ's "Vision," see Introduction, pp.
184–85 above.

benevolent beings who watch over the children of the dust, to preserve them from those evils which will not ultimately terminate in good, and which they do not, by their own faults, bring upon themselves. Look round therefore without fear: observe, contemplate, and be instructed."

Encouraged by this assurance, I looked and beheld a mountain[6] higher than Teneriffe, to the summit of which the human eye could never reach; when I had tired myself with gazing upon its height, I turned my eyes towards its foot, which I could easily discover, but was amazed to find it without foundation, and placed inconceivably in emptiness and darkness. Thus I stood terrified and confused; above were tracts inscrutable, and below was total vacuity. But my protector, with a voice of admonition, cried out, "Theodore, be not affrighted, but raise thy eyes again; the Mountain of Existence is before thee, survey it and be wise."

I then looked with more deliberate attention, and observed the bottom of the mountain to be of gentle rise, and overspread with flowers; the middle to be more steep, embarrassed[7] with crags, and interrupted by precipices, over which hung branches loaded with fruits, and among which were scattered palaces and bowers.[8] The tracts which my eye could reach nearest the top were generally barren; but there were among the clefts of the rocks, a few hardy evergreens, which though they did not give much pleasure to the sight or smell, yet seemed to cheer the labour and facilitate the steps of those who were clambering among them.

Then beginning to examine more minutely the different parts, I observed, at a great distance, a multitude of both sexes issuing into view from the bottom of the mountain.[9]

---

6. Allegorical mountains figure in such earlier essays as *Tatler* 81; *Spectator* 460, 514, 558, 559; *Champion* for 13 Dec 1739.

7. *To embarrass:* "To perplex; to distress; to entangle" (*Dictionary*).

8. "Precipices," a "grove," and a "beautiful meadow" appear in Cebes's "Picture of Human Life."

9. Cf. the "great number of people standing before the portal" to life in Cebes's "Picture of Human Life" (par. 13).

Their first actions I could not accurately discern; but as they every moment approached nearer, I found that they amused themselves with gathering flowers under the superintendance of a modest virgin in a white robe, who seemed not over solicitous to confine them to any settled pace, or certain track; for she knew that the whole ground was smooth and solid, and that they could not easily be hurt or bewildered. When, as it often happened, they plucked a thistle for a flower, Innocence,[1] so was she called, would smile at the mistake. "Happy," said I, "are they who are under so gentle a government, and yet are safe." But I had no opportunity to dwell long on the consideration of their felicity; for I found that Innocence continued her attendance but a little way, and seemed to consider only the flowery bottom of the mountain as her proper province. Those whom she abandoned scarcely knew that they were left, before they perceived themselves in the hands of Education,[2] a nymph more severe in her aspect and imperious in her commands, who confined them to certain paths, in their opinion, too narrow and too rough. These they were continually solicited to leave by Appetite,[3] whom Education could never fright away, though she sometimes awed her to such timidity, that the effects of her presence were scarcely

---

1. *Innocence:* "Purity from injurious action; untainted integrity" (sense 1 in *Dictionary*).

2. *Education:* "Formation of manners in youth; the manner of breeding youth; nurture" (*Dictionary*). The two illustrative quotations read: "Education and instruction are the means, the one by use, the other by precept, to make our natural faculty of reason both the better and the sooner to judge rightly between truth and error, good and evil. Hooker" (*Of the Laws of Ecclesiastical Polity*, 1.vi.5); "All nations have agreed in the necessity of a strict education, which consisted in the observance of moral duties. Swift" ("A Proj-

ect for the Advancement of Religion," *The Prose Works of Jonathan Swift*, ed. Herbert Davis, 11 [1939], 52).

3. *Appetite:* "The natural desire of good; the instinct by which we are led to seek pleasure" (sense 1 in *Dictionary*). The illustrative quotation reads: "The will properly and strictly taken, as it is of things which are referred unto the end that men desireth, differeth greatly from that inferiour natural desire, which we call *appetite*. The object of appetite is whatsoever sensible good may be wished for; the object of will is that good which reason does lead us to seek. Hooker" (*Of the Laws of Ecclesiastical Polity*, 1.vii.3).

perceptible. Some went back to the first part of the mountain, and seemed desirous of continuing busied in plucking flowers, but were no longer guarded by Innocence; and such as Education could not force back, proceeded up the mountain by some miry road, in which they were seldom seen, and scarcely ever regarded.

As Education led her troop up the mountain, nothing was more observable than that she was frequently giving them cautions to beware of Habits;[4] and was calling out to one or another at every step, that a Habit was ensnaring them; that they would be under the dominion of Habit before they perceived their danger; and that those whom a Habit should once subdue, had little hope of regaining their liberty.[5]

Of this caution, so frequently repeated, I was very solicitous to know the reason, when my protector directed my regard to a troop of pygmies, which appeared to walk silently before those that were climbing the mountain, and each to smooth the way before her follower. I found that I had missed the notice of them before, both because they were so minute as not easily to be discerned, and because they grew every moment nearer in their colour to the objects with which they were surrounded. As the followers of

---

4. In SJ's *Dictionary*, sense 3 of *habit* is defined by the following quotation from Locke's *Essay concerning Human Understanding* (2.22.10): "*Habit* is a power or ability in man of doing any thing, when it has been acquired by frequent doing the same thing." Under sense 4, "Custom; inveterate use," SJ cites this passage from one of Francis Atterbury's sermons: "The force of education is so great, that we may mould the minds and manners of the young into what shape we please, and give the impressions of such *habits*, as shall ever afterwards remain" (*Sermons and Discourses on Several Subjects and Occasions*, 8th ed., 1766, II.233–34). For remarks on habits spoken by the tutor in *The*

Preceptor, see Introduction, p. 180 above. For a discussion of the broader context (English homiletic writings of the later seventeenth and early eighteenth century) and the nature of SJ's notions about habits—notions which stress the negative rather than the positive potentialities of habits—see Paul K. Alkon, "Robert South, William Law, and Samuel Johnson," *Studies in English Literature, 1500–1900*, VI (1966), 499–528.

5. In 1775, SJ "observed, that the force of our early habits was so great, that though reason approved, nay, though our senses relished a different course, almost every man returned to them" (*Life*, II.366).

Education did not appear to be sensible of the presence of these dangerous associates, or, ridiculing their diminutive size, did not think it possible that human beings should ever be brought into subjection by such feeble enemies, they generally heard her precepts of vigilance with wonder; and, when they thought her eye withdrawn, treated them with contempt. Nor could I myself think her cautions so necessary as her frequent inculcation seemed to suppose, till I observed that each of these petty beings held secretly a chain in her hand, with which she prepared to bind those whom she found within her power. Yet these Habits under the eye of Education went quietly forward, and seemed very little to encrease in bulk or strength; for though they were always willing to join with Appetite, yet when Education kept them apart from her, they would very punctually obey command, and make the narrow roads in which they were confin'd easier and smoother.

It was observable, that their stature was never at a stand, but continually growing or decreasing, yet not always in the same proportions; nor could I forbear to express my admiration,[6] when I saw in how much less time they generally gained than lost bulk. Though they grew slowly in the road of Education, it might however be perceived that they grew; but if they once deviated at the call of Appetite, their stature soon became gigantic, and their strength was such, that Education pointed out to her tribe many that were led in chains by them, whom she could never more rescue from their slavery.[7] She pointed them out, but with little effect; for all her pupils appeared confident of their own superiority to the strongest Habit, and some seemed in secret to regret that they were hindered from following the triumph of Appetite.

---

6. *Admiration:* "Wonder; the act of admiring or wondering" (sense 1 in *Dictionary*).

7. With the condition of these victims of habits, cf. the plight of those unfortunate persons in Cebes's "Picture of Human Life" who "are conquered, and led along like captives, some by Intemperance, and others by Arrogance; here by Covetousness, and there by Vain-Glory, or any other of the Vices: whose chains they are in vain striving to get loose from" (par. 149).

It was the peculiar artifice of Habit not to suffer her power to be felt at first. Those whom she led, she had the address of appearing only to attend, but was continually doubling her chains upon her companions, which were so slender in themselves, and so silently fastened, that while the attention was engaged by other objects, they were not easily perceived. Each link grew tighter as it had been longer worn, and when by continual additions they became so heavy as to be felt, they were very frequently too strong to be broken.[8]

When Education had proceeded in this manner to the part of the mountain where the declivity[9] began to grow craggy, she resigned her charge to two powers of superior aspect. The meaner of them appeared capable of presiding in senates or governing nations, and yet watched the steps of the other with the most anxious attention, and was visibly confounded and perplexed if ever she suffered her regard to be drawn away. The other seemed to approve her submission as pleasing, but with such a condescension as plainly shewed that she claimed it as due; and indeed so great was her dignity and sweetness, that he who would not reverence, must not behold her.

"Theodore," said my protector, "be fearless, and be wise; approach these powers, whose dominion extends to all the remaining part of the Mountain of Existence." I trembled, and ventured to address the inferior nymph, whose eyes though piercing and awful, I was not unable to sustain. "Bright power," said I, "by whatever name it is lawful to address thee, tell me, thou who presidest here, on what condition thy protection will be granted." "It will be granted," said she, "only to obedience. I am Reason,[1] of all subordi-

---

8. See p. 109, n. 7, above; also cf. Sermon 10 (par. 21).

9. See p. 196, n. 9, above.

1. *Reason:* "The power by which man deduces one proposition from another, or proceeds from premises to consequences; the rational faculty; discursive power" (sense 1 in *Dictionary*). The illustrative quotations include the fol-

lowing: "*Reason* is the director of man's will, discovering in action what is good; for the laws of well-doing are the dictates of the right reason. Hooker" (*Of the Laws of Ecclesiastical Polity*, I.vii.4); "*reason*'s glimmering ray / Was lent, not to assure our doubtful way, / But guide us upward to a better day. Dryden" (*Religio Laici*, ll. 5–7).

nate beings the noblest and the greatest; who, if thou wilt
receive my laws, will reward thee like the rest of my votaries,
by conducting thee to Religion."² Charmed by her voice
and aspect, I professed my readiness to follow her. She then
presented me to her mistress, who looked upon me with
tenderness. I bowed before her, and she smil'd.

When Education delivered up those for whose happiness
she had been so long solicitous, she seemed to expect that
they should express some gratitude for her care, or some
regret at the loss of that protection which she had hitherto
afforded them. But it was easy to discover, by the alacrity³
which broke out at her departure, that her presence had
been long displeasing, and that she had been teaching those
who felt in themselves no want of instruction. They all
agreed in rejoicing that they should no longer be subject to
her caprices, or disturb'd by her documents,⁴ but should be
now under the direction only of Reason, to whom they
made no doubt of being able to recommend themselves by a
steady adherence to all her precepts. Reason counselled
them at their first entrance upon her province, to inlist
themselves among the votaries of Religion; and informed
them, that if they trusted to her alone, they would find the
same fate with her other admirers, whom she had not been
able to secure against Appetites and Passions,⁵ and who

2. *Religion:* "Virtue, as founded
upon reverence of God, and expectation of future rewards and punish-
ments" (sense 1 in *Dictionary*). Two of
the illustrative quotations read: "By *religion*, I mean that general habit of reverence towards the divine nature,
whereby we are enabled and inclined
to worship and serve God after such a
manner as we conceive most agreeable
to his will, so as to procure his favour
and blessing. Wilkins" (*Of the Principles
and Duties of Natural Religion*, 4th ed.,
1699, p. 39); "*Religion* or virtue, in a
large sense, includes duty to God and
our neighbour; but in a proper sense,
virtue signifies duty towards men, and
religion duty to God. Watts" (*Logick*,

1.iv.7).

3. *Alacrity:* "Cheerfulness, expressed
by some outward token; sprightliness;
gayety; liveliness; cheerful willingness"
(*Dictionary*).

4. *Document:* "Precept; instruction;
direction" (sense 1 in *Dictionary*).

5. Under sense 4 of *passion* in his
Dictionary, SJ quotes the following passage from Watts's *Logick* (1.iv.7): "The
word *passion* signifies the receiving any
action in a large philosophical sense; in
a more limited philosophical sense, it
signifies any of the affections of human
nature; as love, fear, joy, sorrow: but
the common people confine it only to
anger." In Sermon 18 (par. 1), SJ declares: "To subdue passion, and regu-

having been seized by Habits in the regions of Desire, had been dragged away to the caverns of Despair.[6] Her admonition was vain, the greater number declared against any other direction, and doubted not but by her superintendency they should climb with safety up the Mountain of Existence. "My power," said Reason, "is to advise, not to compel;[7] I have already told you the danger of your choice. The path now seems plain and even, but there are asperities and pitfalls, over which Religion only can conduct you. Look upwards, and you perceive a mist before you settled upon the highest visible part of the mountain, a mist by which my prospect is terminated, and which is pierced only by the eyes of Religion. Beyond it are the temples of Happiness,[8] in which those who climb the precipice by her direction, after the toil of their pilgrimage repose for ever.[9] I know not the way, and therefore can only conduct you to a better guide. Pride[1] has sometimes reproached me with the narrowness of my view, but when she endeavoured to extend it, could only shew me, below the mist, the bowers of Content;[2] even they vanished as I fix'd my eyes upon them;

---

late desire, is the great task of man, as a moral agent; a task for which natural reason, however assisted and enforced by human laws, has been found insufficient, and which cannot be performed but by the help of religion." For SJ's notions on reason as an auxiliary to religion, see the Introduction (pp. xlix–li) to the edition of SJ's *Sermons* edited by Jean H. Hagstrum and James Gray (Vol. xiv, Yale Edition of the Works of Samuel Johnson, 1978).

6. *Despair:* "Hopelessness; despondence; loss of hope" (sense 1 in *Dictionary*). The definition is followed by this quotation from Locke's *Essay concerning Human Understanding* (2.20.11): "*Despair* is the thought of the unattainableness of any good, which works differently in men's minds, sometimes producing uneasiness or pain, sometimes rest and indolency."

7. Cf. *Idler* 89 (par. 9): "Reason has no authority over us, but by its power to warn us against evil."

8. SJ's second mention of the abode of happiness (p. 208 below) reduces the "temples" to one. In *Dictionary*, sense 1 of *happiness* is "Felicity; state in which the desires are satisfied." Cf. the "Edifice" of "Happiness" which "appears above all the inclosures, as a citadel does above all the buildings in a city" (par. 133) in Cebes's "Picture of Human Life."

9. Cf. *Letters* 578: "There is but one solid basis of happiness; and that is, the reasonable hope of a happy futurity."

1. *Pride:* "Inordinate and unreasonable self-esteem" (sense 1 in *Dictionary*).

2. *Content:* "Moderate happiness; such satisfaction as, though it does not fill up desire, appeases complaint" (sense 1 in *Dictionary*).

and those whom she persuaded to travel towards them were inchained by Habits, and ingulfed by Despair, a cruel tyrant, whose caverns are beyond the darkness on the right side and on the left, from whose prisons none can escape, and whom I cannot teach you to avoid."[3]

Such was the declaration of Reason to those who demanded her protection. Some that recollected the dictates of Education, finding them now seconded by another authority, submitted with reluctance to the strict decree, and engaged themselves among the followers of Religion, who were distinguished by the uniformity of their march, though many of them were women, and by their continual endeavours to move upwards, without appearing to regard the prospects which at every step courted their attention.

All those who determined to follow either Reason or Religion were continually importuned to forsake the road, sometimes by Passions, and sometimes by Appetites, of whom both had reason to boast the success of their artifices; for so many were drawn into bypaths, that any way was more populous than the right. The attacks of the Appetites were more impetuous, those of the Passions longer continued. The Appetites turned their followers directly from the true way, but the Passions marched at first in a path nearly in the same direction with that of Reason and Religion; but deviated by slow degrees, till at last they entirely changed their course. Appetite drew aside the dull, and Passion the sprightly. Of the Appetites Lust was the strongest,[4] and of the Passions Vanity.[5] The most powerful assault was to be feared, when a Passion and an Appetite joined

---

3. Cf. Giant Despair and his dungeon in *The Pilgrim's Progress*, ed. J. B. Wharey and Roger Sharrock (1960), pp. 113–19, 281–83. In Cebes's "Picture of Human Life," Despair ranks among the worst of human ills.

4. Cf. Robert South's comment on lust (defined under sense 1 as "Carnal desire" in SJ's *Dictionary*): "Nothing does or can darken the mind or con-

science of man more [than lust]: nay, it has a peculiar efficacy this way, and for that cause may justly be ranked amongst the very powers of darkness" (*Sermons* [1859], 1.220).

5. *Vanity:* "Ostentation; arrogance" (sense 6 in *Dictionary*); "Petty pride; pride exerted upon slight grounds; pride operating on small occasions" (sense 7).

their enticements; and the path of Reason was best followed, when a Passion called to one side, and an Appetite to
the other.

These seducers had the greatest success upon the followers of Reason, over whom they scarcely ever failed to
prevail, except when they counteracted one another. They
had not the same triumphs over the votaries of Religion;
for though they were often led aside for a time, Religion
commonly recalled them by her emissary Conscience,[6] before Habit had time to enchain them. But they that professed to obey Reason, if once they forsook her, seldom
returned; for she had no messenger to summon them but
Pride, who generally betrayed her confidence, and im-
ployed all her skill to support Passion; and if ever she did
her duty, was found unable to prevail, if Habit had interposed.

I soon found that the great danger to the followers of
Religion was only from Habit; every other power was easily
resisted, nor did they find any difficulty when they inadvertently quitted her, to find her again by the direction of
Conscience, unless they had given time to Habit to draw her
chain behind them, and bar up the way by which they had
wandered. Of some of those the condition was justly to be
pitied, who turned at every call of Conscience, and tried, but
without effect, to burst the chains of Habit:[7] saw Religion
walking forward at a distance, saw her with reverence, and
longed to join her; but were, whenever they approached

---

6. *Conscience:* "The knowledge or
faculty by which we judge of the goodness or wickedness of ourselves" (sense
1 in *Dictionary*). The illustrative quotations include this passage from Swift's
sermon "On the Testimony of Conscience": "*Conscience* signifies that
knowledge which a man hath of his
own thoughts and actions; and, because if a man judgeth fairly of his actions, by comparing them with the law
of God, his mind will approve or con-
demn him, this knowledge or con-

science may be both an accuser and a
judge" (*The Prose Works of Jonathan
Swift*, ed. Herbert Davis, IX [*Sermons*,
ed. Louis Landa (1948)], 150). Cf. *Life*,
II.243.

7. SJ's prayers contain repeated references to his struggles with "evil habits" and the "chain of evil custom"; see
Diaries, Prayers, and Annals, ed. E. L.
McAdam, Jr., with Donald and Mary
Hyde (Vol. I, Yale Edition of the Works
of Samuel Johnson, 1958), pp. 143, 69,
et passim.

her, withheld by Habit, and languished in sordid bondage which they could not escape, though they scorned and hated it.

It was evident that the Habits were so far from growing weaker by these repeated contests, that if they were not totally overcome, every struggle enlarged their bulk and increased their strength; and a Habit oppos'd and victorious was more than twice as strong as before the contest. The manner in which those who were weary of their tyranny endeavoured to escape from them, appeared by the event to be generally wrong; they tried to loose their chains one by one, and to retreat by the same degrees as they advanced; but before the deliverance was completed, Habit always threw new chains upon her fugitive: nor did any escape her but those who by an effort sudden and violent, burst their shackles at once, and left her at a distance; and even of these many rushing too precipitately forward, and hindered by their terrors from stopping where they were safe, were fatigued with their own vehemence, and resigned themselves again to that power from whom an escape must be so dearly bought, and whose tyranny was little felt, except when it was resisted.[8]

Some however there always were, who, when they found Habit prevailing over them, called upon Reason or Religion for assistance; each of them willingly came to the succour of her suppliant; but neither with the same strength nor the same success. Habit, insolent with her power, would often presume to parley with Reason, and offer to loose

---

8. With this paragraph, cf. *Idler* 27 (par. 9), where SJ remarks that "custom is commonly too strong for the most resolute resolver though furnished for the assault with all the weapons of philosophy. 'He that endeavours to free himself from an ill habit,' says Bacon [in "Of Nature in Man"], 'must not change too much at a time lest he should be discouraged by difficulty; nor too little, for then he will make but slow advances.' This is a precept which may be applauded in a book, but will fail in the trial, in which every change will be found too great or too little. Those who have been able to conquer habit, are like those fabled to have returned from the realms of Pluto. . . . They are sufficient to give hope but not security, to animate the contest but not to promise victory."

some of her chains if the rest might remain. To this Reason, who was never certain of victory, frequently consented, but always found her concession destructive, and saw the captive led away by Habit to his former slavery.[9] Religion never submitted to treaty, but held out her hand with certainty of conquest; and if the captive to whom she gave it did not quit his hold, always led him away in triumph, and placed him in the direct path to the temple of Happiness, where Reason never failed to congratulate his deliverance,[1] and encourage his adherence to that power to whose timely succour he was indebted for it.

When the traveller was again placed in the road of Happiness, I saw Habit again gliding before him, but reduced to the stature of a dwarf, without strength and without activity; but when the Passions or Appetites which had before seduced him, made their approach, Habit would on a sudden start into size, and with unexpected violence push him towards them. The wretch thus impelled on one side, and allured on the other, too frequently quitted the road of Happiness, to which, after his second deviation from it, he rarely returned. But if by a timely call upon Religion, the force of Habit was eluded, her attacks grew fainter, and at last her correspondence with the enemy was entirely destroyed. She then began to employ those restless faculties in compliance with the power which she could not overcome; and as she grew again in stature and in strength, cleared away the asperities of the road to Happiness.

From this road I could not easily withdraw my attention, because all who travelled it appeared chearful and satisfied; and the farther they proceeded, the greater appeared their alacrity,[2] and the stronger their conviction of the wisdom of their guide. Some who had never deviated but by short excursions, had Habit in the middle of their passage, vig-

---

9. Cf. *Adventurer* 108 (par. 9): "Habits grow stronger by indulgence; and reason loses her dignity in proportion as she has oftner yielded to temptation."

1. SJ's first mention of the dwelling

of happiness (p. 204 above) is plural ("temples"). Cf. "They congratulate our return" (*Letters* 338).

2. For the meaning of *alacrity*, see p. 203, n. 3, above.

orously supporting them and driving off their Appetites and Passions, which attempted to interrupt their progress. Others, who had entered this road late, or had long forsaken it, were toiling on without her help at least, and commonly against her endeavours. But I observed, when they approached to the barren top, that few were able to proceed without some support from Habit, and that those whose Habits were strong advanced towards the mists with little emotion, and entered them at last with calmness and confidence; after which they were seen only by the eye of Religion, and though Reason looked after them with the most earnest curiosity, she could only obtain a faint glimpse, when her mistress, to enlarge her prospect, raised her from the ground. Reason however, discerned that they were safe, but Religion saw that they were happy.[3]

"Now, Theodore," said my protector, "withdraw thy view from the regions of obscurity, and see the fate of those who, when they were dismissed by Education, would admit no direction but that of Reason. Survey their wanderings, and be wise."

I looked then upon the road of Reason, which was indeed, so far as it reached, the same with that of Religion, nor had Reason discovered it but by her instructions. Yet when she had once been taught it, she clearly saw that it was right; and Pride had sometimes incited her to declare that she discovered it herself, and persuaded her to offer herself as a guide to Religion; whom after many vain experiments she found it her highest privilege to follow. Reason was however at last well instructed in part of the way, and appeared to teach it with some success, when her precepts were not misrepresented by Passion, or her influence overborn by Appetite.[4] But neither of these enemies was she

---

3. Cf. John Tillotson's assertion, in his sermon on "The Care of our Souls, the One Thing Needful," that "religion is a certain way to happiness" and that "there is no other way to happiness but this" (*Works* [1820], III.68).

4. In *Idler* 52 (par. 10), SJ, after urging restraint and self-denial regarding "lawful desires," declares, "No man, whose appetites are his masters, can perform the duties of his nature with strictness and regularity; he that would be superior to external influences must first become superior to his own passions."

able to resist. When Passion seized upon her votaries, she seldom attempted opposition, she seemed indeed to contend with more vigour against Appetite, but was generally overwearied in the contest; and if either of her opponents had confederated with Habit, her authority was wholly at an end. When Habit endeavoured to captivate the votaries of Religion, she grew by slow degrees, and gave time to escape; but in seizing the unhappy followers of Reason, she proceeded as one that had nothing to fear, and enlarged her size, and doubled her chains without intermission, and without reserve.

Of those who forsook the directions of Reason, some were led aside by the whispers of Ambition, who was perpetually pointing to stately palaces, situated on eminences on either side, recounting the delights of affluence, and boasting the security of power. They were easily persuaded to follow her, and Habit quickly threw her chains upon them; they were soon convinced of the folly of their choice, but few of them attempted to return. Ambition led them forward from precipice to precipice, where many fell and were seen no more.[5] Those that escaped, were, after a long series of hazards, generally delivered over to Avarice,[6] and enlisted by her in the service of Tyranny, where they continued to heap up gold till their patrons or their heirs[7] pushed them headlong at last into the caverns of Despair.

Others were enticed by Intemperance[8] to ramble in search of those fruits that hung over the rocks, and filled

---

5. Cf. *The Vanity of Human Wishes*, ll. 99–128, which include the depiction of Cardinal Wolsey's fall from power.

6. Cf. *Rambler* 151 (par. 12): "Avarice is generally the last passion of those lives of which the first part has been squandered in pleasure, and the second devoted to ambition." Also see p. 96, n. 2, above.

7. Cf. *The Vanity of Human Wishes*, ll. 275–90, which describe the prospective heirs and the "unextinguish'd avarice" (l. 285) of an old man.

8. In Prodicus's "Choice of Hercules," the female character of Virtue criticizes her sensual counterpart Sloth for "draining the copious bowl, ere thirst require" and "feasting, ere hunger to the feast invite" (ll. 155–56); for a discussion of the similarities between the "Choice of Hercules" and SJ's "Vision," see Introduction, p. 184 above. In Cebes's "Picture of Human Life," Intemperance figures significantly as a vice or habit.

the air with their fragrance. I observed, that the Habits which hovered about these soon grew to an enormous size, nor were there any who less attempted to return to Reason, or sooner sunk into the gulphs that lay before them.[9] When these first quitted the road, Reason looked after them with a frown of contempt, but had little expectations of being able to reclaim them; for the bowl of intoxication was of such qualities, as to make them lose all regard but for the present moment; neither Hope nor Fear could enter their retreats, and Habit had so absolute a power, that even Conscience, if Religion had employed her in their favour, would not have been able to force an entrance.

There were others whose crime it was rather to neglect Reason than to disobey her, and who retreated from the heat and tumult of the way, not to the bowers of Intemperance, but to the maze of Indolence.[1] They had this peculiarity in their condition, that they were always in sight of the road of Reason, always wishing for her presence, and always resolving to return to-morrow. In these was most eminently conspicuous the subtlety of Habit, who hung imperceptible shackles upon them, and was every moment leading them farther from the road, which they always imagined that they had the power of reaching. They wandered on from one double of the labyrinth to another with the chains of Habit hanging secretly upon them, till as they advanced, the flowers grew paler, and the scents fainter: they proceeded in their dreary march without pleasure in their progress, yet without power to return; and had this aggravation above all others, that they were criminal but not delighted. The drunkard for a time laughed over his wine;[2] the ambitious man triumphed in the miscarriage of

---

9. Cf. *Rambler* 102 (pars. 11–15), part of a dream vision which describes the "'Gulph of Intemperance,' a dreadful whirlpool," whence "Reason" is "able to extricate" few "passengers."

1. *Indolence:* "Laziness; inattention; listlessness" (sense 2 in *Dictionary*). In Prodicus's "Choice of Hercules," the fe-

male character of Virtue, after declaring that "honour . . . spurns the timorous, indolent, and base" (l. 116), accuses Sloth of being "only tir'd with Indolence" (l. 165); see Introduction, p. 184 above.

2. Cf. SJ's comment that a man is "never" happy in the "present" mo-

his rival; but the captives of Indolence had neither superiority nor merriment. Discontent lowered in their looks, and Sadness hovered round their shades; yet they crawled on reluctant and gloomy, till they arrived at the depth of the recess, varied only with poppies and nightshade, where the dominion of Indolence terminates,[3] and the hopeless wanderer is delivered up to Melancholy: the chains of Habit are rivetted for ever, and Melancholy having tortured her prisoner for a time, consigns him at last to the cruelty of Despair.

While I was musing on this miserable scene, my protector called out to me, "Remember, Theodore, and be wise, and let not Habit prevail against thee."[4] I started, and beheld myself surrounded by the rocks of Teneriffe; the birds of light were singing in the trees, and the glances[5] of the morning darted upon me.

.

---

ment "but when he is drunk" (*Life*, II.351).

3. Cf. *Letters* 976: "That voluntary debility, which modern language is content to term indolence, will, if it is not counteracted by resolution, render in time the strongest faculties lifeless, and turn the flames to the smoke of virtue"; and *Letters* 869.1.

4. At the end of Cebes's "Picture of Human Life," the "Old Citizen" exhorts his listeners, "Get a habit of doing right, whatever pain it costs you"; see Introduction, p. 185 above.

5. *Glance:* "A sudden shoot of light or splendour" (sense 1 in *Dictionary*).

THE FOUNTAINS:

A FAIRY TALE

The Fountains
a Fairy Tale.

As Floretta was wandering in a Meadow at the Foot of Plinlimmon, she heard a little Bird cry in such a Note as she had never heard before; & looking round her saw a lovely Goldfinch entangled by a Lime Twig, and a Hawk hovering over him, as at the point of seizing him in its Talons.

Floretta longed to rescue the little Bird, but was afraid to encounter the Hawk, who looked fiercely upon her, ... without any dread of her approach & clapped his wings in Token of defiance. Floretta stood deliberating a few moments, but seeing her Mother at no great distance took Courage & snatched the Twig with the little Bird upon it. When she had perceived him she put him in her Bosom, and the Hawk flew away. Floretta shewing her Bird to her Mother told her from what danger she had rescued them; her Mother after a while advising her Beauty...

Traduzione della Novella detta le due Fontane scritta dal Dottor S. Johnson.

Why this was translated or transcribed, or why the Translation was torn, & the Transcript left, I cannot now make a Guess.
H: L: P: 1807.

EDITOR'S INTRODUCTION

"The Fountains: A Fairy Tale" was Johnson's longest (thirty-one page) single contribution to a collection entitled *Miscellanies in Prose and Verse* ostensibly written by the blind Welshwoman Anna Williams, who was for many years a member of Johnson's remarkable household.[1] Since Miss Williams's own compositions were insufficient to make a satisfactory volume, several persons added assorted pieces—all anonymous—which helped to form a thin quarto published by Thomas Davies on 1 April 1766.[2] Besides Johnson, who managed the undertaking and wrote the "Advertisement" on pp. iii–iv, the contributors included his close friend Mrs. Henry (Hester) Thrale (later Mrs. Gabriel Piozzi), Thomas Percy, John Hoole, and probably Frances Reynolds.[3] Johnson's exact share of the book, patently substantial, remains somewhat unclear even today.

To Mrs. Piozzi we are indebted for precise information about the composition of "The Fountains." Recalling its creation long after the actual event, she remarked that Johnson, intent on eking out Anna Williams's own scanty stock of material for the *Miscellanies,* accepted "instantly" some verses she "had written the week before" and then said, "Come Mistress, now *I'll* write a tale and your character shall be in it; so he composed 'The Fountains' in the same book, a performance little known, and in few hands."[4] On another occasion, with her younger friend Sir James Fellowes noting her remarks, she recollected that

> Dr. Johnson wrote the beautiful tale of the 'Fountains' in a short time in the library at Streatham whilst Mrs. Thrale was sitting by him, telling her that he would describe her as 'Floretta' and that it would serve to fill up the book about to

1. For an account of Miss Williams, see *The Dictionary of National Biography,* xxi.378–79.
2. Hazen, p. 213 (citing an advertisement in the *London Chronicle*).
3. Hazen, pp. 214–15.
4. James L. Clifford, *Hester Lynch Piozzi (Mrs. Thrale)* (2d ed., 1952), p. 61.

be published for the benefit of Mrs. Anna Williams the blind
lady entitled 'Miscellanies in Prose & Verse' 1766. The lines
scored in the tale of the Fountains were by H. L. P.—[5]

Mrs. Piozzi's two groups of reminiscences harmonize perfectly,
although the second obviously contains many more details than
the first. Deferring until later[6] a scrutiny of her supposed fictive
portrait, we may assay her other statements about the creation of
the fairy tale.

First, since it accords with Johnson's habitual pattern of rapid
writing, her specification of the "short time" necessary to produce "The Fountains" can be accepted as probably accurate. Second, the correctness of her identification of the place where the
composition occurred—"the library at Streatham" (the Thrales's
country residence, situated some six miles[7] from eighteenth-
century London)—can be neither verified nor disproved. For the
exact date of composition (presumably late 1765 or early 1766,
well before 1 April, when the Miscellanies was published), the
complete roster of Johnson's visits with the Thrales, and the
latter couple's precise sojourns during this period at Streatham
and Southwark, the location of their London dwelling, all remain
unknown. James L. Clifford, Mrs. Piozzi's most authoritative biographer, places the probable locale of writing "in Southwark
rather than Streatham," but admits that "this . . . is not certain."[8]

Third, Mrs. Piozzi's recollections both of her physical presence
during the composition of the tale and of her contribution to its
text gain a measure of credibility from an examination of the
copy of the Miscellanies which she presented to Sir James Fellowes
toward the end of her life and which is now part of the collection
in the Johnson Birthplace Museum at Lichfield. The volume
contains a number of ink and pencil comments and markings.
Since, as noted below, some of those in ink can definitely be
assigned to Mrs. Piozzi, the earlier annotator, and some in pencil
to Fellowes (with no switching in the kind of instrument used),

5. Clifford, Hester Lynch Piozzi, p. 63, n. 2.
6. See pp. 223–24 below.
7. Clifford, Hester Lynch Piozzi, p. 49.
8. Clifford, Hester Lynch Piozzi, p. 63, n. 2.

one infers that all of those in ink probably belong to the lady and all in pencil to the gentleman. With three exceptions, discussion of the latter may be consigned to a footnote.[9] But Mrs. Piozzi's intimate connection with the production of "The Fountains" necessitates an ampler treatment of her putative jottings.

Her only real note appears on an interleaf at the beginning of the volume and reads: "The Tale of the Fountains was written by Doctor Johnson for purpose [*sic*] of *filling up this Book:* & he asked H: L: Thrale for something of hers beside—She contributed the Three Warnings, & a Translation of Boileau's Epistle to his Gardener"; in the space above the note, Fellowes has commented, "This was written by H. L. P." Other markings by Mrs. Piozzi occur in the text of "The Fountains." One is a correction of the spelling of a word on page 127, "pertinacy" to "pertinacity"; in the right-hand margin beyond the word, Fellowes has written, "corrected by H. L. P." A second consists of two alterations in the punctuation of the passage on page 137 reading "and because she was often doubtful where others were confident,": Mrs. Piozzi seemingly inserted a comma after "doubtful" and changed the comma following "confident" to a semi-colon; she also, intentionally or inadvertently, made a longish ink mark in the left-hand margin beside the punctuation changes. A third mark is a vertical line, resembling an exclamation point, in the right-hand margin outside the passage on page 138 reading "but no friendship was durable; it was the fashion to desert her, and with the fashion what fidelity will contend? She could have"; beyond the line Fellowes has written, "This mark was by H. L. P." Presumably the line denotes Mrs. Piozzi's estimate of the similarity between the plight of the character Floretta and her own subsequent social

9. Apart from the three notes given in the text of this Introduction and another—now illegible—at the top of the first page of "The Fountains," Fellowes's comment is confined to "H. L. P. had no pretention to beauty. J. F.," written in the left-hand margin outside a passage reading in part: "her first desire was the increase of her beauty. She had some disproportion of features" (p. 122). He also apparently drew vertical lines in some margins (notably on pp. 124, 136–37) to signify parallels between Floretta's difficulties with society and the (much later) treatment accorded Mrs. Piozzi as a consequence of her second marriage. By underlining the phrase "most unpolluted purity" on p. 137, Fellowes seems to be defending Mrs. Piozzi's honor and reputation—a little belatedly, to be sure.

isolation during the period leading up to, and culminating in, her marriage to the Italian singer-teacher Gabriel Piozzi (1784).

The rest of the marks are lines drawn beneath five passages of the text: (1) "She [Floretta] could not hear a long story without hurrying the speaker on to the conclusion" (p. 135); (2) "This behaviour made her unwelcome wherever she went" (p. 135); (3) "for she often honoured virtue where she laughed at affectation" (p. 136); (4) "her rest broken *by niceties of honour and scruples of morality*" (p. 137; the italicized words indicate the underlining); (5) "By this time she began to doubt whether *old age were not dangerous to virtue;* whether *pain would not produce peevishness, and peevishness impair benevolence*" (p. 140; the italicized words indicate the underlining). These "scored" lines are apparently those to which Mrs. Piozzi refers in the statement above recorded by Fellowes. Their existence and their content—the fact that they all depict Floretta, Mrs. Piozzi's supposed fictive counterpart—although certainly not conclusive proof, thus measurably enhance the believability of Mrs. Piozzi's remark that she was with Johnson while he wrote the tale and that she had a hand in its creation.[1]

Her reminiscences and the Birthplace Museum copy of the *Miscellanies* do not exhaust the material about the composition of "The Fountains" issuing from Mrs. Piozzi. So far as the work itself is concerned, the most significant document is an English transcription preserved among the Piozzi papers in the John Rylands Library of Manchester University. At one time the group of folios of paper containing the transcription also included an Italian translation of the tale, its position immediately preceding that of the transcription. Later, the translation was torn out of the group, leaving only the signs of its forcible removal and a "title-page" reading: "Traduzzione della Novella detta / Le due Fontane / scritta dal / Dottor S: Johnson. / " Below these phrases is the following: "Why this was translated, or transcribed, or why the Translation was torn & the Trans[cription?] left, I cannot *now* make a *Guess* [.?] H: L: P. 180[?]" In addition to this initialed note,

---

1. Clifford, it should be noted, "greatly" doubts "whether Mrs. Thrale actually supplied any parts of Johnson's Tale, though," he concedes, "she may possibly have suggested some points of the characterization" (*Hester Lynch Piozzi*, p. 63, n. 2).

the Italian phrases, (presumably) the missing translation, and the transcription are certainly written in Mrs. Piozzi's bold, clear hand.

On inspection, the twenty-five page transcription[2] becomes an important source of information about the composition and text of "The Fountains," for it exhibits many differences from the version published in the *Miscellanies*. Numbering more than 140, the variants (those affecting meaning constitute most of the textual notes below [pp. 231–49]) appear on every page of both the manuscript and printed forms of the tale. The largest single group consists of additions of words and phrases in the printed version—for example, the insertion of "apparent" between "any" and "dread" (p. 231), the naming of "the second summer" after "that followed" (p. 235), and the elaboration of "Floretta was not invited" into "it was stipulated that Floretta should not be invited" (p. 246). A second substantial group includes the substitution of one or more words for the originals in the manuscript—for example, "endeavoured" for "tried" (p. 232), "nothing but" for "only" (p. 240), and "was not afraid" for "feared not" (p. 246). A third, much smaller class of changes eliminates from the published text individual words found in the manuscript—for example, "the rosy" becomes simply "rosy" (p. 239), "& the opposition" becomes "and opposition" (p. 240), and "ways had ended" is altered to "ways ended" (p. 240). Finally, a fourth group of printed variants, also small, displays the recasting, sometimes rather complex, of various passages in the manuscript—for example, "thought mankind better than they were found by fairies who knew them better" becomes "thought better of mankind than other fairies found them to deserve" (p. 233), "a hawk (which was herself)" becomes "herself in the shape of a hawk" (p. 235), and "she wished as she drank again to be made" becomes "she drank again, desired to be made" (p. 238).

Regardless of their character, virtually all of the readings in the *Miscellanies* must be judged distinct improvements over their counterparts in Mrs. Piozzi's transcription. Some changes heighten the intelligibility and clarity of parts of the narrative; some

2. That is, thirteen folios minus 13v. Page references in the text refer to pages below.

supply more precise expressions for those deleted; others sharp-
en syntactical patterns, including parallelism; still others increase
the rhythm of particular passages; and so on. It therefore seems
very probable that Mrs. Piozzi's transcription embodies a pre-
rather than a post-publication version of the text of "The Fountains." Her reason for making the copy remains obscure to us, as
it was to her lapsed memory in 180[?]; presumably, however, she
reproduced Johnson's holograph manuscript or, possibly, a fair
copy by an amanuensis. At some time after she had completed
her transcription, Johnson, perhaps when he was reading the
proofs, gave the tale the finishing touches evident in its printed
form, which, one may observe, presents unchanged the few lines
Mrs. Piozzi supposedly contributed to the text.

Granted its likely accuracy, this partial reconstruction of Johnson's process of composition may be extended by a scrutiny of two
discrete parts of "The Fountains"—the epigraph and the setting.
The former consists of lines 1–2 from Boethius's *Consolation of
Philosophy* (Book III, Meter 12): "*Felix qui potuit boni / Fontem visere
lucidum.*" Johnson's use of this passage may well be related to an
unfinished enterprise which he and Mrs. Piozzi undertook soon
after the beginning of their friendship. At the end of the preface
to her edition of *Letters to and from the late Samuel Johnson*, Mrs.
Piozzi, explaining the presence of non-epistolary material in Volume Two, wrote:

> The verses from Boethius will be accepted as a literary
> rarity; it was about the year 1765 when our Doctor told me
> that he would translate the Consolations [*sic*] of Philosophy,
> but said, I must do the Odes for him, and produce one every
> Thursday: he was obeyed; and in commending some, and
> correcting others, about a dozen Thursdays passed away.—
> Of those which are given here however, he did many entirely
> himself; and of the others—I suffered my own lines to be
> printed, that his might not be lost. The work was broken off
> without completion, because some gentleman, whose name I
> have forgotten, took it in hand; and against him, for reasons
> of delicacy—Johnson did not chuse to contend.[3]

3. (1788), I.vi.

Among the "verses from Boethius" referred to above by Mrs. Piozzi is "Book III. Metre 12," described as being "By Dr. Johnson and Mrs. Piozzi." Johnson's (larger) share of the translation appears in roman type, Mrs. Piozzi's in italic. He rendered the first two lines thus: "HAPPY he, whose eyes have view'd / The transparent Fount of Good."[4] His version was a substitution for Mrs. Piozzi's original, which reads: *"Happy He of human Race / Who in Truth's pellucid Glass / Virtue's Fountain clear and true / His reflected Face can view."*[5]

It is impossible to determine whether the definite choice of the epigraph occurred prior to, during, or after the composition of "The Fountains." But we may almost certainly conclude that Johnson's selection of the passage was prompted by the collaboration he and Mrs. Piozzi had carried on no more than about a year (at most) before he wrote the fairy tale. Indeed, without straining the bounds of credibility, one may discern a possible germ of the tale in Boethius's "fontem" and still another in the fact that Mrs. Piozzi, supposedly the model for the tale's central figure, shared the task of translating the *Consolation of Philosophy*.

Mention of Mrs. Piozzi's putative fictional portrait brings us to an examination of the setting of the story. Only a single actual place is named in "The Fountains." The opening sentence begins: "As Floretta was wandering in a meadow at the foot of Plinlimmon" (p. 111); and shortly thereafter the fairy Lady Lilinet remarks to Floretta: "We [fairies] have always been known to inhabit the crags and caverns of Plinlimmon" (p. 114). Numerous other statements make it clear that Floretta lives within walking distance of Lilinet's dwelling. Consequently, most of the action may be presumed to take place in Wales and specifically on and near Plinlimmon, for centuries among the most celebrated of Welsh mountains both in verse and in prose.

Speculation on the reasons behind Johnson's geographical location of the tale is directed by two pieces of pertinent information regarding Mrs. Piozzi and Mount Plinlimmon. First, like

---

4. *Letters to . . . Johnson*, II.423.
5. See *The Poems of Samuel Johnson*, ed. David Nichol Smith and Edward L. McAdam (2d ed., 1974), p. 174. The editors note SJ's use of the two lines from Boethius as the epigraph to "The Fountains."

Anna Williams, the ostensible author of the *Miscellanies,* Mrs. Piozzi was a Welshwoman, born Hester Lynch Salusbury in west Caernarvonshire, who boasted an ancient and distinguished lineage of which she was justifiably if tiresomely proud.[6] Second, the lasting renown of Plinlimmon—that "most mightie hill," as Michael Drayton called it in the seventeenth century[7]—derived partly from its begetting, by means of mountain springs or fountains, two famous British rivers, the Severn and the Wye, and three others not so famous.[8] When he turned his thoughts to composing "The Fountains," Johnson, we may reasonably conjecture, was drawn to a Welsh setting because of Mrs. Piozzi's nativity, and to Plinlimmon in particular because of the springs which give rise to the Wye and Severn rivers—the notion of the "fountains" having perhaps been already suggested to him, at least partially, by the lines from Boethius that form the epigraph to the story. These conjectures, however, it should be stressed— and as the discussion below (pp. 225–26) of the generic antecedents of the tale makes explicit—offer at best only a restricted explanation of individual parts of the work.

The inception of two additional parts—Floretta's mother and, preeminently, Floretta herself—can be linked to Johnson's purported intention of describing Mrs. Piozzi's "character" in the story. The introduction of a single parent (Floretta's father plays no part in the narrative[9]) may have been caused by the commanding presence of Mrs. Piozzi's mother, Mrs. John Salusbury, whose husband had died (1762) before their only child's marriage (1763) to the wealthy brewer Henry Thrale and who during

6. "[I]t has been said of Mrs. Thrale," Clifford writes, "that the only topic upon which she could be dull was her family history" (*Hester Lynch Piozzi,* p. 3).

7. Vol. IV (*Poly-Olbion*) of *The Works of Michael Drayton,* ed. J. William Hebel (corr. ed., 1961), p. 114. The passage reads: "Plynillimons high praise no longer Muse defer; / What once the Druids told, how great those floods should bee / That here (most mightie hill) derive themselves from thee." According to Drayton, the Severn, Wye, and "Rydoll" rivers "issued out of" Plinlimmon.

8. *Encyclopaedia Britannica* (11th ed., 1911), XXI.841 (s.v. Plinlimmon): "Plinlimmon is notable as the source of five streams—three small: the Rheidol, the Llyfnant and the Clywedog; and two larger and famous, the Wye (*Gwy*) and the Severn (*Hafren*)."

9. The closest SJ comes even to mentioning Floretta's father is when he writes that the young woman's suitor "applied to her parents; and, finding her fortune less than he expected, contrived a quarrel and deserted her" (p. 239 below).

1765–66 (and thereafter) was a steady frequenter of the Thrale residences; moreover, Johnson's decidedly unfavorable depiction of the mother may reflect both his initial negative opinion of Mrs. Salusbury—subsequently altered[1]—and also his estimate of her rather domineering attitude toward her daughter (Floretta, we are told, after a period of attempting "to do her own way," "replaced herself under her mother's care" [p. 240]).

Reference to the fictive mother-daughter relationship bears directly, of course, on Floretta herself as Johnson's most evident means of representing Mrs. Piozzi's "character" in the narrative. Quite understandably, previous commentators[2] have limited the characterization to her alone; and the probable reasons, besides those suggested above, for Mrs. Piozzi's persistent identification with her are easy to comprehend.[3] Floretta, while not a flawless paragon of superlative virtues, evinces from beginning to end fundamental goodness and intelligence, which serve to temper notably the succession of her conventional, normally human wishes—for beauty, a lover, wealth, wit, and longevity. All of the latter acquirements, too, she finally retracts, barring one, that of becoming a wit,[4] of acquiring remarkable powers of perception,

1. In Clifford's view, "It was only after a long succession of family sorrows that Johnson and Mrs. Salusbury got over" their early mutual dislike "and became devoted friends" (*Hester Lynch Piozzi*, p. 67). Also see Mary Hyde, *The Thrales of Streatham Park* (1977), pp. 63–65.

2. In his *Autobiography, Letters, and Literary Remains of Mrs. Piozzi (Thrale)*, A. Hayward declares flatly: "The character of Floretta in 'The Fountains' was intended for Mrs. Thrale" (2d ed., 1861, 1.55). Katharine Balderston, in her edition of *Thraliana*, observes that "*The Fountains* . . . held a peculiar interest for Mrs. Thrale," who "paralleled" "the character of Floretta" "with her own, in one of her published letters to Johnson" (2d ed., 1951, II.753, n. 1). Clifford states that Mrs. Piozzi "always believed" that SJ had described "her character" in "The Fountains," "as is shown by remarks in her letters and books; indeed, her copy of the *Miscellanies* has numerous annotations in the margins comparing Floretta with herself." The latter comment requires qualification as a result of a fresh scrutiny of Mrs. Piozzi's copy of the *Miscellanies*. Clifford goes on to say: "Probably all Johnson wished was to make his hostess realize that most worldly ambitions were hollow, and he took this means of advising her to be content with the talents God had given her" (*Hester Lynch Piozzi*, p. 63). My assessment of a larger mass of evidence leads to a different conclusion.

3. See Gwin J. Kolb, "Mrs. (Thrale) Piozzi and Dr. Johnson's 'The Fountains: A Fairy Tale,'" *Novel*, XIII (1979), 68–81.

4. Perhaps significantly, Floretta's mother is never mentioned in the story after Floretta decides to become a wit.

discrimination, criticism, and expression, along with, inevitably, some less attractive qualities, such as impatience, lack of tolerance, and asperity. To Floretta the wit, Johnson allots more space than to the realization of any of her other wishes.

The attribution of this trait, as well as the overall conception of the heroine, probably derives from Johnson's personal opinion of Mrs. Piozzi, who clearly elicited his liking and admiration from the start of their friendship. Moreover, although his overt compliments appear to postdate 1766, his strong tributes to "the first woman in the world" were repeatedly noted by his contemporaries. Boswell, William Shaw, Thomas Tyers, Anna Seward, and Frances Reynolds all report his abundant praise, which apparently often singled out for mention Mrs. Piozzi's "brilliancy of . . . wit."[5] Surveying the entire body of evidence, one concludes that the composition of "The Fountains" was markedly—perhaps decisively—affected by Johnson's "Mistress of Streatham."

GENRE AND THEME

The full title of "The Fountains," presumably supplied by Johnson himself, reveals the genre to which the composition belongs. In its plot, characters, setting, and incidental touches, the work displays numerous traits of a conventional fairy tale, albeit traits suffused with the typically Johnsonian ether. Living near Mount Plinlimmon, a renowned mountain in Wales (itself a traditional haunt of fairies), a young girl (Floretta) rescues a goldfinch from the clutches of a hawk. The goldfinch turns out to be a fairy (Lady Lilinet), small, sparkling, elegant, and a denizen of Mount Plinlimmon, whom the Queen of Fairies, angered by Lilinet's repeated naive benevolence to wicked human beings, had earlier transformed into a bird, to remain such until a person "shall shew thee kindness without any prospect of interest." As a reward for her disinterested rescue, Floretta receives from Lady Lilinet the power of realizing not merely three but almost all of her wishes and also the power (which, Lilinet says, has not been granted a

5. See Clifford, *Hester Lynch Piozzi*, pp. 197; 239, n. 4; 242, n. 1; 307; 356. Boswell, of course, also recorded less favorable comments by SJ about Mrs. Piozzi; see, e.g., *Life*, 1.494.

mortal before and which seems to be very rare, if not unique, in earlier fairy tales) of retracting the same wishes. To make a wish come true, Floretta must drink from the "sweet" Fountain of Joy located in a cavern of Mount Plinlimmon; to undo a wish, she must drink from the adjacent "bitter" Fountain of Sorrow. From youth to old age, the succession of her desires begins with beauty (attained but later retracted), and then proceeds to a faithful lover (unrealized), an independent spirit (attained but later retracted), riches (attained but later retracted), wit (attained and kept), and longevity (attained but finally retracted). The incessant "hunger of the imagination," as Johnson calls it in *Rasselas*, rather than the machinations of a wicked fairy, evidently prevents her from obtaining lasting contentment. At the end, Floretta, in the company of the fairy, desists from wishing and "resigns" the remainder of her life "to the course of Nature."

So far as can be discovered, none of these elements owes anything to other individual fairy tales. But by 1766, after the translation of such popular collections as those of Charles Perrault and Marie Catherine la Motte d'Aulnoy and the appearance of (say) Henry Brooke's *New Collection of Fairy Tales* (1750), the genre was firmly if spottily established in Great Britain; and analogues to most of the motifs in "The Fountains" appear in various earlier works, including those named above. Specifically, similarities can be adduced for at least the following components: the designation of a mountainous cavern as a fairy residence, the punishment of an erring fairy by another fairy, the transformation of a fairy into a bird and back again into a fairy, an act of disinterested kindness performed for a fairy by a mortal, the reward to a mortal by a grateful fairy, and the power exerted by the water of a magic fountain.[6] Awareness of these similarities strengthens one's conclusion, derived from several comments in his edition (1765) of

6. For evidence and examples of these antecedents, see the following works: Jacques Barchilon and Henry Petit, *The Authentic Mother Goose: Fairy Tales and Nursery Rhymes* (1960), pp. 10–11 ("The Fairy"); *The Diverting Works of the Countess A'Anois* [*sic*] (1715), pp. 401, 446–47, 519, 524, 580–81, 594–96, 625; Henry Brooke, *A New Collection of Fairy Tales*, 2 vols. (1750), II.222–23; Thomas Keightley, *The Fairy Mythology* (1860), p. 290; Katharine Briggs, *The Vanishing People: Fairy Lore and Legends* (1978), pp. 16, 79, 84, 146–47.

Shakespeare's plays,[7] that Johnson possessed a rather extensive knowledge of fairy tales and traditions and that this knowledge helped to shape the contents and form of "The Fountains."

Besides amalgamating this lore with an imaginative depiction of Mrs. Piozzi's "character," Johnson utilized in his tale another ingredient—the choice of life theme—which figures prominently, as pointed out above,[8] in "The Vision of Theodore" and *Rasselas*. The former expresses the concept by means of the assorted paths taken by travellers moving upward on the "Mountain of Existence"; the latter conveys the same theme via the Prince's exposure to various conditions of life he could elect to pursue. In the fairy tale, the heroine's succession of wishes and her consequent draughts from the two fountains serve to dramatize still again the same persistent notion, as old as Prodicus's "Choice of Hercules"—that of a human being making choices among alternative modes of life. The consistent aim of Floretta's selections is earthly happiness, an aim whose elusiveness, despite the fulfillment of most of her wishes, exemplifies another variation on a common notion in Johnson's writings, the vanity of human wishes. The same goal likewise motivates the "pilgrims" in "The Vision of Theodore" and Rasselas in his fruitless quest for the best way of life. To the notion of happiness as man's primary aim and his choice of life as an essential means, Johnson's earliest extended fictive work adds the allegorical vision as its literary genre. *Rasselas*, his most famous fictional creation, emphasizes the same end and means but utilizes the eastern or oriental moral tale as its most obvious generic category. And "The Fountains," his final substantial piece of fiction, while continuing to stress the

7. These comments include the following: Ariel "and his companions are evidently of the fairy kind, an order of beings to which tradition has always ascribed a sort of diminutive agency, powerful but ludicrous, a humorous and frolick controlment of nature"; "Fairies are never represented stamping, or of a size that should give force to a stamp"; "Cleanliness was always necessary to invite the residence and the favour of fairies"; "Fairies in [Shakespeare's] time were much in fashion; common tradition had made them familiar, and Spenser's poem had made them great" (*Johnson on Shakespeare*, ed. Arthur Sherbo [Vol. vii, Yale Edition of the Works of Samuel Johnson, 1968], pp. 124, 152, 159, 160).

8. See p. xliv above.

same end and means, turns to the fairy tale for its literary identity.[9]

RECEPTION, 1766–1800

Soon after its publication on 1 April 1766, Miss Williams's *Miscellanies* was briefly but favorably noticed in at least five periodicals, which also printed extracts from the volume. For the *Gentleman's Magazine* the collection is "small but elegant"; for the *Critical Review* the "prose and poetical compositions" are "correct, easy, and humorous [cf. *harmonious* below]; . . . even her trifles have their meaning"; and for the *Scots Magazine,* following the *Critical,* the pieces are "correct, easy, and harmonious."[1] The *Monthly Review,* concluding that "the author of the *Rambler* must be numbered" among the contributors to the book, praised several items, including "The Fountains," which "abounds with many sensible and well-expressed observations on human life." The *Monthly* reviewer then remarked that the "consequences" of Floretta's wit are "agreeably and ingeniously told" and quoted relevant passages from the text.[2] The *Royal Magazine* first labelled the entire assortment "ingenious" and later copied the *Monthly*'s treatment of Floretta's wit.[3]

Additional signs of the fairy tale's modestly positive reception are its independent appearances during the remainder of the century. In 1766 it was reprinted by at least three periodicals—*Universal Museum, British Magazine,* and *Caledonian Mercury* (Edinburgh: a partial text).[4] Three years (1787) after Johnson's death, it turned up in the *European Magazine,* where a correspondent made clear its authorship, pointed out that the piece (which

9. For a highly laudatory appraisal of "The Fountains" as a fairy tale, see Ruth K. MacDonald, *"The Fountains,* the Vanity of Human Wishes, and the Choice of Life," *Children's Literature,* VI (1977), 54–60.

1. XXXVI (April 1766), 187; XXI (April 1766), 291; XXVIII (May 1766), 261.

2. XXXIV (May 1766), 355 n., 357.

3. XIV (April, June 1766), 191, 299.

4. For details about the first two reprintings, see Robert D. Mayo, *The English Novel in the Magazines, 1740–1815* (1962), p. 497. For details about the third reprinting, see Helen Louise McGuffie, *Samuel Johnson in the British Press, 1749–1784: A Chronological Checklist* (1976), p. 50.

"deserves more celebrity") had been omitted from Sir John Hawkins's recent edition (1787) of Johnson's *Works,* and noted that earlier Miss Williams's *Miscellanies* "had but a confined sale, and never was much noticed."[5] Shortly thereafter (1787) the tale appeared in the *Edinburgh Magazine, Northern Gazette,* and *Hibernian Magazine.*[6] Months later it was contained in John Stockdale's supplement (Volume XIV [1788]) to Hawkins's edition and also in the *English Lyceum* (1788), and three years afterwards it was carried by the *Weekly Miscellany* (Glasgow, 1791).[7] On the other hand, it had not been included in Thomas Davies's collection of *Miscellaneous and Fugitive Pieces* (1773–74), which contained numerous writings by Johnson, and it was not included in the 1792 edition of Johnson's *Works.*

Johnson's learned friend Elizabeth Carter, who imputed its authorship to Miss Williams, commented on the tale in letters to Catherine Talbot (1766) and Mrs. Elizabeth Montagu (1775), expressing much the same reaction on both occasions. The work is

> enchantingly beautiful. But the conclusion is faulty, and leaves too melancholy an impression on one's mind. Human folly, the source of poor Floretta's ill-directed wishes, is not irremissible guilt; and the idea of her finally sinking under the miserable consequences of them, is inexpressibly painful. This conclusion is liable to the same objection as Mr. Johnson's *Rasselas.*[8]

Boswell, of course, was also aware of the work's existence and, in the *Life,* lauded it as "a beautiful little fairy tale . . . , written with exquisite simplicity."[9] Subsequently, Robert Anderson, in his *Life*

5. XII (July 1787), 42–47.

6. Mayo, *English Novel in the Magazines,* p. 497.

7. For details about the last two reprintings, see Mayo, *English Novel in the Magazines,* p. 497.

8. *Letters from Mrs. Elizabeth Carter to Mrs. Montagu between the Years 1755 and 1800,* ed. Montagu Pennington, 3 vols. (1817), II.316. In Pennington's opinion, the last of these remarks "shew[s] the critical accuracy of Mrs. Carter's judgment. She was certainly ignorant at that time, and perhaps never knew, that the Fairy Tale, and several of the poems, published under the name of Mrs. Williams, were actually written by Dr. Johnson." See also *A Series of Letters between Mrs. Elizabeth Carter and Miss Catherine Talbot from the Year 1741 to 1770,* ed. Montagu Pennington, 4 vols. (1809), III.136.

9. II.26.

of Samuel Johnson, cited the piece as an instance of its creator's "amazing powers" of imagination and "unbounded knowledge of life and manners."[1]

The sporadic appearances of "The Fountains" between 1766 and 1800 extended neither to the volume of which it was a part nor to the drama based on it. The *Miscellanies,* though it increased Miss Williams's meager assets by £150, was "still for sale in 1770,"[2] and it was never reprinted. Reminiscing long after 1766, Mrs. Piozzi commented that the book "it appears sold miserably: I never saw it on any table but my own. Tis *now* however become a curiosity."[3] The latter sentence also applies to the play—"from poor Dr Johnson's Floretta [i.e., "The Fountains"]" and entitled "The Two Fountains"—which Mrs. Piozzi wrote in 1789–90 and fervently hoped that John Philip Kemble, then manager of Drury Lane Theater, would produce. Both Kemble and his sister, Sarah Siddons, the great actress and a friend of Mrs. Piozzi, "pretend[ed] to like my little drama" (which concentrates on the heroine's quest for a lover); but Kemble finally rejected it.[4] Thus the sole literary descendant of Johnson's fairy tale—certainly not an exceptional artistic achievement—was destined to remain in manuscript, a revealing if justly neglected testament to the original's influence on the creator of the play. "The Fountains," unlike *Rasselas,* could not boast even a moderately popular offspring among the other aspects of its reception. Yet the tale's intermittent life, and the admiration it evoked from at least a few readers, prove that by the beginning of the nineteenth century it had escaped the oblivion attending the *Miscellanies* as a whole.

THE TEXT

As noted above (p. 218), an undated manuscript version of "The Fountains" (English MS. 654)—in Mrs. Piozzi's handwriting—is

1. 3d ed. (1815), pp. 533–34.

2. *Life,* II.479 (citing a remark by Lady Knight that "'Miss Williams ultimately got a hundred and fifty pounds by her poems'"); Hazen, *Prefaces & Dedications,* p. 215.

3. Clifford, *Hester Lynch Piozzi,* p. 61.

4. *Thraliana,* II.752–53, 771, 820–21, 829. See also Kolb, *Novel,* XIII (1979), 76–77.

held, together with other Piozzi papers, by the Rylands Library of Manchester University. This version contains numerous substantive and accidental differences from the text in Mrs. Anna Williams's *Miscellanies in Prose and Verse*, published on 1 April 1766 and never reprinted. The printed text—to repeat what has been said earlier (p. 220)—surely presents a later version of the work than does Mrs. Piozzi's transcript. Johnson, it is plausible to speculate, may have put the finishing touches to the tale during his proofreading.

A collation of four copies of the printed text (Bodleian Library, British Library, Newberry Library, and Northwestern University Library) reveals no variants of any kind, and an additional collation of the text in John Stockdale's supplement (1788) to Sir John Hawkins's edition of Johnson's *Works* discloses no significant differences from the text in the *Miscellanies*. The Bodleian Library copy, therefore, apparently embodying the author's final intentions, has been reproduced here with slight alterations—namely, (1) the regularization of quotation marks, italics, and capitals, and (2) the reduction to lower case of the initial words (save the first letters) of paragraphs and of the names Floretta and Lilinet. All variants affecting meaning (including tone and emphasis) in Mrs. Piozzi's transcript (identified as *PT*) have been included in the textual notes.

THE FOUNTAINS: A FAIRY TALE.

Felix qui potuit boni
Fontem visere lucidum.

BOETHIUS.[a][1]

As Floretta[2] was wandering in a meadow at the foot of Plinlimmon,[3] she heard a little bird cry in such a note as she had never observed before, and looking round her, saw a lovely goldfinch entangled by a lime-twig, and a hawk hovering over him, as at the point of seizing him in his[b] talons.

Floretta longed to rescue the little bird, but was afraid to encounter the hawk, who looked fiercely upon her without any apparent[c] dread of her approach, and as she advanced seemed to increase in bulk,[d] and clapped his wings in token of defiance. Floretta stood deliberating a few moments,[e] but seeing her mother[4] at no great distance, took courage, and snatched the twig with the little bird upon it. When she had disengaged him she put him in her bosom, and the hawk flew away.

Floretta[f] shewing her bird to her mother, told her from what danger she had rescued him; her mother, after admiring his beauty, said, that he would be a very proper inhabit-

a. Boethius *om. PT*   b. its *PT*   c. apparent *om. PT*   d. and . . . bulk, *om. PT*
e. few moments] Moment *PT*   f. *no par. PT*

---

1. *Consolation of Philosophy*, Book III, Meter 12, ll. 1–2. For a translation of these lines by SJ and a possible connection between an unfinished translation of Boethius by SJ and Mrs. Piozzi and the composition of "The Fountains," see Introduction, pp. 220–21 above.

2. In naming Floretta, SJ repeats the designation he had chosen for a different kind of female character in *Rambler* 40, pars. 6–8. For a discussion of Mrs. Piozzi as the model for Floretta,

see Introduction, pp. 223–24 above.

3. For a possible reason for SJ's choice of Mount Plinlimmon—among the most celebrated of Welsh mountains—as the setting of "The Fountains," see Introduction, pp. 221–22 above.

4. For a discussion of Mrs. Piozzi's mother as the possible model for Floretta's mother, see Introduction, pp. 222–23 above.

ant of the little gilded cage, which had hung[g] empty since[h] the starling died for want of water, and that he should be placed at the chamber window, for it would be wonderfully pleasant to hear him in[i] the morning.

Floretta, with tears in her eyes, replied, that he had better have been devoured by the hawk than die for want of water, and that she would not save him from a less[5] evil to put him in danger of a greater:[j] She therefore took him into[k] her hand, cleaned his feathers from the bird-lime, looked upon him with great tenderness, and, having put his bill to her lips, dismissed him into the air.

He[l] flew in circles round her as she went home, and perching on a tree before the[m] door, delighted them awhile with such sweetness of song, that her mother reproved her for not putting him in[n] the cage.[o] Floretta endeavoured[p] to look grave, but silently approved her own act, and wished her mother more generosity. Her mother guessed her thoughts, and told her, that when she was older she would be wiser.

Floretta[q] however did not repent, but hoped to hear her little bird the next morning singing at[r] liberty. She waked early and listened, but no goldfinch could she hear.[s] She rose, and walking again in the same meadow, went to view the bush where she had seen the lime-twig the day before.

When she entered the thicket, and was near the place for which she was looking, from behind a blossoming hawthorn advanced a female form of very[t] low stature, but of elegant proportion and majestick air, arrayed in all the colours of the meadow,[u] and sparkling as she moved like a dew-drop in the sun.

---

g. stood *PT*   h. since] ever since *PT*   i. him in] him sing in *PT*   j. greater:] greater, *PT*   k. in *PT*   l. *no par. PT*   m. her *PT*   n. into *PT*   o. cage.] Cage: *PT*   p. tried *PT*   q. *no par. PT*   r. in *PT*   s. hear.] hear: *PT*   t. of very] of a *PT*   u. Rainbow *PT*

---

5. *Less* is defined in SJ's *Dictionary* as "The comparative of *little*: opposed to *greater*, or to *so great*"; *lesser* as "A barbarous corruption of *less*, formed by the vulgar from the habit of terminating comparatives in *er*; afterwards adopted by poets, and then by writers of prose, till it has all the authority which a mode originally erroneous can derive from custom."

Floretta[v] was too much disordered to speak or fly, and stood motionless between fear and pleasure, when the little lady took her by the hand.

"I[w] am," said she, "one of that order of beings which some call fairies, and some piskies:[6] We have always been known to inhabit the crags and caverns of Plinlimmon. The maids and shepherds when they wander by moonlight have often heard our musick, and sometimes seen our dances.[7]

"I[x] am the chief of the fairies of this region, and am known among them by the name of Lady Lilinet of the Blue Rock. As I lived always in my own mountain, I had very little knowledge of human manners, and thought better of mankind than other fairies found them to deserve;[y] I therefore often opposed the mischievous practices of my sisters without always enquiring whether they were just. I extinguished the light that was kindled to lead a traveller into a marsh, and found afterwards that he was hasting to corrupt a virgin: I dissipated a mist which assumed the form of a town, and was raised to decoy a monopolizer[8] of corn from his way to the next market: I removed a thorn, artfully planted to prick the foot of a churl, that was going to hinder the poor from following his reapers; and defeated so many schemes of obstruction and punishment, that I was cited before the Queen as one who favoured wickedness and opposed the execution of fairy justice.

"Having[z] never been accustomed to suffer control, and thinking myself disgraced by the necessity of defence, I so much irritated the Queen by my sullenness and petulance, that in her anger she transformed me into a goldfinch. 'In

v. *no par. PT*   w. *no par. PT*   x. *no par. PT*   y. thought . . . deserve] thought Mankind better than they were found by Fairies who knew them better *PT* z. *no par. PT*

---

6. Neither *pisky* nor *pixy* appears in SJ's *Dictionary*. Sense 1 of *fairy* is "A kind of fabled beings supposed to appear in a diminutive human form, and to dance in the meadows, and reward cleanliness in houses; an elf; a fay."

7. According to Katharine Briggs (*An Encyclopedia of Fairies* [1976], p. 88), dancing is the "festive exercise most widely attributed to the Fairies, large or small."

8. *Monopolist* (defined as "One who by engrossing or patent obtains the sole power or privilege of vending any commodity")—but not *monopolizer*—appears in *Dictionary*.

this form,' says[a] she, 'I doom thee to remain till some human being shall shew thee kindness without any prospect of interest.'

"I[b] flew out of[c] her presence not much dejected; for I did not doubt but every reasonable being must love that which having never offended, could not be hated, and, having no power to hurt, could not be feared.

"I[d] therefore fluttered about the villages, and endeavoured to force myself into notice.

"Having[e] heard that nature was least corrupted among those who had no acquaintance with elegance and splendor, I employed myself for five years in hopping before the doors of cottages, and often sat singing on the thatched roof; my motions were seldom seen nor[f] my notes heard, no kindness was ever excited, and all the reward of my officiousness[9] was to be aimed at with a stone when I stood within a throw.

"The[g] stones never hurt me, for I had still the power of a fairy.

"I[h] then betook myself to spacious and magnificent habitations, and sung[1] in bowers by the walks[i] or on the banks of fountains.

"In[j] these places where novelty was recommended by satiety, and curiosity excited by leisure, my form and my voice were soon distinguished, and I was known by the name of the pretty goldfinch;[k] the inhabitants would walk out to listen to my musick, and at last[l] it was their practice to court my visits[m] by scattering meat[2] in my common haunts.

"This[n] was repeated till I went about pecking in full security, and expected to regain my original form, when I

a. said *PT*   b. *no par. PT*   c. out of] from *PT*   d. *no par. PT*   e. *no par. PT*   f. or *PT*   g. *no par. PT*   h. *no par. PT*   i. Walk [?] *PT*   j. *no par. PT* k. goldfinch;] Goldfinch, *PT*   l. at last *om. PT*   m. my visits] me *PT*   n. *no par.* [?] *PT*

9. *Officiousness:* "Forwardness of civility, or respect, or endeavour. Commonly in an ill sense" (sense 1 in *Dictionary*).

1. Both *sang* and *sung* are defined as the "preterite" of *sing* in SJ's *Dictionary*.
2. *Meat:* "Food in general" (sense 2 in *Dictionary*).

observed two of my most liberal benefactors silently advancing with a net behind me.[o] I flew off, and fluttering
beside them pricked the leg of each, and left them halting
and groaning with the cramp.

"I[p] then went to another house, where for two springs
and summers I entertained a splendid family with such
melody as they had never heard in the woods before. The
winter that followed the second summer[q] was remarkably
cold,[r] and many little birds perished in the field.[s] I laid
myself in the way of one of the ladies as benumbed with
cold and faint with hunger;[t] she picked me up with great[u]
joy, telling her companions[v] that she had found the goldfinch that sung so finely all summer in the myrtle hedge,
that she would lay him where he should[w] die, for she could
not bear to kill him, and would then pick his fine[x] feathers
very[y] carefully, and stick them in her muff.

"Finding[z] that[a] her fondness and her[b] gratitude could
give way to so slight an interest, I chilled her fingers that she
could not hold me, then flew at her face, and with my beak
gave her nose four pecks that left four black[c] spots indelible
behind them,[d] and broke a match by which she would have
obtained the finest equipage in the county.[e]

"At[f] length the Queen repented of her sentence, and
being unable to revoke it,[g] assisted me to try experiments
upon[h] man, to excite his tenderness, and attract[i] his regard.

"We[j] made many attempts in which we were always[k] disappointed.[l] At last she placed me in your way held by a
lime-twig, and herself in the shape of a hawk[m] made the[n]
shew of devouring me. You, my dear, have rescued me from
the seeming danger without desiring to detain me in cap-

---

o. me.] me: *PT*   p. *no par. PT*   q. the second summer *om. PT*   r. remarkably cold,] very severe *PT*   s. fields [?] *PT*   t. as . . . hunger;] as if faint
with Hunger and benumbed with Cold: *PT*   u. great *om. PT*   v. Friends *PT*
w. might *PT*   x. fine *om. PT*   y. very *om. PT*   z. *no par.* [?] *PT*   a. that *om.*
PT   b. her *om. PT*   c. black *om. PT*   d. 'em *PT*   e. Country *PT*   f. *no*
par. PT   g. it,] it; *PT* h. on *PT*   i. tempt *PT*   j. *no par. PT*   k. always *om.*
PT l. disappointed.] disappointed: *PT*   m. and . . . hawk] & a Hawk (which
was herself) *PT*   n. a *PT*

tivity, or[o] seeking any other recompence than the pleasure of benefiting a feeling creature.

"The[p] Queen is so much pleased with your kindness, that I am come, by[q] her permission, to reward you with a greater favour than ever fairy bestowed before.

"The[r] former gifts of fairies, though bounties in design, have proved commonly[s] mischiefs in the event. We have granted mortals to wish according to their own discretion, and their discretion being small, and their wishes irreversible, they have rashly petitioned for their own destruction. But[t] you, my dearest Floretta, shall have, what none have ever before obtained from us,[u] the power of indulging your wish,[v] and the liberty of retracting it.[3] Be[w] bold and follow me."

Floretta[x] was easily persuaded to accompany the fairy, who led her through a labyrinth of craggs and shrubs, to a cavern covered by a thicket on the side of the mountain.

"This cavern," said she, "is the court of Lilinet your friend;[4] in this place you shall find a certain remedy for all real evils." Lilinet then went before her through a long subterraneous passage, where she saw many beautiful fairies, who came to gaze at the stranger, but who, from reverence to their mistress, gave her no disturbance. She heard from remote corners of the gloomy cavern the roar of winds and the[y] fall of waters, and more than once entreated to return; but Lilinet assuring her that she was safe, persuaded her to proceed till they came to an arch, into which the light found its way through a fissure of the rock.

There[z] Lilinet seated herself and her guest upon[a] a

o. desiring . . . captivity, or *om. PT*   p. *no par. PT*   q. with *PT*   r. *no par. PT*
s. proved commonly] commonly proved *PT*   t. destruction. But] Destruction—but *PT*   u. ever . . . us] ever enjoyed before *PT*   v. Wishes *PT*   w. it.
Be] them—be *PT*   x. *no par. PT*   y. the *om. PT*   z. *no par. PT*   a. on *PT*

3. Although Lilinet's assertion may not be accurate, a reasonably wide survey of earlier fairy stories has disclosed no clear antecedents of the indulgence and subsequent retraction of such wishes.

4. In a note on *Merry Wives of Windsor*, SJ remarks that "fairies [are supposed] to dwell under ground" (*Johnson on Shakespeare*, ed. Arthur Sherbo, Vol. VII, Yale Edition of the Works of Samuel Johnson, 1968, p. 339).

bench of agate, and pointing to two fountains that[b] bubbled before them, said, "Now attend, my[c] dear Floretta, and enjoy the gratitude of a fairy. Observe the two fountains that[d] spring up in the middle of the[e] vault, one into a bason[5] of alabaster, and[f] the other into a bason of dark flint. The one is called the Spring of Joy, the other of Sorrow; they rise from distant veins in the rock, and burst out in two places, but after a short course unite their streams, and run ever after in[g] one mingled current.[6]

"By[h] drinking of these fountains, which, though shut up from all[i] other human[j] beings, shall be always accessible to[k] you, it will be in your power to regulate your future life.

"When[l] you are drinking the water of joy from the alabaster fountain, you may form your wish, and it shall be granted. As you raise your wish higher, the water will be sweeter and sweeter to the taste;[m] but beware that you are not tempted by its increasing sweetness to repeat your draughts, for the ill effects of your wish can only be removed by drinking the spring of sorrow from the bason of flint, which will be bitter in the same[n] proportion as the water of joy was sweet. Now, my Floretta, make the experiment, and give me the first proof of moderate desires.[o] Take the golden cup[p] that stands on the margin of the spring of joy, form your wish and drink."

Floretta[q] wanted no time to deliberate on the subject of

b. which *PT*   c. my *om. PT*   d. which *PT*   e. this *PT*   f. and *om. PT*
g. in *om. PT*   h. *no par. PT*   i. all *om. PT*   j. human *om. PT*   k. shall . . . to] are open to *PT*   l. *no par. PT*   m. and . . . taste *om. PT*   n. the same *om. PT*
o. desires.] Desires: *PT*   p. golden cup] Cup of Gold *PT*   q. *no par. PT*

5. Under *basin* in his *Dictionary*, SJ remarks, "It is often written *bason*, but not according to etymology."

6. From Mount Plinlimmon issue fountains or springs which form the source of five British rivers, including the Severn and the Wye; see Introduction, pp. 221–22 above. In *Rambler* 167 (par. 9), SJ creates a figure strikingly similar to Lilinet's remark: "Our thoughts," write two correspondents, "like rivulets issuing from distant springs, are each impregnated in its course with various mixtures, and tinged by infusions unknown to the other, yet at last easily unite into one stream, and purify themselves by the gentle effervescence of contrary qualities."

her wish;[r] her first desire was the increase of her beauty. She had some disproportion of features.[s] She took the cup and wished to be agreeable;[t] the water was sweet, and she drank copiously; and in the fountain, which was clearer than crystal, she saw that her face was completely regular.

She[u] then filled the cup again, and wished for a rosy bloom upon her cheeks:[v] the water was sweeter than before, and the colour of her cheeks was heightened.

She[w] next wished for a sparkling eye:[x] The water grew yet more pleasant, and her glances were like the beams of the sun.

She[y] could not yet stop;[z] she drank again, desired to[a] be made a perfect beauty, and a perfect beauty she became.

She[b] had now whatever her heart could wish; and making an humble reverence to Lilinet, requested to be restored to her own habitation. They went back, and the fairies in the way wondered at the change of Floretta's form. She came home delighted to her mother, who, on seeing the improvement, was yet more delighted than herself.

Her mother from that time pushed her forward into publick view: Floretta was at all the resorts of idleness and assemblies of pleasure; she was fatigued with balls, she was cloyed with treats, she was exhausted by the necessity of returning compliments. This life delighted her awhile, but custom soon destroyed its pleasure. She[c] found that the[d] men who courted her to day[7] resigned her on the morrow to other flatterers, and that the women attacked her reputation by whispers and calumnies, till without knowing how she had offended, she was shunned as infamous.

She knew that her reputation was destroyed by the envy

r. wish;] wish, *PT*   s. features.] Features, *PT*   t. agreeable;] agreable, *PT*
u. *no par. PT*   v. bloom . . . cheeks:] Bloom, *PT*   w. *no par. PT*   x. eye:]
Eye, *PT*   y. *no par. PT*   z. stop;] stop, *PT*   a. she . . . to] She wished as She
drank again to *PT*   b. *no par. PT*   c. but custom . . . . She] but Content is
seldom lasting: Custom destroys the pleasure of a Crowd. She *PT*   d. the *om. PT*

---

7. The word *today* does not appear in   comments: "Before *day, to* notes the
Dictionary. Under sense 25 of *to,* SJ   present day."

of her beauty, and resolved to degrade herself from the dangerous pre-eminence. She went to the bush where she rescued the bird, and called for Lady Lilinet. Immediately Lilinet appeared, and discovered by Floretta's dejected look that she had drank[8] too much from the alabaster fountain.[e]

"Follow[f] me," she cried, "my Floretta, and be wiser for the future."

They[g] went to the fountains,[h] and Floretta began to taste the waters of sorrow, which were so bitter that she withdrew more than once the cup from her mouth: At last she resolutely drank away the perfection of beauty, the sparkling eye and rosy[i] bloom, and left herself only agreeable.

She[j] lived for[k] some time with[l] great content; but content is seldom lasting. She had a desire in a short time again to taste the waters of joy: she called for the conduct of Lilinet, and was led to the alabaster fountain, where she drank,[m] and wished for a faithful lover.

After[n] her return she was soon addressed by a young man, whom she thought worthy of her affection.[o] He courted, and flattered, and promised; till at last she yielded up her heart.[p] He then applied to her parents; and, finding her fortune less than he expected, contrived a quarrel and deserted her.

Exasperated[q] by her[r] disappointment, she went in quest of Lilinet, and expostulated with her for the deceit which she had practised.[s] Lilinet asked her with a smile,[t] for what she had been wishing; and being told, made her this reply. "You are not, my dear,[u] to wonder or complain: You may wish for yourself, but your wishes can have no effect upon another. You may become lovely by the efficacy of the foun-

e. fountain.] Fountain: *PT*   f. *no par. PT*   g. *no par.PT*   h. Fountain *PT*
i. rosy] the rosy *PT*   j. *no par. PT*   k. for *om. PT*   l. in *PT*   m. content; . . . she drank] Content, till desiring again to taste the Waters of Joy, She drank *PT*   n. *no par. PT*   o. affection.] Affection: *PT*   p. heart.] heart: *PT*
q. *no par. PT*   r. this *PT*   s. for . . . practised *om. PT*   t. with a smile *om. PT*
u. dearest *PT*

8. *Drank:* "The preterite" of *drink* (*Dictionary*).

tain, but that you shall be loved is by no means a certain consequence; for you cannot confer upon another either discernment or fidelity: That happiness which you must derive from others, it is not in my power to regulate or bestow."

Floretta[v] was for some time[w] so dejected by this limitation of the fountain's power, that she thought it unworthy of another visit; but being on some occasion thwarted by her mother's authority,[x] she went to Lilinet,[y] and drank at the alabaster fountain for a spirit to do her own way.

Lilinet[z] saw that she drank immoderately, and admonished her of her danger;[a] but *spirit* and *her own way* gave such sweetness to the water, that she could not prevail upon herself to forbear, till Lilinet in pure compassion snatched the cup out of her hand.

When[b] she came home every thought was contempt, and every action was rebellion: She had drunk[c] into herself a spirit to resist, but could not give her mother a disposition to yield; the old lady asserted her right to govern; and, though she was often foiled by the impetuosity of her daughter, she supplied by pertinacy what she wanted in violence; so that the house was in continual tumult by the pranks of the daughter and opposition[d] of the mother.

In time,[e] Floretta was[f] convinced that spirit had only made her a capricious termagant, and that her own ways ended[g] in errour, perplexity and disgrace; she perceived that the vehemence[h] of mind, which to a man may sometimes procure awe and obedience, produce to a woman nothing but[i] detestation; she therefore went back, and by a large draught from the flinty fountain, though the water was very bitter, replaced herself under her mother's care, and quitted her[j] spirit, and her own way.

Floretta's fortune was moderate, and her desires were not

v. *no par. PT*   w. for some time *om. PT*   x. her mother's authority] her Mother *PT*   y. to Lilinet *om. PT*   z. *no par. PT*   a. and . . . danger; *om. PT* b. *no par. PT*   c. drank *PT*   d. and opposition] & the Opposition *PT*   e. In time,] In Time however *no par. PT*   f. grew *PT*   g. ways ended] Ways had ended *PT*   h. Violence *PT*   i. nothing but] only *PT*   j. her *om. PT*

larger, till her mother took her to spend a summer at one of
the places which wealth and idleness frequent, under pretence of drinking the waters.[k,9] She was now no longer a
perfect beauty, and therefore conversation in her presence
took its course as in other company, opinions were freely
told, and observations made without reserve. Here Floretta
first learned the importance of money.[l,1] When she saw a
woman of mean air and empty talk draw the attention of
the place, she always discovered upon enquiry that she had
so many thousands to her fortune.

She[m] soon perceived that where these golden goddesses
appeared, neither birth, nor[n] elegance, nor civility[o] had
any power of attraction, that every art of entertainment was
devoted to them, and that the great and the[p] wise courted
their regard.

The[q] desire after wealth was raised yet higher by her
mother, who was always telling her how much neglect she
suffered for want of fortune, and what distinctions if she
had but a[r] fortune her good qualities would obtain. Her
narrative of the day was always, that Floretta walked in the
morning, but was not spoken to because she had a small
fortune, and that Floretta danced at the ball better than any
of them, but nobody minded her for want of a fortune.

This[s] want, in which all other wants appeared to be included, Floretta was resolved to endure no longer, and
came home flattering her imagination in secret with the
riches which[t] she was now about to obtain.

On the day after her return she walked out alone to meet

---

k. Water [?] *PT*   l. money.] Money, *PT*   m. *no par. PT*   n. nor *om. PT*
o. nor civility] or Sweetness *PT*   p. the *om. PT*   q. *no par. PT*   r. a *om. PT*
s. *no par. PT*   t. which *om. PT*

---

9. Bath, the most famous of eighteenth-century British watering places,
is located near the Welsh border and
thus fairly close to Mount Plinlimmon.

1. Cf. *Rambler* 131 (par. 2): "Wealth is
the general center of inclination, the
point to which all minds preserve an
invariable tendency, and from which
they afterwards diverge in numberless
directions. Whatever is the remote or
ultimate design, the immediate care is
to be rich."

Lady Lilinet, and went with her to the fountain: Riches did not taste so sweet as either beauty or spirit, and therefore[u] she was not immoderate in her draught.

When[v] they returned from the cavern, Lilinet gave her wand to a fairy that attended her, with an order to conduct Floretta to the Black Rock.

The[w] way was not long, and they soon came to the mouth of a mine in which there was a hidden treasure, guarded by an earthy[2] fairy deformed and shaggy, who opposed the entrance of Floretta till he recognized the wand of the Lady of the Mountain.[x] Here Floretta saw vast heaps of gold and silver and gems, gathered and reposited in former ages, and entrusted to the guard of the fairies of the earth. The little fairy delivered the orders of her mistress, and the surly sentinel promised to obey them.

Floretta, wearied with her walk, and pleased with her success, went home to rest, and when she waked in the morning, first opened her eyes upon a cabinet of jewels, and looking into her drawers and boxes, found them[y] filled with gold.

Floretta[z] was now as fine as the finest.[a] She was the first to adopt any expensive fashion, to subscribe to any pompous[3] entertainment, to encourage any foreign artist, or engage in any frolick of which the cost was to make the pleasure.

She was on a sudden the favourite of every place.[b] Report made her wealth thrice greater than it really was, and wherever she came, all was attention, reverence and obedience. The ladies who had formerly slighted her, or by whom she had been formerly caressed, gratified her pride by open flattery and private murmurs. She sometimes over-heard[c] them railing at upstarts, and wondering whence some peo-

u. beauty . . . therefore] Spirit or Beauty so *PT*   v. *no par. PT*   w. *no par. PT*
x. Mountain.] Mountain: *PT*   y. them] them all *PT*   z. *no par.* [?] *PT*
a. finest.] finest; *PT*   b. place.] Place; *PT*   c. heard *PT*

---

2. *Earthy:* "Inhabiting the earth; ter-   3. *Pompous:* "Splendid; magnificent;
restrial" (sense 3 in *Dictionary*).   grand" (*Dictionary*).

ple came, or how their expences were supplied. This incited her to heighten the splendour of her dress, to increase the number of her retinue, and to make such propositions of costly schemes, that her rivals were forced to desist from contest.

But[d] she now began to find that the tricks which can be played with money will seldom bear to be repeated, that admiration is a short-lived passion, and that the pleasure of expence is gone when wonder and envy are no more excited.[e] She found that respect was an empty form, and that all[f] those who crouded round her were[g] drawn to her by vanity or interest.

It[h] was however pleasant to be able[i] on any terms to elevate and to mortify, to raise hopes and fears; and she would still have continued to be rich, had not the ambition of[j] her mother contrived to marry her to a lord, whom she despised as ignorant, and abhorred as profligate.[k] Her mother persisted in her importunity; and Floretta having now[l] lost the spirit of resistance, had no other refuge than to divest herself of her fairy fortune.

She implored the assistance of Lilinet, who praised her resolution.[m] She drank chearfully from the flinty fountain, and found the waters not extremely bitter. When she returned she went to bed, and in the morning perceived that all her riches had been conveyed away she knew not how, except a few ornamental jewels, which Lilinet had ordered to be carried back as a reward for her dignity of mind.

She[n] was now almost weary of visiting the fountain, and solaced herself with such amusements as every day happened to produce: At last there[o] arose in her imagination[p] a strong[q] desire to become a wit.[4]

---

d. *no par. PT*   e. excited.] excited: *PT*   f. all *om. PT*   g. were only *PT*
h. *no par. PT*   i. to be able *om. PT*   j. the ambition of *om. PT*   k. profligate.]
profligate, *PT*   l. now *om. PT*   m. resolution.] Resolution; *PT*   n. *no par.*
PT   o. produce: . . . there] produce, till there *PT*   p. Mind *PT*   q. strong
om. PT

---

4. In SJ's *Dictionary,* sense 4 of *wit* is "A man of fancy." Sense 1 of *fancy* is   "Imagination: the power by which the mind forms to itself images and repre-

The[r] pleasures with which this new character appeared[s] to teem were so numerous and so great, that she was impatient to enjoy them; and rising before the sun, hastened to the place where she knew that[t] her fairy patroness was always to be found. Lilinet was willing to conduct her, but could now[u] scarcely restrain her from leading the way but by telling her, that if she went first the fairies of the cavern would refuse her passage.

They[v] came in time to the fountain, and Floretta took the golden cup into her hand; she filled it and drank, and again she filled it, for wit was sweeter than riches, spirit, or beauty.

As she returned she felt new successions of imagery rise in her mind, and whatever her memory offered to her imagination, assumed a new form, and connected itself with things to which it seemed before to have no relation.[5] All the appearances about her were changed, but the novelties exhibited were commonly defects. She now saw that almost every thing was wrong, without often seeing[w] how it could be better; and frequently imputed to the imperfection of art these[x] failures which were caused by the limitation of nature.

Wherever[y] she went, she breathed nothing but censure and reformation. If she visited her friends, she quarrelled with the situation of their houses, the disposition of their gardens,[z] the direction of their walks, and the termination of their views. It was vain to shew her fine furniture, for she

---

r. *no par. PT*   s. began *PT*   t. that *om. PT*   u. now *om. PT*   v. *no par. PT*
w. often seeing] seeing often *PT*   x. the *PT In revising SJ may have written* those
rather than these: *his* e *and* o *are hard to distinguish*   y. *no par. PT*   z. the disposition . . . gardens, *om. PT*

---

sentations of things, persons, or scenes of being." For SJ's opinion of Mrs. Piozzi's wit, see Introduction, pp. 223–24 above.

5. Cf. SJ's description of *wit* in *Rambler* 141 (par. 7), 194 (par. 10): "Wit . . . is the unexpected copulation of ideas, the discovery of some occult relation between images in appearance remote from each other; an effusion of wit therefore presupposes an accumulation of knowledge; a memory stored with notions, which the imagination may cull out to compose new assemblages"; see also "Life of Cowley" (*Lives*, 1.20, par. 56).

was always ready to tell how it might be finer, or to conduct her through spacious apartments, for her thoughts were full of nobler fabricks, of airy[6] palaces and hesperian gardens. She admired nothing and praised but little.

Her[a] conversation was generally thought uncivil. If she received flatteries, she seldom repaid them; for she set no value upon vulgar praise.[b] She could not hear a long story without hurrying the speaker on to the conclusion;[7] and obstructed the mirth of her companions, for she rarely took notice of a good jest, and never laughed except[c] when she was delighted.

This behaviour made her unwelcome wherever she went;[8] nor did her speculation upon human manners much contribute to[d] forward her reception.[e] She now saw the disproportions[f] between language and sentiment, between passion and exclamation;[g] she discovered the defects of every action, and the uncertainty of every conclusion; she knew the malignity of friendship, the avarice of liberality, the anxiety of content, and the cowardice of temerity.

To[h] see all this was pleasant, but the greatest of all pleasures[i] was to shew it.[j] To laugh was something, but it was much[k] more to make others laugh. As every deformity of character made a strong impression upon her, she could not always[l] forbear to transmit[m] it to others; as she hated false appearances she thought it her duty to detect them, till, between wantonness and virtue, scarce any that she knew escaped without some wounds by the shafts of ridi-

a. *no par. PT*   b. praise.] Praise: *PT*   c. and . . . except] & laughed only *PT* d. much contribute to *om. PT*   e. reception.] reception: *PT*   f. Disproportion *PT*   g. exclamation;] Exclamation: *PT*   h. *no par. PT*   i. greatest . . . pleasures] greatest Pleasure *PT*   j. it.] it; *PT*   k. much *om. PT*   l. always *om. PT*   m. to transmit] transmitting *PT*

6. *Airy:* "Wanting reality; having no steady foundation in truth or nature; vain; trifling" (sense 6 in *Dictionary*).

7. Mrs. Piozzi may have written the part of this sentence beginning with *She* and concluding with *conclusion;* see

Introduction, pp. 217–18 above.

8. Mrs. Piozzi may have written the part of this sentence beginning with *This* and concluding with *went;* see Introduction, pp. 217–18 above.

cule; not that her merriment was always the consequence of total contempt, for she often honoured virtue where she laughed at affection.[9]

For[n] these practices, and who can wonder, the cry was raised against her from every quarter, and to hunt her down was generally determined. Every eye was watching for a fault, and every tongue was busy to supply its share of defamation. With the most unpolluted purity of mind, she was censured as too free of favours,[o] because she was not afraid[p] to talk with men: With generous sensibility of every human excellence, she was thought cold or[q] envious, because she would not scatter praise with undistinguishing profusion:[r] With tenderness that agonized at real misery, she was charged with delight[s] in the pain of others, when she would not condole with those whom she knew to counterfeit[t] affliction. She derided false appearances of kindness and of pity, and was therefore avoided as an enemy to society.[u] As she seldom commended or censured but with some limitations and exceptions, the world condemned her as indifferent to the good and bad; and[v] because she was often doubtful where others were confident, she was charged with laxity of principles, while her days were distracted and her rest broken by niceties of honour and scruples of morality.[1]

Report[w] had now made her so formidable that all flattered and all shunned her. If a lover gave a ball to his mistress and her friends, it was stipulated that Floretta should not be invited.[x] If she entered a publick room[y] the

n. *no par.* PT   o. too . . . favours] free *PT*   p. was not afraid] feared not *PT*
q. & *PT*   r. profusion:] Profusion; *PT*   s. delighting *PT*   t. would . . .
counterfeit] forbore Condolance with them that counterfeited *PT*   u. She . . .
society. *om. PT*   v. commended . . . bad; and] censured or praised without
limitation or exception, She was charged with Indifference to good & bad, because
PT   w. *no par.* PT   x. it . . . invited] Floretta was not invited *PT*   y. Place *PT*

9. Mrs. Piozzi may have written the part of this sentence beginning with *for* and concluding with *affectation;* see Introduction, pp. 217–18 above.

1. Mrs. Piozzi may have written the part of this sentence beginning with *by* and concluding with *morality;* see Introduction, pp. 217–18 above.

ladies courtsied, and shrunk[z] away, for there was no such thing as speaking, but[a] Floretta would find something to criticise. If a girl was more spritely than her aunt, she was threatened that in a little time she would be like Floretta.[b] Visits were very[c] diligently paid when Floretta was known not to be at home; and no mother trusted her daughter to herself without a caution, if she should meet Floretta to leave the company as soon as she could.

With[d] all this Floretta made sport at first, but in time[e] grew weary of general hostility. She would have been content with a few friends, but no friendship was durable; it was the fashion to desert her, and with the fashion what fidelity will contend? She could have easily[f] amused herself in solitude, but that she[g] thought it mean to quit the field to treachery and folly.

Persecution[h] at length tired her constancy, and she implored Lilinet to rid her of her wit: Lilinet[i] complied and walked up the mountain, but was often forced to stop and wait for her follower. When they came to the flinty fountain,[j] Floretta filled a small cup and slowly brought it to her lips, but the water was insupportably[k] bitter. She just tasted it, and dashed it to the ground, diluted the[l] bitterness at the fountain of alabaster,[m] and resolved to keep her wit with all its consequences.

Being[n] now a wit for life, she surveyed the various[o] conditions of mankind[p] with such superiority of sentiment, that she found few distinctions to be envied or desired, and therefore did not very[q] soon make another visit to the fountain.[r] At length being alarmed[s] by sickness, she resolved to drink length of life from the golden cup. She returned elated and secure, for though the longevity ac-

---

z. slunk [?] *PT*   a. there ... but *om. PT*   b. If ... Floretta. *om. PT*   c. very *om. PT*   d. *no par. PT*   e. in time] soon *PT*   f. have easily] easily have *PT* g. that she *om. PT*   h. *no par. PT*   i. The Faery *PT*   j. to the flinty fountain] to Place [?] *PT*   k. inexpressibly *PT*   l. its *PT*   m. fountain of alabaster] Alabaster Fountain *PT*   n. *no par. PT*   o. various *om. PT*   p. Life *PT* q. few ... very] little to be desired, & did not *PT*   r. the fountain] her Friend *PT*   s. At ... alarmed] Alarmed however *PT*

quired[t] was indeterminate, she considered death as far[u] distant, and therefore[v] suffered it not to intrude upon her pleasures.

But length of life included[w] not perpetual health.[x] She felt herself continually decaying, and saw the world fading about her.[y] The delights of her early days would delight no longer, and however widely[z] she extended her view,[a] no new pleasure[b] could be found; her friends, her enemies, her admirers,[c] her rivals dropped one by one into the grave, and with those who succeeded them she had neither community of joys nor strife of competition.[2]

By[d] this time she[e] began to doubt whether old age were not dangerous to virtue; whether pain would not produce peevishness, and peevishness impair benevolence.[f][3] She thought that the spectacle of life might be too long continued, and the vices which were often seen might raise[g] less abhorrence; that resolution might be sapped by time, and let that virtue sink, which in its firmest state it had not without difficulty supported; and that it was vain to delay the hour which must come at last, and might come at a time of less preparation and greater imbecillity.[4]

These thoughts led her to Lilinet, whom she accompanied to the flinty fountain; where, after a short combat with herself, she drank the bitter water. They walked back to the favourite bush pensive and silent; "And now," said

t. acquired *om. PT*   u. far *om. PT*   v. therefore *om. PT*   w. includes *PT*
x. health.] Health; *PT*   y. her.] her; *PT*   z. wide *PT*   a. Views *PT*
b. Pleasures *PT*   c. her enemies, her admirers] her Admirers, her Enemies
PT   d. *no par. PT*   e. time she] Time too she *PT*   f. benevolence.] Benevolence: *PT*   g. be seen with *PT*

---

2. Cf. *The Vanity of Human Wishes*, ll. 305–08: "Year chases year, decay pursues decay, / Still drops some joy from with'ring life away; / New forms arise, and diff'rent views engage, / Superfluous lags the vet'ran on the stage."

3. Mrs. Piozzi may have written the parts of this sentence (1) beginning with *old* and concluding with *virtue* and (2) beginning with *pain* and concluding with *benevolence;* see Introduction, pp. 217–18 above.

4. *Imbecility:* "Weakness; feebleness of mind or body" (*Dictionary*).

she, "accept my thanks for the last benefit that[h] Floretta can receive." Lady Lilinet dropped a tear, impressed upon her lips the final kiss, and resigned her, as she resigned herself, to the course of Nature.[i]

h. that *om. PT*   i. The End *written below the last sentence of the text PT*

APPENDIX
THE RECEPTION OF *RASSELAS*, 1759–1800

ROBERT DODSLEY'S LAWSUIT AGAINST THE *GRAND MAGAZINE OF MAGAZINES*

As noted above in this volume,[1] all of the reviews of *Rasselas* appearing in serials contain numerous passages from the tale. Ten complete chapters and portions of twenty-three others are reprinted, excluding the extracts that make up parts of the eight notices borrowed from other periodicals.

Additional extracts in the *Grand Magazine of Magazines* produced significant results that should be briefly described. Responding to the action of the *Grand Magazine*, Robert Dodsley, one of the three proprietors of *Rasselas* and representing the other two (William Johnston and William Strahan),[2] brought a suit for infringement of copyright against the *Magazine's* (presumed) owner, Thomas Kinnersley, who, it was asserted, "printed part of the [tale's] narrative . . . but left out all the reflections." The case was argued in the High Court of Chancery before Sir Thomas Clarke, Master of the Rolls, on 15 June 1761. During the proceedings

> Mr. [Jacob] Tonson [III] and two other booksellers were examined for the plaintiffs, who spoke in general, that the sale of the book was prejudiced by its being printed in the Magazine; and Mr. Tonson conjectured, that about two-thirds of the book was printed in the Magazine; but it appeared clearly, that he deposed relating to the whole work, the second as well as the first volume; whereas only part of the first volume was printed in the Magazine when the bill was filed (though great part of the second volume was

---

1. See p. xlv above.
2. For evidence of the proprietorships, see Gwin J. Kolb, "*Rasselas:* Purchase Price, Proprietors, and Printings," *Studies in Bibliography,* xv (1962), 257.

printed afterwards); and according to the passages marked, not above one-tenth part of it was printed.

For the defendant,

> evidence was read, that it is usual to print extracts of new books in Magazines, &c. without asking leave of the authors. That it is often done at the request of the author, as being a means to help the sale of the book. That the plaintiffs published a larger extract of this very book in the *Annual Register*. Also, that the plaintiffs published an extract of it in the newspaper called the *Chronicle* in April, 1759, *before the extract was published by the defendant in the Magazine,* of which paper the plaintiffs with others are proprietors.

After the presentation of the arguments, Sir Thomas Clarke, besides making other remarks, called *Rasselas* "a very good, elegant, and useful book," whose "title may draw in persons to look into it, which perhaps they would not do if it had a graver title"; observed that "it does not appear that one-tenth part of the first volume has been abstracted"; agreed "that a fair abridgment" is "not a piracy"; admitted that "what I materially rely upon is, that [the abstract in the *Grand Magazine*]," which "may serve the end of an advertisement," "could not tend to prejudice the plaintiffs, when they had before published an abstract of the work in the *London Chronicle*"; and "dismiss[ed] plaintiffs' bill without costs."[3]

Most (not all) of the factual allegations made for the defendant in the report on the case of Dodsley v. Kinnersley can be readily verified, and the remainder are almost certainly true too. Specifically, although the portions of *Rasselas* initially reproduced by the *Grand Magazine of Magazines* may come to about 12 rather than 10 percent of the whole text,[4] in 1759 it *was* "usual to print extracts

---

3. Charles Ambler, *Reports of Cases Argued and Determined in the High Court of Chancery*, 2d ed. (1828), pp. 402–05.

4. I estimate the length of *Rasselas* to be about 38,500 words, that of the first *Grand Magazine* installment (II [April 1759], 217–22) to be about 4,700 words, and that of the second installment (II [May 1759], 301–04) to be about 3,500 words. At the end of the second installment, we are told (p. 304) that "this well-imagined tale" will appeal to a wide range of readers. I am indebted to the American Antiquarian Society for photographic reproductions of both installments.

of new books in magazines, &c. without asking leave of the authors," who very likely "often" encouraged the practice as "a means to help the sale" of their works. Moreover, to say that "the plaintiffs published" an "extract" from *Rasselas* in the *Annual Register* is probably an accurate statement, for Robert Dodsley owned the *Register,* which printed a number of passages (but fewer than the number appearing initially in the *Grand Magazine*) as a part of Burke's review of the tale.[5] Further, the *London Chronicle did* print an extensive abstract from *Rasselas* in its issue of 19–21 April (and again in its issues of 28 April–1 May, 3–5 May, and 10–12 May 1759) at the same time the book itself was published, and well ahead of the appearance of the *Grand Magazine*'s April number.[6] Last, at least one (William Strahan, who also printed the paper), and possibly two (Robert Dodsley), of the three proprietors of *Rasselas* owned shares of the *Chronicle;*[7] so Kinnersley's representative was correct in asserting that "the plaintiffs published an extract" of the work in the *Chronicle.*

From the disclosure of the opposing parties before Sir Thomas Clarke in 1761, an unsurprising but sometimes forgotten conclusion can be drawn quite firmly: the immediate printed reaction to *Rasselas,* as to countless other books, good and bad, was tinctured by the profit motive, which should not be confused with the disinterested attention and admiration evinced by some excerpting.

THE RECEPTION IN EUROPE AND AMERICA

The extensive diffusion, as Boswell termed it, of *Rasselas* "over Europe" commenced with French and Dutch translations in

---

5. Dodsley's ownership of the *Annual Register* is well known; see, for example, his entry in the *DNB.*

6. The *London Chronicle* for 28 April–1 May 1759 contains an advertisement announcing the publication of the April number of the *Grand Magazine of Magazines,* which includes, among other pieces, "the story of Rasselas, Prince of Abyssinia."

7. Patricia Hernlund, who has examined relevant entries in Strahan's ledgers, has kindly informed me that Strahan owned a one-ninth share of the *Chronicle* as early as 12 Nov 1757. See also J. A. Cochrane, *Dr. Johnson's Printer: The Life of William Strahan* (1964), pp. 103–04. I am indebted to O M Brack, Jr., for the information (based on a letter of 12 Dec 1758 from Dodsley to William Strahan) that Dodsley may have owned a share of the *Chronicle* as late as 1759.

1760.[8] Apparently the first edition of the tale to name the author on the title page ("Par M. Jhonnson [*sic*]," we are told, "Auteur du Rambler"), the French translation, published "A Amsterdam, et se trouve à Paris, chez Prault Fils," was made by Mme Octavie Belot, who included in her preface probably the earliest printed comparison of *Rasselas* and *Candide*. Part of her comment reads:

> Le succès de Candide semble présager celui de son contemporain Rasselas, Prince d'Abissinie. Ces deux ouvrages renferment trop sensiblement les mêmes vues, pour n'avoir pas droit au même accueil. Cependant comme nous préférons quelquefois le coloris au dessein, je sens quel est l'avantage des choses finement dites sur celles qui ne sont que judicieusement pensées, & je m'en allarme [*sic*] pour mon Prince moraliste & voyageur.
>
> L'analogie du fond des idées de Candide & de Rasselas; certains rapports entre Imlac & Martin; entre l'isle d'Aldorado & l'heureuse Vallée, m'avoient fait présumer d'abord que l'Auteur Anglois pouvoit bien n'être qu'un pyrate littéraire. Mais j'ai réfléchi qu'il ne falloit soupçonner légèrement personne d'un larcin, & que la seule force de la vérité faisoit sans doute penser en Angleterre, comme en France, que le bonheur est une chimère.

Mme Belot then presents her own notions regarding human happiness, paying a lavish tribute to Montesquieu and Voltaire in the course of her discussion.[9] As might possibly have been expected, she also later sent a copy of her work to Voltaire, who thanked her for a book "qui m'a paru d'une philosophie aimable, et très bien écrit."[1]

At about the same time (May 1760), Élie Fréron's *L'Année littéraire* carried an extended review of the translation. The reviewer quotes the opening lines of the tale, states what he takes to

8. "None of his writings has been so extensively diffused over Europe; for it has been translated into most, if not all, of the modern languages" (*Life*, 1.341).

9. *Histoire de Rasselas, Prince d'Abissinie*, pp. iii–iv, xiii. See also L. F. Powell's letter (entitled "*Rasselas*") in the *TLS* for 22 Feb 1923, p. 124, which describes, and quotes from, Mme Belot's preface; *Life*, 11.500.

1. *The Complete Works of Voltaire*, ed. Theodore Besterman (1968–80), CV, 309; *Life*, 11.500.

be its central theme ("On veut prouver dans ce roman philosophique & moral que le bonheur n'est attaché à aucun état, à aucun
âge, à aucune condition, & qu'il faut perfectionner son esprit &
son coeur si l'on veut trouver dans la vie quelques momens
heuréux"), summarizes the principal events of the story, and
finally evaluates both the tale itself and the translation. Seemingly
influenced by Mme Belot's preface, his critical remarks first consider the issue of temporal precedence between *Rasselas* and *Candide*. Then, concentrating on Johnson's work, Fréron rates the
first part of *Rasselas* "supérieure de beaucoup" to the second:

> dans cette dernière, l'action est noyée dans de raisonnemens
> d'une longueur insupportable. L'auteur n'a pas tiré parti de
> la favorite Pekuah; il falloit, pour suivre le fil de la nature, que
> la Princesse commençât à se consoler, que l'idée de Pekuah
> devînt moins forte, que le Prince rallentît ses soins pour ses
> recherches, & qu'après l'avoir retrouvée l'un & l'autre, le
> frère & la soeur se rendissent compte de leurs sentimens,
> qu'ils s'avouassent tacitement qu'ils avoient manqué a l'ami-
> tié, & qu'en rougissant ils convinssent que l'humanité est une
> source d'imperfections. Cela eût formé alors une situation
> intéressante, au lieu que cette favorite n'excite aucun at-
> tendrissement, & qu'elle n'attache que foiblement. Au reste,
> il y a très peu d'imagination dans cet ouvrage; c'est un cadre
> usé; mais que de vérités, que de lumières sur le coeur hu-
> main!

These last notes of approval become still louder when Fréron
reintroduces *Candide* in his discussion. *Rasselas,* he tells us, "est un
miroir moins révoltant que *Candide;* nous nous y voyons cepen-
dant avec toutes nos foiblesses & tous nos malheurs. *Candide* fait
d'abord rire l'esprit, & laisse ensuite le désespoir dans le coeur;
Rasselas nous attendrit, nous fait gémir sur les misères de notre
nature; *Candide,* en un mot, nous rend en horreur à nous-mêmes,
& *Rasselas* nous fait les objets de notre propre compassion; il ne
nous désespère pas; il nous invite seulement à nous corriger."
Thus, he concludes, "ce livre, avec tous ses défauts, ne peut man-
quer de réussir, & d'être placé parmi ce petit nombre d'ouvrages
dont le but est de nous rendre meilleurs." Freron goes on to say

that "on ne sçauroit trop donner d'éloges à Madame B***. Sa traduction est pure, élégante, quelquefois trop asservie au tour original."[2]

Fréron's laudatory opinion of Mme Belot's translation was evidently shared by a crowd of other persons, since later editions appeared in 1768, 1787, and 1788. To this group of four can be added probably six more editions of French translations of *Rasselas* that were issued in various places (including London) before 1800. And the total of ten obviously excludes the version Giuseppe Baretti completed in 1764 (of which Johnson contributed the first sentence) that was not published until 1970.[3]

As noted above, apart from French, Dutch was the earliest foreign language to welcome *Rasselas*. "Published at Amsterdam by Dirk onder de Linden in 1760 and . . . entitled *De Historie van Rasselas, Prins van Abissinien. Zynde een verbloemde Shildery van het Menschenlyk leven. Door den Autheur van De Hollandsche Wysgeer*," the translation, now very rare, "was issued in conjunction with a collective work entitled *De Hollandsche Wysgeer [The Dutch Philosopher]* by the same publisher, consisting chiefly of translations from English periodicals and other works; this work appeared in seven *deelen*, or parts, over the years 1759 to 1763." Unlike Mme Belot's French version, the Dutch translation failed to make clear its derivative character and, of course, to credit Johnson with the authorship of the original. This failure was soon criticized by a reviewer in *De Vaderlandsche Letteroefeningen* (I [1761], 286), who observed: "This little book, although the title does not say so, is a translation. We make this statement because we trust that a Dutch philosopher does not wish to shine by another man's work, as if it were his own." Without identifying the author (if indeed he knew who it was), "the reviewer then proceeds to give an extensive *résumé* of the story covering ten closely printed pages (286–96)."[4]

2. *L'Année littéraire*, VII (1760 [Geneva, 1966]), 223, 227–28.

3. The information in this paragraph about the French translations is drawn from Fleeman; Courtney and Smith, p. 94; *NCBEL*, II. col. 1131; *Life*, II.208, 499–500; Raffaella Carbonara, ed., *Giuseppe Baretti e la sua traduzione del "Rasselas" di S. Johnson* (1970).

4. For information (including the quoted passages) about the first Dutch translation and the review of it, I have drawn on the following: L. F. Powell, "For Johnsonian Collectors," *TLS*, 20 Sept 1963, p. 712; A. J. Barnouw, "'Rasselas' in Dutch," *TLS*, 11 April 1935, p. 244.

His summary—and the work he noticed—clearly satisfied Dutch tastes throughout the rest of the century, for the next Dutch translation did not appear until 1824.[5]

Two years (1762) after the publication of the initial French and Dutch versions, Elieser Gottlieb Küster's German translation of *Rasselas* was issued at "Frankfurth, Leipzig und Zelle" "bey Georg Conrad Gsellius." It was joined by three more German versions (1785, 1786, 1787) before 1800. An Italian translation (by Cosimo Mei), which Baretti labelled "a damned one," came out at Padua in 1764, and another at Florence in 1797. Finally, Russian versions appeared in 1764 and 1795, and a Spanish version in 1798.[6] Thus, at about the age of forty, *Rasselas* had been clothed in six foreign languages and approximately twenty editions, which must have totalled, by a conservative guess, perhaps 10,000 copies.

Five (probably) American editions increased the circulation of the tale among residents of the colonies and fledgling republic. The earliest of these—*Rasselas*, it should be pointed out, was seemingly the first of Johnson's works to receive an American edition[7]—appeared at Philadelphia in 1768 and was published by Robert Bell. He gave the apologue the formal English title of *The History of Rasselas, Prince of Abissinia. An Asiatic Tale;*[8] omitted, like the publishers of all English editions issued in Johnson's lifetime, the name of the tale's author from the title page (although he revealed it elsewhere); and, observing a practice followed by some of his fellows, patriotically announced on the title page that his version originated in "America" and was "printed for every purchaser." Bell also embellished his production with a frontispiece, a crude engraving labelled "A Perspective View of Grand Cairo,"[9]

5. Fleeman; Courtney and Smith, p. 97.

6. The information about the German, Italian, Russian, and Spanish translations is drawn from *NCBEL*, II. col. 1131; Fleeman; *Life*, II.499–500.

7. I draw this conclusion after an examination of Vols. II–IV (1730–73) of Charles Evans's *American Bibliography*, and Roger P. Bristol's *Supplement to Charles Evans' "American Bibliography"* (1970). See also Robert B. Winans, "Works by and about Samuel Johnson in Eighteenth-Century America," in *Papers of the Bibliographical Society of America*, LXII (1968), 540.

8. The title pages of all previous English editions read "*The Prince of Abissinia: A Tale*"; however, the heading on the first page of the text is "The History of Rasselas, Prince of Abissinia."

9. For information about Bell's edition, I am indebted to C. B. Tinker, "*Rasselas*

which started the slow movement, increasingly common in the early nineteenth century, toward illustrated editions of the story. Thanks to the thoughtfulness of the young American William White, a copy of Bell's edition made its way to Johnson, who, on 4 March 1773, acknowledged it cordially. "The impression is not magnificent," he wrote, "but it flatters an authour, because the printer seems to have expected that it would be scattered among the people. The little book has been well received, and is translated into Italian, French, German, and Dutch. It has now one honour more by an American edition."[1]

That honor, however, was rather short-lived. For, despite its introduction of an illustration and its democratic recognition of "every purchaser," Bell's work apparently did not pass beyond a solitary printing, and another American edition did not appear until 1791—again in Philadelphia. Four years later "the little book" and Ellis Cornelia Knight's *Dinarbas* were apparently issued together in both Greenfield, Mass., and New York. And the third year (1803) after the dawn of the new century saw the publication of what was called the "First American Edition" at Hartford, Conn.[2]

Altogether, then—to summarize—between 1759 and 1800 *Rasselas* was available to readers in six foreign languages and some fifty editions, English and non-English.

---

in the New World," *Yale Review*, xiv (1924), 95–107, esp. 99–101; and Robert F. Metzdorf, "The First American *Rasselas* and Its Imprint," *Papers of the Bibliographical Society of America*, xlvii (1953), 374–76. Mary Hyde Eccles has also kindly sent me photographic reproductions of the title page of Bell's edition and of what purports to be an extract from "Dodsley's View of Literature" giving the "Character of the History of Rasselas" and, at the end, naming Johnson as the author of the work. In fact, virtually the entire extract is a passage of Burke's review of *Rasselas*, which appeared in the *Annual Register*. For a discussion of the early illustrations of *Rasselas*, see Paul Alkon, "Illustrations of *Rasselas* and Reader-Response Criticism," *Samuel Johnson: Pictures and Words* (Papers presented at a Clark Library Seminar 23 Oct 1982, by Paul Alkon and Robert Folkenflik [1984]), pp. 3–62.

1. *Life*, ii.207–08, 499.
2. The information about these editions is drawn from Fleeman; *NCBEL*, ii. col. 1130; Evans, x (1795–96), 111; my personal copy of the so-called First American Edition.

INDEX

259